Until You

Also by Bertrice Small
in Large Print:

Rosamund
The Dragon Lord's Daughters

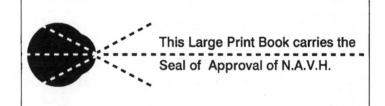

This Large Print Book carries the
Seal of Approval of N.A.V.H.

Until You

Bertrice Small

Thorndike Press • Waterville, Maine

Copyright © Bertrice Small, 2003
The Friarsgate Inheritance # 2

Published in 2005 by arrangement with NAL Signet,
a member of Penguin Group (USA) Inc.

Thorndike Press® Large Print Romance.

The tree indicium is a trademark of Thorndike Press.

The text of this Large Print edition is unabridged.
Other aspects of the book may vary from the original edition.

Set in 16 pt. Plantin by Elena Picard.

Printed in the United States on permanent paper.

Library of Congress Cataloging-in-Publication Data

Small, Bertrice.
    Until you / by Bertrice Small.
      p. cm. — (Thorndike Press large print romance)
    ISBN 0-7862-7261-9 (lg. print : hc : alk. paper)
    1. Scotland — History — James IV, 1488–1513 —
Fiction. 2. Large type books. I. Title. II. Thorndike
Press large print romance series.
PS3569.M28U58 2005
  813′.54—dc22   2004028370

For Pat of SeaAire Limo and
Car Service in Mattituck, N.Y.,
a longtime reader who gets me
where I need to go on time.
Thanks, Pat!

As the Founder/CEO of NAVH, the only national health agency solely devoted to those who, although not totally blind, have an eye disease which could lead to serious visual impairment, I am pleased to recognize Thorndike Press* as one of the leading publishers in the large print field.

Founded in 1954 in San Francisco to prepare large print textbooks for partially seeing children, NAVH became the pioneer and standard setting agency in the preparation of large type.

Today, those publishers who meet our standards carry the prestigious "Seal of Approval" indicating high quality large print. We are delighted that Thorndike Press is one of the publishers whose titles meet these standards. We are also pleased to recognize the significant contribution Thorndike Press is making in this important and growing field.

Lorraine H. Marchi, L.H.D.
Founder/CEO
NAVH

* Thorndike Press encompasses the following imprints: Thorndike, Wheeler, Walker and Large Print Press.

Prologue

THE BORDER

December 1511

"You are absolutely mad," Sir Thomas Bolton said to his cousin Rosamund as they rode across the border into Scotland. It was a cold but clear day.

"Why?" she demanded. "Because for once in my life I would do the unthinkable and dare to be the one to choose? I am tired of being told who I shall marry, and 'tis always for someone else's benefit, not necessarily mine. I was fortunate in Hugh, and again in Owein, but next time? I dare not take the chance. I want to make my own decisions from now on, and I intend to, dear Tom. Besides, I am not particularly interested in being someone's wife again. I have been a wife one way or another since I was three years of age. I am yet young, and I want to visit King James' court quite unencumbered by a husband. Perhaps I shall take a lover."

"You are surely planning some mischief, dear girl, and if you are, you simply must share it with me," he told her with a wicked grin.

"Oh, Tom," she laughed. "Please don't ever leave me! I do not know what I should do without you. You are my best friend in all of this world!"

"Now, wench, don't go getting sentimental on me," he replied, but he was smiling, for he loved his young cousin every bit as much as she loved him. His much younger sister had been like Rosamund. And how lonely he had been when she died in childbirth, and her child with her. And then, thanks to the queen, he had found Rosamund, the heiress to the major branch of his family. She could never take his sister's place, but she had made her own place in his heart.

"Do you think Logan Hepburn will be too upset when he discovers I am not at Friarsgate?" Rosamund wondered aloud.

"You still question his sincerity, then?" her companion said.

Rosamund sighed. "I probably should not, but aye, I yet do, at least in part. I have never before been sought after just because I am me. If he really wants me, he will take my sensibilities into account and

8

be patient. Besides, when Edmund tells him where we have gone, he will certainly come hotfooting it to Edinburgh, or wherever the court is located at the time. But by then I should be well into the round of Christmas revels, and there will be other men to pay me court. Logan Hepburn will have to do more than tell me that he has loved me since I was a child and it is now his turn to be my husband. He does not really love me. He lusts after me, that is all," she concluded.

Sir Thomas Bolton chuckled. "I can foresee that the next few months with you are going to be most interesting, dear girl."

"Until now, dear Tom, I have lived a most circumspect life," Rosamund replied. "I have done what was expected of me, what I was told to do, what I knew was right, what I knew I had to do. Now, however, I mean to do what I want to do, and I want to do something different, something exciting, something that would never be expected of me!"

"Oh my," her cousin said softly, looking at Rosamund with new eyes. "You are, I fear, in a dangerous mood, sweet coz. You are obviously ready to kick over the traces that have constrained you for your whole life. Just be cautious, I beg of you."

"Caution, dear Tom, was for the old

Rosamund. The new Rosamund wants more out of life now. And when I have had it, I shall return to Friarsgate, to my daughters, and aye, probably even to Logan Hepburn if he will still have me."

Tom shook his head, but then he looked up and smiled at her. "I shall be by your side if you wish it, dear cousin, no matter the danger you will probably get us into. I understand these Scots lords are very different from we English. More savage and reckless, I have heard."

"So Meg has written me, and in doing so she has quite piqued my interest," Rosamund responded with a little grin.

"Has she, indeed?" he answered, and then he grinned back at her. "Well, dear girl, it sounds as if we just might have a little bit of fun, eh? If," he noted dryly, seeing the first few flakes of snow beginning to fall, "we don't freeze to death before we get to Edinburgh." Shivering, he pulled up the collar of his cape.

"It should not be much farther to Lord Grey's home," Rosamund said, and then she pointed. "Look! On the next hill! That is our destination for tonight."

"Then, for pity's sake, let us ride faster," Tom said. He turned to the captain of their escort. "Is it possible, dear sir, to move more quickly lest I turn into a block of ice?"

"Aye," the captain said slowly, his tone clearly scornful of this English milord. But then he raised his gloved hand and signaled their troop forward at a much quicker pace, rather surprised that his two charges kept up with them quite well.

"Come, dear girl," Sir Thomas called to his cousin Rosamund. "We are in Scotland, and adventure awaits us!"

Chapter 1

"Who is she?" Patrick Leslie, the first Earl of Glenkirk asked his friend Lord Grey.

"Who is who?"

"The woman who sits on the footstool at the queen's right side," the earl answered his friend.

"Ahh," Lord Grey said, understanding at last. "The lady with the auburn hair in the green gown. She is the queen's childhood friend, the lady of Friarsgate, come from England at the queen's invitation. She is lovely, isn't she? She spent a night at my home on her way to court, but I was not there, of course."

"I would meet her," the earl said.

"What?" Lord Grey chuckled. "You have shown no interest in a respectable woman in over twenty years, Patrick. And you could be her father," he teased.

"Fortunately I am not her father," the earl replied, a faint smile touching his lips. "Can you introduce us, Andrew?"

"I have not yet myself been introduced," Lord Grey said.

It was the Christmas season. The two men stood among the crush of King James IV's court in the Great Hall of Stirling Castle. The hall had been built by the king's late father, James III. It had a hammer-beamed roof, large heraldic stained-glass windows, and five great fireplaces. Above the fireplace that was behind the high board where the king sat, hung his embroidered Cloth of Estate. The interior of the Great Hall was painted a rich lime yellow called King's Gold.

The court of King James IV of Scotland was a very cosmopolitan one. At least six different languages could be heard spoken among the guests. The king was an educated man with eclectic tastes. He could speak on the most modern sciences and theories, architecture, poetry, and history. He was urbane and had great charm. And as well liked as he was by those who peopled his court, he was beloved of the common man as well.

The Earl of Glenkirk stared again at the auburn-haired young woman. Andrew Grey was correct. It had been years since he was last attracted to a woman like the lady of Friarsgate. He had been widowed for twenty-eight years, and when he had lost his wife, Agnes, he had vowed never again to kill a woman with the bearing of his children. Oh, he had enjoyed his share of

13

mistresses, but they had been mostly for the release of his lust — though some of his mistresses had been his friends as well. They had all been women considered of low estate, not women from respectable families, who a man paid court to or married. His boyhood mistress, Meg MacKay, had borne his daughter, Janet; and his wife, Agnes Cummings, had given him his only son. The Earl of Glenkirk sighed, remembering these two women. Never since their untimely deaths had he looked at another woman as he was now looking at the lady of Friarsgate. The very sight of her stirred something in his heart he had long thought immune to such tender emotions. Was he being a fool?

"You really want to meet her?" Andrew Grey's soft voice pierced the earl's thoughts. "I know one of the queen's ladies, Elsbeth Hume. I could speak to her."

"Do it," the Earl of Glenkirk said. "Now, if you can."

"God's foot, Patrick!" Lord Grey said. "I cannot remember the last time you were so eager over a wench." He chuckled. "Very well. Come along, and let us find Elsbeth."

They moved through the crowded hall until finally the lady they sought was found. She was a pretty girl with black hair and dancing blue eyes.

Lord Grey moved next to her and slid an

arm about the lady's waist. "Elsbeth, you adorable and fascinating lass, I have a favor to ask of you, my pet."

Mistress Hume turned to look up at Lord Grey, her blue eyes twinkling. "And just what is it you seek of me, my lord, and what will you give me in return for this favor?" she purred. Her cherry-red lips pursed questioningly.

Lord Grey quickly kissed the offered lips and replied, "My friend the Earl of Glenkirk wishes a proper introduction to the queen's English friend, the lady of Friarsgate. Can you aid him?"

Elsbeth Hume turned and smiled up at Patrick Leslie. "I can, my lord. Rosamund Bolton is a most delightful lady. There is naught high-flown about her, as there is with most of these English who come to our court. From the look in your eyes, I expect you would meet the lady sooner than later, eh?" She smiled mischievously at him.

"I would, Mistress Hume," the Earl of Glenkirk replied with an answering smile.

"Come then, and I will present you. Your intentions will be as honorable as any man at this court, I expect. The lady, however, is no fool, and she can defend herself," Mistress Hume said. "Be warned, my lord. More than one gentleman has felt the sting of her outrage when he exhibited bad behavior before her."

She moved across the hall with Lord Grey and the Earl of Glenkirk following behind her. Reaching the throne where the queen sat, Elsbeth Hume curtsied low and said, "Your majesty, the Earl of Glenkirk would pay his respects to the lady of Friarsgate. May I have your permission to introduce them?"

Margaret Tudor, Queen of Scotland, smiled at Patrick Leslie and Andrew Grey. "You have our permission," she said, wondering what it was the earl could possibly want. "We have not met, my lord earl. You have not been at court in my time here, have you?"

Patrick bowed with an elegant flourish. He might have been a Highlander, but he remembered his manners. "I have not, your highness," he replied.

"What has brought you back to the court, then?" she queried.

"His majesty's personal request, madame, although he has not yet seen fit to share his wishes with me," the earl said. But whatever it was, Patrick considered, it was important to James Stewart or he would not have sent for the Earl of Glenkirk. The king knew how this earl felt about his court, or any other court for that matter. He did not share these thoughts with the queen, however.

"How intriguing," the queen said. "I

16

shall have to ask Jamie about this mystery you have provided me with, my lord." Then she smiled at the earl. "You have our permission to make the acquaintance of our dearest friend, the lady of Friarsgate. Beth, you will make the introductions." Then the queen turned away, her curiosity satisfied for the moment and her attention engaged elsewhere now.

"Lady Rosamund Bolton, Patrick Leslie, the Earl of Glenkirk, and my friend Lord Andrew Grey," Elsbeth Hume said, making the introductions.

Rosamund held out her hand to be kissed, and her gaze met those of the two gentlemen. Lord Grey took her hand, saluted it, and murmured, "Lady Bolton." But when Rosamund's amber eyes met those of the Earl of Glenkirk, she was overcome with shock. The green eyes locked on to hers, and he was not a stranger! She had known him forever, and yet she had never before this day seen the man. She struggled to maintain control over herself while the most disturbing images bloomed in her head, and when his lips touched the back of her hand Rosamund felt as if she had been scorched by a bolt of lightning.

"Madame," he said, his big hand yet holding hers. His voice was deep.

"My lord," she managed to say. She felt

as if they were a single entity. Her voice was soft.

It was patently obvious to their two companions that something extraordinary had just happened. And though neither Lord Grey nor Elsbeth Hume understood, they moved away discreetly, leaving Rosamund and the Earl of Glenkirk alone.

Patrick tucked the small hand still in his possession into the crook of his arm, saying as he did so, "Let us stroll, madame, and we will tell each other of ourselves."

"There is naught to tell," Rosamund began. She felt better now that they were speaking than she had in the odd silence that had enwrapped them previously.

"You are English," he said, "but not from the south, for I understand you too well."

She smiled now. "My home is in Cumbria, my lord."

"And how did a lass from Cumbria come to be Margaret Tudor's friend? A good enough friend to be invited to King James' court?" he asked. He shortened his steps to match hers, for he was very tall, and she, while not as small as the queen, was petite.

"When my second husband died, he put me into the care of King Henry. Not he now upon England's throne, but his father," Rosamund explained. "I was just thirteen."

"At thirteen you had outlived two husbands, madame? Are you so dangerous, then?" he asked, and she heard the humor in his voice.

"I am twenty-two now, my lord, and have buried three husbands," she teased him.

He laughed aloud. "You have children, then." It was a statement.

"Three daughters. Philippa, Banon, and Elizabeth," Rosamund answered. "They were born to me and my third husband, Sir Owein Meredith. I was wed first at the age of three to a cousin who perished when I was five. I was married again at the age of six to Sir Hugh Cabot, an elderly knight chosen by my uncle, who wished to retain control over Friarsgate. Hugh, however, taught me how to be independent and cleverly thwarted my uncle Henry by placing me into the custody of the king when he died. My uncle was furious, for he sought to wed me to his second son, who was but five. It was the king's mother, the Venerable Margaret, and your queen, Margaret Tudor, who chose my third husband for me. Owein was a good man, and we were content together."

"How did he die?" the Earl of Glenkirk asked her.

"Owein loved Friarsgate every bit as much as if he had been born and bred there. He had a peculiar habit of climbing to the top of each tree in the orchards come harvest, so that no fruit was wasted. No one else had ever done it. Usually that fruit was left to rot, or to fall and be scavenged by the deer. But he would not have it. He thought it wasteful. He fell from the top of one of those trees and broke his neck. A branch gave way." She sighed. "I had lost our only son several months before."

"I lost my wife in childbed, but my son survived," he told her. "He is now a grown man with a wife of his own."

"He was your only child?" she asked.

"I had a daughter," he replied shortly, and his tone indicated he did not at this time choose to discuss it further. They had reached the end of the Great Hall. "Let us go out and view the night sky," he suggested. "It is very clear, and the stars are always their brightest over Stirling on a winter's night."

"We have no capes," she answered, but she very much wanted to go.

The Earl of Glenkirk snapped his fingers at a passing servant.

The man stopped. "Yes, my lord?"

"Two warm cloaks for the lady and for me," the earl ordered.

"At once, my lord, if you will wait here," the servant responded, and he hurried off.

They stood silently until he returned a few moments later with the required garments.

The Earl of Glenkirk took a long nut-brown wool cape lined in warm marten and draped it over Rosamund's shoulders. He moved around before her and carefully fastened each of the polished brass frogs that closed the garb tightly. Then he gently drew up the fur-lined hood. Each time their eyes met, Rosamund had this incredible sense of déjà vu. "There," he said and then, turning, took the other cloak from the servant. When he had dressed himself, he thanked the servant and took Rosamund's hand to lead her outside into the winter gardens.

It was very cold, but the air was still. Above them the night sky was ebony in color and dotted with stars that twinkled crystal, blue, and red. They walked in silence until the lights of the castle were but glittering gold points and they could no longer hear the murmur of the many voices within the hall. Then suddenly he stopped. He turned her so that she was facing him, pushing back the hood of her garment, taking her small face within the enclosure of his two big hands.

Rosamund's heart began to hammer with her excitement. Each time their eyes met it was as if this very moment had happened before. She could not for the life of her look away from him, and when his dark head slowly descended, his lips brushing gently over hers several times as if tasting her, it was she who cupped his head in her palms, and drew him down to kiss him hungrily. She shuddered as their mouths met that first time. Or was it for the first time?

Finally he drew away, saying as he did, "I am hardly a young man, madame."

"I know," she replied.

"I have seen a half century," he answered. "I could be your father."

"But you are not my father, my lord," Rosamund told him. "You are older than Owein Meredith, but younger than Hugh Cabot. We are drawn to each other, although I do not know why or how this is. I know that you feel it, too, for I have seen it in your eyes." She reached out and gently caressed his cheek. "So here we are, my lord earl, and what are we to do?"

"Will you believe me when I tell you that I have never before felt with a woman as I do with you, madame?"

"My name is Rosamund," she told him, nodding. "And like you, I have never felt quite this way before, my lord."

"My name is Patrick," he answered.

"Are we bewitched, Patrick?" she asked him.

"By whom or what?" he wondered aloud.

She shook her head. "I do not know. I am new here and know few."

"As am I," he replied. "I have not been to court since I returned to Scotland from San Lorenzo many years ago."

"San Lorenzo?" She looked puzzled.

"It is a small duchy on the Mediterranean Sea. I was sent as the king's first ambassador to set up a friendly port where our trading vessels might find safety, water, and supplies," the earl explained.

"Then you have traveled, Patrick. I have never wanted to travel, for I love my home. I always hated going to court. But now, suddenly, I am ripe for adventure." She smiled mischievously, and his heart contracted almost painfully.

He reached out again and enfolded her in his embrace. "I want to make love to you," he said softly. He kissed her slowly, his mouth demanding yet gentle. "I cannot believe I would be so damned bold with someone I have only just met, and yet I feel as if we have known each other forever. And you feel it, too, Rosamund. I saw the surprise of recognition in your eyes earlier. I do not understand it, and yet it is happening."

"I know," she agreed. "I do not know what to do. Do you? Should we follow our instincts? Or should we decide this is some madness, and part from each other? You must decide for us, Patrick, for I am much too afraid to do so, and I have never before been a coward when facing life."

"Neither have I," he said. "So despite what common sense would tell us, my fair Rosamund, let us follow our instincts and see where they will lead us." He kissed her again. "Are you ready for the journey?"

"My family's motto is *Tracez Votre Chemin* — Make Your Own Path. If we are to follow our instincts, my lord, then that is exactly what I shall do," she told him, looking up into his handsome face. He did not look to her as if he had lived a half century, even if there were small lines about his eyes. And looking into those eyes she once again felt an overwhelming sensation of giddy excitement.

"So, dear cousin, this is where you have gotten to," a familiar voice broke into her thoughts, into the privacy of their new world. "And who, dear Rosamund, is this gentleman who would drag you out into the cold night? God's foot! I am frozen just seeking you, dear girl."

She laughed as his voice brought her back to reality. "This, my lord of Glenkirk, is my cousin Thomas Bolton, Lord Cambridge. He escorted me from Friarsgate, and is, he assures me, enjoying himself immensely, having never believed the Scots could be so civilized, he says."

Patrick knew immediately what Thomas Bolton was, and the irritating jealousy he had felt at the arrival of the other man drained away. He smiled and held out his big hand to shake that of Rosamund's cousin. "I saw her well protected before I brought her out, my lord. The sky above, however, is well worth it." The earl drew up Rosamund's hood again in a tender gesture. "We should nonetheless return to the hall. So you find us civilized, do you?" He chuckled.

"Aye," Tom agreed. "Your court is much more open and less pretentious than our good King Henry's court. Perhaps it is his Spanish queen who requires such formality. Your king, however, keeps a merry company about him, and habits here are far more relaxed. I am quite enjoying myself, and I am tempted to purchase a house in Edinburgh and here in Stirling."

"Would not your king object?" the earl queried.

"Nay. I am not important to Henry Tudor. I am simply a rich man whose wealth comes from trade and whose title comes from the guilty conscience of a long-dead king," Tom said with a chortle. "I am not considered important enough to be bothered with but for my connection with Rosamund."

"Tom!" her voice held a warning note.

"I have no importance in the English court but that I helped our good queen in her time of need once."

"Poor Spanish Kate," he responded, and then he turned to the Earl of Glenkirk. "There she was, dear creature, widowed by one Tudor and considered for another but that her father would not pay all her dowry. The old king was hardly noted for his generosity and would scarce support her. Her attendants were shipped home but for a few who would not leave her, wise creatures they were. They suffered for it though. They were all in rags and half-starved with the old king blowing hot and cold on the marriage. And then Rosamund learned of it. Spanish Kate had been her companion along with Princess Margaret when Rosamund lived at court. My good-hearted cousin sent little purses to she who is now England's queen. They were much for her, but barely enough for the poor princess to keep herself and her few ladies for several weeks. It was gallant of her to do such a thing, and in the end she was rewarded when Spanish Kate finally became England's queen. My cousin stands in the queen's favor, my lord."

"The queen believed she owed me a debt, which she did not, but has now been more than repaid," Rosamund said quietly. "You are most voluble tonight, cousin."

"I was concerned when I could not find you anywhere in the hall, dear girl," he answered her smoothly.

"And what brought you out into the cold night?" the earl inquired, amused.

"I overheard one of the queen's ladies saying she had introduced the lady of Friarsgate to the Earl of Glenkirk and they had left the hall together," he replied. "You cannot deny me my curiosity. And there are others in the king's hall equally as fascinated. I understand, my lord, that you have not been to court in many years."

"I do not enjoy the court with its gossip and intrigue," the Earl of Glenkirk said pointedly, "but I am a loyal servant to Jamie Stewart, and when he calls, I come."

"Not another word, Tom!" Rosamund scolded her cousin. "And before you even ask, he does not know yet why he was summoned."

"Rosamund, I am crushed, dear girl, that you would think me a common gossip," Lord Cambridge said dramatically, his hand going to his heart.

"You could certainly never be called a common gossip, Tom," she replied wickedly.

Patrick laughed. "My lord, when I learn of why I have been sent for, I assure you it will not be long before the entire court learns of it. I admit to being curious myself, for the king knows I am not a man of the court and that I am content to remain on my lands at Glenkirk. But he also knows my son is there to oversee our estates in my absence."

"You have a wife, then, my lord?" Tom asked.

"I am a widower, my lord," the earl replied, "or I should not have approached your cousin Rosamund. I am pleased to see what a gallant protector she has in you."

Lord Cambridge nodded slowly. "Rosamund is dear to my heart, my lord. She and her daughters are my only living family. I should not like to see her hurt, you understand."

"Of course," the Earl of Glenkirk said quietly.

"Dearest Tom, I cannot explain to you what has happened," Rosamund began, "for I do not even comprehend it myself, but we have always trusted each other. You must believe me when I tell you that whatever is to be between myself and Patrick, it will be all right." She turned to the earl. "Will it not, my lord?"

"Aye," he said, amazed to realize that he actually believed it. She did not know what was happening between them? Well, neither did he! He had walked into the Great Hall of Stirling Castle this evening and seen this young woman for the first time.

And yet something within him had refused to believe it was the first time. And speaking with her he felt that he had known her forever. And he instinctively knew that she felt exactly the same way.

Tom could feel the magic that surrounded the pair, and it startled him. What sorcery was this? he wondered, and yet there was nothing dark in it at all. But at the same time he could feel himself almost fading into the background as the intensity between them began to grow once more. "I will bid you both good night, then," he said as they reentered the castle. Then he hurried back to the Great Hall to consider just what was happening. He needed to get away from his cousin and the Earl of Glenkirk if he were to think clearly, for the atmosphere surrounding them was simply too deep and too ardent. And it was most disquieting, as well!

"Do you reside within the castle?" Rosamund asked Patrick as they watched Tom disappear.

He nodded. "I have been given a chamber for myself, as I am a guest of his majesty," he told her. "And you?"

"As the queen's invited guest I have been given a chamber, as well, for myself and my servant Annie," she told him.

"We will go to my hidey-hole, then, madame, as I have no servant to dispossess," he told her. "If your Annie is seen spending the night in another place, there will be gossip. I am not of a mind to share what is between us at the moment. Are you?"

"Nay," she agreed. "Whatever this magic is, I want to keep it for ourselves, Patrick. For the first time in my life I am being selfish, but I don't care!" Then she slipped her hand back into his and followed him as he led her down several corridors and finally up a flight of stairs.

He opened an oak door, ushering her into a simple room with but two pieces of furniture: a bed and a stool. There was no fireplace, and the room was cold. There were wood shutters drawn across the single window, but no curtains. It was spare, but they were unlikely to be disturbed. He laid his cloak upon the stool, then gently unbuttoned the frogs fastening her outdoor garment, and, removing it, put it with his own. Taking her face in his hands he smiled down into her eyes. "This is not fine enough for you," he told her. Then he found the candle and lit it, before closing the door behind them and turning the key in the lock.

"Kiss me," she responded softly.

With a sigh he complied, his chill lips warming atop hers.

Rosamund slid her arms about his neck,

drawing him closer. Her full breasts pressed against the velvet that covered his chest. Their kisses blended one into another until her mouth ached. Finally she drew her head away from his, saying as she did, "I can but hope you are a good lady's maid, my lord."

He laughed softly. "It has been many years since I have undone such finery, Rosamund, but I hope I may remember," Patrick told her. Then he turned her about and began to unlace her bodice while placing small kisses upon the back of her neck. She smelled fresh, and of a scent he recognized as white heather. He put the elegant little bodice atop the pile of cloaks. Next he unknotted the drawstring holding her skirt up and let the heavy material drop to the wood floor. Then he lifted her from the velvet heap, setting her back upon the floor. "Now, what is that thing you have fastened about you?" he demanded, puzzled. Rosamund giggled. " 'Tis called a shakefold, and it is used to plump my skirts out in a fashionable manner," she explained.

"It looks dangerous," he said. "Can you get the damned thing off without me?"

She unfastened the shakefold and stepped from it, kicked it over to the stool, where her other garments were piled. Then she added her flannel petticoats.

"Sit on the edge of the bed, and I will remove your stocking for you," he said.

Rosamund sat, watching him as he first removed each of her square-toed leather shoes and then set about unrolling her wool stockings. When her feet were finally free, she wiggled her toes in an attempt to get some warmth back into them.

"Get beneath the coverlet," he said, and then he turned away to undress himself.

She watched him in the pale flickering light of the single candle. He had lived a half century, he had said, yet his body was hard and firm. He was obviously not a man who was idle or lazy. His buttocks were tight, and his hairy legs long. His back was broad, and he was very fair of skin. Entirely naked, he turned about to enter the bed, and she caught a glimpse of his manhood. At rest it was large, and she shivered with anticipation, then blushed with her own lustful thoughts. What was she doing here, in bed with a stranger? And yet it was right.

He drew her into his arms, his fingers undoing the ribbons that held her chemise closed. When the delicate fabric spread itself open, he looked upon Rosamund's breasts, and then his dark head bent. He rubbed his face against the perfumed skin, gaining the most intense pleasure as he did so. She shivered and held his head against her bosom, enjoying the act every bit as much as he was.

"I have never . . ." she began.

"I know," he said, understanding instinctively what she was trying to say. He raised his head to look into her face. "I have conceived little of what has happened between us tonight, Rosamund. All I know is that you and I are meant to be together like this. You are not one of the ladies of the court with their light morals. This is as much a surprise to me as it is to you. There is yet time. If you wish to leave me now, you may go unimpeded."

"I cannot," she admitted. "I feel exactly as you do, though it be confusing to me." Then she removed her chemise and let it fall to the floor. "I am a practical woman, Patrick, and have not garments to waste."

He drew her back into his embrace so he might caress and fondle her lovely round breasts. He had never before seen such perfectly luscious spheres. Her skin was firm and silken to his touch. She sighed with her pleasure as his hands petted her tenderly. Singling out one breast, his head dropped. He rained kisses across her sentient flesh. His mouth fastened upon a taut nipple, and he began to suckle upon her eagerly.

Rosamund had always loved the touch of a man's mouth on her breasts. She almost purred her contentment. How long had it been since she had lain in a man's arms enjoying his attentions? It seemed like forever. Her fingers glanced over the nape of his neck. His hair was dark and just lightly sprinkled with silver. She entwined her hand into his locks, kneading his scalp with what became a growing urgency.

He raised his head, and his green eyes were glazed with his rising passion for her. He began to kiss her hungrily, their bodies twining and untwining with their lust. His mouth touched her throat, her shoulders, her chest. Their lips met and burned as they kissed seemingly without end. He could feel her heart beating wildly. The pulse at the base of her throat leapt like a netted salmon. His lips moved to her breasts again, then down her torso. Rosamund was making little mewling noises that alerted him to her pleasure. The white heather that scented her body warmed, growing stronger with her passion. It intoxicated him, and he could feel himself growing harder with his desire for her. He could not ever remember a time when he wanted a woman so very much.

"God help us!" she half-sobbed, and he understood her concern.

His fingers began to brush the curls on her mons. A single finger explored.

She whimpered softly, her thoughts jumbled. But then, for a moment her practical nature pushed to the fore, and again she questioned what she was doing. Yet when his long fingers began to brush the insides of her thighs with a seductive stroking, she felt herself concentrating only upon her need for him. But why him? *Because it is he for whom you have waited,* her voice within replied. "Oh, yes," she said aloud, knowing, but not quite understanding.

The big hands caressed her, pulling her into his arms again, sweeping down her back to cup and fondle her buttocks. "I cannot get enough of you," he said quietly. "Your skin is like silk. Your body perfection."

"I need you inside of me, Patrick," Rosamund heard herself telling him.

"I need to be inside of you," he replied. Then his big frame covered her, the fingers of their two hands intertwining as he slowly possessed her.

She felt the lengthy hardness tenderly seeking entry into her body. He was bigger than the two men she had previously known, but Rosamund opened like a flower for him, absorbing his length within her love sheath until he filled her. Their eyes met again, as they had earlier when this madness began. She felt as if her soul were flowing into his, and for a moment she was frightened.

He saw the look upon her lovely face and quickly reassured her. " 'Tis all right, my love," he told her. "I sense it, too. We are one now in every sense." Then he began to move upon her, and within moments Rosamund found herself lost in passion as they sought to satisfy each other.

Her eyes now closed, she was enveloped in sensation. The rhythm their bodies created overwhelmed her. She moved from delight, past pleasure, to pure, hot ecstasy. She cried out as stars and moons exploded behind her eyelids, her voice rising to a scream of utter satisfaction as her nails raked down his long back. The thrust and withdraw of his manhood did not cease. He drove her further and further, until her cries of gratification echoed again and again within the stone walls of the small chamber.

And his own shouts of enjoyment mingled with hers until, with an intense howl of triumph, his love juices gushed forth in a tremendous rush, flooding her body with their heat. With a groan of repletion he rolled off of her, pulling her into his arms as he did so. "I have no words," he finally gasped.

"Nor I," Rosamund sighed deeply. She had never, never, never, ever been made love to with such tender, such passionate, such fierce intensity. Owein had never taken her like Patrick Leslie. And as for Henry Tudor, his only desires were for himself. What just happened between herself and the Earl of Glenkirk had been achieved by the two of them together. There was almost something mystical to it. It was as if they had been together like this before. From that first sensation of sudden recognition until now, it was as if they were old and dear friends. Lovers.

"I cannot be parted from you," he said quietly. His hand smoothed down her auburn hair.

"Nor I you, my lord. But shall I shock you if I tell you I do not wish another husband now?" She almost held her breath waiting to learn what he thought.

"I can understand your feelings, Rosamund, but someday you may change your mind. I, however, will not. Like you, I do not choose to wed again. I have a son, older than you, I suspect. He is wed and has sons. And there is the matter of why the king has asked me to leave my Highland home and come to Stirling."

"I shall be your mistress, then, and gladly," Rosamund told the Earl of Glenkirk. "Something happened tonight, my lord. You know it, and I know it. I suspect you do not understand what it is any more than I do. But there it is. Something deep within me knew you at first sight. That same something bids me stay with you for now. There will come a time when I will seek to return to Friarsgate. Or perhaps you will need to return to Glenkirk. And when that time comes, we will know it, and we will part again as we obviously did at some other time and in some other place. My poor cousin Tom will be most shocked, for this behavior is very unlike me. And there is something you should know. I have a suitor — Logan Hepburn, the laird of Claven's Carn. He expected to wed with me on St. Stephen's Day, though I told him nay. He will come to court seeking me and attempting to foist his will upon me. But I do not wish to remarry."

"Do you become my mistress to thwart him, Rosamund?" he wondered aloud.

She propped herself upon an elbow and looked down into his face. "I become your mistress because I choose to be and because there is something obviously unfinished between us from that other time and place. You know it, Patrick!"

"Aye, lass, I know it," he said. "I am a Scot, and I understand these things." He reached up and pulled her down into his embrace once more, kissing her. "I loved you once, Rosamund."

"I know," she replied softly. "And I loved you."

"I will love you again," he told her.

"I know," she said with a little smile. "I already love you, though it be madness to say it, Patrick."

He laughed softly. "The king has the *lang eey*, or long eye as you English would say. I shall ask him about this wonderful insanity that has afflicted us, my love." He drew her even closer and pulled the coverlet about them. "Will you remain with me?"

"For a little while, my love," she responded. "My poor Annie will wonder where I have gotten to, and fret. She is one of my own Friarsgate folk. And I would prefer that what we have be between us alone for now. Soon enough there will be talk and speculation about the Earl of Glenkirk and the queen's English friend."

"You are very discreet," he teased.

"I don't want to be discreet," Rosamund told him. "I want to shout from all the rooftops of Stirling that I am in love and am loved in return." She chuckled. "People would think me mad, especially if they knew the circumstances of our love, my lord."

He nodded. "I can hear the gossips now. There is old Glenkirk, come down from his Highland eyrie, and carrying on wi a lass young enough to be his daughter."

"But there will be others who say old Glenkirk is a lucky devil to have such a lusty young mistress and keep her satisfied, too," Rosamund teased him back.

He laughed. "I suspect you care no more than I do what people say, Rosamund."

"I don't care," she admitted. "Once I might have cared, but no more. I have outlived three husbands. I have spent my entire life doing what was expected of me, doing what I was told, for I am naught but a mere woman. But I have given Friarsgate three little heiresses, and I have kept the land well and will continue to do so with the help of my uncle Edmund. Now I wish to live for myself, if only for a little while."

"Tell me about Friarsgate," he said.

"It is beautiful and fertile. The house sits above a lake. I raise sheep. We prepare our own wool and weave our own cloth, which is highly sought after by the mercers in Carlisle and the low countries. I have cattle and horses, as well. We are safe from our border neighbors because the land about my valley is ringed with steep hills. No one can steal our livestock because they cannot escape with it without being caught. I love it there! It is the best place in all the world, Patrick. Now, you tell me of Glenkirk."

"It sits in the eastern Highlands between two rivers. My castle is small. Until I was sent to San Lorenzo by our Jamie, I was naught but the laird of Glenkirk. The king wished to honor the Duke of San Lorenzo by sending a nobleman, and so I was created the Earl of Glenkirk. We raise sheep and Highland cattle. I have two children: a daughter, Janet, and a son, Adam."

"Yet you speak only of your son," Rosamund noted.

"My lass was stolen away by slavers when we were in San Lorenzo. She was to wed with the duke's heir. We had just celebrated the betrothal when she was taken. We tried to regain her custody, but could not." His face wore an expression of intense pain. "I cannot speak of it, Rosamund. Please understand and ask me no more."

She kissed him tenderly. "I understand," she said.

For a moment all was silent in the chamber, and then the earl said, "Tell me of this Logan Hepburn who pursues you."

"A most irritating man," Rosamund replied. "He claims to have been in love with me since I was six years of age. He says he saw me at a cattle market at Drumfie with my uncle. He appeared at Friarsgate just before I wed with my Owein. He had, he said, come courting. I told him I was to marry, and then the bold creature showed up at my wedding with his brothers and their pipes! They brought whiskey and salmon. I should have sent him packing then and there, but Owein found it amusing. After Owein's death, Queen Katherine asked me back to court. She thought to cheer me, though if the truth be known I hated to leave my home and could scarcely wait to return. And when I did, there was Logan Hepburn! He announced we were to wed on St. Stephen's day, and he would come for me then."

"He's a bold fellow," the earl said thoughtfully.

"He is irritating and brash," Rosamund said heatedly. "Thank God your queen sent me an invitation to come to this court. I should have had to fortify my house to keep that damned borderer out. He wants a son and an heir of me. Well, he had best find someone more willing, for I will not be broodmare to his stallion!" Then her hand flew to her mouth. "Oh, Patrick! What if . . ."

"There is no possibility, lass," he told her. "Before I returned home from San Lorenzo, I contracted an illness. My face blew up like a sheep's bladder, and my manhood ached and burned by turns. The old woman who nursed me told me that my seed would be barren from that point on. I have had several mistresses in the intervening years, and none has claimed a bairn by me. I have never cared until now, though I swear I do not consider you a broodmare to my stallion," he finished with a small smile.

She giggled, and reaching down, stroked his now-flaccid rod. "You do, however, my lord, have some most impressive stallion-like qualities." Her fingers teased his length and found their way beneath to fondle his twin pouches.

He closed his eyes and enjoyed the sensations she was engendering with her daring play. "I had been told you English were cold creatures," he bedeviled her wickedly.

"Whoever gave you such an idea, my lord?" she murmured, and then she squeezed him, causing him to groan with his budding arousal.

"I cannot remember, madame, but I am relieved to learn it a lie," the earl said.

"I suspect his majesty could tell you that. It is said King Jamie is hot-blooded by nature. So, too, is his queen. Considering the bairns born to them, it would seem truth."

"Aye, but among those bairns not a living heir," the earl noted.

"This time will be different," Rosamund said. "Come the spring the queen will deliver a healthy son, my lord. We all pray for it."

"Do you have the *lang eey* like our Jamie, then?" he asked. His hand cupped a breast, and he tenderly fondled it. The little nipple instantly thrust itself forth to salute him. He bent his dark head and kissed it. His tongue licked at it in a leisurely fashion.

Rosamund sighed deeply. Every touch of his hand, his mouth, offered her the most incredible pleasure. While she had loved Owein, it had never been that way with him. Not like this. Nor her own king, who had taken her briefly for his mistress on her last visit to court. Nay. Henry Tudor was always interested in only one thing: his own gratification. This man, however, Patrick Leslie, Earl of Glenkirk, a man she knew hardly at all, this man opened her eyes in a single night of passion to the reality of what love truly was. "I think I will die if you leave me now," she said, voicing her thoughts to him with daring audacity.

He kissed her sweetly, his lips brushing hers tenderly. "We are not meant to part for now, my love, but one day we will, for your heart is at Friarsgate and mine at Glenkirk. This is how it should be, for we are both loyal to our lands and our people. Once, I think, we may have neglected our responsibilities in favor of our love. We are being given the chance now to right that wrong. Do you understand me, Rosamund?"

"Nay," she replied. "I do not."

"What I believe, my love, is considered a heresy, but nonetheless I believe it. I think that we live other lives, in other times and places. I recall that when I arrived in San Lorenzo I had the most incredible sense that I had been there before. I would find my way to certain locations without the benefit of direction. Throughout my life it has been that way. An old clanswoman on my lands has the *lang eey*, and she told me I have lived before, as have most souls. I believe her. Tonight, when we first met in this time and this place, we both experienced a sense of familiarity, a strong feeling that we knew each other well. You are not a woman with loose morals, yet here we lie together in our bed, and I am about to make love to you for a second time this night. Do you understand now, Rosamund?"

She nodded. "Aye and yet nay," she told him.

"Can you accept this magic between us, or shall we part and pretend that it never happened?" he asked her.

"How could I possibly deny the wonder of what is between us?" she cried softly. "I cannot! I hear what you tell me, but it seems so impossible. Still, I do lie here in your arms, and I feel as if I never want to leave you, that I shall die if you send me away!"

"I will not send you away, Rosamund. Yet there will come a time, as I have said, when we will both know we must part for the sake of others. But that time is not now. For a while the fates will allow us this idyll, and we will be grateful," he told her.

"Could you not have found me sooner, my lord?" she said with utmost seriousness.

He smiled down on her, his green eyes filled with pure love. Then he kissed her mouth and said, "Be silent, my love, and let me join with you once more."

"Yes!" She said the single word, her own love shining forth from her amber eyes. Then she opened her arms to him and took him into her embrace.

For a second time they met passion. For a second time they cried aloud as it swept over them, rendering them both weak with satisfaction. The length and breadth of him filled her love sheath. The rhythm they created was overpowering in the pleasure it offered. Her body arced against him in her great desire. He forced her down, thrusting and parrying with his lance as he brought them to a perfect heaven once again.

"I die!" she sobbed as her desire grew and grew until it burst in a frenetic rush of his love juices that left them both half-conscious and gasping for breath.

"You are the most incredible woman," he finally managed to say, his dark head resting upon her white bosom.

"And you astonishing, my dear lord of

Glenkirk. You tell me you are past fifty, and yet you make love like a younger man," she said with admiration.

He chuckled. "It is only young men who claim excess virility and work to make the myth a truth. A man of my years knows his limits, although tonight I have surpassed even myself, my love, but that is due to you, I suspect. You inspire me."

"Take your ease, then, my lord, for soon you must help me find my way back to my own chamber. I have absolutely no idea where I am right now," she told him laughing.

"You are in my arms, where you should be," he said. "I will help you find your way back," he promised, "but first let us regain our strength, Rosamund."

She nodded in agreement and closed her eyes, feeling safer and more content than she had felt in many months. This was what it was like to be really loved, she thought happily. If only the whole world could feel just like this.

They dozed for a short time, wrapped in each other's arms, savoring the warmth of their love. But finally the Earl of Glenkirk rose reluctantly and dressed himself. When he was clothed, he handed her the garments he had discarded upon the stool earlier, ordering her to dress within the comfort of their bed, for the air was bitterly cold. Finally he led her from his little chamber through the darkened corridors of the castle, asking her as they went exactly where her own chamber was. She told him, and to her surprise, they were quickly there. They kissed hungrily, desperately, as if they would never again be together. Then he turned swiftly and hurried off, back into the darkness of the hallway.

Rosamund slipped quietly into her little chamber. Annie was dozing in a chair by the embers of the fire. She started awake as her mistress entered. "I am glad you were not worried," Rosamund said to her.

"Lord Cambridge come to me, my lady. He said you might be very late." She rose from her place, yawning and stretching. Then, peeping through the heavy velvet curtain covering the single window, she said, " 'Tis already false dawn. You had best get into bed, my lady, if you are to have any rest before the mass."

"Build up the fire," Rosamund ordered her, "and heat some water. I stink of passion and cannot enter the queen's presence until I have washed. Neither will I enter my bed until I am fresh."

Annie looked shocked with her mistress' pronouncement.

"I have taken the Earl of Glenkirk as a lover, Annie," Rosamund said bluntly. "You will not gossip about it with the other servants even if they ask you. Do you understand me, girl?"

"Aye, my lady," Annie said. "But it ain't right, a respectable lady such as yourself!" she burst out.

"I am widowed, Annie, and were you not my confidante when I was with the king?" Rosamund asked her servingwoman.

"That was different," Annie said. "You was just obeying our king. There was no harm in it as long as good Queen Katherine didn't know or be shamed by it."

"Nay, Annie, 'twas no different than all of my life before it," Rosamund said. "I have always done what I was asked. What was expected of me. Now, however, I shall do what I want. I shall live my life to please myself and no one else! Do you understand?"

"What of the laird of Claven's Carn?" Annie asked. "He ain't going to marry with a lady who lifts her skirts so easily, my lady."

Rosamund slapped her servant. "You presume upon our friendship, Annie," she said. "Do you wish me to send you home to Friarsgate? I shall do it, for there are plenty who would be willing to serve me — and keep their tongues silent. I will tell you what I told Logan Hepburn. I do not wish to marry again! And I will not be forced to it. Friarsgate has an heiress, and two more

49

besides. I will unite my daughters one day in marriages that will bring honor and wealth to our family. Logan Hepburn wants a son. He needs an heir for Claven's Carn. Let him get it upon some sweet young virgin who will adore him and be a good wife to him. I am not that woman. King Henry's mother, she who was my guardian, once told me that a woman must marry first for her family. Twice at the most. But after that, the Venerable Margaret said, a woman should marry where it suited her. Twice my uncle Henry Bolton has made marriages for me. My third husband was the king's choice. Now it is my choice, and I choose no husband! Do you understand me, Annie? I will do as I please now."

Annie rubbed her cheek and sniffled softly. "Yes, my lady," she said.

"Good. Then we are agreed, and you will serve me without question, eh?"

"Yes, my lady."

"Go about your duties, then," Rosamund instructed her servant, and she sat down upon the bed while Annie built the fire back up and began to heat the water for her ablutions.

What a night it had been! She had been at court only a short time, yet now, as the day of Christ's Eve dawned, she was filled with a joy such as she had never known.

She knew not where this was all leading, but she realized, to her surprise, that she had no fears in the matter. She was truly, deeply in love for the first time in all of her twenty-two years. She would follow where the road led, and when it ended . . . well, she would worry about that when it happened. For now she meant to live for the moment, and the moment was Patrick Leslie, Earl of Glenkirk.

Chapter 2

King James looked closely at his old friend the Earl of Glenkirk. "By the rood, Patrick, if I did not know better I would say you were in love!" he exclaimed.

Patrick smiled. "Why do you think it impossible for me to be in love, Jamie?" he inquired of the king. "Am I not a man like any other?"

"A man, aye, but like any other? Nay, Patrick, you are not. You were my ambassador to San Lorenzo. It was an important assignment for an unimportant Highland laird. I created you an earl to honor San Lorenzo's duke. And you served me well until the tragedy of your daughter, Janet. Then, without even waiting for my permission, you packed up your family and returned home. You stopped at court only long enough to give me your report, and then you disappeared into your Highland eyrie for the next eighteen years. You would still be there had I not called you back to me. I do not know of any other man so loyal to my crown who would do that, Patrick. You were ever my friend, even from the very beginning, unlike some whom I must smile at, praise, and bestow honors upon. You do not dissemble. Your word is your bond. I can trust you."

"So you said when you asked me to go to San Lorenzo," the earl replied dryly. "And suddenly you have called me back to your side, Jamie. Why?"

"First you must tell me who the lady is, Patrick," the king teased his old friend.

The earl smiled. "A gentleman does not gossip like a cotter's wife," he said. "I know you possess a good soul of patience, Jamie. I will tell you in time, but not now."

The king grinned. "Ahh, then it is love," he chortled. "I shall be watching you, my lord of Glenkirk." Then he grew serious again. "Patrick, I need you to return to San Lorenzo for me."

"You have a competent ambassador there," the earl responded.

"Aye, Ian McDuff is indeed competent, but he is not the diplomat that you were, Patrick. And I very much need a diplomat. You know that the pope is forming what he refers to as the Holy League. He wishes the French out of the northern Italian states, and he cannot do it himself. So he is declaring a righteous war against them, inviting others to join in his cause with promise of eternal salvation, among other rewards. My bombastic young brother-in-law, Henry of England, is his loudest supporter. I am invited to join them, but I cannot. Will not. This aggression is wrong, Patrick!"

"And the French are our auld alliance. You are an honorable man, Jamie, and I know that you would not turn upon a friend without good reason. And there is no good reason, is there?"

"Only Henry Tudor's intense desire to please the pope in order to gain more power than England now has," James Stewart replied. "Spain, of course, joins the pope and England. Venice and the Holy Roman Empire have joined, as well, but before it goes any farther, I would make an attempt to stop them. I must do it in secret and in a place no one would suspect if they knew of my plans. I do not want the most powerful of the Christian states fighting with one another when we should be mounting a crusade against the Turks in Constantinople. And, too, my brother-in-law knows that, unlike him, I am an honorable man. I will not betray an ally even for my own advantage, as he would. He knows I cannot join this league against the French. He seeks to turn the Holy Father against me — against Scotland. You must meet with Venice's and the emperor's representatives in San Lorenzo,

Patrick. You must convince them that this league is but England's plan to achieve a dominant hold over us all. There are parties within each of these countries who understand this. I am in contact with them, and they will arrange for delegates from their governments to be in San Lorenzo to hear you out. Instinct tells me it is unlikely we can succeed, but we must try, Patrick."

"There will be war with England sooner than later," the earl sighed.

"I know," the king replied. "My *lang eey* tells me so, yet I must do what I know is right in this matter. I do it for Scotland, Patrick."

"Aye, and we have never had a better king then you, Jamie, the fourth of the Stewarts. But you should not have wed with England. You should have married Margaret Drummond. The Drummonds had given Scotland two queens, and good queens they were." He sighed. "I mean no disrespect to your wee wife, Jamie."

"I know," the king answered, "and you are right. I knew I should not wed with England, and I avoided it as long as I could. But when my beloved Margaret and her sisters were poisoned, I had no more excuses. Many desired the match with the Tudor princess, and they believed that it would bring peace between our two nations. The peace has been a fragile one at best. But since my father-in-law's death and the ascension of his son, I fear for us all. My wife's brother is a determined man, and the wealth built up so carefully by his father makes him a powerful one, as well."

"But Scotland is more prosperous and peaceful under your rule, Jamie, than it has been in centuries," the earl noted. "It is obvious that we desire nothing more than peace in order to continue on as we have."

"Aye, but Henry Tudor is an ambitious man, I fear," the king replied. "He is jealous of the fact that I have been on good terms with the Holy See. He attempts to destroy that trust by his enthusiasm for the pope's war, and he will succeed, I fear. You have heard about the matter of my wife's jewels, have you not?"

The earl shook his head, puzzled. "Nay, I have not."

"Of course," the king said. "You are only just back at court. My wife's grandmother, the Venerable Margaret, and her mother, the late Elizabeth of York, left their jewelry in three equal parts: to my Meg, to her sister, Mary, and to her brother's good Queen Katherine. But the King of England refuses to send his elder sister her portion, making all sorts of excuses as to why he will not. Finally my wife wrote to her brother that she didn't need the jewelry as much as she desired

these mementos of her mother and grandmother, for I, her husband, would gift her
with double their value. I can but imagine
the sting that gave arrogant King Hal. Meg
tells me he used to cheat at their nursery
games, and whined and raged if he did not
win. These are traits he has obviously carried with him into his manhood."

"When do you want me to leave?" the
earl asked.

"Not until after the Twelve Days of
Christmas are over and done with," the
king answered. "I want it to appear as if I
have just lured you back to court for the
Christmas season for old time's sake. And
you came because it had been many years
since you had paid your respects to me.
The fact that you have involved yourself
with a lady is all to the good. After the holidays have ended, you will disappear, and
all will assume you have returned to
Glenkirk. You know that there are spies
here at my court, Patrick, and should they
know my plans they would report back to
England or Spain or even the pope himself.
Your mission must be secret. I realize there
is little chance of its success, but I do not
want the waters muddied before I have at
least attempted to stop this madness.
Three years ago the Holy See formed an
alliance with France to humble Venice.
Now France is the enemy. I despair, Pat-

rick, of this chess game my fellow monarchs play. And no one ever really wins! These politicians will be the ruin of the world."

"So, what you actually desire of me is to convince some of the players of the foolishness of this matter," the earl said. "Which ones, Jamie? Which are the weak links?"

"Venice, who is suspicious of everyone, and possibly the Holy Roman Empire, who never quite trusts Spain. Spain will side with the pope no matter, especially as the English queen is Spanish born and bred. If I can but weaken the league, the pressure will be off of me to join it and betray the auld alliance we honor with France. And learning of this new coalition, the Turks are bound to make some hostile move that should turn the pope's attention in other directions. After all, he is the father of the Christian church." The king chuckled wickedly.

"So, Venice's and the emperor's representatives will be in San Lorenzo?" the earl said.

The king nodded.

"Well," Patrick said, "my son, Adam, is a grown man and can manage our lands without me for a short time. And while I do not imagine my trip across a winter's sea will be a pleasant one, January and February in San Lorenzo, as I recall it, are

58

most benign. It has been a long time since I have enjoyed a mild winter."

"And you will not regret leaving your lady?" the king queried.

"Leave her? Nay, Jamie, I shall not leave her. I intend to take her with me to San Lorenzo. You are correct when you say I am a man in love. I am. I adored my daughter's mother. I married my son's mother, a sweet and gentle girl whom I came to care for most deeply, because I needed a legitimate son and heir. Her sudden death broke my heart. It was not fair that Agnes die as Janet's mother had. She was so damned good, even making me promise to legitimatize Janet when our son was born. But I have never, never until this moment in time, been truly and deeply in love. I am a man long grown. I have grandchildren. But nonetheless I am in love. I feel like a young man again, Jamie."

"Will her absence from this court be noted?" the king asked his friend.

The Earl of Glenkirk considered a long moment, and then he said, "Mayhap. She is the queen's friend."

"Does she have a husband we should be concerned about?" the king wondered aloud. "Is her family an important one?"

"She is widowed and of unimportant lineage," the earl said. "It will be said that she has returned to her own home."

"Unless," the king responded, suddenly knowing of whom the Earl of Glenkirk spoke, "my wife wants her here for the birth of our child in the spring."

"You know? That damned *lang eey* of yours, Jamie," the earl said with a small smile. "Or are you merely guessing?"

"You have fallen in love with the little lady of Friarsgate, Patrick, haven't you?" was the king's answer.

The earl nodded. "We met two nights ago," he began.

"But two nights ago?" the king exclaimed, surprised.

"Hear me out, Jamie. It was the oddest experience I have ever had. I saw her across the chamber. Suddenly I had the most overwhelming urge to meet her. Lord Grey managed the introductions through his friend Elsbeth Hume. Our eyes met, and we both knew in that instant that we had known each other in some other time and place and that we were meant to be together for the here and now. I cannot explain it any more plainly than that. There are many who would think me mad, but I know you do not, Jamie Stewart."

"Nay," the king agreed, "for it was the same with Margaret Drummond and me. Rosamund Bolton is lovely, I will concur. But she is English, Patrick. And she was, according to my information, briefly mistress to my brother-in-law."

"Was she?" The earl was intrigued. Rosamund had not told him that, but why would she? "Nonetheless, Jamie, I do not believe the lady is politically involved, whatever her past," he said. "You cannot believe she seeks to curry favor with her king. I do not believe that of her. She need not know why I go to San Lorenzo, just that I would take her there that we might be lovers in peace, far from the prying eyes of your court and our friends. Arcobaleno, the capital, is a most romantic place. I am certain that Rosamund, having never until she entered Scotland been out of England, will find it delightful."

"The affair was most discreet. Neither my wife nor Queen Katherine knew of it," the king said. "Brother Henry had attempted to seduce the lady when she was a young girl at court. He was prevented from doing so, and she was wed to her husband on the king's orders. He obviously sought her out when she returned to court a grieving widow, to correct his previous failure. He does not like losing at games, I am told."

"You are extremely well informed, Jamie," the earl noted admiringly.

"Almost nothing a king does is truly secret," James Stewart replied. "There is always someone, in this case a servant of her cousin Lord Cambridge, with information to sell to the appropriate buyer. I think this fellow thought I might be interested in bedding the lady myself. I have at the moment, however, a perfectly satisfactory mistress in Isabel Stewart, the daughter of my cousin, the Earl of Buchan. And my wife is again with child. I would not distress Meg, as I know that this child she delivers in the spring will be a son, and he will survive — unlike the other wee, frail bairns she has borne me."

"The queen does not really need Rosamund, but I do," the earl said. "I am your most loyal servant, Jamie, and well you know it, but I will not go to San Lorenzo without my lass. I will speak with Rosamund when the time is right, and she will convince the queen that she must return home to her beloved Friarsgate, but that she will return in the spring when the queen has her bairn. A lad, you say? The *lang eey* again, eh, Jamie?"

"Aye, a lad!" He sighed. "I can but hope I live to see him grown, but I will not."

The earl did not argue, for he did not want to know what the king knew. James Stewart was known for having incredible intuition and sensitivity to supernatural forces. Patrick knew if the king was concerned, then this mission was of great importance. "I'll be an old man, Jamie, before I serve your son," he said comfortingly.

The king laughed, his mood now suddenly lightened. "You've already bedded her!" It was a statement, not a question.

"Within hours of our meeting. Jesu, Jamie! I feel like a man of thirty again when I am with her. God knows I have had mistresses aplenty in my lifetime, but none of them ever captured my heart as this girl has."

"They say she has a suitor," the king replied.

"Aye, the Earl of Bothwell's cousin, the Hepburn of Claven's Carn. She told me," he chuckled. "He told her he would come on St. Stephen's Day to wed her. I think he will be most surprised not to find her waiting meekly and eagerly for his arrival."

"St. Stephen's? That's today," the king exclaimed, laughing. "What a wench she is, Patrick. Are you certain you would have her?"

"As long as it is meant to be, Jamie," the earl said.

"Ah, then," the king remarked, "you do not believe it is forever. You will not wed her."

"I would wed her if she would have me. But though she will have me as a lover, she will not have me as a husband," the earl explained. "She has no wish to remarry, and I know she would not leave her beloved Friarsgate any more than I would depart Glenkirk forever. But one day I will ask her," he finished with a small smile. "So we may both be satisfied that I truly love her. That is why she has rejected the Hepburn of Claven's Carn. She believes his only interest in her is getting a son. I pity the lad. For what can he possibly do to convince her otherwise that he loves her? If he does."

The king nodded. "You may expect him here at court, Patrick, when he finds the lass gone, I have not a doubt. Hepburns are not noted for giving up easily. And he will have his cousin Bothwell plead his case for him, as well."

"Rosamund is English, and you cannot order her to wed with this man," the Earl of Glenkirk said quietly. "Can you?"

"Such will be my defense, but Meg will undoubtedly become involved in the matter. My wee English wife is a romantic, a discovery I find astounding in a Tudor. Rosamund will have to confide in my queen or Meg will not be silent or rest in her quest to gain her dear friend another husband. The queen believes that no woman can be truly happy, or even content, without a lawful mate. In that mood she becomes dangerous, Patrick. Your affair may become public knowledge."

"Perhaps it will be better if it does," the earl said thoughtfully. "The better to deter the queen, the Earl of Bothwell, and this Hepburn of Claven's Carn. But I must consult with Rosamund first. She is not a woman to be surprised in matters that are important to her."

"Ah, to be in love once again," the king chuckled. "You are a fortunate man! I have not felt that way since Margaret Drummond."

"I am," the Earl of Glenkirk agreed with a smile.

The two men were seated companionably in the king's privy chamber at Stirling Castle. Settled before a roaring fire, handleless silver drinking vessels containing peat whiskey cupped between their hands, they talked on into the night, while the king was thought to be with his mistress.

"A French vessel will ferry you across the sea to France," the king said. "From there you will travel by land to San Lorenzo. I would not risk your life at this time of year crossing the Bay of Biscay. With a woman, however, it may take you longer than I had anticipated," James Stewart considered.

"Rosamund is a country girl, as is her servant. A coach with all its accoutrements would but attract someone's attention. We will ride. My lass has said she wanted adventure in her life after all those years of doing her duty." Patrick chuckled. "This will surely be an adventure for her."

"And her clothing and all the gewgaws so dear to a woman's heart?" the king wondered aloud.

"We will carry what we need, and I shall have an entire new wardrobe made for her when we arrive," the earl said.

"I will be interested to see if your lady is so eager for adventure when you tell her that," the king remarked with a broad grin.

"She will come," the earl said quietly. "We cannot be parted yet."

"We will talk again before you leave, Patrick," the king told Glenkirk. "Go and find your bed, as I am going to find mine."

The two men arose from their places by the fire, shook hands, and went their separate ways. James Stewart to visit his current mistress, Isabel, and the Earl of Glenkirk to find his Rosamund.

Rosamund had decided that her chamber with its small fireplace was a better space for she and the earl to inhabit. Annie had been banished to the dormitory shared by many of the young servant women. When a tiring woman who usually shared her mistress' bed appeared in those quarters it was always assumed her mistress had taken a lover. Annie had been warned by her mistress to be discreet, but she kept her ears open for any tidbit of gossip that might be of interest or use to Rosamund.

Rosamund was sleeping when the earl entered her room. He quietly divested himself of his garments, and after climbing into bed, drew her into his arms, kissing the nape of her neck as he did so. She murmured a sound of distinct contentment, and he whispered in her ear, "Are you awake, lovey? I have news." One hand moved to cup a breast, and he caressed it tenderly.

"What news?" she asked him softly, and she ground her hips into his body suggestively.

"You're a bad lass," he teased her, his lust being aroused at a fierce pace. What was this sorcery she possessed to do that to him, and at his age?

"Because I want to fuck?" she queried, turning about to face him, pulling off her chemise as she did. Her arms slipped about his neck, and her round, full breasts pressed against his broad chest.

He yanked her against him by her buttocks. "Because your delicious little body and your eagerness set me aflame as no other woman ever has, my Rosamund," he told her. "Because now that you have caught my fancy in this manner, I shall have to satisfy us both before I share my news with you, you wicked wench!" His mouth found hers in a hot kiss, demanding, insisting, and she returned his ardor. "You know I love you, sweetheart, don't you?" he said breaking off their kiss.

"Aye, my lord, I do. And you will not be surprised to learn that I return your lordship's passion. I am mad for you, Patrick! I feel as if my whole life has been leading up to this moment in time. How in the name of God is that possible? I loved Hugh, for he was a father to me. I loved Owein, for he loved me and Friarsgate. But this is different. This lunacy has naught to do with Friarsgate. It is only us! I could stay in this chamber with you forever!"

He lay her back against their pillows and covered her small body with his big one, the fingers of their hands intertwined as had become their custom. Their eyes met as he entered her, and she sighed deeply. He stopped all motion for a brief time, enjoying her as she absorbed his size with such pleasure it almost brought him to tears. Then he began to move upon her again, and finally her eyes closed and she sighed once more as he brought them to passionate perfection.

"Oh, Patrick, I love you so very much! Perhaps too much," she admitted when she once again came to herself, her head upon his chest.

"I wonder," he replied, "if we can ever

love enough, let alone too much." His big hand stroked her auburn tresses. "Your hair is so soft."

"Annie thinks me mad, for I insist it be washed weekly. She says it is a wonder I have not caught my death of cold, putting my head in water so much," Rosamund said.

"Is she very angry at being banished?" Patrick asked.

"I think she actually likes the company of the other servingwomen," Rosamund replied.

"Do you think she would like to travel, my love?" he queried casually.

"I don't know," Rosamund responded. "Why?"

"I am of a mind to spend the winter in a warmer climate. I want you to go with me, Rosamund," the Earl of Glenkirk said quietly.

"Which means crossing the sea in the worst weather," she noted. Then she said, "Do not treat me as you would some foolish lass, Patrick."

He understood at once and told her, "It is for the king, lovey. I can say no more now, which I know you will comprehend. Even saying that much, I put my fate in your two little hands, Rosamund."

"Why would you say that?" she wondered.

"Because you were once King Henry's mistress," he answered bluntly.

"How on earth did you learn that? Only Tom and Annie know. It had to be a servant. Not mine I hope! Nay. It is not Annie, or you would not have asked me if she liked to travel, since you expect her to come with me. And having learned this fact, your king fears that I will betray you. Please tell me that Meg does not know."

"Nay. Nor Queen Katherine, either," he reassured her.

"I did not seek to attract Hal," Rosamund began. "But he would have me, willing or nay. For my family's sake I acquiesced as graciously as I could, Patrick. There was no real love between us, and while I am loyal to England, I do not believe whatever you do in your king's service will harm my country. King James appears to be a man of great intellect and peace. I know Henry Tudor well enough to know he is ambitious and vain. He has a bad habit of always making it appear that God is on his side alone. It would be amusing if it were not so dangerous. I would not under any circumstances betray you, my lord," she concluded.

"I know that," he told her, and then he kissed her mouth again. "You will come with me, my Rosamund?"

"I will come with you, Patrick Leslie, for

where you are, my heart is, I fear," she responded.

"And what of Logan Hepburn?" he queried her.

"Logan needs a son and an heir. He should have married long ago but that he has this fancy for a child he saw at a cattle fair when he was sixteen. I was the child he saw, but I am no longer a child. Nor do I wish to be married because I am considered good breeding stock," Rosamund told the earl.

"A man expects — is entitled to — children on his wife's body," the earl said quietly.

"I will not disagree," she answered him, "but that and his silly story seem to be his whole rationale for wanting to marry me. He says he loves me, but does he really? I don't know, but I will not take the chance of marrying him to discover that it is only my fecundity that attracts him. I have never known love, Patrick, until you. I will not give that up for what is considered a respectable marriage. I won't!"

"We might marry, you and I," he said softly.

"Only when you are ready to give up your Glenkirk, and I, Friarsgate," she replied with a small smile.

"How can you know me so well on such short acquaintance?" he chuckled.

"And you me," she responded. "Ohh, Patrick! I do not care what anyone else may think. I love you! I do not need to be your wife; nor do you need to offer me the honor of your name for me to know that you love me. From the moment our eyes met, we knew it was so."

"Aye," he agreed. "It was, sweetheart."

"When are we to depart court?" she asked him.

"After Twelfth Night," he said. "It will be thought that I have returned home to Glenkirk, as I am not a man of the court. Your departure must be considered a return home, as well, Rosamund. Will it be difficult for you to take your leave of the queen?"

Rosamund was thoughtful for a few moments, and then she said, "Aye, but I will tell her one of my daughters has taken ill and Maybel has sent for me. She will accept that, although I know she will be disappointed. She wanted me to remain with her until her child was born. She fears so that she cannot give her husband a son."

"The king's *lang eey* tells him the child will be a healthy lad. He frets that he will not live to see the boy grown," the earl noted.

"Then I need not feel so guilty about my wee lie," Rosamund said.

"And your cousin Lord Cambridge? A

most amusing fellow, but very astute beneath his droll wit, I think," Patrick said.

"Tom is clever, but I will have to tell him the entire truth of the matter. He is the best friend I have ever had, and no one, not even my husbands, have been as good to me as Thomas Bolton has. Frankly, he will be very disappointed not to be invited along with us," Rosamund chuckled. "However, I will need him to return to Friarsgate to explain to my uncles and to Maybel where I have gone and why. I will need him there to watch over my lasses and wield my authority in my absence. My uncle Henry may still have hopes of gaining Friarsgate through one of his sons. Edmund could not prevent his mischief, but my darling Lord Cambridge certainly can. I need not fear to return home eventually to discover my Philippa wed to one of my wretched cousins, as long as Tom is there to watch over her." She leaned forward and gave her lover a quick kiss. "I shall feel very guilty about leaving Tom behind. He is a most amusing traveling companion."

"Yet I prefer that our idyll be more private than familial," the earl said.

"Will Glenkirk be all right while you are gone so far? Will you tell your son?"

"Adam is a man grown. He is a little bit older than you are, my darling love. He has a sound head on his shoulders, and as Glenkirk will one day be his, it is past time he handled its responsibilities on his own." He drew her closer into his embrace, his lips brushing the top of her head.

"Is he a married man?" Rosamund asked.

"Aye, though why he wed with Anne MacDonald I will never know. They met at the Highland games one summer. She was young and pretty. She knew he was an earl's heir, and he was vulnerable to her flattery. Adam is much like his mother, though he never knew my sweet Agnes. He is kind and gentle. His saving grace is that he has a Leslie's head for common sense. Nonetheless, he is not at all like me. He had no lasses mooning after him, and so Anne easily captured his innocent heart. The family was a good one. I had no cause to deny the match. So they wed. Only afterwards he discovered he had married a shrew. She fears me, however, and so my son's life has not been intolerable. Oddly, I sometimes feel sorry for Anne, and God knows she has done her duty. I have two fine grandsons and a wee granddaughter born just last year and named after Adam's mam, the sweet Agnes. She's a bonnie little lass, not in the least like her mother. Anne is content letting her daughter be looked after by her nursemaid. I expect my daughter-in-law will very much enjoy being in charge while I am away," the earl finished with a small grin.

"Then neither of us need fear for our lands and our families while we are in San Lorenzo," Rosamund said.

"We have earned this time together, sweetheart," he answered her, and he enfolded her closely in his arms. "Let us sleep now. Tomorrow we must begin planning. We can take little with us, as once we reach France we must ride the rest of the way. A coach and all that goes with it would attract the interest of those who earn their livings selling information. A small party of horsemen will not. Do you mind riding so great a distance?"

"Nay," she answered. "I think perhaps it would be best if I dressed in boy's clothing, and Annie, too. It would be easier, and it would attract even less attention."

He nodded. "Aye, lass, it would. Can you ride astride?"

"I certainly can!" she laughed. "Even in skirts, my lord. Do you think I shall make a pretty boy in trunk hose and doublet?"

He chuckled. "Aye. Perhaps too pretty. Now, go to sleep, Rosamund. The morning will come quickly enough, and you are expected at mass with the queen."

She lay against his chest, the beat of his

heart beneath her ear, the comforting rhythm of his breathing lulling her to slumber. When she finally awoke he was gone, and Annie was bustling about their chamber. It was still dark outside Rosamund saw, so she was not late. She yawned and stretched. "Good morrow, Annie," she said.

"Good morning, my lady," Annie replied. "The earl has gone already, and he says he will see you later. He also says you are to speak to me. Oh, my lady, I hope I have not displeased him, or you, again!" Annie's face bore all the hallmarks of her distress.

"Nay, you have displeased neither of us." Rosamund sat up in her bed. "Put a bit more wood on the fire, Annie, and bring me a basin to wash myself." She swung her legs over the side of the bed, shivering as she came from beneath the shelter of the coverlets and her feet touched the cold stone floor.

Annie handed her mistress the chamber pot, and Rosamund peed. Then she washed herself as thoroughly as she might using a flannel and the little basin. She longed for her daily bath, but the servants at Stirling grudged her even her weekly ablutions, grumbling as they brought up the water to fill her little oak tub. But they dared not deny her, for they knew the Englishwoman was the queen's dear childhood friend.

"What will you wear today, my lady?" Annie asked.

"Give me the tawny orange velvet," Rosamund said. "Tom always likes me in that gown, although I wonder if the gold embroidery isn't perhaps too showy."

" 'Tis beautiful, my lady. I'll fetch it from the trunk and see the wrinkles smoothed out." She bustled about the room as Rosamund climbed back into the warm bed.

"I would speak with you privily, Annie," Rosamund began. "I have never enjoyed having my life decided for me by others, and so I will share a confidence with you that you may choose what it is you will do. I am going away with Lord Leslie, Annie. I would like you to come with us. No one is to know. They are to believe that each of us has returned to our own homes. If you choose not to accompany me, I shall see you safely returned to Friarsgate with Lord Cambridge, and I shall not hold it against you. But however you decide, you can say nothing to anyone of what I have just told you. Do you understand, Annie? No one must know."

Annie was more than surprised by her mistress' speech. She drew a deep breath and asked, "Will we be going back to

Friarsgate ever, my lady?" The velvet gown in her hands felt very heavy.

Rosamund laughed softly. "Annie," she chided the servant, "you know I should not leave my girls. And Uncle Henry so close by?" She laughed again. "Why, all three should find themselves wed to my uncle's odious sons if I were to desert them. And there is Friarsgate itself. I love it so! I gain my strength from Friarsgate. I must always eventually go home, Annie."

Annie nodded slowly. "When would we come back?" she queried.

"I don't know, but I suspect in a few months' time. No more," Rosamund responded. "We just want a little time together before we must part again."

"Why don't you just wed the earl?" Annie questioned her lady. "Begging your pardon, mistress. I do not mean to be forward, but I do not understand."

"The Earl of Glenkirk can no more abandon his home than I could forsake Friarsgate, Annie. Were my lasses not so young I might consider a union with him, but they are too young for me to leave."

Annie nodded again, understanding, but not quite understanding. She lay the orange tawny gown out on the chamber's single chair. "Where would we go?"

"Across the sea," Rosamund replied simply.

"Across the sea? I ain't ever been on any boat, my lady!" Annie exclaimed.

"Neither have I," Rosamund chuckled. "It will be quite an adventure for us."

"And how long would we be at sea?" Annie asked nervously.

"A few days at the most," Rosamund promised her.

"And we'll come home after you have all this adventure out of yourself?" Annie pressed her mistress. "You swear on the Blessed Mother's name?"

"I swear," Rosamund said with utmost seriousness. "I expect we will be back by autumn at the latest, Annie. Probably sooner."

Annie drew a long, deep breath. Then she said, "I'll come, my lady. But what will Mistress Maybel and Master Edmund say? And who is to tell them?"

"Lord Cambridge will tell them, Annie," Rosamund answered the girl.

"Have you told him?" Annie persisted as she unrolled two pairs of stockings.

"I shall tell him today, Annie. Now, remember, this is a great secret. I shall have to lie to the queen, I fear, for she would not understand my leaving her now. And it is not yet time for all the dissembling to begin. Put it from your mind now, and I shall tell you when you may recall it again," Rosamund said. "Now, I would get dressed before I am late for the mass."

Margaret of Scotland signaled to her friend to come and be by her side just as the mass was beginning. This was an honor, and Rosamund well knew it. For a moment she felt almost guilty at the deception she would play on her old friend. But then her eyes met those of the Earl of Glenkirk across the royal chapel, and her guilt vanished. When the morning services were over, the queen linked her arm in Rosamund's, and they walked together towards the Great Hall where the morning meal would be laid out.

"What is this gossip I hear about you and Lord Leslie?" the queen asked bluntly.

"I do not know the gossip to which you refer, madame," Rosamund answered formally, for they were in public.

"It is said that you have become lovers," the queen replied. Then she lowered her voice. "Is it true, Rosamund? Have you? He is very handsome, even if he is old."

"He is not that old, Meg," Rosamund whispered, a twinkle in her amber eyes.

"Ohhh, then it is so!" the queen chortled. "What a naughty girl you have suddenly become, Rosamund."

"I would not offend your highness," Rosamund quickly said.

"Offend me? Nay, I envy you!" the

80

queen answered. "Do you remember how my grandmother always said a woman married first, perhaps a second time for her family, but after that she should find her own happiness? Does Lord Leslie make you happy, Rosamund? I hope so! Have you ever had a lover before?"

The first lie, Rosamund thought to herself. "Nay, Meg," she murmured softly. "Never before." And in a sense it was the truth, for she had not really loved Margaret Tudor's brother, England's king. But she was surely in love with Patrick Leslie.

" 'Tis rather sudden, isn't it?" the queen pressed her friend further.

"I cannot explain it," Rosamund said. "Our eyes met, and we both knew."

The queen laughed softly. "You sound like my husband with his *lang eey,*" she said. Her hand went protectively to her belly. "I don't want to be an empty vessel like my brother's wife. Pray God and his Blessed Mother that this child is a strong son, Rosamund. Pray hard for me!"

"I do," Rosamund said. "Every day, Meg."

"Your highness." The king's page was before them. "His majesty would break his fast with you this morning," the lad said. "I am here to escort you."

The queen nodded, and Rosamund gracefully slid into the background, seeking

81

either Glenkirk or her cousin Lord Cambridge. It was Lord Cambridge who found her first.

"My darling girl, you have set the court upon its ear, I fear. Is it true? Has Lord Leslie become your lover? I have never before heard such delicious tittle-tattle. The Scots court is far more fun than the English court, where poor Spanish Kate and her mate, our stodgy King Henry, hold sway. There everything is proper and ordered while the king casts his eye boldly about and then swives his little conquests in secrecy — no offense, my darling cousin."

"None taken, dearest Tom," Rosamund replied dryly.

"But in this delightful court," Lord Cambridge continued, "people are not so damned *au fait* about their passions. I quite like it! Now come along, dear girl, and tell me absolutely everything!" He linked his velvet-clad arm in hers.

"I am hungry, Tom," Rosamund protested. "We have only just celebrated the mass, and I have not eaten since last night."

"We shall go to my house, and my cook will feed you," he responded. "And that will allow us our privacy, cousin, for I do indeed mean to hear all."

"You bought a house in Stirling Village!" Rosamund exclaimed.

"Nay, I have just rented it. It is little more than a cottage, but quite charming, and the old woman who owns it cooks like an angel. I had no intention, dear girl, of sleeping in the king's hall with those other poor disenfranchised souls who are at court. You were given a little box to nest in, cousin, but I am not the queen's friend. I only accompanied you. Therefore I was on my own. The royal hospitality does not mean to be niggardly, but you see how many follow this court. There is simply no room to house them all decently, Rosamund. Now, come along, my darling. Shall we invite Lord Leslie?" he teased her wickedly, and he gave her arm a little pinch.

"Do I need my horse?" she asked, ignoring his teasing.

"Nay, darling girl. 'Tis only a short walk down the hill. The house is but a few yards from the castle gates. The old woman used to cook for the royal nursery when it was at Stirling. Your little friend, the queen, however, objected to the king housing his bastards in a castle she had a particular fondness for, and she threw such a tantrum when she first discovered the little by-blows there that the king moved his nursery to a more discreet location out of his queen's sight. The king wanted to make his eldest son, Alexander, his heir, you know, and the queen still fears he might if she doesn't give him a nice healthy babe."

"Alexander Stewart is the bishop of St. Andrew's," Rosamund said.

"Aye, he is, and he is amazingly well suited to the task despite his youth. He and the king have a great bond of love between them. The queen is jealous. She knows that even if she gives her husband a healthy son and heir, Alexander will always be his favorite. But then, of course, he is the firstborn."

"How do you learn all this gossip, and in such detail?" Rosamund demanded of her cousin. "We have been here scarce a week," she laughed.

They had exited the castle, walked across the great courtyard, and were now passing through Stirling's open gates into the street beyond. It was a cobbled byway lined in well-kept stone houses with dark slate roofs. Three houses down on the left Lord Cambridge stopped and turned to enter the building, calling as he did, "Mistress MacHugh, I have brought my cousin home, and we are hungry, having just come from the mass."

A tall, thin woman appeared from the depths of the darkened hallway. "Yer cousin, is it, my lord?"

"Rosamund Bolton, the lady of Friarsgate and the queen's good friend, Mistress

MacHugh. I've spoken of her," Lord Cambridge said. He divested himself of his cloak and took Rosamund's from her.

"Ye've done naught but chatter away since ye rented my dwelling from me," Mistress MacHugh replied sharply. She looked directly at Rosamund. "Does he ever stop speaking, my lady?" But her gray eyes were twinkling.

"Not often, I fear, Mistress MacHugh," Rosamund answered with a smile. Then she shivered involuntarily.

The lady saw it and she *tch*ed. "Come into the parlor, my lady. I have a good fire going there. It's the coziest room in the house. I'll bring yer meal there." Then she bustled off.

The parlor of the cottage was indeed warm with the blazing fire. Rosamund sat down in a tapestried chair next to the warmth. Tom placed a small goblet of wine in her hand, advising her to drink it to restore the heat to her slender frame.

"I'll not press you until the meal is served," he said. "I don't want to be interrupted, and you, I am certain, don't wish to share your news with the entire world."

She nodded and slowly sipped at the sweet wine.

"You are wearing one of my favorite gowns," he noted. "The fur-trimmed sleeves make it a whole other garment, I vow. It complements your lovely hair, cousin."

"It is pretty, isn't it?" Rosamund agreed. "And I thank you for the new sleeves. The marten is just wonderful in both texture and color."

The door to the parlor opened, and Mistress MacHugh came in carrying a large tray. She set it on a sideboard, then said, "My lord, help me with this table." And together the landlady and Lord Cambridge set a sturdy oak table before the fire. Rosamund immediately drew her chair up. Their hostess filled two pewter plates with small trenchers of oat stirabout, fluffy eggs, ham, and individual cottage loaves that were hot from her ovens. She placed a stone crock of fresh butter, another of cherry preserves, and a generous wedge of cheese between them. Then, with a small curtsy, she departed the chamber.

They ate in silence until both plates were empty and half the cheese was devoured between them. The wine, Rosamund thought, was really quite good. Finally satisfied, they sighed in unison, laughed, and Tom said to his cousin, "Well, now, dear girl, I would know absolutely all! Hold back nothing!"

"We are lovers," Rosamund began, and he nodded, not in the least surprised. Anyone at court who thought otherwise was a simpleton and a fool. "I am going away with him shortly, Tom. I would have you understand everything, but you must keep what I tell you a secret, for many lives depend upon it. Can you do that, cousin?"

He nodded. "You know, Rosamund, that while I love England, I am not a man to involve myself in politics. Do you swear to me that this will not be treason on your part or mine by hearing you out?"

"There is no treason, Tom," she assured him.

"Then I will keep secret all you tell me, but haven't I always, dearest girl?"

"You have, Tom. But this is very different. Hal has entered into an agreement with the Holy Father in Rome to attempt a removal of the French from northern Italy. Venice, Spain, and the Holy Roman Empire have joined them. They call themselves the Holy League. Hal has been pressing King James to join them. This Scots king has always been in high favor with the pope. That favor is now endangered by England insisting that Scotland join their cause. Patrick has told me what King James would do."

"Ahh," said Lord Cambridge, seeing the problem immediately. "The auld alliance, of course. King James is an honorable man. He has no cause to break his word."

"Exactly," Rosamund replied. "So the

king is sending Lord Leslie to San Lorenzo, where he once served as Scotland's ambassador, to meet secretly with Venice and the Empire in hopes that he may convince them to withdraw from this league, and by doing so weaken the alliance. Then Scotland will not seem so out of step. But if there is any chance of this plan succeeding, it must be done clandestinely. When Lord Leslie disappears from court it will be assumed that he has gone home. He hasn't been to court in eighteen years, after all, and is hardly considered among the powerful or influential. He has asked me to go with him. I have said that I would, but my absence would be questioned, as I was asked to come to court by the queen and am considered her friend. I must lie to Meg. I will tell her that I have been sent a message that one of my daughters is very ill. That I must return to Friarsgate immediately, but that I will return to her as soon as possible — and indeed I will."

"You want me to go back to Friarsgate and tell Edmund and Richard? Is that it?" he asked her.

"Aye, I do, Tom, but there is more. I would give you authority over my lands and my daughters until I return home again. I will not allow Henry Bolton any opportunity to steal my lasses, and by doing so, steal Friarsgate from me. He

88

would try to bully Edmund and even Prior Richard, but he will not bully you. You are Lord Cambridge, and he just plain, ordinary Henry Bolton. I realize that I am asking a great deal from you, cousin. You thought to spend the winter here with me at the Scots court, escort me home, and then return to your own holding near London."

"True," Tom said. "And I am more disappointed that I cannot travel with you to San Lorenzo. I have heard it is a most beautiful little duchy."

"I told Patrick you would be disappointed not to be accompanying us," Rosamund responded with a small smile.

Lord Cambridge chortled. "And I am certain he expressed his regrets at losing my company, dear girl."

She laughed. "Forgive us, dear Tom. Unexpectedly, and quite to our mutual surprise, we have fallen madly in love with each other. We must have this time to be together before it ends."

"You do not expect to marry him, cousin?" Tom looked troubled.

"I will not leave Friarsgate, and neither can he leave his Glenkirk. We both understand this, Tom, and are content to have what time fate will allow us. That is why when the king asked Patrick to go to San Lorenzo he said he would only obey if I might come with him. Soon enough our duties will call us to our own holdings, Tom. I do not comprehend really what has happened, and I certainly do not understand why it has happened, but for the first time in my life I am in love. And I am loved in return. I have spent my life doing what was required of me. Now I require this little time for myself, and I shall have it."

"I will keep your secret, cousin. I will help you create this subterfuge, and then I will return to Friarsgate with your authority to watch over your daughters for you. Edmund guards your lands, and he is an amusing companion, although he will persist in beating me at chess. It is not quite the winter I had envisioned, but you are my beloved Rosamund, and I will do it. When must we leave?"

"Not until after Twelfth Night," she said.

"And Logan Hepburn? What of him? What am I to say when he comes calling? What if he comes here to court before you escape?"

"I shall cross that bridge if we come to it," she said. "And if he comes to Friarsgate seeking me, you will tell him I went off with a lover, and 'tis all you know," Rosamund instructed her cousin. "I will not be bullied by that wild borderer!"

"He's in love with you, cousin," her companion said.

"He wants a son of me," she replied. "I will not be his broodmare, Tom. Let him get his son on another!"

"His family may force him to it now, dear girl. What will happen when you and Lord Leslie part and you decide that you want Logan Hepburn after all?" he asked her candidly.

"Then I shall allow him to become my lover," she answered pertly. "If he indeed does love me for myself and not my fecundity, he will be content with that, Tom."

"You have changed, my darling, since Owein's death," he told her. "Once you were a sweet innocent, but now you have become a willful wildcat. I love you nonetheless, however, and I do understand."

"Then you are probably the only one who does, Tom, and I am grateful for it," she responded softly. "Thank you for being the best friend I have ever had or ever will have!"

He shook his head at her. "Lord Leslie will not hurt you, I know. 'Tis you, I fear, who may hurt yourself. Do not lose your common sense, Rosamund. Enjoy this idyll you are about to embark upon, but keep a clear head, I beg you."

"I will, dear Tom," she promised. "I am in love, but I am not a fool. And Patrick, I suspect, will protect me from myself."

"But who, I wonder," he said quietly, "will protect Glenkirk?"

Chapter 3

Logan Hepburn came to court on the last day of the old year. He should have arrived a day earlier, he told his cousin, the Earl of Bothwell, but the weather had slowed him down. "I've come to wed with my lass," he said with a grin.

Patrick Hepburn's look was disturbed. "Why have you set your heart on this English girl, Logan? Are there not plenty of fine Scots lasses for you to choose from, cousin? This woman is not for you."

Logan's blue eyes were at once curious and wary. "You have seen her?" he said.

"Aye, and I will agree that she is fair and charming, Logan, but she is not for you, I fear," the Earl of Bothwell said quietly.

Logan shifted his large frame in the too-small chair in which he was seated. "And why is Rosamund Bolton not the lass for me, cousin?" His tone was decidedly dangerous.

Patrick Hepburn sighed. He was annoyed by the position in which he found himself and troubled by his cousin's insistence that he marry this Englishwoman. "Did you ever consider, Logan, that Rosamund Bolton might not want to marry you or any other man right now?" he asked the younger man.

"But I love her!" the laird of Claven's Carn replied.

"It isn't enough to just love a woman, Logan," his cousin began.

"What has happened?" Logan demanded.

There was no help for it, the earl decided. Candor was the best route to take in this matter. "The lady has taken a lover, cousin. He is the Earl of Glenkirk, and their passion for each other is both public and palpable. You cannot possibly wed her now."

"I will kill this Earl of Glenkirk!" Logan shouted, jumping from his chair. "I warned Rosamund that I should destroy any man who tried to take her from me! Where is she? Where is he?"

"Sit down, Logan," his cousin ordered in a hard voice. "The Earl of Glenkirk is a cherished friend of the king's. He is a widower with a grown son and grandchildren. He has not been to court in almost two decades, but the king invited him to Stirling this Christmas, and he actually came. He and Rosamund Bolton took one look at each other, and while I do not pretend to understand it, they were lovers that same night, I am told. They have contracted that rarest of conditions: love. You can do nothing about it, Logan. Their hearts are engaged, and that is an end to it."

"She knew I wanted her for my wife," the laird said, and he slumped again in the chair by the fire in his cousin's apartments. *Why did Rosamund not understand?*

"Did she say she would wed you, Logan? Was there an agreement legal and binding between you?" the earl probed. "If there was, you are at least entitled to damages for her betrayal."

"I told her I would come on St. Stephen's Day to marry her," he answered.

"And what did she reply?" the earl asked quietly.

Logan's blue eyes grew thoughtful with his memories of that day. He and his clansmen had helped Rosamund entrap the thieves who had been pilfering her sheep. He had told her that while he was named for his mother's family, Logan, his Christian name was Stephen, after the saint, and so he would come to wed her on St. Stephen's Day, 26 December. She had sat there on her horse, and her amber eyes had looked directly at him when she said, "I will not marry you." But she hadn't meant it! She couldn't have meant it. She was just being coquettish as all women were apt to be in situations like that.

"What did she reply?" his cousin repeated.

"She said no," Logan told him. "But she was surely being coy."

"Obviously she was not," the earl told him tartly. "I have seen her since she arrived here at Stirling, Logan. She does not strike me as a woman who dissembles or who blows this way and that. And her passion for Patrick Leslie is startlingly pure, as is his for her. When you see them together you will understand."

"You say he is an older man?" the laird asked his cousin.

"Aye," the earl answered.

"Two of her husbands were older than she. While the second of them got children on her, they were but lasses. Is it possible, cousin, that she fears to wed with a young and vigorous man? Is that why she appears to fancy this graybeard lover?"

Patrick Hepburn laughed aloud. "Put such notions from you, Logan," he advised. "While the Earl of Glenkirk has seen a half century, he cannot be considered a graybeard. He is handsome and vigorous. Indeed, he seems to be in his prime, and his devotion to Rosamund Bolton cannot be questioned. I would swear there was sorcery involved if I believed in such things, which I don't."

"I will not give her up!" the laird of Claven's Carn said desperately. "I love her!"

"You have no choice, Logan! You have no other choice!" the Earl of Bothwell shouted angrily. "Now, your brothers have been importuning me for months to find you a wife. I have put them off, respecting your pursuit of this Englishwoman. I can no longer, as head of this clan branch, ignore my duty to Claven's Carn. I will find you a suitable wife, Logan. And you will wed with her and get heirs on her for the sake of your family. Put Rosamund Bolton from your mind."

"It is not my mind in which she has entrenched herself, Patrick. It is my heart," the laird said sadly. "My brothers have sons. Let one of them take my place one day as laird. I will wed no one but Rosamund Bolton. Now, where is she?"

"I cannot permit you to instigate difficulty over this woman," the Earl of Bothwell said. "If I bring her to you and she tells you that she does not wish to wed with you, will you give up this foolishness, Logan?"

"Bring her to me," he said.

The Earl of Bothwell looked closely at his cousin. "What madness do you plan?"

"Bring her to me," the laird repeated. "You may remain in the room to assure

97

yourself that I plot no mischief, cousin."

"Very well," Patrick Hepburn said. "Tomorrow after the mass. Until then you will remain here in my apartments, Logan. I suspect it is better for us all that way. Will you agree?"

"I am content to stay here, cousin," came the reply.

The Earl of Bothwell sent a message to the king informing him of his cousin's arrival at Stirling and one to Rosamund informing her of the same thing and asking that she attend him in his apartments on the morrow after the morning mass. A page returned from the king acknowledging his missive and also saying that the lady of Friarsgate would come to speak with the earl, but as she was to accompany the queen riding, she would come before the main meal of the day.

"Tell the lady of Friarsgate that the time is suitable," the earl told the page.

"Yes, my lord," the child answered, then hurried off.

"The queen rides in her condition?" the laird asked.

"Her ladies ride. She travels in a padded cart," the earl replied.

The following day Rosamund came to the Earl of Bothwell's apartments. She was accompanied by her cousin Lord Cambridge. Patrick Hepburn felt a moment of sorrow for his young cousin, for the wench was exceedingly lovely. She wore a dark green velvet gown trimmed in rich brown beaver, the bodice embroidered with gold threads. Her little cap, which was set back on her head, allowed a glimpse of her rich auburn hair. The earl smiled to himself, for the woman had the lush sleek look of someone who was well loved. Aye, Logan had lost a prize, but lost her he had.

"You wished to see me, my lord Bothwell," Rosamund said.

" 'Tis my cousin Logan Hepburn who wishes to see you, madame," he replied.

Rosamund paled slightly, but then she responded, "He is here?"

"He awaits you in the room beyond," the earl said, pointing to a door.

"He knows, of course, for you will have told him," she said quietly.

Bothwell nodded silently.

"And he is angry." It was a statement.

"Did you expect he would be otherwise, madame?"

"I never agreed to wed him, my lord. I would have you know that, for I am not a woman to give her word and then take it back. My cousin will attest to my honesty."

"She told him nay, though why I cannot fathom," Tom said. "The lad is quite bonny as you Scots are wont to say. And he seems to have a passion for her."

99

The earl could not refrain from the small smile that touched his lips. "We Hepburns do not take lightly to refusal, be it the surrender of a castle or the surrender of a lady's heart, my lord. I am but the intermediary in this matter. The lady of Friarsgate and my cousin Logan must settle this themselves. Will you take a dram of whiskey with me while we wait for your relation and mine to resolve the difficulty between them?"

"I will," Tom replied. He patted his cousin upon her shoulder. "Run along now, dear girl, and conclude this unpleasant business so both you and the laird can get on with your lives." He gave her an encouraging nod.

Rosamund sighed. "Why could he not have just accepted my refusal?" she grumbled. She looked to the earl. "Have you settled on a wife for him? His brothers will want him to marry with all possible haste, my lord, and he should."

"I have a prospect or two, madame, but he is stubborn. You will have to work hard to convince him that you will not marry him."

"Then I shall, my lord, for God help me, I am so in love with Glenkirk I can barely stand to be away from him, even to keep the queen company," Rosamund said.

The Earl of Bothwell nodded. "Go then,

madame, and try to instill some sense of that truth into my cousin."

Rosamund moved past Patrick Hepburn and opened the door to which she had been directed, stepping through into a small paneled room beyond and drawing the portal closed behind her. "Good morning, Logan," she said softly. "Did you not believe me when I said I should not wed you?"

"Nay, I did not!" he said belligerently. "What is the matter with you, lass? I am a man of property, and I have offered you the honorable estate of marriage and my good name. You would bear my bairns and mother the next laird of Claven's Carn, Rosamund. I should never take Friarsgate from you, if that is your fear. Philippa is its heiress. I have already told you that." His wonderful blue eyes scanned her face for some sign of hope.

Rosamund sighed deeply. "You do not understand, Logan, and I wonder if you ever will," she told him. He was a handsome man, but he was not complex in character.

"Understand what?" he demanded of her. "What is there to understand?"

"Me," she replied. "You do not understand me, Logan, or how I feel, widowed for the third time in twenty-two years. I do not want another husband! At least not now. And if one day I again decide that I do want to marry, I will do the choosing! My uncle Henry shall not decide for me. Margaret Tudor shall not decide for me. No one shall decide for me but me! I have always done my duty. Done what was expected that the lady of Friarsgate do. Now I would do what I want to do."

"And playing the whore to some ancient Highlander is your choice? If that is so, Rosamund, I question your judgment," Logan said scathingly.

"Patrick Leslie has seen a half century, it is true," she replied quietly, "but he is not old in any way. But most important to me, Logan Hepburn, is the fact that he loves me. Not once have you said you really loved me. You have told me the story of seeing me in Drumfie as a child and wanting me for a wife because I was such a pretty lass. You say you would give me your name and the honorable position of wife. You say you want me to bear your bairns. But not once have you said that you really loved me. You lust after me, I know. Well, Patrick does love me, and I him. Our eyes met that first time, and it was like being struck by lightning. We both knew in that instant, and neither of us has looked back since."

"Of course I really love you, you daft woman!" Logan shouted. "Did you not know it?"

"How could I know? You did naught but babble about bairns," she answered him.

"And you could not divine it, Rosamund?" he demanded of her. "There was more between us than just neighborly camaraderie."

"There was nothing between us," she said firmly. "How could there be? I do not really know you, Logan Hepburn. And what I do know I am not certain I even like. You are bold, my lord, and arrogant! You insinuated yourself into my wedding day with Owein Meredith. And then, when I was widowed of that good man, you informed me that I would wed with you, and bear your bairns. You do not ask, sir. You inform me of your wishes. Well, I will not have it! I am a free woman of property, and I have wed thrice to please others. Now I will please myself and Patrick Leslie. No others! Find yourself a wife, Logan! There must be one woman in Scotland who would please you besides me. It is your duty as lord of Claven's Carn to sire an heir and the next generation to follow you and your brothers. You are a good man, and you deserve a woman who will love you. I love Patrick Leslie."

"So you seek to be a countess?" he snarled cruelly.

"I do not seek marriage with the Earl of Glenkirk, Logan. He is no more capable of deserting Glenkirk than I am of deserting Friarsgate. But so you understand, he would have me if I would have him. But I will not. What I will have is my small bit of happiness before I must return to my duty as the lady of Friarsgate. I have found that happiness with the Earl of Glenkirk. Your duty as the lord of Claven's Carn is to marry. I have heirs. I have done what I should. You have not."

"My brothers have legitimate bairns," Logan said stubbornly.

"But you are the direct line of descent at Claven's Carn," she reasoned with him. "It is your sons who should inherit. Do not be so damned difficult, Logan. You are behaving like a child who is hungry and given a bowl of porridge but wants meat instead. Eat your porridge, Logan. Eat it, and be happy."

"I cannot be happy without you," he insisted.

"Then you shall never be happy," she told him. "Besides, it is not up to me to make you happy. Each of us must seek and find our own happiness. I have found mine. Go and find yours, Logan Hepburn. Now I shall bid you farewell." She turned to leave.

"He cannot love you as I would," Logan said bitterly.

Rosamund turned back, and her face was

lit by a happiness he could not even conceive. "You have no idea how he loves me, but it pleaseth me right well," she said.

"One day you shall have the good fortune to make the comparison, Rosamund, and then I shall be interested to hear what you say," he told her.

She swallowed back the sharp retort that came to her lips and laughed instead. "Will you always be so overly proud, Logan?" she wondered aloud.

"A young man loves a woman differently than an old man. Your husband was old and your lover is old. I think you may fear a young man," he said softly.

"I fear no man, Logan Hepburn, especially you," she replied. Then she swept him a deep curtsy and left the room.

"Did you slay him, cousin?" Tom asked her humorously as she came forth into the Earl of Bothwell's dayroom again. He was warm with the earl's good whiskey.

"He is quite unharmed but for his pride," Rosamund replied with a smile.

"And is he convinced you will not marry him?" Bothwell queried her.

"He is an enigma to me, my lord. I can make myself no plainer than I did, yet I think he still harbors the hope I will wed with him. My advice to you is to find him a very pretty and complaisant lass and marry him to her as quickly as you can. If he is allowed to persist in this futile pursuit of me, his brothers' sons will inherit Claven's Carn one day. But that is a matter for the Hepburns to decide. I thank you, my lord, for intervening in this concern between your cousin and me." She curtsied to him. "I bid you good day. Coming, Tom?" She departed Bothwell's apartments.

Lord Cambridge scrambled to his feet. "My thanks for the whiskey, my lord," he said, and he followed after Rosamund.

When they had gone, Logan came forth from the little privy chamber where he and Rosamund had been speaking. He took the chair lately vacated by Thomas Bolton.

"Well," the Earl of Bothwell said, "are you now satisfied that the lady of Friarsgate is a lost cause?"

"She says they will not marry," Logan told his cousin. "There is yet hope for me when she has tired of this love affair and he goes back to his Highlands."

"Have you no pride, cousin?" the earl said.

"I love her, but the fault here is mine, Patrick. I never convinced her of it. I assumed that she must know my devotion all these years bespoke my love for her, but I never convinced her of it, and women, it seems, must hear those words convincingly to believe them. How could I have been such a fool?"

"Did she say she loved you, Logan?" his cousin queried pointedly.

"Nay, but when she is quit of this passion she has for the Earl of Glenkirk she will return to Friarsgate. I will court her properly this time, Patrick, and she will love me. I know it!"

"There is no time, cousin," the earl said. "You are past thirty now, and you must sire a legitimate heir. I have found a bride for you, and you will marry her before you leave Stirling. She is a distant cousin on your mother's side. Her name is Jean Logan. She's just sixteen. She is an only daughter, and her mother has birthed her father five sons, as well. It's a good match for you. The lass has a generous gold dowry and a respectable trunkful of linens, silver, and other bridal gewgaws. The king has given his approval."

"You went to the king without my permission?" Logan was outraged. "You had no right, Patrick! I'll not have this lass! Nay! A thousand times nay!"

"I have every right, cousin, as clan chief, and as such I will sign the betrothal papers today. You have no excuses not to marry. Rosamund Bolton will not have you, and there is no other engaging your heart, Logan. You must marry for the sake of Claven's Carn. Jeannie Logan is a good lass. Pretty, too. She will make you an admirable wife. She will make a good mother for your sons."

Logan slumped forward, his head in his hands. "I will not lose her," he said brokenly.

"You have already lost her to Glenkirk, cousin. Wed with little Jeannie Logan, and take your bride home. By this time next year you should have a son if you do your duty by your wife, and you will, I know," the Earl of Bothwell told the younger man.

"But I cannot love this girl," Logan protested.

"You will learn to love her, and if you don't, you will not be so different from most men. We wed to sire bairns. Try to get along with the lass, treat her kindly, and all will be well," the Earl of Bothwell advised the laird of Claven's Carn.

"Let me see Rosamund with Glenkirk first. I must be certain before I marry another, Patrick."

"Tonight, then. The king and queen are giving a masque, and the court is invited. You will see what we have all seen. The passion between Rosamund Bolton and Patrick Leslie is unique and unusual. I have never seen its like; nor has anyone else."

"I will see for myself," Logan said.

His cousin nodded in agreement. "And when you have seen it, you will allow me to set the date for your marriage?"

The laird of Claven's Carn was silent for a long moment. Then he sighed and said, "Aye, I will, Patrick."

"Good, good," the earl murmured, pleased. "Your family will be content now and will cease importuning me over this matter. You will not be unhappy with my choice, Logan. The girl is gentle of spirit, and a virgin. Her father was planning to put her with the church when I asked him for the lass for you. She is convent bred, well mannered, and knows everything she should about housewifery. She will be an obedient wife, and because she is devout to the Holy Mother Church, she will bring order into your family and will raise your bairns to be equally pious. You are fortunate in this lass."

Logan looked glum. A pious virgin. What more could a man ask for in a wife? he thought. He sighed again. "Is she at least pretty, Patrick?" he asked.

The earl chuckled, considering his cousin's question a good sign. "Aye, she is quite pretty," he repeated for the third time. "Her eyes are as bonnie a blue as are yours. Her hair is the color of wildflower honey. Not light, but not dark either. Her skin is unblemished, and she has all of her teeth. Her form is nicely rounded where it ought although her bubbies are small. Still, she is young, and with regular caressing she will fill out nicely. Your sons will nurse comfortably from her teats."

"And when do you propose I meet this pious virgin with the small bosom, cousin?" Logan asked the earl.

"I will point her out to you tonight. She is among the queen's ladies for her own safety, Logan, although how safe she is there I cannot guarantee. Let us set the wedding for Twelfth Night. After I am certain you have breached her, you may take her home."

"You do not trust me, then," the laird said with a sarcastic smile.

"It is a requirement of her father's that the marriage be consummated immediately," Bothwell soothed the laird. "Robert Logan is an old-fashioned man, cousin. He would see the bloodied sheet made public the morning after the marriage is celebrated. It is his right, and it gives Jeannie the protection she deserves. Surely you cannot object, for your motives are honest, laddie."

"If I agree to the match, aye, my motives will be honorable," Logan said.

"Then, in a few hours you will see Rosamund Bolton and Patrick Leslie together. Afterwards you will see wee Jeannie Logan, and the die will be cast. You will not regret wedding this lass. 'Tis a good decision you have made."

"You and my family have forced me to it, Patrick. I do not do this thing willingly," the laird said quietly.

"You cannot wait forever for the lovely lady of Friarsgate to decide she wants to be your wife, Logan. She has made it plain to you that she does not," Bothwell said.

"Nay, what she has made plain is that I was an arrogant fool, and I will now pay for it," came the distraught reply.

"Accept what fate has handed you, Logan," the earl advised, "and make the best of it. You will be unhappy otherwise."

Logan laughed bitterly. "Rosamund advised me in similar terms to do the same thing just a little while back," he said.

"I begin to admire this lady myself, cousin," Bothwell said. "She is wise beyond her years. If you will not heed me, then heed her."

"I have no other choice," Logan said. "Fear not, Patrick. I will not make this little lass unhappy. If I take her for my wife I will treat her with kindness and respect. It is not her fault that I am a fool and the lady of Friarsgate does not love me."

"Good, good," the earl said, relieved. He had painted Robert Logan a rosy picture of his only daughter's life as mistress of Claven's Carn. He didn't want it any other way. The lass was a perfect choice for his cousin.

When evening came, the Earl of Bothwell, his cousin in his company, went to the Great Hall to join the rest of the court. The minstrel's gallery was full, and music wafted throughout the chamber, which overflowed with revelers. Serving-men and wenches dashed back and forth with trays, bowls of food, and pitchers of wine and ale. The hall was decorated with holly and pine. Beeswax candles and tapers burned everywhere. The fireplaces, full with huge logs, burned bright. They found their way to a table and sat down, and the earl was greeted by many, and introduced his companion. Goblets of wine were set down before them. There were silver plates quickly filled with food and bread.

"There, at the table next to us," the earl said softly to Logan.

The laird turned, and he felt his breath catch in his throat as he beheld Rosamund Bolton and her lover. They were totally absorbed in each other, and he had never seen her so beautiful as she was at that moment. Her face glowed with the open love she had for the man by her side. His expression as he gazed back at her was utterly adoring. "God's blood!" Logan said under his breath. Then he turned back to his cousin. "Set the match with Jean Logan," he said.

The Earl of Bothwell nodded quietly.

"Now, laddie, look to the end of this table. Do you see the lass in the blue gown? That is Jean Logan. What do you think?"

Logan turned and looked quickly, for he did not wish to appear as if he were staring. The lassie had a sweet face and a quick smile when the young man by her side spoke to her. "She has an admirer," he noted, "but, then, she *is* fair. She would. Tell me, Patrick, that her young heart is not involved with another. I would not take her away from someone who loved her."

"She has been schooled for the convent since age eight. She is newly come to court under the queen's protection. There is no one that I know of, cousin," the earl said.

"Do you know her, Patrick?"

"I do. Her father and I are friends of long standing," came the answer.

"Does the lass know of your plans, cousin?" the laird asked the earl.

"She has an inkling," Bothwell responded. "She was told there was a possible match for her, and she was to come to court to meet the gentleman."

"What if Rosamund Bolton had not fallen in love with another and had agreed to be my wife?" Logan queried.

"Then I should have found bonnie Jean another suitable husband," the earl replied. "But I do not have to, do I, Logan?"

"Nay, you do not. She is pretty, she is young, and being convent bred undoubtedly amenable. If I cannot have Rosamund, this lass will do as well as any," Logan said, resigned.

" 'Tis not such a bad fate, cousin," the earl noted.

"Come then, and introduce us, my lord," the laird of Claven's Carn said. "The sooner, the better, if you want me wedded and bedded on Twelfth Night. We should give the lass a little time to know the man she is to be shackled to for the rest of her life." He arose from the table, the earl with him.

Together the two men walked to the end of the long board, and Patrick Hepburn stopped within the young girl's gaze. She looked up, stood quickly, and curtsied to him.

"My lord Bothwell," she said breathlessly, her curious gaze going to the earl's companion. Her cheeks were pink, and her heart was beating rapidly.

"What, my bonnie Jean, it was Uncle Patrick the last time we met," Bothwell said jovially. He tipped her small face up and gave her a quick kiss upon her lips. "You are being treated well in the queen's household?"

"Oh, yes, Uncle Patrick!" she replied.

"Well, lassie, you'll not be there much

longer, for you are to be married. But, then, your father told you it might be so, didn't he?"

"Aye," came the soft answer. Her blush deepened.

"Then, allow me to present my cousin, whose mother, God assoil her good soul, was a member of your own clan. This is Logan Hepburn, the laird of Claven's Carn, Jean. You will be married to him on Twelfth Night here at Stirling."

"Mistress Jean," Logan said, bowing over the girl's little hand as he took it up and kissed it. The small hand trembled in his, and he immediately felt protective of her.

She blushed again, but she looked directly at him. "My lord."

He smiled at her, thinking the blush charming. Poor little lass, she had no choice in the matter and knew not what she was getting into at all. And then in a flash he understood what Rosamund had been forced to endure. "We have little time in which to get to know each other, Mistress Jean," he said to her.

"We will have a lifetime together, my lord," she answered, surprising him. "Besides, many girls never meet their bridegrooms until they are standing at the altar."

"Which," he remarked, "can often be a shock."

She giggled. "On both sides, my lord," she replied quickly.

In that moment he decided he was going to like her. He could only hope that she would like him.

"I shall leave you two to become acquainted," the Earl of Bothwell said to the pair, and he moved quickly off.

There was a long, awkward silence, and then the laird of Claven's Carn took Jeannie's hand and said, "Let us stroll away from the revelers and talk, mistress."

"I should like that," Jean Logan responded, moving by his side. She was very petite, and he towered over her.

"I would tell you, Mistress Jean, that I require honesty above all things, and so I must ask you if you are content to make this marriage with me."

"I am, my lord," she said. Her voice was soft, but it did not quiver.

"And your heart is not engaged by any other?" he asked her. "For if it is, I would not force you into a match."

"My heart will be yours, my lord, and no other's," Jean Logan said honestly.

He nodded. "I have two brothers," he began. "Claven's Carn is in the borders. We are not rich, but we are comfortable. The house is snug, and it will be yours to rule."

"Have you ever been wed before, my lord?" she asked.

"Never, Mistress Jean," he answered her.

"Why not?" she wondered.

"It is a long story," he said.

"I like stories," she responded quietly.

He laughed. "I see that I shall be unable to hide anything from you, Mistress Jean. Very well. I have for many years sought the hand of an English neighbor. Her guardian would not consider a match, and after he had seen her wed to two husbands — for she was a child when those marriages were celebrated — I thought to have my chance with her. But the English king matched her with one of his own knights. It was a good marriage. There were children, and then her husband was killed in an accident. I sought her hand, but she would not have me. Since I am past thirty, my family appealed to Lord Bothwell to make a match for me, as we are kin. And so he has."

"I think her a foolish lady, my lord," Jeannie said softly, having stopped so she might look up at him when she said it. "I shall not be unhappy to be your wife at all."

He smiled down at the young girl. It might have been far worse, he thought, and while he would always regret Rosamund, he was going to be a good husband to this sweet lassie. "Then I will certainly be con-

117

tent as well, Mistress Jean, and I think myself fortunate in having found you." He bent down and kissed her lips softly. "To seal our bargain, lassie," he told her.

She blushed again. "I have never been kissed before by a lover," she told him naively.

"And now mine are the only lips your sweet ones shall know, Jean Logan," he said to her. "I shall take you back now, and we will tell Lord Bothwell that we are content with this bargain." He took her hand again, and they reentered the crush of guests in the hall. He sought out Bothwell telling him, "We are agreed, Mistress Jean and I, cousin. You may affix Twelfth Night as our wedding day."

"Excellent!" the Earl of Bothwell declared. "Let us go and speak with the king now." And he led them to where James Stewart sat observing his court.

"Well, my lord, and what have you come to say, for you are looking most arch this night?" the king remarked.

"I do not believe, highness, that you have met my cousin, Logan Hepburn, the laird of Claven's Carn," the earl began, "and this is his betrothed wife, Mistress Jean Logan, who is a relation on his mother's side. They seek your highness' permission to be wed here at Stirling on Twelfth Night Day."

James Stewart's dark eyebrows quirked. Was this not the man who desired the lovely lady of Friarsgate for a wife? He considered asking, but realized that if this was the man of whom he had heard, the sweet-faced lass by his side might not have known of her future husband's lust for Rosamund Bolton. It mattered not. The Englishwoman was enamored of the Earl of Glenkirk, and this border lord was to wed another. "They have our permission," the king said, "and the marriage may be celebrated in my chapel. The queen and I will serve as witness to this union." Then he smiled at them, delighting in Jean Logan's blue eyes, which grew round with her excitement. "Come here, lassie," he said, "and give your king a kiss, now." He held out his hand to her.

"Oh, sir!" she exclaimed, rosy with her blushes. "Oh, sir!" And catching up the outstretched hand, she kissed it fervently. Then, releasing the hand, she curtsied deeply. "Thank you, my lord, for this great honor."

"And you, Logan Hepburn? Are you satisfied with this matter?" the king probed. His look was sharp and very direct.

"I am advised by my cousin, the earl, and the rest of my small clan branch that it is past time for me to wed, my lord. Mistress Jean should make me a fine wife," the laird of Claven's Carn said politically.

The king smiled cynically. "May God and his Holy Mother bless you both, then, and give you many bairns," he said. The impulsive laird had obviously seen the truth of Rosamund's infatuation with Lord Leslie and given in to his family's pleas. Well, the little lass was pretty and obviously well bred. She would probably suit Logan Hepburn far better than the lovely Englishwoman, although right now he undoubtedly did not realize it.

They were dismissed, and the trio made a final obeisance to the king and moved back into the crowd of courtiers.

James Stewart leaned over and murmured to his queen, "The laird of Claven's Carn will be wed in our chapel Twelfth Night Day to a young cousin."

"Who?" Margaret Tudor asked her husband.

"A little lass called Jean Logan," the king replied quietly.

"I know her," the queen said. "She has been among the women in my household for a fortnight. Bothwell brought her to me. A sweet child."

"You will want your fair English friend to know," the king advised softly.

"Aye, I will tell her. I wonder if she will care. She is so wrapped up in her passion for Lord Leslie that I doubt it," Margaret

Tudor said. "How she has changed from our days at my father's court. She was so young and ingenuous then. Now she is proud and fierce in her determination to have her own way."

"I imagine that you are not the girl you once were either, my queen," the king said, amused by his wife's astute observation of her old friend. "Many years have passed since you were together, Meg. A great deal has happened in each of your lives since that time."

The queen nodded. "Aye, she has borne three daughters and lost another husband, while I have lost four bairns. But I will not lose this child, Jamie! I feel different this time! This bairn is strong. It virtually leaps in my womb." She looked up at him, her pretty face both sure and hopeful.

"Aye," the king told his wife. "This child will live, Meg. I know it."

Relief flooded the queen's face as she understood what he was saying to her. She took his hand up and kissed it ardently. "Thank you, Jamie! Thank you!"

"Now, lass, you will have the whole court saying that the queen is in love with her husband if you go on like that," he said, gently disengaging himself from her grasp.

"But I do love you!" she protested. "I do, Jamie!"

"I know, Meg," he replied. "And I love you, too." He patted her cheek, then turned away to speak with a courtier who had been attempting to catch his royal eye.

The evening was coming to an end. The queen signaled to her little page, and he was immediately at her side. "Find the lady of Friarsgate and tell her that I would speak with her now in my privy chamber."

"Aye, highness," the child answered, and he hurried off.

The queen arose, and her ladies were instantly clustered about her. "Nay," she said to them. "Stay and enjoy yourselves. I will be in my privy chamber and am not yet ready for bed. Remain here." Then she glided off, moving silently across the chamber and down the corridor to her own apartments. Entering, she told her servingwoman, "The Lady of Friarsgate is coming. Send her to me when she arrives."

"Aye, highness," the servant said, curtsying.

Margaret Tudor entered her privy chamber, and after sitting down by the blazing fire in the fireplace, kicked off her shoes, wiggling her toes with pleasure. The door opened, and Rosamund entered. "Fetch us some wine," the queen said, "and then come sit with me. I have some rather interesting news to impart."

Rosamund did as she was bid, and then

after seating herself opposite her old friend, she, too, kicked off her shoes. "Ahh, that is much better," she said, and she took a sip of wine.

"Do you have any feelings for Logan Hepburn?" the queen queried her friend.

"Nay. What on earth do you mean, Meg? I still find him as arrogant and as irritating as I ever have. He is here at Stirling, you know. I saw him at Bothwell's insistence. I told him I would not wed him. That I loved Patrick Leslie."

"He is to be married Twelfth Night Day!" the queen exclaimed.

"Who is to be married?" Rosamund asked, puzzled.

"Logan Hepburn! He is to marry that sweet little Jean Logan who has been in my household these past few weeks."

"That quiet little lass with the big blue eyes who hardly says a word?" Rosamund asked. "God's blood! Bothwell did not wait long to propose that, although I suspect he had it planned all along."

"Then you do not mind?" Margaret Tudor sounded disappointed.

"Nay, Meg, I do not mind. It is past time Logan Hepburn gave up this childish fantasy about me, and married. He needs an heir, and he has a duty to his family. Nay, I am pleased he has seen reason at long last."

"You really are in love with Patrick Leslie, then?" the queen asked.

"I really am in love with him," Rosamund replied.

"I hold myself responsible for what has happened to you," the queen said. "If I had not invited you to visit me, you should never have met Patrick Leslie. Logan Hepburn might have even forced you to the altar, Rosamund! I have saved you once again, as I saved you from my brother all those years ago!"

Rosamund laughed. "It is true, Meg! Though until now I never thought of it that way. If I had not come to see you at this moment in time, I should not have met Patrick Leslie. But believe me when I tell you, Logan Hepburn would have never forced me to the altar. If I ever marry again, it will be for love alone, and the choice will be mine to make and no one else's."

"You remember Grandmother's advice," the queen chuckled.

"I do indeed, Meg. The Venerable Margaret was a great woman, and I admired her muchly."

"I wonder what she would think of us today. I think she would approve of your exchanging Logan Hepburn for the Earl of Glenkirk, no matter he is an old man. She always considered a woman advancing her status in life a good thing. Will you marry Lord Leslie?"

"Nay," Rosamund said quietly. "And before you ask, Meg, or attempt to interfere, let me explain. Patrick has a duty to Glenkirk. I have a duty to Friarsgate. Neither of us will eschew our duty. We both comprehend that, and we are content. This is the way it must be between us. I know you will not understand, but you must not meddle, Meg. Promise me that you will not involve yourself in this matter."

The queen sighed. "I just want you to be happy," she said.

"We are happy," Rosamund told her.

"But one day you will part from each other," Meg replied.

"I know," Rosamund said. "That is what makes whatever time we have together all the sweeter, Meg. No one is ever happy constantly. I should rather have these days with the Earl of Glenkirk than with any other man. I should rather know this perfect happiness for even a short span in my life than to never know it at all. What memories we are making together. What dreams of the past we shall cherish when we are no longer with each other in the years to come."

"You are far braver than I am, Rosamund, and I should have never thought it of you," the queen said softly. She sighed.

"I need the security of a marriage. I need to know that my husband is there for me even if he does stray now and again. You are really alone, and you are not afraid."

"I think I have been alone my entire life until now," Rosamund answered.

"But you wrote that Owein loved you," the queen protested.

"Oh, he did, Meg, and I was so fortunate to have him as my husband. But Owein was raised to a life of service to his betters. He always stood slightly in awe of me as the lady of Friarsgate. He always deferred to me, bless him. Not once did he ever corrupt my authority. And he loved Friarsgate."

"Did you love him, too?" the queen wondered. "He seemed like the right match for you back then when we were girls at my father's court."

"Aye, I learned to loved him, which is why I know what I have with Patrick Leslie is so much more. My love for the lord of Glenkirk is something that comes only rarely, Meg. That is why I will not let it go until I have to let it go." She smiled. "What a serious conversation we are having, and all because you wanted to tell me that Logan Hepburn is to be wed in a few days. I wish him good fortune."

"Wish the bride good fortune," the queen said, and she chuckled. "She is certain to tell him if you do so, and you will have your own back on him for teasing you the day you wed with Owein. I am certain that he still loves you, Rosamund. This marriage is for his family's sake."

"All he could talk about was his need for an heir when he was with me. I felt like a prize mare or heifer. Yet when I spoke with him in Lord Bothwell's apartments he said I should have understood that he loved me even if he didn't say so," Rosamund replied. She shook her head.

"How just like a man!" the queen exclaimed, and she laughed.

"Aye," Rosamund agreed. "How just like a man." Then she sipped her wine thoughtfully. "I hope he will be happy, for I am so happy myself I can but wish him the same."

"You always had a good heart," the queen said. "I am glad to have you with me again, Rosamund. Do you miss your Friarsgate as much as you ever did?" She smiled.

"Not as I did when I was a young girl," Rosamund answered the queen. "It is my lasses, Meg, that I miss the most. Kate insisted after Owein's death that I come to their court, and I could not disobey, but it was hard. Philippa, the eldest, knew that I was gone and missed me the most, though Maybel says she is like me, and is a good child. The two little ones, however, did not understand. I was almost a stranger to them when I returned."

"And then my invitation came," Margaret Tudor said.

"I might have refused you, Meg, but we were such good friends I could not. Besides, it is not as long a journey as going down into England," Rosamund replied with a small smile.

"And my invitation was a convenient excuse to escape the laird of Claven's Carn," the queen said, laughing mischievously.

"Aye, it was," Rosamund agreed, grinning. "The priest at Friarsgate is his kinsman, but he would not have forced the issue if I said nay. Still in all, it would have been difficult. Here at Stirling, Logan is overruled in his intentions by the Earl of Bothwell. I do not think Patrick Hepburn was pleased with the idea his cousin might marry an Englishwoman. When I told him he need not fear I would wed his cousin, I asked if he had a lass for Logan. He told me one or two, the devil, when all along he had the little Mistress Jean in mind."

"He's a clever man, this particular Hepburn," Margaret Tudor noted. "He supported my husband even before the breach with the late king. Jamie never forgets those who are loyal to him. He was simply the Hepburn of Hailes until Jamie created him the first Hepburn Earl of Bothwell. He has risen high in the hierarchy of this kingdom, and he brings his family along with him, as is right and proper. My husband has a good friend in him. If he had asked Jamie for you for Logan Hepburn, Rosamund, you would have been wedded and bedded whether you would or nay."

"But I am English!" Rosamund cried, shocked.

"That would have made no matter," the queen told her. "If the Earl of Bothwell had desired it, it would have been so. Had you not fallen so publicly and passionately in love, Rosamund, you would not have escaped Logan Hepburn here at Stirling. Indeed, you would have been shoved directly into his arms." She laughed softly. "But fate did indeed intervene to save you. I have never particularly believed in fate, but perhaps in light of all that has happened to you, I will now."

Rosamund had gone pale, but now she laughed weakly. "Mayhap I, too, will believe in fate, as well, from now on, Meg."

There was a discreet knock upon the door of the queen's privy chamber.

"Come in," the queen called, and the door opened to reveal one of the queen's chamber women. "Yes, Jane, what is it?" Margaret Tudor asked.

"Little Mistress Logan would speak with

you, madame. She says she will not take a great deal of your time," Jane said.

Margaret Tudor's blue eyes twinkled wickedly as she looked to Rosamund. "Tell Mistress Logan that she may come in, Jane," she replied.

The chamber woman stepped aside, and Jean Logan entered the room. She curtsied deeply to the queen, but her eyes were surprised to see the queen's companion.

"Madame, I have come to tell you that the king has given his permission for my marriage to Logan Hepburn, the laird of Claven's Carn, to be celebrated on Twelfth Night Day. I hope that we may also have your highness' permission and blessing." Jeannie Logan stood before Margaret Tudor, her head modestly lowered, her hands folded neatly.

"This is sudden, child, isn't it?" the queen said. "Tell me how this has all come about so quickly. I hope that you have not been forced to any imprudent decision."

"Oh, nay, madame! I am more than content to marry the laird. I was to enter the convent, where I had been schooled, but Uncle Patrick . . . the Earl of Bothwell, madame . . . was seeking a good wife for his kinsman and asked my father for me. While I venerate our dear Lord and his Blessed Mother, I have no calling to the church. But my dower portion is not large, and none had asked for me. My father thought in that light that perhaps the convent was the place for me. When my father said my dower was slight, Uncle Patrick added a purse to it. At first my father protested, but Uncle Patrick said since I was his goddaughter and he had scarce seen me in the last few years, it seemed only right that he do it. Then he told my father what a fine man his kinsman was and how he had put his family and their welfare ahead of his own needs, but now he was ready to wed. My father could not refuse under such circumstances. Then Uncle Patrick told my father that his kinsman's mother had been a member of the Clan Logan, but we are not closely related or within the forbidden bonds of consanguinity, and so the church has given us a dispensation to marry."

"You already have the dispensation, my child?" the queen purred solicitously.

"Oh, yes! Uncle Patrick said his kinsman was eager to wed and so the sooner the better," Jeannie Logan confided ingenuously.

"How fortunate you are to have your uncle Patrick," the queen murmured. "The Earl of Bothwell has always been known for his kindness. But, my child, how rude of me. This is my friend, Lady Rosamund Bolton of Friarsgate."

131

"Oh, I know who she is," Jeannie said innocently.

"Do you?" Rosamund answered her. "And who am I, Mistress Logan?"

"You are Lord Leslie's — friend, my lady," the girl replied.

"I am," Rosamund admitted.

"And you shall be neighbors," the queen said wickedly. "Friarsgate is just over the border in England. It is practically a stone's throw from Claven's Carn. Do you not know Logan Hepburn, Rosamund?"

"Slightly," Rosamund responded through gritted teeth. "I believe he and his brothers were guests when my late husband and I were wed." Had Meg not been a queen, Rosamund thought, she would have smacked her. "But, madame, it is late and in your delicate condition you need your rest." She arose. "I shall leave you, taking Mistress Logan with me. Do give her your permission and blessing, for that is what she came for — didn't you, Mistress Logan?"

"Aye, my lady," Jeannie said.

"You have both, then, my child. My husband and I shall come and bear witness to your vows on Twelfth Night Day. And, Rosamund, you will come, too, with Lord Leslie?" The queen's eyes were dancing with mischief.

"If you so command, madame," Rosamund responded. "But your chapel is small, and Mistress Logan will want her family there."

"Oh, no, my lady. My family is in the north and will not be here. I think it would be lovely to have a neighbor with us on our happy day. Please come!"

"Make your curtsy to the queen, Mistress Logan," Rosamund said. "I will speak with Lord Leslie." She practically pushed the girl from the queen's little privy chamber, murmuring softly to Meg as she did, "I shall repay you in kind for this, you bad creature!"

"God bless you, my child," the queen called, and grinning from ear to ear she closed the door into her anteroom behind them.

Chapter 4

There was a storm on Twelfth Night Day. Outside Stirling Castle the snow swirled in twisted whorls that were blown about by winds that howled mournfully through the narrow streets of the town and about the castle's stone towers. In the Earl of Bothwell's apartments the laird of Claven's Carn adjusted his garments as he prepared to depart for the royal chapel.

"You can have your privacy here tonight," Patrick Hepburn said. "I'll find another place to sleep. You won't be able to leave Stirling until this storm has blown itself out and down into England."

"Thank you," Logan replied glumly.

His cousin laughed. "All men feel this way on their wedding day. A thousand questions run through your head. Did I do the right thing? Will I love her? Will she give me sons and not daughters? Will she object if I take a mistress? Will I have to beat her?" He chuckled. "But we marry nonetheless, Logan, and young Jeannie will make you a fine wife. She's already half in love with you and eager to please. Keep her that way, laddie, and your life will be a happy one."

"Rosamund is coming to the wedding," Logan answered. "What the hell is she coming to my wedding for, Patrick? I didn't ask her to come. Is it possible she regrets her hasty decision?"

"Put the idea from your thoughts, laddie," the earl advised. "She is coming to your wedding because the queen insisted she come. And she will be on Lord Leslie's arm. She has no regrets at all. Why would she trade a simple border lord for her earl? The lass is no fool, Logan, but you stand in danger of being one if you allow your bruised heart to overrule your common sense this day. Let her go, and concentrate on the lovely lassie who will be your wife shortly." He adjusted the fur collar of his cousin's mid-calf–length burgundy velvet coat. The garment was lined in the same fur, as were its sleeves, which were flared. Beneath the gown he wore haut-de-chausses and silk hose striped in burgundy, black, and gold. A linen shirt with a ruffle was visible beneath his fur collar. "You look quite handsome, cousin, if I may say so."

"I feel like a damned prized goose all done up for roasting," Logan grumbled. "I think you had these wedding clothes waiting for me, Patrick."

"I did," the earl admitted with a broad grin.

"You had this whole damned affair planned, too, I'll vow," the laird continued.

"I did," Patrick Hepburn said.

"What if Rosamund had agreed to marry me? What then, cousin?" Logan demanded.

"Come now, cousin. It is time for us to depart for the chapel," the earl replied, ignoring the question. He took the younger man by the arm, and together they walked from the earl's apartments.

The queen and her women had kindly seen to the young bride, Margaret Tudor giving the girl one of her own gowns, which had been quickly altered to fit the reed-slim girl. It was peach-colored velvet with an underskirt embroidered and quilted with large gold flowers. The neckline was low and square and fitted tightly. The long, tight sleeves had fur cuffs. An embroidered hanging girdle was wrapped about the bride's waist.

"Gracious," Rosamund murmured so that only the queen might hear her. "There is enough material here for another gown, I'll vow. I do not remember you this plump, Meg." She smiled sweetly.

"Jamie likes a woman with meat on her bones," the queen murmured back. "Besides, this girl is very slim. Still, her husband will put a bairn in her belly no matter. Do you think Logan Hepburn is a good lover?"

"I wouldn't know, Meg," Rosamund said softly. "Do watch your tongue, else poor Jeannie will hear you."

"Then take back what you said about my being plump," the queen muttered.

"My memory of our youth grows faulty, madame," Rosamund said.

The queen giggled. "I accept your apology," she whispered. "Now, what shall our bride wear on her head, ladies?"

"Oh, madame," said Tillie, the queen's chief tiring woman, "do you not remember? A virgin going to her wedding wears her hair loose to indicate her virtue. You did on your wedding day, and I will wager that Mistress Rosamund did, too."

"I did indeed, Tillie," Rosamund replied.

"Where is your jewelry?" the queen asked Jeannie Logan.

"I have none, madame," the bride answered.

"Here, take these pearls," Rosamund said generously, removing a strand from about her neck. "They are a wedding present, Jeannie Logan, from your neighbor, the lady of Friarsgate." She slipped the long strand about the girl's neck. "There! They make the gown even lovelier."

"Oh, Lady Rosamund, I could not!" the girl cried, but she was already fingering the pearls longingly.

"Of course you can," Rosamund replied. "They are perfect, as are you. Logan Hepburn is a fortunate man. Make certain he knows it, Jeannie."

"Thank you, my lady! I shall tell him how kind you have been to me," the girl said ingenuously.

"Yes," Rosamund agreed, "do tell him, and say I wish you both much happiness, Jeannie. Perhaps you will allow me to entertain you when I return to Friarsgate." She smiled at the girl.

As they escorted the bride to the royal chapel, Margaret Tudor leaned over and whispered to her old friend, "You do have a bit of the bitch in you, Rosamund. This is another revelation."

"I have naught against the lass, Meg. It is her arrogant mate my words were for, and I know she will repeat them as I have said them, and they will sting him. This is repayment for what he did on my wedding day to Owein."

At the chapel door, the Earl of Bothwell was waiting to escort the bride. They left her with him and entered. The queen moved swiftly to the front of the room where her husband awaited her. They would formally witness the vows. Rosamund slipped into her seat next to Patrick. He took her hand immediately in his.

"No regrets, my darling?" he asked softly.

"None," she told him, smiling.

The bridegroom came forth, and the bride was led to him by the Earl of Bothwell. The priest shook his censer of incense over them while the candles on the altar flickered and the storm outside moaned mournfully. The mass began. Logan's eye went just once to Rosamund. She was standing next to the Earl of Glenkirk, gazing up at him adoringly. It was as if a hand had reached out and squeezed his heart to half its size. Then he felt the small hand slipping into his, and he looked down into the sweet face of his bride. She gave him a tremulous smile, and unable to help himself, he smiled back at her. Poor lassie. She wasn't responsible for his heartbreak. Nay! 'Twas that brazen, false bitch boldly standing with her lover! He would put her from his heart and give what was left of it to this sweet lass who was about to become his wife.

The bride spoke her vows in a soft but clear voice. The bridegroom spoke his in a loud, almost defiant voice. The ceremony over, the wedding party adjourned to the Great Hall of Stirling Castle to join the rest of the court in the Twelfth Night celebration. The long holiday was about to come to an end, and the winter was setting in with a vengeance. The entire court drank to the health and long life of the newly wed couple. There was much jesting, and the bride was soon rosy with her blushes.

Patrick took Rosamund aside. "We must depart in two days," he said in a low voice. "Remember, you can take but a few necessaries, my love."

"I know. But Annie must pack for me as if I am leaving court for home," she answered. "I can but hope the weather clears."

"It may be better if it doesn't," Glenkirk told her. "We're less apt to encounter the English at sea if the weather remains foul. They have no real navy, although the king's brother-in-law, seeing our Jamie's success in building ships, is embarking on the same course. You're sure you would come?"

"Absolutely," Rosamund told him. "Are you having second thoughts, my lord?"

"Nay! I cannot imagine my life without you now, Rosamund," he told her.

"One day . . ." she began.

He stopped her lips with his fingers. "But not now."

She nodded. "I hope the queen believes me," she said. "I had best speak with her now, while I can." She leaned over and gave him a quick kiss upon the lips, then rose from the board where she had been seated with him and other guests. Finding her way to the High Board, Rosamund caught the queen's eye. Margaret Tudor beckoned her forward, and Rosamund hurried to her side.

"I have just received word, highness, that Philippa, my eldest daughter, is dangerously ill. How the messenger got through in this storm is a miracle, but I must depart for Friarsgate as soon as the storm clears," Rosamund said.

"One of your own people came?" the queen said. "I would see him and commend him for his diligence."

"Nay, madame, not one of my people. They are simple folk and would not know how to travel to Edinburgh and then on to Stirling. It was a messenger hired by my uncle Edmund. I didn't even see him. He asked for me and was directed to Annie. She took the message and came to find me immediately after the mass," Rosamund said.

"Ah," the queen said, disappointed. "Must you leave me, Rosamund? I did so want you here for this birth. I have missed you, and we have had such fun these last few weeks."

"You have had fun teasing me," Rosamund said with a smile. "I will try to return in time for the prince's birth, Meg." She felt guilty lying to her old friend, especially in light of how good Margaret Tudor had always been to her. But the queen could not know the truth about the Earl of Glenkirk's mission to San Lorenzo, and Rosamund knew she could not allow her lover to leave her at this point.

The queen nodded. "You are a good mother, Rosamund. Go home and tend to your daughter, but please come back when you can."

"We will speak again before I leave you," Rosamund responded. Then she curtsied and moved off.

The festivities went on the day long and into the evening. There was food and drink in abundance. There was music and dancing. A troupe of entertainers was allowed into the hall. They had a bear with a polished brass collar on a chain that danced to flute and drum. There were several men who juggled shiny balls and pastries from the tables. There was a blind girl who sang like an angel while accompanying herself on a small harp. And finally there were acrobats who tumbled and leapt across the hall, causing the spectators to *ooh* and *ahh* with delight. When the entertainers had departed the hall, it was time to put the bride and groom to bed in the

Earl of Bothwell's comfortable apartments. Rosamund did not join in this rough rite.

"It is as good a time as any for us to make our escape," Patrick whispered to her with a smile.

Rosamund nodded. "I cannot imagine what poor Logan would think if he found me among the women who prepared his wife for the bridal bed," she chuckled. "I gave the lass my pearls as a wedding gift, which should prick him enough."

"Revenge for your own wedding day, my sweet?" Lord Cambridge said as he came to her side. "You are learning how to fight back, my pet. I am proud of you."

"I have nothing against the lass, Tom," Rosamund said. "Actually, she is perfect for him. She will obey his every wish and whim. She will dutifully produce children and keep his house in perfect order. And she'll get little thanks for it, for Logan will believe it is his due. If the pearls pleased her, good! If it distresses him each time she wears them, good!"

"Would you believe that she was once as meek and mild as one of her lambs?" Tom said with a grin to the Earl of Glenkirk.

"I like a woman with a wee bit of spice," the Earl of Glenkirk responded with a smile.

"Then you have surely found her in Rosamund," Lord Cambridge chortled.

"I have told the queen I must return to Friarsgate because Philippa is ill," Rosamund said quietly to her cousin.

"Ah, so our time at this delightful court is finished," he noted. "It was too short, my pet. We must come back one day. Promise me we shall. If I am to spend my winter watching over your lasses I must have my reward."

"You shall have it, Tom," she promised. "If it were not for my girls, I should leave you here to pursue all manner of naughtiness."

"And there are so many delights for a discreet gentleman to enjoy," he sighed. "Of course, one must really be quite discreet. There are still those who remember this king's father and his favorites. The Stewarts do seem to blow this way and that." Tom Bolton grinned.

Glenkirk laughed. "And you have indeed been discreet, Tom. I have heard no rumors of bad behavior at all. In fact, several of the ladies have remarked that it is a pity a gentleman of your breeding has no wife."

"What they mean, the wicked creatures," he laughed, "is a gentleman with my purse, Patrick. But I prefer an unencumbered life, my dears, and Rosamund and her daughters are my heirs. She is my nearest kin. We are like brother and sister."

"And a better friend I never had, dear

Tom," Rosamund told him. "Patrick and I will now retire, but you are free to enjoy as much of this court as you can until we must go in a few days." She blew him a kiss as she departed the Great Hall.

In the little bedchamber that was their sanctuary, Rosamund and her lover undressed each other slowly as they prepared for bed. He was teaching her the lesson of patience, although it was not easy for her. Again she silently asked herself how it was possible that she had fallen so deeply, so desperately, in love with this man who less than a month ago was totally unknown to her. She had no answers today any more than she had had answers yesterday or would have them tomorrow. She knew only that she must be with Patrick, in his arms, in his bed, in his heart.

"What would your son think of us?" she asked him as she undid the silk ribbons holding her chemise closed.

"He would think me fortunate to have found love again," Glenkirk said. "My daughter-in-law, however, would think me mad. She would say things like 'At your age, my lord!' and she would purse her narrow lips in disapproval. Anne has a hard heart. Would that Adam had known it before he wed with her, but he is content. He seems to know how to manage her, though she be shrewish." He pushed the chemise from her shoulders and lifted her naked from the silken pile of material now about her ankles.

"I wonder if we shall ever meet," she said, unlacing his shirt and pulling it off him. "Does he look like you? Or does he favor his mother?"

"He is tall and is said to have my features, but his eyes are his mother's. Agnes had the bonniest blue eyes I have ever seen on a woman, and Adam has those eyes. I think that is what first attracted his wife to him." He drew Rosamund's naked form against his bare chest. "I love the feel of your nipples on my skin," he told her.

She grew dizzy with the simple pleasure of his body against hers. "You are nothing like Owein, or even Hugh," she told him.

"I'm glad," he answered, and his lips brushed lightly over hers.

Rosamund's breath was coming in small quick bursts. She could feel the hard length of him against her. "Will you get out of those damned haut-de-chausses?" she said through gritted teeth. Her hand smoothed down along the rigid stretch.

"*Tch, Tch,* lassie," he scolded her. "Have you no patience?"

"Not where you are involved, Patrick Leslie," she told him. "I admit that I am a shameless wench where you are concerned."

"I must teach you better, Rosamund. Passion is best savored and enjoyed slowly. You want to gobble, but I will not allow it." He loosed his hold on her and pulled off the last of his garments. Then, reaching for her again, he turned her so her back was to him and he might gather her lovely round breasts into his hands to enjoy. He fondled the fleshy globes tenderly all the while rubbing his manhood against her buttocks and between the cleft that separated those twin moons.

Rosamund sighed and relaxed against him. He was right. This was much better than a quick coupling. The teasing anticipation was arousing her to new heights. "Oh, Patrick," she said softly, "that is so very, very nice, my darling."

"We have only just begun, my love," he told her. Then he turned her about to face him and kissed her deeply, his mouth hot and eager.

Their tongues met, caressed, dueled for superiority. They tasted each other, and then he lifted her up and carried her to their bed, laying her gently down and joining her. His big hands brushed over her torso, and she sighed. He turned her over onto her stomach and began massaging her back and her shoulders. His fingers dug into her prettily rounded bottom and then her thighs. He massaged her feet, rubbing any soreness that might have been there from them. "It is better, of course, with lotion or oil," he explained. "In San Lorenzo they make the most delicious treats for the body, Rosamund, and I intend to introduce you to them all. They are lush and sensuous, and you will love what they do to your body, my love."

Then he murmured a soft command to her, and when she positioned herself with raised buttocks he entered her womanly passage slowly and then began to pump her vigorously until Rosamund was whimpering with her pleasure. "That's it, my pet," he whispered hotly in her ear. "Enjoy the delights I can offer you. It has been a very long time since I wanted a woman as much as I want you. And even having you, it is not enough!" He thrust harder and deeper until she was screaming softly with her lustful satisfaction.

"Oh, God, Patrick! Please don't stop! I could not bear it if you stopped!" she half-sobbed.

"There is more, my love," he promised her, and then he continued on until he could no longer hold back his own desires. His love juices flooded her, and she wept.

"I cannot bear to think of the time when we must part," she told him, her face wet with her tears.

"Do not consider it, my love," he counseled her. "We have much time ahead of us, I promise you." And he was kissing her face, her lips, and she was sighing with her happiness in their love while outside the single window in the room the storm raged on, but they neither knew nor cared.

The following afternoon the snow had finally abated, and the late day was clear, as was the night that followed. They would leave on the morrow. To Rosamund's surprise, the laird of Claven's Carn and his bride were to travel with them.

"Then he shall know that I have not gone home to Friarsgate!" Rosamund said, distressed.

"I have already spoken to the king, but he says there is no help for it. The queen made the arrangements, for she thought it would be safer for you to travel with the laird's party. The king can say nothing lest he reveal his plans. He dare not, or England will learn of Scotland's plans," Glenkirk said. "I can but appeal to Logan Hepburn's patriotism when we leave them for the Leith road. He can certainly keep his wife quiet."

"And I shall keep her friendly and amused for the journey," Tom added. "She will be feeling a bit strange going to her new home for the first time, and I will help to ease her fears. I shall keep Logan Hepburn's friendship for Friarsgate despite your bad behavior, cousin," Tom teased, and he grinned at her with a wicked wink.

Glenkirk laughed. "You are a valuable ally, Tom, and I thank you for it."

"Do not think to wheedle me, my dear lord," Tom said. "I am still quite put out that I must go back to Friarsgate in the snow while you whisk my fair cousin and best friend off to the balmy shores of San Lorenzo. I shall expect a great favor in return one of these days."

"And you shall receive whatever it is your good heart desires," Glenkirk replied. "Within reason, of course."

"One man's reason is another's unreason," Tom said with a chortle. "You must bring me sweet Mediterranean wines and some of your own whiskey if I am to be recompensed."

"And I shall bring you jars of olives, stored with lemon and oil in stone crocks for a year. San Lorenzan olives are considered a rare delicacy," the Earl of Glenkirk told Lord Cambridge. "I wish you could taste their grapes. They are the sweetest I have ever known."

"Say not another word, dear man, for I am already regretting my decision to remain at Friarsgate!"

"Oh, Tom, you must! My lasses will not be safe without you there," Rosamund cried.

"Dear cousin, I have given you my word, and I will indeed go to Friarsgate to watch over those three little angels you spawned. But I will nonetheless regret that I am not with you," Tom said.

"You can teach them court manners," Rosamund teased him.

"They can certainly use my tutelage," he sniffed. "Especially Philippa, who should know better than to squat and pee when she is outdoors with the other children and nature calls to her. A proper young lady uses her chamber pot."

"You will tell her that, of course, dear Tom," Rosamund said, laughing.

"You are quite enjoying my distress," he grumbled. "Well, I am not the one whose bottom will be red each day from all the riding you have ahead of you. While you gallop through the worst of the winter weather I shall be snug at Friarsgate with your good Maybel watching over me and cosseting me with her kind heart and good cooking. And what am I to tell her, cousin?"

"I have written a letter to her, Tom. She will ask you all manner of questions despite it, but you may answer her honestly," Rosamund told him quietly. "She will blame poor Meg for my behavior, of course," Rosamund concluded with a smile.

"Aye, she will not believe this reckless behavior of you, my dear girl," he agreed.

"I must go and bid the queen farewell now," Rosamund said, and she left the two men together by the fire in the Great Hall where they had all been seated.

The queen was feeling quite well when Rosamund arrived to see her.

"I have never felt better in these circumstances," she declared.

"The king's prediction will be a true one, then," Rosamund responded.

"His predictions are always true," Margaret Tudor replied. "It is sometimes quite eerie. So, you are leaving me, my old friend."

"My visit has been wonderful!" Rosamund declared. "And I promise I shall come back to see you when I can."

"You will not let the war separate us?" the queen asked.

"What war?" Rosamund was puzzled.

"The one that my brother, Henry, will certainly force upon my husband and Scotland," the queen said. "This marriage between us was to settle the matter for good and all, but it has not. And it is all Hal's fault! He presses Jamie at every turn. My husband, however, is far wiser than my brother; but eventually Hal will make war on Scotland, and you and I will be separated again, Rosamund."

"If there is indeed a war, I shall not allow it to harm the friendship that we formed back at your father's court when we were children, Meg. Whatever the men of this world may do, we women shall remain friends. I shall try and be here for your son's christening," she promised, "if not sooner."

"What of Lord Leslie?" the queen asked, unable to help herself.

"He is coming with me," Rosamund said. "He says he is not needed at Glenkirk now as his son is capable of managing their lands. And besides, it is easier for him to come with me to Friarsgate than to get back into his Highland eyrie with this weather."

"Then you shall not be separated," the queen said. "Oh, Rosamund, I am glad! For all I have teased you, I can see that you love him and he you. It is so strange, but there it is. God bless you both!"

"Why, thank you, Meg," Rosamund said, and then she embraced the queen.

The following day dawned clear and very cold. It would take them two days to ride to Leith, Scotland's main port on Firth of Forth. Logan assumed that they were riding to Edinburgh. They might have made the journey in a single day but that Lord Leslie did not feel young Mistress

Hepburn was up to such a trip.

"She is young, but delicately made," he noted. "It will be a hard enough venture for her, I fear."

They overnighted at an inn near Linlithgow. It was a small establishment, and the two women were put into a chamber with another female traveler and Annie, while the men were shown into a dormitory with others of their sex. Rosamund found their situation very amusing until the bride sought to confide in her.

"Madame," Jeannie began, "you are a lady of some experience, and I mean you no disrespect when I say that, but I need a woman's advice."

God's boots, Rosamund thought to herself, but she drew a deep breath and said, "Are you certain you are not violating a confidence, Mistress Hepburn? Some things are meant to remain between a wife and her husband."

"Nay, I do not believe I tell a tale I should not. I simply wish to know whether all men are so enthusiastic in their bed sport. And how often is it proper for a husband to couple with his wife?" She blushed as she spoke, the color rising swiftly to stain her pale cheeks.

"You are fortunate in your husband's enthusiasm," Rosamund replied. "It means he enjoys your company. And he may have your favors as often as he desires them, unless, of course, you are well along with child or your monthly courses are upon you. Men enjoy their bed sport differently than women do. It is the way God made them."

"Aye, you are right," Jeannie said slowly. "Thank you. My mother died when I was ten, and I was sent to the convent. The nuns do not know about such things; nor would they speak of them if they did. It is too worldly."

Rosamund asked, "Were you unhappy to leave the convent, Mistress Hepburn?"

"Nay. But I had no sister or friend or other lady with whom to speak about these intimate things and I went to my marriage bed quite ignorant. But my husband was very kind and most patient with me," Jeannie concluded.

"I am glad," Rosamund told her. "Men sometimes do not understand innocence. They can be rough creatures. They mean no harm usually. It is just their way."

"Oh, thank you, madame!" Jeannie said, and the gratitude in her voice was palpable. "I did not know what to think. May I ask one more question of you?"

Oh lord, save me! But Rosamund nodded, smiling. "Of course."

"Is it proper that I enjoy it when my husband and I couple?" came the naive query.

"Did you enjoy it?" Rosamund was fascinated in spite of herself.

"Oh, very much!" Jeannie admitted, blushing deeply once again.

"It is proper," Rosamund told her. "Indeed, it is good that you do."

"I suppose we should get some sleep," Jeannie said softly. "I expect tomorrow and the days to follow will be long ones. Is it far to Claven's Carn?"

"If the weather holds it will take you several more days past Edinburgh," Rosamund told the young girl. "Your home is on the border, and you are nearer to England than anything else Scotch."

"I have been told the English are very fierce, madame. Is it true?" Jeannie's blue eyes were wide with her interest.

"I am English, Mistress Hepburn. Do you find me fierce?" Rosamund teased the girl gently.

Jeannie giggled. "Nay, madame."

"Go to sleep, then, lass, and do not worry yourself so much. You have married a good man, and you will be happy at Claven's Carn," Rosamund told her.

In the morning they departed even before the sun was up, riding for several hours until they reached a fork in the road where there were two directional signs. One said "Edinburgh" and the other said

"Leith." The Earl of Glenkirk stopped in the crossroad, and Tom rode up next to him.

" 'Tis here we part company, Tom," Patrick said quietly, and he signaled to Logan to join them. "Keep the ladies company, and make your farewells to your cousin while I speak with the laird."

"Godspeed, Patrick!" Lord Cambridge said. "I hope we will meet again." He shook the earl's hand, then moved off to join Rosamund and Mistress Hepburn.

"What is this about, my lord?" Logan demanded. He was not at all happy that he had been traveling with this man and Rosamund for the past two days.

"What I am about to tell you, Logan Hepburn, must go no farther. I tell you this on the king's order. Do you understand?"

The laird nodded, now intrigued. "I understand, my lord, and you have my word that whatever you tell me I will not repeat."

"The queen," the earl began, "enjoys a good jest. She found it amusing, not aware of why we were really departing the court, to put us together in our travels. She believes that Rosamund's daughter is ill, and Rosamund is going to her. She believes I am accompanying Rosamund. She is fully aware of the relationship you desired to forge with the lady of Friarsgate and thinks it humorous that you and your bride travel with us. But Rosamund's daughter is not ill, and we are not going to Friarsgate. The king has delegated me to undertake a secret diplomatic mission for him. As you are aware, I have not been to court or out of my Highlands for eighteen years. Consequently, no one would even consider that the king would appoint me to such a duty. Nor is anyone other than the king aware of what I am to do or where I am going. I cannot even tell you, Logan Hepburn. I told the king I would do his bidding if Rosamund could come with me."

"What if she hadn't wanted to go?" the laird demanded. He was, in spite of it all, jealous of this man who had somehow stolen Rosamund from him. "Rosamund loves Friarsgate and dislikes being away from it for very long."

"Nonetheless she agreed to go with me," the Earl of Glenkirk said quietly.

"How can you love each other so on such short acquaintance?" Logan burst out, unable to help himself from the question.

"I do not know," the earl admitted honestly. "All I can tell you is that until Rosamund I had just existed, and I never even knew it. From the moment our eyes met we have desired nothing more than to be together."

"She will never desert Friarsgate," Logan said.

"Nor will I desert Glenkirk. But until the time comes when we must return to our duties, however long a time that is, we shall be together."

"Do you love her?" he asked, his look tortured.

"I have always loved her," came the strange reply.

"She loves you," Logan said, almost bitterly.

"Aye, she does," Patrick said simply.

"That you are leaving us here says you are going to Leith," the laird of Claven's Carn said.

"We sail tonight," was the reply.

"Rosamund was never a girl for adventure," Logan remarked. "She has changed so suddenly that I cannot believe she is the same girl. Have you bewitched her, my lord?"

The Earl of Glenkirk laughed. "Nay," he said, "although we both considered such a thing that first night. She has told me she isn't adventurous, and yet she is willing to come across a sea with me. Such is the power of our love. But it is not witchcraft, Logan Hepburn. Now, Tom Bolton will travel with you as far as Claven's Carn, and Rosamund would appreciate it if your clansmen would escort him over the border back to Friarsgate. He holds her authority so that her uncle Henry cannot interfere should he learn she isn't there. She fears for her lasses. Will you do that for her?"

"There is nothing she could ask me that I would not do," Logan said.

"Laddie, laddie," the earl replied, shaking his head at the younger man, "Bothwell gave you a sweet wife. Be true to her, and put my fair Rosamund from your thoughts. She would not have wed you even if we had not met. She is not ready to remarry, and I know she tried to explain that to you, but you would not hear what she had to say. You wanted a wife upon whom to get your heirs. You have one. Take her back to Claven's Carn and put a bairn in her belly. Rosamund and I will be far away from Scotland."

"And when you return, my lord?" the laird asked.

"I do not know. But when we do return I hope we shall hear that you have a healthy son, Logan Hepburn." He held out his hand. "Now, shake my hand, for I already have your word that you will not divulge what we have discussed. Then bid us Godspeed. If I can accomplish what the king desires, we may prevent a war."

The laird of Claven's Carn took the Earl of Glenkirk's big, gloved hand and shook it. "Then I do bid you Godspeed, my lord, and reassure you again that my lips are sealed in your secret matter. Tell Rosamund that I will see Tom Bolton is brought safe and sound back to Friarsgate." Then he turned his mount and rejoined his wife and the clansmen who were accompanying them.

Rosamund and Tom moved forward. The Englishman took his cousin's hand in his. "Be careful, dearest girl, and come home safe to us when you can," he said.

"You have the letter for Maybel and Edmund?" she asked him for the third time.

"I do," he said, and he kissed her hand. "Godspeed, cousin," Tom told her, and then he rejoined the laird's party as they moved off down the road to Edinburgh.

"You are certain?" Patrick asked Rosamund.

She nodded. "I am." Then she turned to Annie. " 'Tis now or never, lassie."

"I'm coming!" Annie said firmly. " 'Twill be something to tell my grandchildren one day," she finished with a grin.

"Then, let us go," the earl said, and he signaled to his manservant, Dermid More.

The little party of four, each mounted, turned onto the Leith road and headed for the port. The day remained very cold, but bright. They reached Leith in the late afternoon as the sun was setting behind them, making their way to the Mermaid Inn on the waterfront.

It was a large and prosperous establishment, and its courtyard was bustling busily. Dermid dismounted first and went into the inn. He returned a few moments later.

"Captain Daumier is awaiting us in a private room, my lord," he reported.

"We'll go in, then. You know the way, Dermid?" the earl asked, sliding off his horse and then helping Rosamund from hers.

Dermid nodded, then aided Annie to dismount.

"My bottom is fair sore," Annie said with a sigh. She followed her mistress and the earl into the inn as Dermid led the way. It was a back route, and they neatly avoided the public rooms by taking it. At the end of a narrow hallway was a door, and Dermid knocked upon it, then opened the portal to usher his master and their party inside.

A portly gentleman arose from a chair by the fire and came forward. "Lord Leslie?" he asked.

"I am Patrick Leslie," the earl replied.

The gentleman nodded. "Jean-Paul Daumier, captain of *La Petite Reine*," he said.

"I was told we are to sail tonight, captain. Is everything on schedule?" Patrick Leslie queried.

"But, of course, my lord!" came the firm answer. "The weather is fair, and will remain that way for a few more days, thanks to *le bon Dieu*. We have good northwest winds, and your passage should be a swift one. Be advised that I will be hugging the English coast for several days so that if the weather turns we can make port safely. We'll cross the Strait of Dover to Calais, then sail on to Boulogne, and if the weather is still good I can get you as far as Le Havre, but no farther. The weather will turn sooner than later, and I'll not cross the Bay of Biscay at this time of year. I'm just a coastal freighter."

"I understand," the earl said. "And having made that passage several times, I will certainly agree with you, Captain Daumier. Will we be safe, however, within sight of the English coast?"

"*Oui!* The English, for all they proclaim the French their enemies, are always happy to see me, my lord. Especially the wine merchants and their rich customers!" Captain Daumier said with a broad smile. "If we should be boarded, I have enough empty barrels aboard to confirm my story, and you are just a gentleman running away from his wife with his amour, eh?" He chuckled.

The Earl of Glenkirk laughed. "Nonetheless, I hope we are not stopped."

"It is unlikely," the captain told him. "These English are not good sailors. But their king, I am told, seeks to build a great navy, so maybe one day they will be. For now they fish near the shore and run for land at the slightest blow. We will be safe."

The earl nodded. "When do we sail?" he asked.

"You have time for a good supper, my lord, but then you should come aboard. I will send my cabin boy for you and your party," the captain responded. Then he bowed, and taking up his cloak, departed.

"I am ravenous!" Rosamund announced. "It has been a long, cold ride."

"Dermid, find the landlord and order us supper. Do it discreetly, and try not to be seen by any who might recognize you. Leave your plaid and badge here, man," the earl instructed his servant.

"Aye, my lord," Dermid said, and hurried out.

"Why did you instruct Dermid as you did?" Rosamund asked Patrick.

"Because Leith is a port, and it is full of spies seeking whatever bits of information they can find to sell. A Leslie tartan would give rise to questions in certain quarters, and so I prefer that we not be seen or identified," he explained to her.

"But the landlord? How did we get this private accommodation, and how will we pay for it?" she questioned him.

"The landlord of the Mermaid is in the king's pay. He collects bits of information for Jamie Stewart. He was instructed to have this room available for Captain Daumier and his friends. And he was paid well to be silent about it," the earl explained to her.

"This is certainly a world of which I had no idea," Rosamund said to him.

"Why would you, my love?" he said in answer. "You are the lady of Friarsgate, a prosperous estate in the borders of England. Intrigue is not something with which you would be familiar, but you will soon learn much of it, for you are with me. This is more than likely a useless business I undertake, but the king will attempt every means he can to avoid a war with England. Would that your king were as careful."

"Henry Tudor has a great sense of his own importance," Rosamund began. "When he decides that he is right, he will follow a course to its end. And God is always on his side," she finished with a smile.

The Earl of Glenkirk laughed aloud at this. "I think, my darling," he said, "that you have a very sharp eye and will be very useful to me in this matter."

"I will not act against England, Patrick," she told him. "I am no traitor."

"Nay, lovey," he responded. "We do not act against England, but Scotland's king is older, more experienced, and has more wisdom than your Henry Tudor. And do not forget that Scotland's queen is England's sister. But we would prevent a war, and our king will not betray his alliances to serve his own ends, as your king attempts to make him do. It is most dishonorable, Rosamund."

"I know," she sighed. "Meg always said her younger brother was a bit of a bully. And now he is England's king."

"And jealous of King James' good relations with His Holiness. He attempts to destroy that relationship for his own ends," the earl noted.

"He is not a man who likes to lose, or even take second place," Rosamund admitted. "Patrick, tell me exactly what it is you go to do."

"When we are aboard *La Petite Reine*," the earl said.

"You do not trust me?" She was astounded and hurt.

He took her in his arms. "Aye, I trust you, but I cannot know who is listening at the door, my love. Do you understand me?"

Her amber eyes grew wide with surprise,

and then she silently nodded.

A moment later the door opened to admit Dermid and a servingman bearing a tray. The tray was set upon a table, and the servant left after a swift glance about the room. There was nothing of note, and it was just as his master had told him. Lovers escaping to another land. No one would pay good coin for that unless they were people of importance, and while their clothing was fine, it was not extravagant, and the gentleman wore neither a plaid, nor a badge that would identify him. Disappointed, the servingman was swiftly gone.

"He's got a sharp eye in his head," Annie noted pithily.

"Nothing to see here." Dermid grinned at her.

The two young servants served their master and mistress the meal that had been brought, and then, invited, sat down to eat with them. There was a joint of beef, a fat capon with apple, and bread stuffing. There was a bowl of mussels steamed in white wine and bread that was freshly baked and still warm from the oven, with softened butter melted on it. A wedge of cheese had been supplied along with a pitcher of October ale. They ate in silence, and they had barely finished when there was a soft knock upon the door. It opened to reveal a young boy.

"Madame and monseigner will follow me," he said, turning to go.

Annie set her mistress' fur-lined cloak around her shoulders and then stuffed the pockets of her own cloak with the apples and pears that had come with their meal. Then she and Dermid followed after the ship's boy. They exited the inn through the same back entrance through which they had entered, and followed their guide away from the courtyard and down a narrow alley, out onto a long, wide dock. At the end of the wharf was their vessel, a fair-sized boat that appeared to be in good condition. They boarded, and the boy led them through a door at the ship's stern.

"This will be your cabin," he said, and then he left them.

Rosamund looked about the room. It wasn't very big, she thought nervously.

"There is still time," he said to her.

"Nay," she responded.

A large wide bunk was built into the wall, and above it was a single bunk.

"You and Annie will sleep here," the earl said. "Dermid and I will take turns sleeping and watching."

" 'Tis cold," Rosamund said.

He nodded. "We won't be warm again for several weeks," he told her. "Traveling in winter is never very pleasant, but we will manage. You and Annie get into bed now, for that is how you will stay warmest. Remove only your shoes, lovey."

The two young women climbed into the larger of the two bunks after taking their shoes off. They burrowed beneath a surprisingly warm down coverlet.

"It's better here," Rosamund agreed.

"You can sleep safely. Dermid and I will not leave you," he told her.

"I think I am too excited to sleep," Rosamund told him, but both she and Annie were soon snoring lightly.

"Get your rest. I'll take the first watch," the earl told Dermid, and the servant climbed into the top bunk without another word. Patrick settled himself in the small window seat of the stern window. He listened while the ship was freed from its moorings. He felt the shift of the vessel as it began to get under way, slipping out into Firth of Forth, riding on the outgoing tide. He could see the royal shipyard with the black masts of *Great Michael*, the king's pride and joy. The night was fair, and as they moved farther down Firth of Forth and away from the port the stars began to appear in the dark skies above them.

Patrick thought back to the last time he embarked for San Lorenzo. His daughter, Janet, was no more than ten, and Adam, six. He traveled as King James' first royal ambassador to San Lorenzo. He hadn't wanted to go, to leave Glenkirk, but duty had called him; the king had said it would not be for more than a few years. When he had returned again to Scotland his daughter was lost to him forever. He and his son and Mary MacKay, who had been his daughter's maternal grandmother, had gone back into their Highlands. Mary had died several years later, in her cottage, where his daughter had been born. Jan. Janet Mary Leslie. What had become of her? Was she even alive today?

And now here he was once again on his way to that exquisite Mediterranean duchy, traveling this time with a girl younger than his daughter would be now. What madness, he thought, with a small smile. And what incredible happiness he was experiencing, such as he had never known in all of his life. Silently he thanked the fates for giving him Rosamund. That she was as passionate about him was astounding. The mode of their travel was hardly romantic. It would take them several days to reach France traveling as they were, and then a long and weary ride stretched before them. He had been mad to ask her to go. He had been mad to consider going himself. It was a fool's errand the king was sending him upon, but James Stewart would do whatever he had to do to keep the peace with England.

Amazingly, the weather held as they sailed south down the coastline, never letting the land disappear from their sight. It was cold, but the brisk winds sent their vessel speeding along. And then, one morning as Annie and Rosamund stepped from the cabin for a walk about the deck, Captain Daumier approached and pointing, said, "France, madame. We crossed the Strait of Dover in the early hours of the morning. As the weather is holding, we shall make for Le Havre. With luck we will be there by the morrow."

"That is very good news, captain. Does Lord Leslie know?" Rosamund asked him.

"Aye, madame. 'Twas he who told me to come and tell you. He is at the wheel even now. Look up," the captain replied.

Rosamund did, and to her surprise saw her lover piloting their vessel. Laughing, she waved at him and called, "Be sure, my lord, that you do not bring us back to England!"

The next morning *La Petite Reine* sailed into Le Havre and was made fast to a sturdy stone wharf. To Rosamund's great surprise, their horses were brought forth from the belly of their ship and led out onto the pier.

"I never thought about the beasts from the moment we dismounted at the Mermaid," she said.

"It's less noticeable if we retain our own animals and do not seek to purchase new ones. The fewer people we deal with, the fewer remember us. These ports, and many of the inns, are nests of intrigue. The buying and selling of information is a brisk trade," the Earl of Glenkirk said. Then he turned and thanked Captain Daumier for their safe passage.

"It was *le bon Dieu*'s own good fortune, my lord," the seaman said. "You know this is not a good time to cross from Scotland. We were very lucky. Certainly *le bon Dieu* is smiling on your endeavor, whatever it may be." Then he shook the earl's hand and turned away.

Rosamund, Annie, and Dermid were already mounted. The earl joined them.

"We have the day before us, and we have eaten aboard ship. Let us get away from the port and be on our way as quickly as possible," Glenkirk said.

They rode each day that followed from sunup to sunset, bypassing Paris, moving cross-country, usually staying off the main roads. Both Rosamund and Annie were garbed as young men, and anyone who noticed the riders saw four gentlemen.

Rosamund remembered her trips to the English court from her northern home. They had been far more civilized than this travel was. There had been monasteries and nunneries in which to stay the night. In France they sought their shelter where they might find it, but mindful of the two women, the earl did seek out farms with good barns in which they might overnight, offering the farmer a coin in exchange for his hospitality. More often than not, the farmer's wife would offer new bread, which they gratefully accepted. They purchased food occasionally in the market towns along their route.

The weather, which was at first cold and some days wet with rain or snow, began to grow milder as they traveled south and east. Suddenly it was spring, and the sun shone more often as they rode along. Finally, after many days on the road, the earl said, "We will reach San Lorenzo tomorrow."

"The first thing I want is a bath!" Rosamund said fervently. They had settled into a comfortable barn for the night, having been invited to the farmer's table for a hot supper.

"We shall not meet the duke until we have bathed and are properly clothed," he promised her, putting an arm about her shoulders.

"I am to meet the Duke of San Lorenzo?" Rosamund was surprised by this revelation. She sat up. Then she said, "But, of course. It will complete the illusion of two lovers running away together."

"You are my beloved companion, sweetheart," he said. "The duke is a most urbane gentleman. I look forward to seeing him again, although I admit I wish I did not have to see his son and daughter-in-law."

"The boy who was to wed your daughter?" Rosamund asked.

"Aye," the earl said softly. "I always thought he wed that princess from Toulouse too quickly. I wonder if he ever really loved my Jan."

"Let the past be done with, my lord," Rosamund said softly. "Nothing will change by allowing bitterness to take hold of you. You are here on a specific mission for your king. Do your duty, and let what happened all those years ago remain but a dim memory. You are not here to treat with San Lorenzo, but rather with Venice and the Holy Roman Empire."

He nodded at her. "You speak wisdom, sweetheart," he responded. "How is it a little girl from Cumbria should be so clever?"

"I think it is due to Hugh Cabot, my second husband, who taught me to have a care for myself and Friarsgate; and I think it is due to my youth at King Henry the seventh's court. Most of my care was in the household of the old king's mother, called the Venerable Margaret. She was very wise."

"You obviously learned your lesson well, Rosamund," he complimented her.

"Go to sleep, my lord," she advised. "Tomorrow will be a busy day for us. I will be glad to sleep in a bed once again, bathe, and wear beautiful garments. I am weary of being a lad." She leaned over and gave him a quick kiss on the lips. "Good night, my dearest love," she told him.

"And I am eager to have you in my bed again the way you should be," he murmured in her ear, and then he nibbled teasingly upon it. "I very much need you, Rosamund."

"And I you," she whispered back. "If the duke can supply us with a large tub, we shall bathe together," Rosamund murmured meaningfully.

"If we do, you know what will happen," he told her, and he nuzzled her neck.

"I certainly hope so!" Rosamund replied. "Now, go to sleep, Patrick. You will not get much rest tomorrow," she promised him.

And the Earl of Glenkirk laughed, drawing her into his embrace, one hand cupping a breast. "Nor will you, sweetheart," he agreed. "Nor will you!"

Chapter 5

The capital city of the duchy of San Lorenzo lay before them as they looked down from the mountain road on which they had been traveling.

"I have never seen houses in so many colors!" Rosamund exclaimed. "Our houses are either natural stone or whitewashed."

"The town's name is Arcobaleno. It means rainbow in the tongue of the Italians," he explained to her. "The people of San Lorenzo, their duchy set between France and the Italian states, speak both tongues equally."

"I speak some French," Rosamund told him. "I understand better than I speak, however. That can prove to be to my advantage. I shall learn a great deal more in my ignorance," she told him with a smile.

He laughed. "You are too clever by far, sweetheart," he responded.

They moved down now into Arcobaleno. About them, the hills were turning emerald green in the mid-February sunshine. They had come up the hills from a valley newly plowed and planted. Grain, Patrick had told her. On the heights about the town he pointed out the vineyards to the south. San Lorenzan wine was excellent, he assured her, as she would shortly learn. The town itself was perched on the hillsides above the blue sea. Not one house set along the neatly cobbled streets was of the same color, and Rosamund was amazed to find so many hues in the spectrum of the rainbow.

"What is that building?" Rosamund asked the earl, pointing to a complex set just above the town itself.

"The palace of the duke," he responded. "And see the pink marble villa facing the sea? That is the Scottish ambassador's residence. We are going there first. Soon enough it will be known that I am here, for like everywhere else, this is a hotbed of spies. For now I'd like to keep it secret. The duke will not be officially involved in this matter for his own safety and the safety of San Lorenzo."

"Will the ambassador be expecting us?" Rosamund asked.

"Nay," the earl chuckled. "We shall be quite a surprise to him. But I am carrying a letter from the king, and so it will be all right."

They rode past the duke's palace. At the open gates were guardsmen in sea-blue and gold uniforms. Peering into the courtyard beyond, Rosamund saw, to her surprise, a gentleman she recognized. She stared hard at the man dismounting his horse. "Do the English have an ambassador here, my lord?" she asked Patrick.

"Aye, but only recently. Why?"

"As we passed the palace courtyard I saw a gentleman I recognized from the English court," she explained.

"Would he recognize you, sweetheart?" the earl asked her, concerned.

"I do not know, Patrick. We were never introduced, nor did we ever speak, but I know who he is. He is one of the Howards. Not an important one, just a distant cousin."

"But he has obviously been given this posting to please his more powerful relations," Glenkirk noted. "We will have to see he does not become involved in our little business. It would not do for Henry Tudor to learn we are attempting to weaken the alliance the pope seeks to build."

They rode farther down towards the town, coming to the pink villa that was the residence of Scotland's ambassador. Patrick felt the years sliding away as he remembered his own tenure here. Like San Lorenzo itself, he had never thought to see it again. They rode through the open gates into the courtyard, and immediately there were servants to take their horses. The majordomo came out to greet the visitors.

He was an elderly man, but his eyes widened with recognition as he approached them. "My lord Leslie!" he said. "Welcome! Welcome back to San Lorenzo!"

"Pietro! How wonderful to find you still here!" Glenkirk said, wringing the old man's hand. "Is your master inside? I have brought a message from our king."

"Come in, my lord! Come in!" He led them out of the sun, which was surprisingly hot.

"I will tell my master that you are here. We were not expecting visitors," Pietro said. He led them into a beautiful light-filled chamber overlooking gardens. "If you will wait here, my lord. There is wine for refreshment." He hurried out as fast as his old legs could carry him.

"He was my majordomo when I served the king here," Patrick noted.

"He obviously likes you," Rosamund said.

"His daughter liked me, too," came the mischievous reply. "She had dark hair and eyes and golden skin."

"From what I have seen along the road, my lord, I imagine she is now a plump and well-settled matron. A grandmother, perhaps?" Rosamund murmured sweetly.

"You are jealous, sweetheart," he said, and his tone was exceedingly pleased.

"Why are men so vain?" Rosamund wondered aloud.

"Ouch!" he cried, falling back, clutching his chest in mock distress. "Your claws are all the sharper for these weeks on the road, my sweet Rosamund." Then he chuckled.

"My lady!" Annie said excitedly. "Look out in the gardens. There are flowers blooming, and 'tis but February. And didn't the sun feel good, and it still winter?"

"Winter does not visit San Lorenzo, Annie," the earl explained, "except on very rare and quick occasions."

"You mean it's like this all the time?" Annie was astounded. "Surely you've brought us to paradise, my lord."

"I once thought it so," he replied.

The door to the salon opened, and a tall, grizzled gentleman walked through. "My lord earl!" he said, and he bowed.

"Lord MacDuff," Patrick said. "Is there someplace we may speak privily? And if my lady and her servant might be taken to comfortable quarters . . . We will be staying with you. Dermid, go with Annie and Lady Rosamund." The Earl of Glenkirk's voice rang with authority.

"Of course, my lord," the ambassador replied. "Pietro!"

The majordomo was immediately in the room. "My lord?"

"Show the lady to our guest quarters, and see that everything is done to make her and the earl comfortable. My lord, come with me." And Lord MacDuff led Patrick from the salon.

Pietro bowed. "I speak English, a little bit, my lady," he said.

"And I speak French a little bit," Rosamund told him with a smile.

The majordomo smiled back. "Then if my lady will follow me," he responded.

They followed him from the lovely salon out into the round marble foyer and up two levels of a wide marble flight of stairs. On the third landing he opened the gilded walnut doors and ushered them into a spacious apartment.

"Is there anything you need at the moment, my lady?" he asked her.

"We have been on the road for many days, Pietro. I should love a bath," she told him.

"At once, my lady," he told her, and he hurried off.

"And what will you be wearing after I take these stinking clothes and have 'em burned?" Annie demanded to know.

"Do I not have at least one clean shirt or chemise?" Rosamund asked.

"Well, you can hardly meet anyone in

just your chemise," Annie replied pithily.

"Well, then, I suppose after my bath I shall need to see a seamstress," Rosamund told her servant. "The earl has promised me that he would have a suitable wardrobe made for me. And you will need new garments as well, Annie."

"I'd actually like to have a bath myself, and some clean clothing," Annie admitted. "Don't think I'll ever get the stink of horse out of me hair."

"Let's explore this apartment and see what we have while we are waiting for my bath," Rosamund suggested.

Together the two young women began walking about and opening doors. The apartment had its dayroom in which they now stood, but it also had two bedchambers adjoining each other and two small chambers each containing a single bed, a chest, and a little table.

"You have your own room," Rosamund told Annie, "and there is one for Dermid. Choose now, you two, and set your possessions inside. Dermid, I did not ask you before, but were you with the earl when he was last here in San Lorenzo?"

"Nay, 'twas my uncle," Dermid said. "I was just newly breeked when the lord came home. My uncle chose me to go with the earl when the king sent for him. He has no lads of his own, just daughters," Dermid explained. "He said he was too old to go traipsing about any longer, and so was the master. But when the king called, a loyal man answered, and that man would need his servant. He'd been training me to take his place these last few years anyway. He'll be surprised when he learns where I've been."

"If you can tell him," Rosamund said quietly.

"Aye, lady. I may not be able to say," Dermid answered her.

"Oh, my lady, look!" Annie had opened the windowlike doors across the dayroom. Beyond was a balcony that stretched across the villa, and beyond it was the blue sea. "Ain't it beautiful!" Annie said.

"Yes, it is," Rosamund replied, joining her servant. "I don't think I have ever seen anything as beautiful outside of Friarsgate."

"That's the first time I've heard you mention home in weeks," Annie noted. "I wondered if you had forgotten it."

"Nay. Friarsgate is my first love, and it will always be my love, Annie. We will go home eventually, but this is so exciting. I never thought to see a place like San Lorenzo, or live through a winter without chilblains on my hands. Once I should have been content to never leave Friarsgate, and one day I will feel the same way again. But not now. Not today."

The door to the apartment opened, and a line of footmen, led by Pietro, began to enter. He signaled with his hand to Dermid. "Here, man, help me," he said. Then he entered the more feminine bed-chamber, pressed a hidden lock on one of the walnut-paneled walls, which sprang open to reveal a huge bathing tub, and with Dermid's aid wrestled the tub from its place out into the room. "Where will you have it, my lady?" he asked her.

Rosamund looked about the room, and then seeing that the windowed doors opened onto the terrace, said, "Put it out there, Pietro."

The majordomo smiled broadly. "Ah," he said as he and Dermid wrestled the tub to its desired location, "Madame is a ro-mantic."

Rosamund smiled back at him. "It seems a perfect place," she murmured.

The tub was set out upon the marble ter-race, and the footmen began to fill it with their buckets, slowly climbing the twin sets of steps placed on either side of the tub and dumping the water into the large vessel, which was made of hard oak and bound in polished brass bands. It was a labor-intensive effort, but finally the tub was filled.

"I shall need a seamstress, Pietro,"

Rosamund said. "The earl and I traveled swiftly and upon horseback all the way from the French coast. None of our party has suitable clothing for the duke's court. That must be remedied as quickly as possible."

"At once, madame," Pietro answered her with a bow. "My daughter is the finest seamstress in all of Arcobaleno. I shall send her to you."

"Is she the one who was once Lord Leslie's mistress?" Rosamund inquired.

"The very same, madame," he answered her with a twinkle. "His lordship will not recognize her, for she has grown well rounded with her marriage, her children, and her enterprise." He bowed again, and then turned and left her.

"Send her to us late this afternoon," Rosamund called after him.

"After *siesta*, of course, madame," the majordomo replied. "And she will bring a fine selection of fabrics, too." Then he was gone.

"Maybel wouldn't approve of your being so bold, my lady, and you can smack me for it if you will, but 'tis so," Annie said.

Rosamund laughed. "I am at a disadvantage here, Annie, and I know that Lord Leslie had a mistress when he was last in San Lorenzo. I would prefer no surprises.

Now, help me out of these clothes and into that lovely tub."

"You're not going naked out on that terrace, my lady?" Annie fretted.

"We are facing the sea," Rosamund replied. "There is no one to see me." She sat down and pulled off her boots. "Whew!" she exclaimed, peeling her stockings off her feet. "Dispose of it all, Annie, and I mean it. It's beyond washing."

Annie nodded as she helped her mistress to undress. "I've saved one clean chemise, my lady," she told Rosamund. "When you are clean you can put it on. Dermid, go and bring in our packs," she instructed the earl's man.

Dermid gave her a wink and left them.

"Cheeky Scots devil," Annie muttered.

"He likes you," Rosamund noted.

"Aye, and I like him, but that's as far as it will ever go," Annie said.

"Why?" Rosamund wanted to know.

"Because you ain't never going to leave Friarsgate, and I ain't never going to leave you," Annie said.

"Nay, Annie," her mistress said. "If you love him, and he you, then you are free to wed him and go with him. I will not have you unhappy on my account."

"Well, as it ain't got that far yet, my lady, I don't have to think about it, do I?" Annie remarked with a small smile.

"One day you may, and when you do, I would advise you to follow your heart, Annie. I have, and what is sauce for the goose is surely sauce for the other goose," she chuckled.

"Oh, my lady, you say such funny things," Annie giggled. She picked up a coverlet that was lying upon the bed and wrapped it about her mistress. "You ain't going out to your tub as naked as the day God made you, my lady," she said firmly.

Wrapped in the fabric, Rosamund walked out onto the terrace. "I'll have to unwrap it sooner or later," she said, and after climbing up the steps to her tub she flung off the makeshift gown and stepped carefully into the hot water with a deep sigh. "Ahhh," she said, seating herself on the little stool within the tub. "This is wonderful!" Reaching up, she unbraided her long hair and began to wash it with the fragrant soap that had been placed upon the tub ledge.

Annie climbed up the steps with a bucket and rinsed her mistress' soapy hair with water dipped from the tub. Three times Rosamund soaped her auburn hair and scrubbed it and her head free of the dirt of the long road that they had traveled. And each time Annie poured several buckets of water over the young woman's head until Rosamund bid her to cease.

"Give me a drying cloth to wrap my head in while I wash," she said, and she took the item from Annie to enfold it about her head in turbanlike fashion. Then she set about washing the rest of her body. When she had finished, she exited the tub and said to Annie, "Get in, girl! 'Tis not likely you will be given another opportunity."

Annie didn't argue. Forgetting completely where she was, she stripped her filthy clothes off and climbed into the still-warm water to bathe her hair and her body. Rosamund sat upon a bench on the terrace, wrapped in a large drying cloth and brushing her hair with her pear-wood brush, the one luxury item she had carried with her from Scotland. The warm air and the bright sunlight quickly dried her thick hair. When Annie had finished bathing, her mistress handed her another drying cloth, and the servant came forth from the tub, smiling.

"Ah, my lady, thank you," she said. "I'm not much for all the washing you do, but after our travels it was good to have a bath."

"But now, Annie, we have another problem. What are you to wear?" Rosamund laughed.

"I got a chemise like you, my lady, but naught else. I expect that Pietro will be able to find me a skirt and shirt however. When Dermid gets back I'll send him off to ask." She wrapped herself in her drying cloth and sat down next to her mistress.

Rosamund handed her the brush. "Dry your hair," she said.

"Oh, I couldn't use your brush, my lady," Annie protested.

"Then your hair will dry a tangle, Annie," Rosamund said.

"I'll use my fingers," Annie told her. " 'Tis what I do anyhow."

While Annie was drying her hair Dermid returned with their packs from the horses. He flushed at the sight of the two women wrapped in their drying cloths. "I'll leave your pack there, my lady," he addressed Rosamund, his eyes averted from her. "And I'll distribute the rest as they ought to be." He tossed one of the saddlebags on Rosamund's bed and scurried away.

Annie giggled. "He ain't too brave now, is he?" she said.

"Go and put on your chemise," Rosamund instructed her. "I can put my own on, and then I'm going to lie down and have a nap on that soft-looking bed. You should do the same, lass. Until the seamstress comes after *siesta*, whatever that is, there is naught for us to do." She lay down upon the bed, suddenly tired and unable to even pull out her chemise. "Just for a little bit," she said to herself softly, and she closed her eyes.

"I'm sending Dermid for that Pietro. I can't go around without my clothes until something new can be made for me," Annie said, and after putting on her chemise she went off to seek out her fellow servant.

Patrick finally appeared to find Rosamund sleeping. Seeing her upon the bed, wrapped in the drying cloth, so much of her bare to his view was tempting. Then he spied the tub still out on the terrace. He stripped off his travel-worn garments, then walked outside and climbed into the tub. The water was lukewarm and well used, but he was nonetheless able to wash himself thoroughly using the scented soap upon the tub's shelf. He sniffed and smiled. The fragrance was a familiar one, one he had not smelled in years.

Annie returned to the terrace in her chemise and gave a little squeak to see him so ensconced. "Oh, my lord!" She blushed furiously.

"Give me your drying cloth, lassie, as I can see you are quit of it, and then find your own place," he ordered the serving girl gently.

"Aye, my lord," she answered him. "Pietro is sending the seamstress to us after *siesta*. What is *siesta*?"

"The time following the midday meal and the late afternoon when the sun is less hot," he explained. "It is the custom to nap, or otherwise amuse oneself, Annie."

"Thank you, my lord!" she answered, giving him a bobbing little curtsy. "Shall I wake my lady?"

"Nay, Annie. She is fair worn, I can see. Let her sleep. I will shortly join her. Run along now, lass." He took the drying cloth from the girl.

"Yes, my lord," Annie said obediently, and she was quickly gone.

Patrick pulled himself out of the tub and dried himself off before wrapping the cloth about his loins and seating himself on the marble bench. The sun on his shoulders felt wonderful. He had forgotten how good one's body felt when exposed to the air and the heat of the sun. And he realized now that if Rosamund was tired after their exhausting journey then so was he. He stood and went back inside, lying down next to her. She murmured softly, but made no other indication that she was even aware of him. His eyes closed, and he was swiftly asleep.

When he awoke several hours later, Rosamund was gone from their bed, but he could hear her in the dayroom beyond. He gave himself a few moments for his head to clear, and then he stretched before arising to walk towards the sound of her voice.

"Ah, you are awake," she said, seeing him. She was seated at a table, eating ravenously. "Come and eat so we may siesta again," she told him, and she licked her fingers clean of grease from the chicken wing she was devouring. "I am going to enjoy this southern style of living, my darling."

He sat down opposite her with a grin and helped himself to the full bowl of oysters, which he began cracking open and swallowing whole.

"I left them for you," she said sweetly. "I thought you might need your strength, my lord." She picked up her goblet. "You are right. This San Lorenzan wine is delicious." Then she reached out for the pitcher and poured a generous measure into his goblet. "The seamstress is coming later," she said.

"So Annie said," he replied as he picked up the goblet to drink some wine.

"She is Pietro's daughter, an old friend of yours, I believe," Rosamund said innocently.

He choked upon his wine. "Celestina? Jesu! Maria!"

Rosamund giggled mischievously. "Pietro says you will not recognize her, for she has grown with age, bairns, and her busy enterprise. I shall be fascinated to meet her."

"You will behave yourself, madame," he said sternly.

"Now, Patrick, it is not often that the current mistress is permitted to meet the mistress of one's youth," she teased him wickedly.

His green eyes narrowed. "You're a bad wench," he said.

"I am," she agreed, "but I promise to behave. Will you have some of this delicious roast kid?" She carved several slices and put them on his plate together with an artichoke that had been steamed in wine, some fresh bread, and a wedge of soft cheese. "The ambassador has an excellent cook," she noted, and then she returned to her own meal.

"If you continue to eat like that, you shall end up like Celestina obviously has," he teased her.

"I have almost starved these past few weeks," she complained. "You did not tell me that food would be so scarce, or cold, or tasteless along the road, my lord. I shall eat like this every day and bathe daily as well," she told him.

"Was it you who suggested the tub be put out on the terrace overlooking the sea?" he asked her.

She nodded. "I thought how lovely to bathe while looking out at the hills and the sea and the town below."

He smiled at her. "Then we shall keep the tub there while we are here, sweetheart."

"How did your meeting with Lord MacDuff go?" she queried him.

"He was surprised to see us, of course, but once he had read the king's letter he understood. You were right. The English ambassador is Richard Howard, and he is an unctuous little man, always bowing and scraping to the duke when he isn't being arrogant and making demands on behalf of his master."

"And does the duke of this place know you are here and for what purpose?" Rosamund asked her lover.

"I brought a missive for Duke Sebastian, and MacDuff will deliver it tomorrow," Glenkirk answered her. "I do not believe the representatives from Venice and the emperor have arrived yet."

"Have you not taken a chance coming without the duke's knowledge, my lord?" she wondered.

"Duke Sebastian was sent a letter in advance of our arrival saying that I was returning to San Lorenzo sometime this winter, but that my coming must remain secret," the earl told Rosamund. "He is intelligent enough to know that something is afoot. And he will cooperate until it is convenient for him to do otherwise," Glenkirk explained. "Sebastian di San Lorenzo is a politic and clever man. He never does anything without reason, or anything that will not benefit him or the duchy. Slow and steady is the path we must take, unlike your king who wants everything immediately if not forthwith."

"Henry Tudor is an ambitious man," Rosamund responded. "They say he looks like his grandfather, King Edward the fourth, and some say he is like him in character, with lofty, grandiose plans and ideas for England. I repeat what I have heard, for I cannot vouch for his character. He was determined to bed me although I was not pleased by his attentions. He is a man who thinks only of himself and what he wants. Perhaps that is a good thing in a king. I cannot say."

"It is a good thing in a king when that king is thoughtful of his rule," Patrick replied. "How long were you his mistress?"

"A very brief few months," she answered. "I lived in terror that the queen would learn of my betrayal, for she was my friend when I was a girl at court. Owein and I aided her in the years in which King Henry the seventh could not make up his mind if he still wanted her for a daughter-in-law or not. She was treated very shabbily. It was she who invited me back to court after Owein died. I did not want to go, but one does not refuse a queen."

"Or a king," he noted bitterly.

"You are jealous," she said, surprised. "You need not be jealous, my love."

"I am jealous of all the men who have been in your life before me, Rosamund," he told her. "I am jealous of the men who will know you after I have passed from your life. I have never loved a woman as I love you. When you are gone from me, whatever is left of my life will be cold and bleak." Reaching out, he took her hand and kissed it tenderly.

"Do not speak of our parting yet, my darling," Rosamund answered him. "We have much time before us. I know it!" She caressed his cheek with the hand he had kissed. "Are you going to shave that dreadful beard away, my lord? Certainly there is a barber in Arcobaleno who could service you."

"You do not like my beard?" he teased her.

"Nay! I know you could not shave it on the road, but we are no longer on the road," she said.

"I do not need a barber. Dermid will do the deed. Dermid!" he called to his man-servant, and the young man was immediately at his master's side. "My lady will have my beard off, laddie. Let us do it, for I am now clean and well fed and ready for my *siesta*."

"At once, my lord! I'll get a bowl and the razor," came the answer.

"I'll await you, my darling," Rosamund told him, and she got up from the table, wiping her mouth and hands with the linen napkin that had been in her lap. With a seductive smile, she walked slowly to her bedchamber and shut the door behind her.

Dermid grinned. "I've been told that Englishwomen are cold, my lord, but it certainly don't seem so, if you don't mind my saying."

"You've had your eye on my lady's Annie," Glenkirk said. "She's a respectable lass, Dermid, and her mistress would be most distressed if you treated her badly."

"Oh, nay, my lord! No man will ever treat Annie badly. She'd lay them out, she would, if they tried. I'm thinking of courting her, for there is none at home who pleases me as well. She's got a good temper on her, does Annie. She'll make fine bairns for a man. I'd even be willing to stay in England for her."

"If she loves you as well, Dermid, she will come home to Glenkirk with you," the earl said. "But there is time before either of you must make such a decision."

Dermid nodded. Then he went to fetch what he would need to shave his master, and after returning quickly, he set to work removing the growth of dark beard, streaked here and there with silver, that the earl had grown in the last few weeks. When he had finished, he said frankly, "Well, you look better without a beard than with one, my lord. Younger by far, I'd say."

Patrick winced at the remark. Dermid had meant nothing by it, but it was a reminder of the years that separated him and Rosamund. He arose from the table, and thanking his servant, went into his bedchamber. Stripping off the drying cloth, he looked at himself in the full-length mirror by the wardrobe. He was still lean and hard of body despite his years. He knew men far younger grew flabby, but he had not. His hair was yet dark, though here and there he saw silver. He had all his teeth, and none were rotting. His gaze was still sharp, and his appetite for Rosamund's fair body grew with each passing day. He was, he knew, still a very vigorous lover. Turning, he looked for the hidden door that would connect their chambers, and finding it, pressed the lock, and when the door opened, he stepped through into the next room.

She lay dozing again, the graceful curve of her back to him. He realized how difficult a journey it had been for her, though she had never once complained. She had removed her cloth and was as naked as he was. He lay down next to her, and she murmured softly as she felt the bed sag.

"Patrick?" she said.

"Nay, 'tis the king of your heart," he told her, and she rolled over into his arms to face him. He gave her a slow, sweet kiss.

"That is nice," she whispered against his mouth when he had broken off their embrace. "I have missed the leisure of laying in bed with you, my lord."

"Is that all you have missed?" he teased her. The touch of her, the fragrance that emanated from her lovely body, excited him. He was shocked by his body's swift reaction to the mere touch and smell of her. "My God!" he said quietly.

Rosamund laughed softly. "I am as bad as you are, my darling." Reaching out, she caressed his love rod. "I am more than ready, Patrick. I shall surely die if you do not put yourself into me now!"

He complied, finding her hot, wet, and indeed very ready to receive him. He had barely begun the rhythm when he felt the head of his manhood drenched by her love juices. Now it was he who laughed. "Rosamund! Rosamund!" he groaned against her ear, and his own juices burst forth to flood her womb. "I need make no apologies, sweetheart," he told her. "And now that we have satisfied our lust, we shall begin anew, slowly, slowly until you are weeping with your satisfaction." He withdrew from her.

She sighed happily. "I have missed our passion so very much, Patrick. Forgive me for my eagerness, which was but matched by yours." She propped herself up on an elbow and stared down into his face. "I love you so much, my lord. I regret we cannot make a child together."

"So do I," he told her, and he drew her down so that her auburn head was against his broad chest. "Are your daughters like you, Rosamund?"

"Philippa and Banon are said to favor me, but not Bessie. She is her father's lass. He was a good father, Owein Meredith. You were a good father too, I think."

"I tried," he said. "If loving my son and daughter was being a good father, then aye, for I loved them both well. Janet's loss broke my heart. Yet now that I am here again with you, it is different, sweetheart. I remember that time, but it somehow does not seem so cruel to me anymore. We tried to get her back, you know, but we could not."

"You have never told me what happened," Rosamund said.

"The long and the short of it was she was kidnapped by slavers and sold in the great market of Candia for a large sum of money. She was young, a virgin, and very beautiful. My son, Adam, still seeks for her, despite the years that have passed. He is determined to find her, though she may be long dead. I do not know. She is lost to me."

"I am sorry," Rosamund told him. "I think it is better to know that someone is dead than to not know what has happened to them."

"You know that I love you, don't you?" he replied, changing the subject adroitly.

"And you know that I love you," she answered him, understanding that he did not wish to speak on the subject of his daughter any longer.

"I shall have Celestina make you a wardrobe to suit a princess," he said. "You cannot meet the duke until you are properly garbed. I am so proud of you and of your beauty that I would flaunt you, Rosamund."

"I am not beautiful," she protested. "Perhaps very pretty, but surely not beautiful."

"If another woman demurred so," he told her, "I should think her being coy, but not you, my darling. However, I find you beautiful, and so will the duke. He has a roving eye, Rosamund, so beware of him. He will charm you as he does all the lovely women who cross his path. He has been widowed for years, but is content to remain so."

"As you have been," she teased him. "You widowers do not dupe me. You love being able to flit among the ladies like a bumblebee among the flowers."

"Buzz! Buzz!" he harried her, nuzzling the soft hollow between her neck and her shoulder. "I am your bumblebee, my darling, and like the bumblebee, I wish to make love to my beautiful English rose."

Rosamund giggled as his tongue tickled the whorl of her ear and a frisson of a shiver rippled down her spine. "Will you sting me, Master Bumbles?" she asked mischievously.

"Indeed, madame, I will, for I have a rather large stinger just waiting to dip itself deeply into your honey pot," he growled in her ear. His tongue licked at her shoulder and then slowly climbed the column of her slender throat. "You taste delicious," he said softly.

She stretched her full length before him, and he lowered his dark head and began to draw his fleshy tongue over her offered body. Rosamund closed her eyes and relaxed in the feel of the warm wetness, which was followed by the warm breath from his nostrils cooling her moist flesh. His head moved slowly, for he did not miss an inch of her skin. He licked at her breasts and suckled upon the pointed nipples, then lower across her torso, sliding across her taut belly, finding the soft insides of her thighs, which he spread without resistance. He opened her secret place to his view, his tongue touching her with the most delicate and exquisite finesse.

"Oh, Patrick!" she half-moaned. "Yes!"

The marauding tongue lapped at the pearlescent juices that dappled the rose flesh. It found the core of her womanhood and began to harass it with just the tip of his tongue. He was becoming dizzy with his burgeoning lust and the hot scent of her.

"Don't stop!" she begged him. "Oh, God! 'Tis so wonderful, my love!"

"You are a wanton," he groaned, unable to help himself. She was open to him, and he thrust his tongue into the cave of her sex, pushing it as far as he could, using it as he might his manhood, hearing her whimper with her need for more.

Rosamund was almost mindless with the pleasure he was giving her. She wanted to give him pleasure as well. When he raised his body to cover hers, she pulled him forward so that he was kneeling over her breasts. Reaching out, she drew him closer until she was able to draw his manhood into her mouth. Tugging on it gently with her lips and tongue, she heard him moan. She held him steady so she might lick the length of him, run her tongue about the fleshy tip, lap the pearl of his juices.

"Enough!" he finally groaned, and he loosened her grip so he might enter her body in another way. She wrapped her slim legs about him and helped him to thrust deeply into her eager and waiting body. He almost wept to feel her love sheath tightening about him.

"Yes!" she whispered fiercely. "Yes! Dear heaven, how you fill me, Patrick!" She ached with the sweetness he offered, and her arms drew him as close as they could.

She was tight. She was hot. She was an endless delight of which he could not get enough. He thrust and withdrew. Thrust and withdrew, moving slowly at first, and then as their desires burgeoned, his rhythm increased, as did hers. He heard her low keening and his own groans of satisfaction. His head was spinning. He felt her sharp fingernails raking down his long back and swore softly at her, his fingers closing hard about her wrists and forcing her arms up where she could not damage him again. "Bitch!" he growled against her mouth.

"Devil!" she hissed back, and then she screamed softly as her body was convulsed with a series of shudders. "Ohhh, Patrick," she sighed.

His own completion met hers, and he

flooded her with his juices. "Rosamund! Rosamund!" he half-sobbed.

They lay together until their breathing became slower and softer once again. Reaching out, he took her hand in his, kissing each finger as he did. Rosamund closed her eyes and sighed, well satisfied. She knew, as she had known from the moment their eyes met, that this passion they shared could not be forever, but for now it was wonderful, and she would not think about tomorrow. If she died in her sleep tonight, what they had was more than enough. She reached out lifted the hand holding her, and kissed it. Then she placed it on her heart. Neither of them said a word. Words were not necessary.

They slept, awaking a while later to a tentative knock upon the bedchamber door.

"Yes?" Rosamund called.

"Master Pietro has come to say the seamstress will be here in half an hour, my lady," Annie called.

"We will be ready for her," Rosamund called back. She poked her lover gently.

"We have to get up, my lord, and wash the scent of our lust away. The tub will be cool now, but it will suffice."

They went back out upon the terrace, and to Rosamund's surprise the water was not at all icy, for the sun had kept it lukewarm. She and Patrick climbed into the oak vessel and quickly bathed again. She had forgotten to pin her hair up, and the tips of it were wet when she exited the water. She dried herself quickly and then dried Patrick as well.

"Well, I have a chemise to wear," she said, "but what will you wear? Not that Signora Celestina hasn't already seen what you have to offer, my lord," she taunted him.

He chuckled. "Dermid has had Pietro find me some haut-de-chausses and hose, and I have a shirt. I shall be more than respectable when I meet with Celestina again."

"Then go and dress, my lord, so we may at least give the impression of respectability," she told him.

He nodded and walked back into her bedchamber and through the door into his own quarters.

Rosamund looked for the saddlebag and found it on the floor by the bed. Opening it, she pulled out a lace-trimmed chemise. It was clean and of excellent quality. She put it on and then sat upon the edge of the bed to brush her hair out and braid it up neatly. She was eager to wear a gown again.

She heard voices in the dayroom beyond. Then came a knock upon her bedchamber door, and Rosamund opened the portal and stepped through into the dayroom. At the same time, the Earl of Glenkirk came from his bedchamber. The large woman with the black hair and black eyes ignored Rosamund and shrieked as she saw the earl.

"Patrizio! Santa Maria be blessed, for I never hoped to see you again!" She flung her arms about him, enveloping him in a suffocating hug.

Patrick was hard-pressed not to burst into laughter. This was Celestina after eighteen years. He remembered the seductive, sulky-mouthed girl who had become his mistress all those years ago. He managed to squirm from her embrace, and taking her by her broad shoulders, he kissed her firmly upon her red lips. "Celestina! Santa Maria, there is three times as much of you to love now!" Then he set her back. "You have changed little, cara," he told her.

"I've changed a lot," she said with a hearty laugh. "For every bit of flesh I have put on my bones I have put as much in my purse, Patrizio! I have six children, as well."

"And how many husbands have you buried, cara?" he teased her.

"Husbands?" She burst into laughter. "Who has time for husbands, Patrizio?"

Now her gaze swept across the room and lit on Rosamund. "This fair little girl is your latest mistress? We will have to feed her, for she does not look as if she eats. Does she speak some language with which I can communicate with her?" They had been speaking in Italian.

"French, Celestina, but speak slowly, cara. And do not attempt to cheat her. She is the owner of a large estate, which she manages herself, and quite successfully."

"Scotch?" Celestina inquired.

"English," the earl replied. "And your father has explained to you that I am here privately to visit my old friend, the duke. You will not gossip, cara, eh?"

"There is an English ambassador here now," Celestina said, gauging his reaction.

"I know," the earl replied, "but Rosamund would not be anyone of importance that he should know about. She is not connected with the royal court."

Celestina nodded. "Madame," she said, walking across the room to Rosamund, "I have brought a gown that will serve you until I can make you a wardrobe." She was now speaking French.

"Thank you," Rosamund replied. "May I see it?"

"Maria! Quickly!" She called to the young girl accompanying her.

The gown was brought, unwrapped from

its covering, and displayed. It was pale green watered silk with a very low neckline and full puffed sleeves trimmed lavishly in ecru-colored lace. The seamstress and her helper spread the gown over a chair.

"The color is certainly right," Celestina said, "considering I did not know what madame looked like."

"It is plain," the earl said.

"It is lovely, and Celestina could not waste time or materials decorating a gown without a buyer, Patrick," Rosamund replied. She smiled at Celestina. "May I try it on?"

The seamstress nodded, and then she smiled at Rosamund. "He says you are a clever woman with a taste for trade, madame. You were right about the gown."

"My cotters weave wool from the sheep I raise," Rosamund said. "My wools are noted for their quality."

"You do not send your raw wool to the low countries to be woven?" Celestina was surprised.

"Why should I pay good coin to have done in a foreign clime what my own people can do? Besides, it keeps them occupied in the winter months when the fields cannot be cultivated. And, too, I am able to maintain the highest caliber in my product," Rosamund said in practical tones. "Can you put some decoration upon the bodice? Just a little gold thread embroidery perhaps?"

"Of course, madame. The gown but waited for an owner," Celestina said. "I can have it by tomorrow. Try it on now, and we will see what other alterations need to be done to it. And I have brought a variety of materials for madame's inspection as well."

"I will choose the materials for both the earl and myself," Rosamund said. Then she let Celestina and her helper aid her in getting into the gown and bodice.

Celestina spoke in rapid Italian to her companion, who from the look of her was the seamstress' daughter. "The waist will need to come in, Maria. And she is larger in the bosom than I would have anticipated, given her slender stature. The length seems fine. The sleeves will need alteration. This lady is delicately made."

"But she is strong," the earl murmured, and Celestina gave him a broad grin.

"Aye, Patrizio," Celestina said. "Your heart is engaged, my old friend, and it does me good to see you happy again. When you left us, your poor heart was broken. This lady has obviously mended it."

"She has," he admitted.

"What are you speaking about, Patrick?" Rosamund asked. "I do not understand the tongue in which you babble."

"Celestina is more comfortable in the Italian tongue, lovey. She says you have mended my broken heart, and I agree," he told her.

"You flatter me, especially under the circumstances," she told him.

"I should rather have a year with you, Rosamund," he told her, "than a lifetime with any other woman on the face of this earth. Now, sweetheart, let us decide upon the materials we are going to want."

The pale green gown had been pinned where it needed alteration, and so Rosamund removed it carefully.

Celestina snapped her fingers at Maria, and the girl brought forth a silk garment in the most incredible shade of blue that Rosamund had ever seen. "Wear this instead of that pretty chemise," she said, proffering it.

"What is it?" Rosamund asked.

"The people across the sea here, where they are ruled by the Turkish sultan, wear them. They call them caftans. They even go out into the streets there in them, I am told. I thought it might make a better garment for you indoors than your chemise. Do you like the color? It is the color of the Persian turquoise."

"It's lovely," Rosamund said. "Thank you, Celestina! I shall very much enjoy wearing this . . . caftan."

"And now," the seamstress said, "let us look at the materials I have brought for you and Patrizio, madame. Maria! The samples. *Vite! Vite!*"

The fabrics were brought, and they were indeed a rich assortment in wonderful colors. Silks and brocades and lightweight velvets along with delicate cottons and linens.

"How Tom would love all of this," Rosamund said to her lover. "He has such exquisite taste. I can but hope I have learned from him." She fingered a brocade in a rich shade of green. "It would suit me," she noted.

Celestina nodded. "And this sea-blue silk and the russet velvet that matches your lovely hair. Perhaps this cream and gold brocade?"

"It's beautiful," Rosamund agreed, and the seamstress set it aside. "Oh, what a wonderful shade of lavender!"

Patrick watched indulgently as she chose. And then she turned to him and began to seek his advice on the colors he would wear. "I am a gentleman, and so will be less flamboyant," he told her.

The two women gave each other a look and ignored him after that, picking and choosing what they thought was right for the earl's garments. When they had finished, Celestina gave orders to her helper to pack everything up again.

"It but remains for me to measure Patrizio," she said with a wicked smile. "Come, my lord, and let me see how you have grown over the years. You do not look greatly changed, but one can never tell." She took out her tape and began, muttering to herself beneath her breath, making little scratches with her charcoal stick on the tiny piece of parchment she had brought with her. When she had finished, she arose and tucked the notations she had made into the pocket of her skirts. "You are as fine a figure of a man as you ever were," she chuckled. "I shall be back for a fitting tomorrow, and I shall bring the pale green gown with me when I come, madame. Its bodice will be nicely, but simply, embroidered," Celestina promised. Then she turned and was quickly gone from the apartment.

"She moves swiftly for a lady of such girth," Rosamund noted.

He chuckled. "So you are no longer jealous?" he teased her.

"I did not say that, my lord, for her hands were all over you, especially when she measured the length of your legs. I thought she came a bit too close to your manhood, and I thought that you seemed to enjoy it," Rosamund said with a small smile.

"Celestina always had the most clever hands," he remarked, and then, pulling her into his arms, he kissed her soundly. "But you, my darling, seem to be clever all over, and I adore you for it."

"Is there anything that we need to do now, my lord?" Rosamund asked him.

"See that Dermid and Annie have supper on the sideboard when we want it and then disappear so we may be wanton together without fear of being disturbed?"

"Are you suggesting, my lord, that we go back to bed?" she asked him innocently.

"Aye, lass, I am," he replied, a slow smile lighting his eyes. "We have several weeks of loving to make up for, Rosamund, and I am ready to begin."

She smiled back at him. "Then I shall not need this caftan for a while," she said. "Shall I, my lord?"

"Nay, sweetheart. You will not need it for some time to come," he agreed, and taking her hand in his, he led her back into her bedchamber.

Chapter 6

Sebastian, Duke of San Lorenzo, was a man now closer to sixty than he was to fifty. He was still what would be considered a fine figure of a man, if perhaps a bit portly. His once black hair was now steely gray, but his black eyes were as sharp as they had ever been. He pinned his gaze upon the man he had never again thought to see. They had not parted amicably. How could they have? The Earl of Glenkirk's daughter was to have married his heir, Rudolpho. But then the girl was stolen by slavers. Even if they had gotten her back, and the Blessed Mother knew he had attempted to retrieve Janet Leslie, there could no longer have been a question of her marriage to his son. She would certainly have been despoiled. His negotiations with Toulouse for one of their princesses had been, he thought, secret. But Patrick had known immediately, even before it was confirmed his daughter was lost forever, that her match with Rudolpho di San Lorenzo was no longer a possibility and that the formal betrothal celebrated just a brief few weeks before was annulled and San Lorenzo's duke was seeking another bride for his son. The duke and the Scots ambassador's previously cordial relationship had soured badly. They had parted formally, neither expecting to ever see the other again.

"While I am certainly astounded to see you, Patrick," the duke said, "I welcome you back to San Lorenzo. I can see the years have not been unkind to you."

"I thank you, my lord duke," the earl replied.

"Patrick, my old friend," the duke said jovially. "Surely we may still be friends? Has time not softened the memories?"

"Perhaps yours, Sebastian, but not mine," Patrick responded, but his tone was mild. "Still, here I am in San Lorenzo again."

"And returned with a beautiful lady, I am informed," the duke chuckled. "You were ever a man for the fairer sex, my friend. But why are you here?"

"The lady and I wished to escape the harsh northern winter and the curiosity of King James' court," the earl said.

"Nay, I do not believe that. I have a letter from your king asking me to extend to you every courtesy," the duke answered. "If you were just an ordinary man with his lover, I might accept your explanation, but you are not, Patrick Leslie," the duke said.

"The less you know of the purpose of my

visit, Sebastian, the better for you and for San Lorenzo," the earl answered him. "I am here to meet with some people, but it is better that our concourse remain most private."

"So your king has suggested, but he has also said that if I am not content with that explanation you will give me a better one."

Patrick sighed. He did not trust Sebastian di San Lorenzo. Not after what had happened. Still, he had no choice in the matter. To gain the duke's cooperation and goodwill he must tell him the truth. "You know of the Holy League?" he asked.

The duke nodded. "Papal politics in God's name once more," he said dryly.

The Earl of Glenkirk found himself smiling. He might not trust the Duke of San Lorenzo, but Sebastian had never been a stupid man. "Aye, but it has put my king in a very difficult position."

"Why? James Stewart has always been a favorite of this pope. I believe that Julius even presented him with the Golden Rose for his devotion and piety to Holy Mother Church," the duke countered.

"All that is true," Patrick agreed. "But Scotland is married to England's sister. This match was conceived by King Henry the seventh in order to foster peace between Scotland and England. It has done just that, with only minor border skirmishes over the years. Queen Margaret is devoted to her husband and loyal to Scotland. Now, however, her brother sits on England's throne. He is young, ambitious, envious, and filled with a great sense of his own importance and destiny.

"King James is a man of peace. He has brought much prosperity to Scotland. Prosperity that comes through an absence of war or strife. It has made him a distinguished figure among the other rulers of Europe. And Henry Tudor is very jealous of him. He seeks to destroy what he perceives as Scotland's influence, for England, he believes, is more important. It is not meet in his eyes that Scotland take precedence over him. And he is ruthlessly clever, Sebastian. Make no mistake about it. He will have his way in this. The first step in his plan was to encourage the pope, who has previously had good relations with King Louis, to demand that the French give up their possessions north of the Italian states. You will recall that previously the pope was allied with the French in a campaign against the Venetians in the north of Italy."

"The same Venetians who are now members of the Holy League," the duke murmured. "Ah, the vagaries of mankind."

"And, of course, pious Spain is a part of the league, along with Maximilian and his

Holy Roman Empire," the earl said.

"But conspicuously absent is Scotland," the duke noted.

"Aye. Scotland has an alliance with France. It is an auld alliance going back many years. My king is a man of honor, and he can find no reason to break that alliance. So he will not. Henry Tudor is not a man of honor. He has engineered this situation in order to harm my king's good relations with Pope Julius and the Holy See."

"Would your king send troops to France's aid?" the duke asked Patrick.

"Only if absolutely forced into it, if there were no way in which he could eschew it. You know how well a ruler may avoid a situation like this when acting in the best interests of his country, Sebastian."

"So in actuality Scotland would remain neutral," the duke noted.

"Aye, which under any other circumstance would suit the pope," the earl said.

"Except that the English king is pressing the point and making an issue of it. Us or them. Aye, Patrick. This Henry Tudor is indeed ruthless and clever. Now, tell me why you have come."

"King James hopes that perhaps he might weaken the alliance and in doing so take the attention away from what our nation will or won't do. If the pope must struggle to maintain the allies that he already has, he is unlikely to be overly concerned with Scotland's position as long as it is not overtly hostile towards his league. I am here to meet with two gentlemen. One from Venice and the other from Germany. My king considers them the weaker links. Spain will not be moved because England's queen is Ferdinand's daughter."

"It is a bold idea, but you are not likely to succeed," the duke said.

"King James knows that. But he also knows he will not break the auld alliance, and if he does not, England will use it as an excuse to invade Scotland. This means we must invade them first, a faux invasion, mind you, for we have no interest in conquering England. But we must direct Henry Tudor's attention away from this mischief he is causing between the pope and James Stewart," Patrick replied.

The Duke of San Lorenzo nodded thoughtfully. Then he asked, "Why have they sent you, Patrick?"

"For two reasons. Once I was Scotland's ambassador to San Lorenzo. Its first ambassador. And second, since I returned from here eighteen years ago, I have not left my Highland home at Glenkirk. I am barely known by the court, and it is unlikely that I would be considered a candidate for such a mission as this one. If indeed anyone knew of why I have been sent here. And no one does."

"Not even the lovely lady who accompanies you, my friend?" the duke pried.

"Not even Rosamund," the earl lied facilely. "She is English, and the queen's friend. I didn't want her put between her love for me and her loyalty to Margaret Tudor and England. She departed the court under the excuse of an ill child. It is assumed I have gone with her, for our passion was hardly secret."

"Rosamund," the duke said. "It is a charming name. When am I to meet her?"

"Because we traveled secretly, we came quickly with but one servant apiece, a-horse. We carried only the bare essentials. A wardrobe is now being fashioned for us both, Sebastian. I come before you today in altered secondhand garments. They are neat and serviceable, but hardly what I would normally wear, remembering your most elegant court."

"I should be less splendid in my later years but that my daughter-in-law insists that we keep up appearances," the duke remarked.

"How is Rudolpho?" the earl asked.

"Fat. Content. And the father of ten daughters and two sons. The eldest of my grandsons, Henrico, the firstborn actually, is my heir after his father. The second son, who is only a little lad of five, will go to the church, of course, unless something happens to his brother. It is good they are so far apart in age. Roberto is the youngest. But ten granddaughters! Marone! I do not know if I can find husbands for them all. Some will have to go into the nunnery. And you, Patrick? Has your son wed and given you grandchildren?"

"Aye. Two lads and a lassie," the earl said. "He did not choose a warm wife."

The duke nodded. "Neither did I," he remarked. "But my wife was young and fair, and I was filled with lust for her." He chuckled. "It was the same with your son, I assume."

Patrick nodded. "Aye," was all he said.

"Do you want it known you are in San Lorenzo?" the duke asked his companion. "We have an English ambassador now."

"I know. Richard Howard, I believe," the earl answered.

"Your ambassador told you, of course," the duke said.

"Rosamund saw him in the street as we entered San Lorenzo and recognized him, although she could not remember his name," Patrick replied.

"Your lady is a member of the English court?" The duke was interested now.

"Rosamund spent part of her youth as a ward to King Henry the seventh. That is how she became friends with our queen.

They were girls together. But since she was wed, in the same year in which our queen married our king, she has remained home on her estates, which are in the north of England."

"And her husband?" The duke was even more curious.

"She is a widow," the Earl of Glenkirk replied.

"Ahhh," the duke sighed. "A woman of experience as well as beauty. You are indeed a fortunate man, Patrick."

"Our demeanor here will be discreet, Sebastian, as is fitting for a man who has run away with his lover. Let the English ambassador learn of our presence when he learns of it and report it to his master if he thinks it would be of interest to King Henry, but I doubt he will. As I have told you, I am not known to the English or the Scots courts. I am unimportant, as is Rosamund. Hence my value to King James."

"You are remembered here, Patrick," the duke noted.

"If the English ambassador should learn of my former position for Scotland, I will explain it by saying we are here because I thought this a romantic place to bring my lover. Does Lord Howard prefer the English winters? And Scots winters are far worse." He grinned. It suddenly had occurred to Patrick that he was enjoying this adventure, and he had certainly not thought he would.

The duke laughed, seeing his companion's grin. "I believe you like this game that you find yourself playing, Patrick," he chuckled.

The Earl of Glenkirk nodded. "I think I do, Sebastian," he agreed. "It has been a long time since I have enjoyed myself. I am always filled with a sense of my duty, but now I feel like a lad released from his studies. I remember I like the feel of the winter sun on my back and the fragrance of mimosas in February. I have not smelled mimosas since the day I departed San Lorenzo last."

"Were you always this romantic, Patrick, or is it just that you are in love?" the duke teased him.

"I could not tell you, Sebastian," the earl replied. "But, aye, I am in love."

"I look forward to meeting her." Sebastian di San Lorenzo smiled toothily. "Will you marry her?"

"If she will have me," Patrick said, feeling that the wily duke need not be privy to the truth of his relationship with Rosamund. Perhaps the white lie he told would protect her from an attempted seduction. But he would warn her nonetheless of the duke's easily aroused nature.

"Who is doing your wardrobes? Celestina, I assume," the duke queried.

"Aye."

"I well remember how you stole her from me," the duke said. "Her first daughter is mine, you know. We gave her to the church to expiate our sin," he said with a grin.

"Celestina had a generous nature," Patrick remembered with a smile.

"She still does, but alas I am much too old to please her now. But, still, we remain friends," the duke said. "I will see her girls work quickly so you may attend a small party I am giving in three days. It is to welcome the artist Paolo Loredano, who is coming from Venice. He has decided to spend the winter painting in San Lorenzo. It is a great honor to have him here. I hope to commission him to do our portraits. He is a member of the doge's family, and has studied not only with Gentile Bellini, but his brother, Giovanni, as well. It will be a festive evening, Patrick."

"Will the English ambassador be at your gathering?" the earl wondered aloud.

"Of course," the duke said. "But you must come. If you do not, it will seem odd. Little is secret in San Lorenzo, as you well know. Lord Howard has probably already been informed of your presence. He will be curious, of course. You can allay his fears by coming with the Lady Rosamund and being lovers for all to see."

"You have not lost your knack for intrigue, Sebastian, but you will keep the real purpose of my visit secret, of course," the Earl of Glenkirk said quietly. "Sandwiched as you are between France and the Italian states, you would not want to be considered disloyal by either side, I know."

The duke chuckled. "And eighteen years in your Highland eyrie has not lessened your acute abilities to conspire successfully, Patrick. As far as I am concerned, your visit is just what it appears to be. An older gentleman running away with his young lover."

The earl winced. "Am I so old, then, Sebastian?" he asked.

"A bit younger than I am, I will admit," the duke said. "You cannot be so old, however, for you have attracted a young lover. Or is she after your wealth?"

"She has wealth of her own," the earl said. "Nay. We have, for whatever reason, fallen in love with each other, Sebastian."

"Does your son know? What was his name? Adam!" the duke remarked.

"He knows nothing but that I am on a mission, sub rosa, in the king's service," the earl answered. "But I do not believe he would be distressed by my love for Rosamund. His wife, however, is a different matter. But he thought he loved her and the family was acceptable, so I had no cause for complaint," the earl concluded with a small grin.

"How many marriages are made for love, my friend?" the duke said sanguinely. "Marriages are made for wealth and land and power. If there is more, one is fortunate. My late wife, God assoil her good soul," the duke remarked, crossing himself piously, "was not a woman to inspire passion. She understood it and accepted her lot. She was loyal and devoted. She did her duty. I could ask no more of her, and I gave her my respect and loyalty in return. I found love in other places, although I wonder if there was not more lust than love."

"It is usually more lust," the earl said quietly. "But not this time. I am old enough, and hopefully wise enough, to know the difference."

"Then I envy you, Patrick Leslie," the Duke of San Lorenzo said. "Now, let us have some of our good wine and toast the memories we have made and the memories we will make." He clapped his hands, and his servitors were immediately by his side.

Afterwards, the Earl of Glenkirk returned to the ambassador's residence, walking in a leisurely fashion through the city. He stopped in the main market square to purchase a large and colorful bouquet of mimosas from a flower vendor. Walking on, he entered a narrow street, going into a jeweler's shop, where he bought a delicately wrought filigreed golden collar dotted with pale green peridots. It would adorn the green silk dress very nicely. It was the first piece of jewelry he had ever obtained for Rosamund. He hoped that she would like it. The late afternoon was warm, and he was damp about his collar when he finally reached the top of the hill where the Scots embassy was located.

Lord MacDuff greeted him as he entered the building. "You have been to the palace? Come and tell me what has transpired between you and the wily fox, yon duke."

The earl signaled to a servant. "Take these to Lady Rosamund," he said, handing the woman the bouquet of mimosas. "Tell her I will see her shortly."

Smiling, the servingwoman curtsied, then took the floral tribute and hurried up the stairs.

Patrick joined his host. "He hasn't changed," he began, accepting a small silver goblet of wine as he sat down.

"What did you tell him?" Lord MacDuff wanted to know.

"What he needed to know. We have put him in a delicate position, situated as San

Lorenzo is between France and Italy," the earl chuckled. "If the truth should ever come out, Sebastian di San Lorenzo will profess ignorance, outrage, whatever the situation calls for, my lord. He will protect San Lorenzo at all costs, which he should and which is his right. And if Lord Howard is curious as to my presence, you will adhere to the story that I am here with my lover. You will profess ignorance of all else."

"Do you believe we can weaken the alliance, Patrick?" the ambassador asked.

"Nay, and neither does the king, but he felt that we must make an attempt at it. Even if Venice and the Holy Roman Empire insist on adhering to their agreement with the Holy League, they will have certain doubts, which I shall plant in the minds of those who come to treat with me. They will be less enthusiastic and more cautious than they have been. That is the best that we shall do, Ian. But we shall do it! Henry Tudor has not won yet."

"Do you know who it is you will meet with yet?" Lord MacDuff asked.

"Nay. But I have a suspicion that the artist from Venice who is arriving in another day or two, and who the duke is feting, may be one of the gentlemen I am to deal with. He is a member of the Loredano family, and he has made a name for himself as a former student of both the Bellini brothers. No one would suspect a Venetian artist of political intrigue," the earl chuckled. "But I do not know. I shall have to wait and see. Sebastian insisted that Rosamund and I attend this fete. He is curious, of course, to meet her, and still, I suspect, fancies himself a great lover."

"His adventures have not been quite so public in recent years," Lord MacDuff said with a smile. "As he has grown more portly and less fleet of foot, he is not so apt to want to find himself facing an angry husband or father."

"His son, I imagine, has taken over for him," the earl said dryly.

"Nay! Lord Rudolpho keeps a mistress, but he is discreet," the ambassador noted.

"I thought he would be like his father," Patrick said. "I remember saying so to my daughter once. He has fathered enough children."

"Aye, and all those lasses, to boot," Lord MacDuff chortled.

The earl stood up, draining his goblet. "I want to thank you for your hospitality, Ian MacDuff. Rosamund has never been out of England until now, except for her brief visit to our court. She has been made to feel most welcome."

"She is a fair lass, Patrick," Lord MacDuff said, "and has beautiful manners,

according to Pietro, who, as you will remember, values such things. The servants
are happy to have a woman in the house
being that I am a crusty old bachelor."

"I would like to remain until spring," the
earl said.

"You are more than welcome," came the
smiling reply. "I think if I had such a
lovely woman to love, I would want to remain here until spring, too."

Patrick left the ambassador and hurried
upstairs to his apartments, where he found
Rosamund being fitted for her gowns. He
sat down to watch, giving Celestina a
friendly nod.

"I hear," the seamstress said, "that you
are going to the fete for the Venetian,
Patrizio. It will be a grand event, for the
duke will be anxious to impress the artist
Loredano. The festivals and fetes they have
in Venice are said to be spectacular. Our
duke will have to go to some effort to af-
fect any admiration from his visitor." And
she chuckled.

He laughed. "How the hell do you know
we are going to the duke's fete? I have only
just now come from the palace."

She rolled her black eyes at him, a gesture he realized he well remembered.
"Patrizio, this is San Lorenzo. Here, everyone knows everyone's business. The
English ambassador is curious to meet you,

by the way. He wonders why a former Scots ambassador to the duchy has suddenly shown up here. Now."

"The English are always suspicious of the Scots," the earl said casually. "Is that not so, my love?" He addressed Rosamund.

"Always," Rosamund agreed pleasantly. "The Scots, you see, cannot be trusted, Celestina. Should the neckline be that low?"

"It is the fashion here, madame," Celestina answered her.

"It is higher at the Scots court," Rosamund noted.

"It is colder at the Scots court," the seamstress said pithily. "Here in the south we like the breeze to caress our skin on a warm winter's night. Is that not so, my lord?"

"I think the neckline is most correct," Patrick agreed with her.

"Will you think it so correct when this duke ogles my breasts?" Rosamund asked innocently.

"He is permitted to ogle, my darling," the earl told her. "But nothing more."

The two women laughed.

"I am doing the bodice of the pale green gown more elaborately, madame," Celestina said. "You will wear it to the duke's fete along with the gift Patrizio has purchased for you on his way from the palace."

"You bought me a gift?" Rosamund squealed. "I mean, besides the flowers? — which are lovely, my lord. What are they called? And where is my gift?"

"The blooms are mimosas, and as for your gift, I am not certain I shall give it to you now. You are much too greedy," he teased her.

"That is your decision, of course, my lord, but I should dislike seeing a lovely piece of jewelry go to waste," Rosamund murmured.

"How can you be certain it is jewelry?" he asked her, smiling.

"Isn't it?" she asked mischievously. "Or perhaps you have bought me a villa here and could not carry it with you."

Celestina chortled. "You have finally met your match, Patrizio, and how glad I am to be here to see it. There! I am done. Maria! Take madame's gown, and be careful, girl. The fabric is delicate." She gathered up her tools and put them in her basket. "In just a few more days' time, madame, you will have a new and beautiful wardrobe to get you through the winter here." Then, with a curtsy, she departed the earl's apartments.

"We are remaining the entire winter months?" Rosamund asked Patrick.

He nodded. "It will be easier traveling in late spring or early summer, my love."

"I had not thought to be away so long," she replied.

The Earl of Glenkirk put an arm about her. "Your uncle Edmund and your cousin Tom are husbanding Friarsgate for you, Rosamund."

" 'Tis my lasses I worry more about, Patrick," she told him.

"And do you not trust Maybel to watch over them?" he asked.

"Aye, but I do not like it that my daughters are so long without their mother," she answered him. "Still, Maybel raised me. At least my girls are not being forced into marriages by Uncle Henry, as I was."

"And have you not said that you never think of yourself, only your duty. I understand because I am the same way; but now, for just this little space of time, you and I are together, away from those responsibilities. I mean for us to enjoy ourselves."

"But how will you tell the king what he needs to know?" she wondered.

"When the die has been cast, Lord MacDuff will see a message is sent to the king under his diplomatic seal. And you and I will remain here to bask in the sunshine, make love, and drink the wine of San Lorenzo."

Rosamund sighed. "It sounds wonderful," she said softly, turning in his arms to face him, raising her head up for a kiss, which he placed upon her ripe lips. "Now," she said, "where is my present?"

Patrick burst out laughing and reached into his doublet to draw out the flat white leather case. "Here, you vixen," he said, handing it to her.

Rosamund struggled to maintain restraint. She looked at it, the fingers of one hand running over the soft leather. Finally she snapped the small catch and raised the lid. Her amber eyes grew round. "Oh, Patrick, it is beautiful!" she said, lifting the filigreed gold collar from its velvet nest, setting the box aside. "What are these tiny green gemstones? I have never seen any like them."

"They are peridots," he told her. "Their color matches the gown Celestina first showed us. There is a larger stone that can be mounted on a ribbon to be worn in the middle of your forehead. I should like to purchase it, but I wanted to be certain first that you like this."

"Patrick, you are too good to me," she told him.

"Has any other man ever given you jewelry?" he asked her.

She nodded. "Aye," she said, and her lashes brushed her creamy cheek.

"Who?" he demanded, his tone jealous.

"My cousin Tom," Rosamund laughed, unable to taunt him. "Tom, as you know, is an unusual gentleman. He has a passion for beautiful things and possesses a great deal of lovely jewelry. When we were in London, he gifted me with many lovely pieces, but none as beautiful as this collar, my lord." Standing on tiptoes Rosamund kissed him. "Thank you, my darling!"

"Then I shall get the ribbon jewel?" he asked her.

"Would I be too greedy if I said yes?" she wondered aloud.

"No," he told her, smiling down into her eyes. "It will suit you, and every minute of the duke's fete I shall be jealous of all the men admiring you."

"Oh, Patrick, you never have to be jealous over me," Rosamund told him. "I love you as I have never loved any man! I knew nothing of love until that night our eyes met across the Great Hall at Stirling."

"Did Logan Hepburn never attract your notice?" he pressed her.

"Aye, he did attract my notice. He is young and handsome and a very beast of a man. But I never loved him," Rosamund said.

"I don't know how it is possible you love me and not him," the Earl of Glenkirk said quietly. "Why have we met now, in the autumn of my years? And why are we both so duty bound to our families and lands? Sometimes I think I should like to run away from it all. But, of course, I won't, and you won't."

"Nay, we shall both do our duty in the end, Patrick," she replied. "But for now we have each other, and we have San Lorenzo. Do not speak on our parting again. It will come in its time, and we will know it. But not yet."

He drew her back into his embrace, his arms tightening about her. He said nothing further, but his lips touched the top of her auburn head. How could they know each other so well on such brief acquaintance? He didn't understand, but he also didn't care. She was here, with him, and he loved her. It was all he needed to know for now. He smoothed her silken hair with his big hand, and she sighed contentedly.

The afternoon of the duke's fete Celestina and Maria arrived with Rosamund's gown.

"It cannot be the same garment!" Rosamund cried as she looked at the beautiful gown spread across the bed. There was an underskirt embroidered with gold thread in a design of leaping fish, shells, and sea horses. The bodice was sewn all over with pearls. The full sleeves were slashed to reveal delicate natural-colored lace sleeves beneath. The slashings were tied with gold cord. The pale green watered silk overskirt had been left plain, for in combination with the rest of the gown it needed no further artifice. "It is beautiful!" Rosamund said, looking to Celestina. "I cannot thank you enough!"

Celestina nodded. "You will have all the gentlemen clustering about you tonight, madame. It is a beautiful gown, and Patrizio will pay dearly for it," she laughed with good humor. "I brought you shoes. Your Annie loaned me one of your boots to match for size. I hope they will not be too big." She then produced from her voluminous apron pocket a pair of squared-toed slippers covered with the same pale green watered silk as the gown and held them out for Rosamund to take.

Rosamund shook her head. "They are lovely, Celestina. And thanks to you, I will be suitably dressed for the fete."

"I shall go and have something to eat with my father," Celestina said. "Then, when you are ready to depart, I shall make certain that everything is in order."

"Does she think I don't know how to prepare you?" Annie said, just a little irritated by the seamstress' attitude.

"She is an artist in her own right, Annie, and you will admit that this gown is one of the most beautiful gowns I have ever possessed," Rosamund said.

Annie nodded her head in agreement. "Even Sir Thomas would approve of it, though the neckline still looks too low to me."

"Have a bath prepared," Rosamund instructed the servingwoman. "Wouldn't it be wonderful if we could fill my tub as easily as we empty it?"

Again Annie nodded. It was necessary to fill the brassbound oak tub with bucket after bucket of water, but to empty it was a far simpler operation. At the bottom of the tub was a small flexible tube that fit into the side and was unrolled over the terrace-edge. At the end of its length was a cork, which when removed allowed the tub to drain down onto the rocks below.

While the tub was being filled, Rosamund ate. She was given a dish of fluffy eggs and half of a sweet melon. Until she arrived in San Lorenzo she had never tasted melon. Now she insisted on having it every day. When the tub was filled and Annie had scented it with Rosamund's favorite white heather fragrance, she arose from her table, carrying her goblet of sweet wine. Annie took the caftan from her mistress, and naked, Rosamund walked out onto the terrace, handing the goblet to her servant and climbing into her tub. Annie handed the goblet back when Rosamund was settled, then pinned her mistress' hair up.

"Leave me for now, Annie. I will wash eventually, but for now I just want to enjoy sitting here in the sunshine and watching the blue sea."

"You'll want to siesta afterwards, my lady," Annie said. "I'll move your new gown from the bed and set it safely aside." She turned and went back into the apartment.

Rosamund sipped her wine and stared down into the harbor of Arcobaleno. There was a most magnificent ship sailing majestically into the port. It had royal-purple-and-gold striped sails, and on its bow was a full-bosomed golden mermaid with scarlet tresses. Rosamund smiled. Obviously, some very important person was aboard such a gorgeous vessel.

"It's bringing the artist, Paolo Loredano," Patrick said as he joined her on the terrace.

"Perhaps the ship belongs to the doge himself," Rosamund remarked.

"Or perhaps it belongs to Maestro Loredano himself," the earl suggested. "He is famed for his portraits, as was his first master, Gentile Bellini. The duke is anxious to have him do portraits of himself and his family. Loredano, however, is very particular about whom he paints. He will not take just any commission offered, and has offended more than a few."

"What is the duke like?" Rosamund asked.

"Older even than I am," the earl teased her. "Of medium height, a bit corpulent from too-good living. His hair was once dark, but now it is gray. He will appear the good host and will go out of his way to charm you, but never forget that he is clever, he is ruthless, and he is a seducer."

"Should I fear him, then?" she wondered.

"Nay," he said. "You have treated with kings, Rosamund. Just use your own charm, and remember he is but a duke," Patrick said.

"I will remember," she told him. "Do you want to share my tub, my lord?"

He smiled a slow smile. "I have been waiting for you to ask, my darling," he said.

After stripping his clothing off where he stood, Patrick climbed into the great tub with her. She offered him a sip of her wine, which he accepted. Then, setting the goblet aside on the tub's edge, she took up the flannel cloth, rubbed her soap over it, and began to bathe him herself.

"They say in earlier days, the lady of the castle and her serving girls always washed important guests," Rosamund told him. "They do not say if she got into the tub with her guests, however." She gently washed his face, saying as she did, "You must have Dermid shave you again before tonight. I can already see the shadow on your jaw, my lord." She kissed his mouth quickly.

He yanked her hard against him, and she felt his manhood pressing with some urgency against her thigh. His eyes blazed down into hers. His mouth fused itself against hers, his tongue sliding into her mouth to play with hers. Her full breasts were flattened against his broad chest. He held her face between his two hands while he continued to kiss her, his passions rising even as he felt her passions rise. "I do not believe," he said in a hard voice, "that I have ever fucked you in our tub, Rosamund, but I am about to do it now," he growled. His hands plunged beneath the warm water, and pressing her back against the side of the tub, he lifted her up, impaling her on his hardness. "Ahh, my love," he groaned. She was tight and hot.

Rosamund's eyes closed with her pleasure as she slid her arms about his neck. He filled her with his passion, and her head fell onto his shoulder as he loved her until their combined desire burst, leaving them both weak but sated. "I adore you, Patrick Leslie," she said softly in his ear. "I shall never love another as I love you."

His tongue licked at her face, her throat, her chest and shoulder as he stood, his manhood still hard and deep within her. "You consume me," he groaned softly. "I cannot get enough of your sweetness, Rosamund."

She entwined her legs about him, enabling him to press farther, and he groaned again. "I want to soar," she whispered in his ear, and she licked at the curled flesh.

Their bodies tightly locked together, he began to thrust and withdraw until they were both dizzy with the rapture their enthusiasm in each other gave them. The intensity of their mutual desire was intoxicating, and as their carnality overcame them, they both cried out, finally satisfied, if only briefly. Her arms still about his neck, her legs fell away from his firm body.

"If I let go of you," she said, "I shall drown here, for my limbs are as weak as a newborn's, Patrick."

He laughed softly. "You are an outrageous woman, Rosamund. I have never known anyone like you, nor do I expect I ever will."

"We have to get out of this water," she told him, but she still clung to him.

"Did you enjoy our little water sport?" he teased her.

"Aye," she murmured, and then, to his delight, she blushed. "I never considered making the beast with two backs in water, Patrick."

"But you liked it?" His gaze caressed her face.

"I did! It was most stimulating. I do not believe I have ever been made love to other than in a bed," she admitted.

"One day I shall take you in a stable on a pile of sweet-smelling hay," he promised her, and he laughed. "Or perhaps I shall catch you in a linen cupboard, my love."

"I think I am feeling stronger now," Rosamund answered him. It was said that the older men grew the less well they performed in bed. But, Rosamund thought, she had had a husband considered an older man and a young lover in King Henry, but neither of these men had made love to her with such unflagging enthusiasm or suggested such a variety of passion as did Patrick Leslie, the Earl of Glenkirk. She let go of him now and climbed from the tub. The water sluiced down her lush form as she reached for the drying cloth.

He watched her appreciatively until, finally satisfied, she invited him from their bath, and standing naked in the sunshine, began to dry him off.

"Be careful, madame, lest you arouse my baser nature again," he warned her.

"Oh, no!" she scolded him, laughing. "I do not intend to go to the duke's fete tonight, meeting the man for the first time, with the scent of lust hanging about me, Patrick. You will behave yourself, for you shall not have me again until after the fete. Your head must be clear, my lord, for it is likely you will meet one or both of your contacts tonight."

"And it does not disturb you that Scotland will attempt to undo Henry Tudor's ambitions?" he asked her, as he had on several occasions.

"I have told you, Patrick, that I do not consider trying to stop a war treasonous to England. Hal might, for anything interfering with his plans is anathema to him, but no reasonable man or woman would. Do what you must. If you Scots come over the border, it is my home that will be in danger first, not Henry Tudor's," Rosamund said.

He laughed. "Ever the practical lady of Friarsgate," he teased her. Then he looked about him. "Do you think we can be seen?" he asked.

"I doubt it," Rosamund said. "There is but one villa just above us to the east, but no one seems to be inhabiting it." She took his hand and led him back into their apartment. "Go to your own bed, and rest," she instructed.

"I should rather rest in your bed," he said with a small grin.

"Neither of us would get any rest if we shared my bed, my lord, and well you know it. Celestina brought you a beautiful set of clothing for tonight. Now, go make certain Dermid laid it out so it will not be creased."

"You are a hard woman," he grumbled.

"I will see you later, my lord," she told him firmly, but she smiled when she spoke.

He left her, and Rosamund put on a clean chemise and laid down. She could hardly believe the incredible turn her life had taken over the last few months. She had found true love. And she was hundreds of miles from Friarsgate, yet she was happy. She missed her daughters, but there was something both thrilling and wonderful about being loved by a man like Patrick Leslie. They would love each other forever, even if they would part eventually to return to their own lives. This was but a fantasy, a beautiful daydream. She wished it might be otherwise, but she knew it could not. Neither of them could eschew their responsibilities, and neither of them would give up what was theirs.

But they had today, and they would not think about tomorrow until it was done and past.

Annie came and brought her a light supper as the sun was setting. Rosamund was well rested, for she had actually slept for several hours. Her mind was clear, and while she intended being nothing more this evening than Lord Leslie's beautiful mistress, she would keep her ears open for whatever tidbits she might gather. Her French had improved considerably since their arrival a few days ago. She had just needed to use it again. She remembered how patient Owein had been as he had taught her French so she would not appear ignorant when she first came to court. It all seemed like a hundred years ago.

Annie helped her dress. Another chemise, one that would fit perfectly beneath the gown, was substituted for the one Rosamund had been wearing. Cream-colored silk stockings embraced her legs. The neckline of the gown was even lower than it had appeared when the bodice had been lying innocently on the chair. Rosamund's round breasts swelled dangerously over the lace edging of the gown's pearl-strewn top. Her shoulders and part of her upper arms were bare. The slashed sleeves were almost gauzy. Annie fitted her mistress with several silk petticoats and then brought the underskirt.

"Is there no shakefold?" Rosamund asked, looking for the stiffened hooplike garment usually worn beneath her gowns at home.

"Celestina says just a couple of petticoats, my lady. She says it permits the fabric to drape gracefully, showing the gown and its wearer to better advantage," Annie parroted. She tied the laces of the undergown tightly, then fitted the overgown atop it, fastening it neatly. Then the servant stepped back. "Oh, my lady, it is so beautiful, so elegant, and I think a bit naughty. But Celestina assures me that it is the fashion here."

Rosamund nodded. "She would not lie. She is long past her passion for the earl, and her father's position would be endangered if she did me a disservice." She twirled, seeing how the gown moved, and was pleased. "Let us finish my hair," she said.

"Celestina's daughter Martina has been sent to do it, my lady," Annie said. "I am to learn from her."

"Have her come in, then," Rosamund replied, sitting down at a little table.

Martina looked nothing at all like her mother. She was tall and lanky, but she did have Celestina's direct manner. "Ah, madame is ready," she began. She moved quickly behind Rosamund. "First," she said, "I must see what kind of hair madame has." She began brushing the thick auburn locks. "Ah, excellent!" The brush worked vigorously.

"You will wear no cap," she said. "I am told that you have a jeweled ribbon to be worn." She found the part in the center of Rosamund's head. "Now, here is a style I particularly like and that will suit madame. It is simple. It will not detract from her beauty. I fold the hair thusly, fastening it with pins. Girl! Hold up a mirror for your mistress to see. I call it a chignon." And as Rosamund viewed herself in the mirror, Martina attached a half-moon of delicate silk flowers in cream, gold, and pale green across the top of the chignon. Lastly, she fastened the pale green silk ribbon with the oval green peridot set in its center about Rosamund's forehead. Then she held up a second mirror behind her client that Rosamund might see the full effect.

Rosamund stared. "I do not believe I have ever seen such a beautiful hairstyle," she said honestly. "In England we keep our hair beneath caps and hoods mostly. Thank you, Martina. Please teach Annie how you do this."

"It is simple, madame, and your servant does not seem stupid," Martina answered.

"What did she say?" Annie asked.

"That she will be delighted to teach you how to do this style, Annie. Really, you must try to learn the language better," Rosamund scolded gently.

There was a knock on the door, and

Dermid stuck his head through. "His lordship wants to know if her ladyship is ready
to leave yet. The ambassador's carriage is
already waiting outside."

"Give me my shoes," Rosamund said;
then she slipped her feet into the slippers
that were placed before her and arose,
turning as she did to say, "I thank you
both." Then she hurried from the bedchamber out into the dayroom where the
Earl of Glenkirk awaited her. "Oh my!"
she said as she caught her first glimpse of
him.

His dark green velvet breeches were
striped in deep forest green and cloth of
gold. His fine silken hose were deep green
with a tied gold cord garter on one shapely
leg. His short coat was silk brocade, the
sleeves padded and puffed. It was trimmed
in dark brown marten fur. The doublet beneath, which was embroidered in gold
thread with a floral design, was also
slashed to show the cream-colored silk
shirt beneath. His matching hat had a soft
crown but a hard turned-up brim and a
white ostrich plume. His shoes were fine
brown leather. He had a large heavy gold
chain about his neck, and both his hands
were beringed. There was a bejeweled
dagger at his waist.

"May I return the compliment?" the earl
said, admiring Rosamund.

"You may," she replied.

"Then let us go, madame. Lord Mac-Duff awaits us below. I think it is time you met your host." The earl took Rosamund's arm and led her from the apartment and downstairs, where Ian MacDuff stood along with Celestina who nodded her approval at the couple, but said nothing.

The Scots ambassador's gray eyes widened as he saw them descend. He came immediately forward, taking Rosamund's hand up and kissing it. "Madame, I am pleased to have you as my guest. It is an honor to entertain the queen's good friend."

"Unfortunately, the queen does not know I am here," Rosamund admitted. "She would be most vexed with me, I fear."

"Then we shall keep your secret, Lady Rosamund," the ambassador said with a smile. "But the queen is generous of heart and would certainly want her friend happy," he finished with another smile. "Shall we go?" He led them outside where the open carriage awaited them.

Lord MacDuff obviously did not know Meg well, Rosamund thought, amused. Margaret Tudor wanted what she wanted when she wanted it. Still, the man was an ambassador, and obviously a good one.

Rosamund allowed a footman to help her

into the vehicle. She had never seen an open coach, for in England and Scotland such a thing would be considered ridiculous. Here, with the warm evening and the sun setting as they started off to the palace, it was quite perfect.

They moved down the hill upon which the ambassador's residence was located and along a narrow street into the cathedral square. The carriage crossed the square traveling into a broader avenue lined with large and elegant houses. It eventually gave way to a thoroughfare lined with tall trees. They began to ascend a hill, coming finally to the duke's palace at the mount's summit. They passed through great gates and traveled along a drive of perfectly raked white gravel. As their coach passed, servants came out from the shrubbery to re-rake the drive that it might be perfect for the next vehicle.

The palace itself was built of cream-colored marble. They stopped before its entry porch, which was lined with elegant marble pillars speckled with green. There was a large marble fountain before the palace with a bronze statue of a boy on a dolphin, which sprayed water into the pool. Lanterns were hung everywhere in the trees. Their carriage stopped, and they were helped from it by servants in the duke's blue and gold livery. The two gentlemen escorted Rosamund into the palace where a majordomo greeted them obsequiously.

"My lord ambassador, Lord Leslie, Lady Rosamund," he said, and he ushered them towards the exquisite hall where the duke was holding his fete.

Now, how, Rosamund wondered to herself, did this servant, whom she had never before in her life seen, know her name?

They were announced by a second majordomo, the first having left them at the entry to the hall to return to his place in the entry foyer.

"His excellency, the ambassador from his most noble and Catholic majesty, King James of Scotland, Lord Ian MacDuff. Lord Patrick Leslie, the Earl of Glenkirk. Lady Rosamund Bolton," the majordomo called out in ringing tones.

They moved down several marble steps into the lovely hall, so different from what she was used to, Rosamund noted. For one thing, there were no fireplaces, and one wall of the room opened to a terrace that she could see beyond the pale gold marble pillars. There was a ducal throne at one end of the hall, and they now moved towards it.

Sebastian, Duke of San Lorenzo, watched them come and struggled to maintain his surprise. When he had learned that his old friend Lord Leslie traveled with a lovely female companion, he had not anticipated she would be so . . . so . . . so young and so deliciously ripe. He would not have expected such a thing from a man from the north. Lord Leslie, while enjoying San Lorenzo during his tenure as ambassador, had always been most correct. A man his age did not travel with so exquisite and youthful a mistress unless he was very much in love. Sebastian di San Lorenzo had never considered that Patrick Leslie would be in love at any age.

He arose from the ducal throne, and stepping off the dais, offered both his hands in greeting to the Earl of Glenkirk. To any watching it would certainly appear as if they were just meeting. "Patrick!" His voice boomed for all to hear. "Welcome back to San Lorenzo!" He turned his head slightly and gave a sharp look to his heir, Rudolpho, who immediately stood up and came forward, bowing to the earl. "You will remember my son, of course."

"Of course," Patrick said. He would never as long as he lived forget Rudolpho di San Lorenzo. Had it not been for this man now before him, his daughter might not have been lost to him. He bowed curtly.

"And this is his wife, Henrietta Maria," the duke said, drawing his daughter-in-law forward.

"Madame," the earl said, bowing low over the outstretched hand. She might have once been pretty, he thought, but she was worn and wan with all of her childbearing.

"You are most welcome to San Lorenzo," Henrietta Maria said in a soft voice. Her warm brown eyes were sympathetic.

So she knew, the earl thought, and then he smiled at her. "I thank you, madame," he said quietly.

"MacDuff," the duke greeted the ambassador.

"My lord duke," was the equally short reply.

The duke's gaze now fastened itself on Rosamund. "And who is this?" he almost purred, his black eyes plunging into the valley between her breasts.

"May I present the lady of Friarsgate, Rosamund Bolton," the ambassador said, and Rosamund curtsied low, allowing the duke an even better view of her ample charms.

"My dear lady," the duke said, oozing charm, "so fair a flower is most welcome to my duchy." And he took her hand up to kiss, but he did not release it.

"I am honored, my lord," Rosamund said quietly in perfect French, withdrawing her hand from his in a smooth motion.

The duke then introduced her to his heir

and his heir's wife before they were able to move off into the crowd of other guests.

"What happened to his wife?" Rosamund asked Patrick.

"She died about five years after my daughter disappeared," he responded.

"And the duke did not remarry?"

"He had a grown heir, and by then Rudi had one son and three daughters. I imagine he saw no need. Besides, he has always enjoyed the attentions of many women. The duchess Maria-Theresa was a patient woman with a good heart. I suspect he might even have loved her."

Rosamund nodded. "Where is the guest of honor, I wonder?" she said.

And at that moment the majordomo at the entry to the lovely hall called out, "My lords and my ladies, Maestro Paolo Loredano di Venetzia!"

And all eyes turned to the man atop the steps.

Chapter 7

Paolo Loredano was a tall, slender man with bright red hair. He was dressed in the most elegant and fashionable garb. His silken breeches were striped in silver and rich purple, and his hose was cloth of silver with a gold rosette garter on one leg. His doublet was lavender and gold satin brocade embroidered in deep purple. His short silk coat was of cloth of gold and cloth of silver with large puffed and padded sleeves. On his head was a purple velvet cap with an ostrich plume. The gold chain that fell from his neck and lay on his chest was studded with sparkling gemstones. His round-toed shoes were purple silk, and on each of his fingers he had a ring of some sort. He carried a single silver glove in his hand, and at his waist was a light dress sword with a cruciform hilt.

He stood a moment atop the steps leading down into the hall, observing. Then, with mincing steps, he descended as the duke came forward to greet him.

"My dear maestro, I bid you welcome to San Lorenzo. We are so honored you have decided to make it your winter home," the duke said.

"*Grazia,*" Loredano said. "Anywhere is preferable to Venice in February, my dear duke. Your little enclave, however, has everything I like. Sunny weather, the sea, and an abundance of good light for painting. I have taken a villa overlooking the harbor for my servant and myself." He took in the hall again. "And," he continued, "you seem to have many beautiful women and young men as well. I think I shall be quite content here, my dear duke. The doge sends you his greetings."

"He is well, I hope," Duke Sebastian replied.

"Considering his age, he is indeed well. We fully expect him to continue to rule for at least another ten years, if not more," Paolo Loredano answered.

"Excellent! Excellent!" the duke said jovially. "Come now, and meet my son and some of our guests." And he drew the artist forward by the arm so he might be introduced to his son and his daughter-in-law. One by one the other guests came forward to meet the Venetian. "And here is another visitor to my duchy. She joins us each winter," the duke said. "May I present to you Baroness Irina Von Kreutzenkampe of Kreutzenburg."

"Baroness," the artist, said bowing over

the beautiful woman's plump beringed hand, his bright black eyes surveying her bosom. "You must pose for me," he said, smiling. "I shall paint you as a barbarian warrior queen."

The baroness' blue eyes looked directly at the artist. "And how shall I be costumed?" she asked. Her tone, while quiet, was also teasing.

"You shall have a helmet, a spear, and a discreet drapery," he told her, "but your bosom must be bared. Barbarian warrior women were always bare breasted," he finished.

The baroness laughed a low and smoky laugh. "I shall consider it," she said.

"I would gift your husband with the painting," the artist murmured.

"I am a widow, maestro," Irina Von Kreutzenkampe answered him, and then she moved away.

"And this is Lord MacDuff, the ambassador from King James of Scotland," the duke continued, sorry that the previous conversation had been ended.

Lord MacDuff bowed, nodded, and moved on.

"And the Earl of Glenkirk, who was King James' first ambassador to me many years ago. He has returned this winter with his companion to escape the cold. May I present Lady Rosamund Bolton of

Friarsgate," the duke said.

The earl bowed, but the artist's eyes went past him to fix themselves on Rosamund.

"You are beautiful, Madonna," he said softly.

"*Grazia, maestro,*" Rosamund responded. She was beginning to learn the Italian language now.

"I shall paint you, too," the artist said enthusiastically. "You, I shall envision as the goddess of love, Madonna. Do not say no to me."

Rosamund laughed lightly. "You flatter me, maestro," she said.

"But you have not said yes," he cried.

"I have not, have I?" she answered him, and then, taking Patrick's arm she moved off.

"You flirted with him," the earl said, sounding slightly aggrieved.

"I did," she agreed, "but I did not say I should allow him to paint me with my breasts bare or otherwise." And Rosamund laughed.

"If it would help me to gain my ends with Venice, would you?" he asked wickedly.

"Yes!" she told him. "Yes, I would, Patrick! He wants to seduce me, you know. But before or after he has had his way with the baroness I am not certain," she giggled.

He laughed. "You are probably right. Now, the baroness interests me very much. My information tells me that she is the daughter of one of Emperor Maximilian's contemporaries. She comes to San Lorenzo each winter. MacDuff thinks she is the emperor's eyes and ears here, for the duke is much in favor with the Germans, who visit his port on a regular basis. Who would suspect a woman of spying?"

"She is very beautiful," Rosamund noted.

"If you like large-bosomed women with gold hair, blue eyes, and an inviting smile," Patrick said mischievously.

"Well, she has had her eye on you this evening," Rosamund muttered, "but don't you think she is a bit, er, large?"

"These Germanic woman tend to be big-boned," he replied. "They make a right armful, I am told. Are you jealous, my love?"

"Of the baroness? No more than you are of the Venetian, my lord," Rosamund responded smoothly. And she looked up at her lover and smiled.

Before he might reply, however, the lady in question glided to his side. "My lord Leslie," she said. "I believe there are matters we must discuss soon. When may we speak?"

Close up, Rosamund could see the baroness' face was lightly pockmarked. She did not speak to the earl's companion.

"My ambassador will be giving a small feast in a few days. You will be invited, madame, and there we may speak with each other in the privacy of the embassy and not arouse suspicions by doing so," the Earl of Glenkirk told her.

She held out her plump hand to him. "That is suitable," she said.

"I shall look forward to our next meeting," he murmured, kissing her hand.

"I did not know Lord MacDuff was giving a feast in a few days' time," Rosamund said.

"Neither does MacDuff," the earl replied with a grin. "I would prefer it if I could speak with Venice first. That is why you will tell the artist that you are considering his invitation but that you would like to see his studio first. I will come with you. If he is our man, he will use that opportunity to approach me. Our visit to his studio will not arouse anyone's suspicions. Neither will the baroness' visit to the embassy for a feast."

"I think that if you come with me the Venetian will not approach you. He will have his guard up and consider that you come because you don't trust him to be alone with me. He may even think I am King James' emissary. Let me go alone, and then you shall call for me. When you do, you shall ask to see his studio and say you are considering allowing the maestro to paint me. I shall feign weariness and retreat to the street for fresh air at that point. If he is your contact, he will certainly speak with you then, and no one shall be the wiser."

The Earl of Glenkirk smiled admiringly at Rosamund. "You really do have a taste for intrigue, my love," he said. "I think King Henry has lost a valuable ally in you."

"Hal does not consider women intelligent enough for much more than futtering," she answered him dryly. "I do not understand it, for his grandmother, the Venerable Margaret, was highly intelligent, and his father respected her for it. Everyone who knew her did. Everyone but Hal. I always thought he was a little afraid of her."

"I like your plan, my love, but we shall execute it together, lest the maestro think you otherwise interested in his advances," the earl said. "Come, and let us tell him."

They crossed the room together to where Paolo Loredano was now standing surrounded by a bevy of young women. Rosamund almost laughed aloud at the look in his eye as he contemplated each lady with the delight of a boy offered an entire plate of his favorite sweets all for himself. The artist, she decided, was vain and had obviously been quite spoiled by the women in his life. But their path to him was suddenly blocked by Lord Howard, the English ambassador.

"What," he demanded of the earl without any preamble, "are you doing here, my lord? I find it odd that James Stewart should send his first ambassador back to San Lorenzo after so many years."

Patrick looked almost scornfully at the Englishman. "I am no longer a young man, my lord. Highland winters are difficult for me now. It is not your affair why I am here, but I shall tell you, for you English have such an untrusting nature. This lady is my mistress. We wished to be out of the eye of the court at Stirling in order to enjoy each other's company without interference. San Lorenzo has a marvelous climate in the winter, and so I chose to bring us here. There is nothing more to our visit than that. What could have possibly made you think otherwise?"

"Who would care what you do, my lord?" Lord Howard said scathingly. "Except for the brief time in which you served your king as ambassador here, you are unimportant."

"The lady is a close associate of the queen's, my lord," the earl replied. "Does that satisfy your curiosity? Now, step out of my way, please. I wish to speak with the artist about painting my lady's portrait."

Lord Howard moved aside without another word. The woman with Lord Leslie was vaguely familiar to him, but he could not quite place her. He would have to think upon it. Was she one of Margaret Tudor's English ladies? But no. They had all been returned to England years ago. Still, he knew he had seen the woman with the Earl of Glenkirk at some time and place before today. And he did not believe for one moment that Patrick had casually decided to come to San Lorenzo to escape the cold of Scotland's winter. Yet that part might actually be true. Scotland's winters could be vile.

But no ships from Scotland had put into the port of Arcobaleno recently. How had Glenkirk and his companion gotten here? A French ship? Most likely, as the Scots were so tight with the French. He would consider it, for his instincts told him that all was not quite as it appeared.

"I believe he has recognized me," Rosamund said softly when they were well past the English ambassador. "He does not know who I am, but he knows he has seen me before. We have not ever been formally introduced, so hopefully he cannot make the connection."

"Even if he did, what would he make of it? You are a beautiful woman who has run away with her lover. There is nothing more to it," Glenkirk reassured her. They had now reached the Venetian and his admirers. "Maestro!" the earl said jovially. "I believe I may want you to paint my lady's portrait, but she is hesitant. May we come and see your studio one day soon?"

"But of course," Paolo Loredano said in equally jocund tones. "I will receive guests between ten o'clock in the morning and siesta, and again in the evening. Send to me when you are to come." His black eyes caressed Rosamund's features. "Ah, Madonna, I shall make you immortal!" Then he took her small hand up in his and kissed it lingeringly, releasing it with reluctance.

"You flatter me again, Maestro Loredano," Rosamund murmured, and her lashes brushed against her cheeks but once before she looked up at him again and smiled a brilliant smile. "I shall look forward to visiting your studio, but I am not yet certain if I will allow you to paint me. Are you a very famous painter in Venice?"

He laughed at what he considered her naivety. "Only my friends Il Giorgione and Titian surpass me, although it is said my portraits are better than theirs," the artist bragged. "If I paint you, Madonna, your beauty will be everlasting even if you grow old and haggish."

"I suppose you mean to reassure me." Rosamund pretended to consider. "But first I must see just what it is an artist does to obtain a portrait."

"Come, my love," the earl said. "The dancing will soon begin. *Grazia, Maestro* Loredano. I shall inform you when we are coming." He took Rosamund's arm and moved them away, back into the crush of the duke's guests. "Must you flirt with him?" he demanded of her.

"Yes," she answered him. "If I am to keep him intrigued long enough for you to learn if it is he you are to treat with, I must flirt with him. He is not, I can see, a man who would take rejection lightly. It would offend his sense of who he is, my lord, and so I flirt with him, and he is flattered enough to want to continue what he thinks is his pursuit of me along the road to eventual seduction. It means naught to me. He is a popinjay of the sort I cannot really abide. I met many like him at my king and your king's court. Surely you are not jealous, Patrick? You have no need to be. You must certainly know that! When our eyes first met, my love, I knew I had not really lived, or loved, until you. I would hardly throw all of our happiness away over that Venetian braggart."

He stopped, drawing her into an alcove of the hall. His hand cupped her face tenderly. "I am not a young man, Rosamund, and I fear you will one day realize it. I had the same feelings when we first met, but sometimes I am afraid I will lose you too soon when the truth is that I do not want to lose you at all. I know one day we must part, but if we were to part because you loved another man, I do not think I could bear it, though I would, for your happiness is all that matters to me now."

Her eyes shone with bright tears. "If my girls were older, Patrick, I should leave Friarsgate for you, which is something I never thought I would say, for I love Friarsgate with every fiber of my being. If I knew for certain that it was safe from my uncle Henry and his kin, if Philippa, my eldest, were old enough to manage without me, then, my love there should be no question of our ever parting. But none of this is so, nor is it likely to be very soon, and so we shall eventually part — you to return to your Glenkirk and I to go back to Friarsgate. However, until then we shall be together, and we shall love each other for a lifetime of being apart." She stood on her tiptoes then and kissed him sweetly.

"I am too old to have my heart broken," he told her.

"I will not break it, my lord," she promised him.

"You must remarry one day, Rosamund," he told her.

"Why?" she asked. "Friarsgate has its heiresses, and I shall want none after you, Patrick Leslie."

"A woman needs a man to protect her and to love her," he replied.

"You love me and will even from the distance that will one day separate us. And as for me, I am perfectly capable of defending what is mine. I always have."

He shook his head. "You are an amazing woman," he told her.

"So it has been said of me before," she teased him, and now he laughed again, which had been her intent.

They could hear music now, and they stepped from the alcove to watch the dancing, for Rosamund was not ready yet to join the merriment. The duke's musicians played well. His guests all seemed to be beautiful, and the clothing was colorful and magnificent. While her gown was far more daring in design than one she would have worn in England or in Scotland, Rosamund could now understand the difference in style. Even in the summer, the climate at home was not as delicious as was San Lorenzo in late February. She had never known such warm weather, and she was not certain she could live year-round in such a climate. But for now it seemed just right to her.

They finally joined in the dancing, and together they entered the figure, twirling and intertwining with the other dancers. At one point Rosamund found herself dancing with the duke's heir, Rudolpho.

"He still hates me," her partner told her.

"You cannot expect him to forgive you," Rosamund answered. "It was you who gave Janet Leslie the blackamoor who betrayed her."

"But I never anticipated such treachery from the creature," Rudolpho di San Lorenzo protested.

"You could not have anticipated it," Rosamund agreed, "but it happened nonetheless, and it cost Lord Leslie his beloved daughter. You cannot expect him to forgive you for that. Until this winter he has never ventured from his home. Had we not met at King James' court he would not even be here now."

"Why is he here?" came the question.

"Because we did not wish to share our passion with all the gossips at King James' court. Our love, like most loves, will not last forever, but in the meantime is not San Lorenzo a wonderful place in which we may share it?" She smiled as he passed her on to her next partner, the English ambassador.

"Where have we met before, madame, for I never forget a face," Lord Howard said.

"We have never before tonight been introduced, my lord," Rosamund answered him honestly, and her look was direct.

"But you are English," he said. "I am sure of it!"

"I am," she agreed.

"Then what are you doing with a Scots earl?" he demanded of her.

Rosamund laughed almost derisively. "Come now, my lord. You have surely evaluated the nature of my relationship with Lord Leslie. Must I spell it out for you? I am his mistress. There is nothing sinister in it."

"But how did you meet?" he persisted.

"Really, my lord!" Rosamund protested. "I find your curiosity most unseemly and quite indelicate." And at that moment he was forced to hand her off to another partner, the duke himself.

"You are enjoying yourself, *cara?*" Sebastian di San Lorenzo murmured, his eyes going to her breasts, which swelled over the neckline of her gown.

"Very much so, my lord," Rosamund agreed, and she laughed as he twirled her about in the elegant figure of the dance.

"King James' court is most delightful, but your little court is not just delightful, but also charming. Perhaps I find it so because of the warm weather. I have never known such soft air, my lord duke."

"Your beauty graces my court even more," the duke said.

"You flatter me, my lord," Rosamund responded to the compliment.

"Beautiful women are meant to be praised," he told her.

"Perhaps I should have come to San Lorenzo sooner," Rosamund answered him, and she gave him a smile as she was passed along to her next partner, the Earl of Glenkirk. "I have never known men to chatter so much in the dance," she said as the music finally ceased and they moved from the floor to accept goblets of sweet iced wine.

"Were you praised for your loveliness?" he asked her.

"The duke's heir yet feels guilt over what happened to your daughter, and he realizes you dislike him. For some reason it distresses him. The English ambassador is certain he has met me, but I was honestly able to tell him we had never been introduced. But I am certain now he has seen me before. It is only a matter of time before he will recall where. The duke, however, ogled my bosom and told me I was beautiful and should be praised," Rosamund reported to her lover with a mischievous smile.

He laughed at her recitation. "Then, you are enjoying yourself here," he said.

"I am," she admitted to him. "I have been to England's court and to Scotland's court, but I have never had such a good time as I am having here in San Lorenzo. Why is that, Patrick? Is it the weather, or the delightful informality that persists? It is like a wonderful fete one would give in their own home, and not at all stuffy."

"It is because we are in love," he told her. "Everything is perfect when two people are in love." Then he looked into her eyes and was lost for a long moment.

"Must we remain?" she asked him softly.

"Nay. I think we may sneak out and return to the villa," he said.

"Leave the carriage for MacDuff. The streets are well lit, and the moon is full. We can walk back, for it is not really that far," she suggested.

"Agreed," he told her. The streets of Arcobaleno were safe, and he knew it. They moved discreetly from the duke's hall, through the marble foyer, and outside. They waved the ambassador's driver away. "We'll walk," the earl called to him, and the man nodded, smiling.

Hand in hand they traveled back down

the perfectly raked driveway and out through the gates of the palace onto the street beyond. It was late, but here and there a window cast a friendly glow, and the street torches lit their way. They entered the main square of Arcobaleno, and Patrick stopped a moment, staring at the great cathedral that fronted one side of the square.

"Memories?" she asked softly.

"Aye," he admitted. Then he shook his head. "I didn't want her betrothed so young," he said. "I didn't want her married young. I feared an unfortunate end for her, as I had had with her mother and with my wife. But Janet would not have it. My daughter wanted to be betrothed and wed to Sebastian's son. The betrothal ceremony was in the cathedral. I can still see my daughter, all garbed in white and gold, standing atop the cathedral steps with Rudi after all the papers had been signed. Together they made a most spectacularly beautiful couple, and how the people cheered them."

"Oh, my dearest love," Rosamund attempted to comfort him. "I am so sorry!"

"Coming here has brought it all back to me so strongly," he said. "If only I knew what happened to her. That she was all right. That she was alive. My son continues to seek her out. We know she was sold in the great slave market in Candia to one of the Ottoman sultan's representatives. Sebastian sent one of his own cousins to try to buy her back even as he began entertaining an offer of marriage from Toulouse for his son. Under the circumstances, a marriage between my daughter and the duke's son could not possibly have taken place. All I wanted was my daughter safely returned. But she was lost to us, and I could not forgive either the duke or his son for what happened. The duke had to consider his family's good name, but not once did that spineless offspring of his come to my daughter's defense. I had not realized how strongly I felt about it all these years later."

"And you would not have," Rosamund said, leading him across the square and into the hilly street that led up to the Scots ambassador's villa, "except that you came back, Patrick. The past is past, my love. As painful as this is for you, you owe your king a duty in this matter. Do what you must do, and we shall leave."

"But when we leave it but brings us closer to parting," he groaned.

"Come home with me to Friarsgate," she said. "Your son is capable of looking after Glenkirk. Stay with me, Patrick. You will like Friarsgate. The hills tumble down into my lake. The meadows are filled with my sheep and cattle. It is a peaceful place, and

I would give you some peace, my love. You lost your own dear daughter, but I have three little girls. They would love you, Patrick. You do not have to leave your beloved Glenkirk forever. You can go back, and mayhap I will go with you one day. But when you have done what you must for Scotland, come home to Friarsgate with me."

They had reached the top of the hill where the embassy was situated. He stopped, and she saw he was seriously considering her words. "I could come with you," he said softly. "But would we wed, Rosamund?"

"Nay," she told him. "Our love for each other is not dependent upon marriage. I suspect it would upset your son and daughter-in-law greatly. There is no need to do that. It is easier if everyone believes you are just visiting me, or I, you."

"I should like to come back to Friarsgate with you," he said slowly and thoughtfully. "There is no need for me to be at Glenkirk all the time."

"I do not feel the time is propitious for us to be parted," Rosamund told him.

"Nor do I," he admitted.

"Then it is settled between us, Patrick. You will come home to Friarsgate with me after you have seen the king and made your report to him."

"It is settled," he agreed as they entered the villa.

For the next few days they played publicly and privately at being lovers, and nothing more. And then, several mornings after the duke's fete, they rode their horses to the villa where the Venetian artist was now residing. Rosamund left the earl and entered the artist's villa, where she was met by a servingman.

"Tell the maestro that Lady Rosamund Bolton is here to visit his studio as agreed," she said.

The servant bowed and hurried off. He returned a few moments later, bowing and saying, "If the Madonna would follow me, I shall take her to the maestro." He led her into a large light-filled room where Paolo Loredano was even now painting a landscape of the scene outside his windows. He was wearing dark breeches and hose, and when he turned to greet her, she saw that his linen shirt was open, revealing his chest. He was, she had to admit to herself, very virile in appearance.

"Madonna!" He greeted her effusively, throwing down his paintbrush to take her two hands up in his and kiss them. "You have come at last!"

"Good morning, maestro," she replied, pulling her hands free. "So this is an artist's studio. How can it be so cluttered, and you here barely a week?" Rosamund laughed as she looked around.

"I know exactly where everything is," he assured her. "Carlo, biscotti and vino at once!" Then, grasping a single hand, he led her to a large high-backed chair. "Sit down, Madonna! I shall begin my sketch now."

Rosamund retrieved her hand a second time. "But I have not said I should pose for you, maestro. Tell me, has the baroness been here yet?"

He laughed. "Are you jealous, Madonna?" he taunted her.

"Nay, maestro, for I have no need. I was merely curious," Rosamund said.

"You will break my heart, Madonna! I sense it. I am very intuitive," he cried dramatically.

Now it was Rosamund who laughed. "I do believe that you are a complete fraud, maestro," she teased him.

"Have you come to torture me, Madonna?" he asked her.

"I have come to see your studio and to see if I should enjoy posing for you," she told him.

"And what have you decided?" he queried her. "Ah, here is Carlo again. Put the tray down and get out," he instructed his servant in their native tongue. "How can I proceed with my seduction if you are lingering about?"

"*Sì, maestro,*" Carlo answered his master with a toothy grin, and he departed the studio.

"What did you say to him?" Rosamund inquired. "I am just learning your tongue."

"I told him to leave us so I could make love to you," Paolo Loredano said boldly, and drawing Rosamund up from her chair, he pulled her into his arms and kissed her passionately even while his hand was plunging into her bodice to fondle her breast.

"Maestro!" she shrieked, yanking his hand from her gown. "You are far too bold, and if you think to have a commission from the Earl of Glenkirk, you must behave!"

"I must have you!" he groaned, lunging at her again.

Rosamund dodged his advance and slapped his face as hard as she could. "How dare you behave in such a dishonorable manner, maestro!"

"Your lips are like the sweetest honey, and your skin is silken to my touch. How can you deny me? How can you deny yourself? I am considered an incomparable lover, Madonna. And your earl is hardly a young man." He rubbed his cheek.

"Nay, he is not a young man, but neither

is he an old one. And as for his skills in bed sport, he is vigorous, tender, and passionate," Rosamund said. "Now, pour us some of that lovely San Lorenzan wine, maestro. I will forgive your breach of good manners, and you will promise me it will not happen again."

"I cannot," he said, handing her a goblet of wine. "But I will hold my passions in check for now, Madonna." He offered her a biscuit.

"Are all artists mad?" she asked him, nibbling at the biscuit and sipping her wine.

"Only the great ones," he assured her with a grin.

"I like the landscape you are doing of the harbor," she said, getting up and going over to the large canvas upon which he was working. "You have caught it exactly, and I can almost smell the sea looking at it." She eyed him warily as he set down his goblet.

"I have something to show you, Madonna," he told her, and he drew forth from a table several sketches and handed them to her.

She took them and began to peruse them, her eyes widening with surprise and shock. She stared at him questioningly.

Paolo Loredano grinned audaciously at her, and taking her by the hand, led her out onto his terrace. "I have," he said, "a most excellent view from here. I saw you bathing the afternoon that I arrived in Arcobaleno. I have sketched you several times since, Madonna. You have a beautiful body, which is why I would portray you as the goddess of love. Your breasts, in particular, are very fine."

"I thought you found the baroness' bosom most excellent," Rosamund answered him. She was shocked by the charcoal sketches of her nudity that he had so accurately captured. She felt it a terrible invasion of her privacy.

"The baroness' bosom is quite excellent for a woman of her years, but yours!" He kissed his fingertips enthusiastically. *"Magnifico!"* he said.

"My lord Leslie will not be pleased, maestro," Rosamund responded.

In reply, he handed her another small sheaf of sketches. They were of Patrick and also of the two of them together.

Rosamund gasped audibly. "You are much too bold, maestro. You had no right to trespass upon those moments privy to only us. My lord will not be happy by what you have done, I fear."

"But he will manage somehow to overcome his aversion to my behavior, for he must treat with me, as I represent Venice."

"I do not understand you, maestro,"

Rosamund said, but she did. Patrick had been correct. This artist spoke for the doge. Still, she put on a face of confusion.

He reached out and ran a single finger down her cheek to her jaw. "Mayhap you do not. I know if I were your lover I should discuss naught with you but the ways in which we might please each other. But I do not like seeing you distressed, Madonna." The artist handed her the group of sketches. "Keep them as a memento of your visit to San Lorenzo, or destroy them if they embarrass you."

"I could not destroy your work, maestro. It would be a sacrilege, for your art is wonderful. I shall, however, keep them well hidden from my impressionable daughters," she told him.

"You have *bambini?*" he exclaimed. "Aye, your body has that lushness, yet it has not been spoiled by your birthings. How many?"

"Three," Rosamund answered him.

"Are they Lord Leslie's?" he questioned her.

"They are the children of my late husband," Rosamund answered him, smiling. "Do you have children, maestro?"

"At least fifteen that I know of," he said casually. "Sometimes the ladies are not certain, or they are angry at me and do not want me to know, or in some cases they do not want their husbands to know. I have ten sons, but none of them shows a talent for painting, to my sorrow. I have one daughter, however, who could one day be famous, were it not for her sex. A woman in Venice may become a shopkeeper, a courtesan, a nun, or a wife, but never an artist."

"How unfortunate, particularly if your daughter is talented, and you obviously think she is," Rosamund responded.

There was a discreet knock upon the door to the studio, and it opened to reveal the artist's servant, Carlo. "Maestro," he said. "The lord Leslie is here now to see you."

"Send him in!" the artist said.

"You will want to speak with Lord Leslie alone," Rosamund said quietly, gathering up the sheaf of sketches. "I will leave you."

"So you do know," he said with an amused smile.

"I know nothing, maestro. You must remember that I am English and Patrick Leslie is a Scot. It is better this way." She moved gracefully past him, smiling as her lover entered the room. "I will await you outside, my lord," she told him, and was gone.

Patrick closed the door behind him. "Good day to you, Paolo Loredano," he said in his deep voice. "Do we have anything to discuss between us?"

"Sit down, my lord, and have some wine," the artist said, pouring a goblet for the earl and then joining him as he sat down in the opposite chair. "You have already ascertained that I am here on behalf of my cousin, the doge. We need play no silly games, you and I. What is it that Scotland wants of Venice?"

"So, you are not the fool you pretend to be," Patrick noted.

Paolo Loredano laughed. "Nay, I am not. But the pose gains me far more than if I did not play the fool, my lord."

The Earl of Glenkirk nodded. "His Holiness, the pope, has put my master, King James, in a difficult position," Patrick began.

"Pope Julius has always favored your master," Loredano said.

"Aye, he has, but now he needs something that my master cannot give him," the earl continued. "Scotland and England have ever been the most contentious of neighbors, as everyone knows. King James married an English princess in order to ensure peace between the two kingdoms. Peace has helped Scotland grow prosperous, and prosperity is good for the people who share in it. Jamie Stewart is a good king. He is intelligent, and he governs well. His people truly love him. He is devout and loyal to the Holy Mother Church. But most of all, James Stewart is the most honorable and loyal of men. While his father-in-law ruled England all was good between us. Now, however, his brother-in-law, the eighth Henry, sits on the throne. He is young and reckless. He is jealous of his brother-in-law, and he wants above all things to be known as the greatest ruler in all of Europe. He believes that King James, so long favored by the pope, stands in his way.

"Last year Pope Julius the second sided with France against Venice. Now, at King Henry's instigation, he would stand with Venice and others against France. And he has demanded that my master do so, too."

"He is very clever, this English king," the artist noted softly.

"He is ruthless," the Earl of Glenkirk said. "England knows that Scotland has an old alliance with France. My king cannot break that alliance without just cause, and there is no cause. At England's insistence, the pope demands Scotland join his Holy League against France. We cannot."

"And Venice?" the artist asked.

"My master seeks to weaken the alliance so that the pope has greater concerns than Scotland. I was sent to speak with the representative of Venice and of the Holy Roman Emperor. Frankly," Patrick said, "I see little hope in this plan, but King James is desperate to avoid the war that is sure to ensue between Scotland and England should we refuse to betray our alliance with France and join the league. King Henry will use our refusal as an excuse to attack Scotland. He will declare us traitors to Christendom. There is no profit in war, as I am certain you understand, Maestro Loredano. Venice is a great commercial empire. Should you not be looking to the east and the Ottoman to protect yourselves? If you allow your troops to join with the league's, do you not enfeeble Venice's power?"

Paolo Loredano chuckled. "You present a good case for your king, my lord, and your argument is a fine one. However, the doge is determined to keep on Pope Julius' good side in this matter."

"Could you not remain neutral?" the earl asked. "Could you not plead your own city's danger from the Ottoman and promise not to interfere on either party's behalf?"

"That," Paolo Loredano said, "would be the best course, I agree, but the doge will not do it. He thinks if the Ottomans attack us, the league will come to our aid. I, frankly, cannot imagine the English king, or Spain, or the emperor sending troops to deliver us, but I am not the doge. He is old, and sometimes when I see him I think he does not even know who I am. I have no real influence on him. I am his messenger sent here to listen and to report back to him. But I tell you, your mission, as you well know, is a useless one. I am sorry, my lord."

Patrick nodded. "King James expected as much, but he must try for his own country's sake. Will you, however, send a messenger to Venice with what we have spoken on today?"

"Of course," the artist replied. "I have a fine, well-trained coop of pigeons for just that purpose. I must remain the winter, not an unpleasant task, so as not to incur any suspicion. Will you be staying, as well?"

"Aye. I always found the winters here salubrious. Now, do you really want to paint Rosamund? If you do, I shall commission the painting from you."

Loredano sighed. "She is very fair and most in love with you, my lord."

"In other words," the earl chuckled, "you attempted to seduce her, and she rebuffed you."

"She did," he admitted, "but strangely, I was not offended, as I might have been with another woman. She slapped me and scolded me, but there were no tears or recriminations. And then we continued on as if I had not approached her so boldly at all."

"She is a practical country woman," the earl said quietly.

"And you do not wish to challenge me to the duel?" the artist asked.

"If Rosamund is no longer offended, then neither am I, Maestro Loredano. Besides, you are too young for me to engage in battle," he concluded with a smile.

The artist laughed. "There are, I am beginning to see, certain advantages to old age. You may speak freely and do as you choose to do. And have a lovely young mistress. I have always been afraid of growing older, my lord. Now I think I am not."

Patrick rose from his seated position, as did his companion. He towered over the Venetian by at least four inches. "I shall," he said, "accept your conclusions as a compliment, Maestro Loredano. You may come to the ambassador's villa tomorrow to begin your portrait of Rosamund Bolton." He bowed slightly, but politely. "I bid you good day."

"And you also," the Venetian said, bowing a deeper, more respectful bow.

The Earl of Glenkirk departed the artist's villa and joined Rosamund outside. They mounted their horses, and they began their ride back to the Scots villa. The day was actually growing quite warm, and the earl suggested, a gleam in his eye, that perhaps they should have their tub filled and enjoy the afternoon together.

Rosamund laughed. "We will not be using our tub until I can have an awning put up, Patrick. Our terrace, it seems, is visible from the artist's studio. He has sketched us in our tub and out. I have the sketches with me, but we must see his view is compromised so we may retain our privacy."

Patrick didn't know whether or not to laugh. "He's a bold fellow, this Paolo Loredano. Tell me, Rosamund, have you ever been swimming in the sea?"

"I have never really been swimming at all," she told him. "I paddled about a stream at Friarsgate as a child, but I do not really know how to swim."

"Then I shall teach you," he said. "This afternoon we shall go to a little hidden beach outside of town. The sea here is gentle and warm."

"Can we take a picnic?" she asked him.

" 'Tis a fine idea, sweetheart," he replied.

They arrived back at Lord MacDuff's villa to find the servants bustling about for the supper party that the earl had promised the baroness was to be held late the next afternoon. There was much preparation to be done before then. Still, the cook in the embassy kitchens was happy to make up a basket for the earl. He filled it with fresh bread, a soft wax-covered cheese wrapped in cheesecloth, half of a cold chicken, some thinly sliced ham, and a large bunch of green grapes. Lastly, he tucked in a bottle of wine and sent his helper off to bring the basket to the earl.

Rosamund had gone to their apartments to change into something less formal than she had been wearing. She slipped into a dark-colored skirt and a shirt. Annie was nowhere to be found, but Rosamund was quite capable of dressing herself. The earl entered, and she spread the charcoal sketches that the artist had given her upon a table for him to see. There was one of her in the tub, another of her completely naked as she stepped from the tub, and several studies of her using the drying cloth. There was a sketch of the earl as God had made him and another of him in the tub with her. Rosamund blushed again as she looked at that particular view, for it was obvious that they were coupling in the tub.

"He has a good eye," the earl remarked dryly as he studied the sketches.

"It is too sharp for my taste," Rosamund said. Then she picked up the last sketch, which had been lying facedown, and turned it over. "God's foot!" she exclaimed.

Patrick chuckled wickedly.

"It is not funny!" Rosamund said angrily. "I am responsible for the girl!" The sketch they viewed was of Annie and Dermid, who had been caught in a most compromising pose. The earl's man had Annie against the wall of the villa, and he was obviously futtering her for all she was worth. Annie's eyes were closed in utter bliss, her arms about her lover, her legs about his middle while his hands cupped her bottom. "He must marry her!" Rosamund declared.

"I agree," the earl responded. "Your Annie is not foolish, and I am certain that Dermid has made promises that you and I will see he keeps; but for now, let us go down to the sea and spend a quiet afternoon."

They left their apartments and went out to where fresh horses were awaiting them. The picnic basket was already attached to the earl's saddle. The animals moved slowly off out into the road, Patrick leading and Rosamund following. They did not ride through the town, but rather turned off on a small side path. Following it as it twisted and turned brought them at last to a small crescent of golden sand. They left their horses to graze in the little shady grove of trees at the foot of the hill they had just descended. The earl spread a cloth on the sand and set the basket down. He began to unlace his clothing.

"What are you doing?" she asked.

"We cannot swim in our clothes," he told her.

"I thought we would swim in our undergarments," she answered.

"And then they will be wet when we must dress and ride home," he replied.

"Very well," Rosamund said, and she undid her skirt, letting it fall to the ground. She stepped from it and laid it neatly aside, setting her slippers next to it. "The sand is warm!" she exclaimed as she pulled her blouse off, putting it with the skirt. Lastly came her chemise. She was nude now.

"Go into the water," he said to her, pulling the last of his own garments off. And he took her hand and ran down to the sea with her.

"Oh, it is cold!" Rosamund said.

"No, it isn't!" he laughed. "If you had ever been in the seas off of Scotland you would know what cold really is, my love. Duck under a moment, and then you will see. The air is cooler, I'll vow."

"I don't want to go any farther," she said nervously.

"You are as far out as you should be," he said. "The water is at your waist, and now I shall teach you how to swim, my love."

And he did, much to Rosamund's surprise. Soon she was paddling about in the shallows with confidence. Gradually, he lured her out into deeper water, and she suddenly discovered the water was over her head. A look of panic swept her face.

He quickly took her hand, reassuring her as he did. "The water is calm, my love, and warm. You are just slightly over your head. See? I am still standing. Now kick and paddle as I have taught you as your make your way back towards the shore."

Her heartbeat calmed itself, and no longer frightened, Rosamund swam slowly back, finally standing to discover the water just up to her knees. She turned about, grinning proudly.

"Now swim back out to me," he said.

Bravely, she obeyed his command, swimming out into the deep water again, turning, and going back into the shallows. The water was wonderful, Rosamund thought. It caressed her skin, and she was amazed at how buoyant it made her. He stayed near her wherever she swam so she would not be frightened. Eventually they began to play, as Rosamund's confidence grew, and finally, unable to help himself, the Earl of Glenkirk drew the deliciously wet lady of Friarsgate into his arms and kissed her passionately.

"I adore you," he told her. "Where you

are, I must be. You have breathed life into me again after so many years of sorrow." He brushed her face tenderly with his fingertips. "I shall always love you, Rosamund. Always!" Then he picked her up in his arms and returned to the beach with her, laying her gently on the sand, his big body covering hers as he entered her. He moved on her slowly at first and then with increasing urgency as his need sought to be satisfied. He felt her fingernails raking sharply down his long back. Her teeth sunk into the fleshy part of his shoulder.

"Yes! Yes! Yes!" she sobbed in his ear, clinging to him. Her breasts were aching as their embrace flattened them. Her nipples tingled. Closing her eyes, she concentrated on his manhood filling her, hungering for her, wanting her. She allowed the walls of her love sheath to enclose him, squeezing him until he groaned with delight. He probed her fiercely until she was weeping with her pleasure, and then together that pleasure burst to wrap and enfold them in a sweetness that for a brief moment seemed neverending. "Oh, Patrick!" was all she could whisper when it all faded away.

They lay together for a time, the sun warming their nakedness. Then he drew her up, and they entered the sea together to cleanse themselves of their heated passions. When they came again from the water they sat upon the cloth he had spread upon the sand and opened the picnic basket. Their appetites were great, and in no time at all the basket had been emptied of the chicken, the thinly sliced ham, the bread, and the cheese. Then they sat together in the afternoon sunlight feeding each other from the great bunch of grapes, and drinking the sweet wine of San Lorenzo.

"Tell me what happened with the artist," Rosamund said quietly.

"It is as King James suspected. Venice will not weaken the alliance. I suggested they be neutral, but the doge wants no difficulties with the pope. However, I believe I have given the Venetians more insight into Henry Tudor than they had. I have warned them that he is a ruthless, determined man. I think they did not realize that of him, for he is so young a king and not yet well known. I also reminded them of the Ottoman menace that touches them first should the sultan decide to move farther west. While Venice will give lip service to the pope, I think they will be slow to commit their troops, but commit them they will. We are still no better off than we were."

"You still have the baroness to speak with, my love," Rosamund said.

"It is even more unlikely the emperor

will cooperate with Scotland. Without the pope's blessing he cannot rule at all. His alleged empire is but a group of German states, each governed by its own prince, or count, or baron, and very loosely held together by Maximilian the first. I must try, but I hold out even less hope."

"What do you think of the maestro?" she asked him, a twinkle in her eye.

"He is far more intelligent than he would have the world at large know. He is more valuable to his family by appearing to be nothing more than an artist. I have commissioned him to paint your portrait," the Earl of Glenkirk told her.

"With or without my clothes?" she inquired sweetly.

"With, I think. The without I prefer to retain within my mind's eye, sweetheart," Patrick replied with a grin. "The artist comes tomorrow. I shall be curious to see what he does with this opportunity I have given him."

"I will expect Annie with me while I pose for him," she said.

"I will expect Annie with you," he said. "And Annie and Dermid must wed before any unfortunate incident is brought to light by the enthusiasm Loredano's sketch exhibited to us. I warned Dermid. That he was unable to help himself, and seduced her, I have not a doubt."

"And I did warn Annie," Rosamund said. "Aye, they must be wed quickly." She lay back on the cloth again. "Kiss me again, Patrick, for I am yet starved for your love."

"With pleasure, madame," he responded, and then he complied most willingly.

Chapter 8

The Scottish ambassador's villa rang with
laughter as the entertainer with the dogs set
his animals to dancing. The early evening
was fair and warm. The great terrace,
where the rectangular oak dining table had
been set out, was lit by delicate lanterns
strung over the area and great footed can-
delabras set about the red tiled floor. The
guests had eaten well and now were being
diverted by a traveling troupe of players
who sang, danced, and provided other
amusements for the ambassador's guests.
No one paid a great deal of attention when
the Earl of Glenkirk left the table to be followed shortly thereafter by Baroness Von
Kreutzenkampe. The lady moved discreetly
through the terrace doors back into the
villa.

"This way, madame," she heard the
earl's voice directing her, and following the
sound, she moved across the salon and out
into the hall where he awaited her. "Come
with me, my dear baroness," Patrick said,
and taking her hand, he led her into the

ambassador's private library, where he seated her.

"You are a careful man, my lord," she murmured. "That was very well done, but that the artist was watching us."

"He represents the doge as you represent the emperor," Patrick replied.

"*Gott im himmel!* That popinjay?"

The earl laughed. "He does give that impression publicly, but believe me, madame, he is a clever fellow."

"The buffoon is a pose, then?" she asked, and when he nodded she smiled. "I would not have thought the old doge so clever yet. It is said his mind wanders. I thank you for telling me, but then you meant to put me on my guard with the Venetian, my lord. What is it that you want of the emperor?"

"I come from King James of Scotland, baroness. My master is concerned that this alliance your emperor has formed with the English king may not be to his advantage."

Irina Von Kreutzenkampe laughed her throaty laugh. "Your master has been Pope Julius' favorite for many years, my lord. Now the pope treats with the English king. Is King James jealous? I know little of him but that he is said to be noble and devout."

"He is extremely honorable, baroness,

and it is this very honor that prevents him from joining your Holy League. France has ever been Scotland's ally. King James has no just cause to betray King Louis, and he will not. King Henry knows this, and he uses his knowledge to incite the pope to another way while driving a wedge between Scotland and the Holy Father. Henry Tudor is an ambitious and dangerous man. I think your emperor has little idea of how treacherous an ally he is dealing with, baroness."

"What is it you want of the emperor, my lord?" she asked him. "Emperor Maximilian is also an honorable gentleman. He has committed himself to the pope's cause. You know he has little choice, as he reigns at the pope's pleasure."

"I know your master will no more break his word than will mine," the earl replied. "But Scotland would warn Maximilian that he is dealing with a ruthless man in Henry of England. My master asks nothing more of yours than that he understand that England does nothing that is not to its full benefit. Do you really believe that King Henry will commit his troops to war here on the continent? Perhaps. And perhaps not. What he does he does so that when he decides to go to war with Scotland, he has the full support of the pope, Spain, Venice, and your emperor. Yet what benefit would

England's war with Scotland have for you? And Scotland is both prosperous and peaceful. They desire to war with no one."

"Is not your queen Henry Tudor's sister?" the baroness inquired.

"She is. But it matters not to England's king. Perhaps you have heard the story of how Queen Margaret's grandmother left her jewelry to be equally divided between her two granddaughters and her grandson's queen. Yet King Henry has refused to part with the share meant for Queen Margaret. Our queen finally, and most regretfully, told her younger brother he might keep it all, for King James would give her the cost of her grandmother's jewels twice over. It was a gallant thing to say, for it was not the worth of the gems that meant anything to Queen Margaret. Their value for her was sentimental, for the queen loved the grandmother for whom she was named most dearly. This is the kind of man Henry Tudor of England is."

"This is most interesting information, my lord, and I appreciate your candor in revealing it to me. Still, your master must know that Emperor Maximilian will not break this alliance he has made with the pope and the pope's allies." But her look was very thoughtful as she spoke. The Earl of Glenkirk had indeed brought her valuable information. She regretted she must disappoint him. She smiled sympathetically. "I am sorry."

"King James would never ask another honorable gentleman to break his trust, baroness," the earl replied, smiling back at her. "He but hopes the insight he has to offer will cause the emperor to move cautiously when dealing with Henry Tudor."

"I will see that the emperor knows everything that you have told me, my lord," the baroness responded. Then she rose from her seat. "I think it is best that we now return as discreetly as we may to the terrace, lest gossip ensue regarding our relationship. I would not want to distress your mistress. She is very beautiful. But she is not Scottish."

"Nay. She is English," he answered the baroness, amused. She was really quite transparent in her desire for more information. "Rosamund is the queen's dear friend."

"Ah, so you met her at King James' court. Of course."

"Aye," the earl replied, and he took Irina Von Kreutzenkampe by the arm and led her from the library and back to where the other guests were assembled.

"Does Lord Howard know her?"

"She tells me they have never met," he answered as they walked onto the terrace.

"And you believe her?" The baroness

was curious now about this Scots earl with the English mistress who was the queen's friend yet did not know the English ambassador. If the lady was the queen's friend, they must have known each other from the English court.

"Why would I disbelieve her?" Patrick asked.

"My lord, I cannot believe you are that naive!" Irina Von Kreutzenkampe exclaimed.

It was then he understood her, and Patrick laughed. "Rosamund was briefly with the English court as a child. It was there she became friends with Margaret Tudor, but she lives in Cumbria, in the borderland between England and Scotland. She has no connection at all with King Henry's court."

"And no husband obviously," Irina murmured, still probing.

"She is a widow," he replied with a small grin. "With three daughters and a rather large estate full of sheep. Is that what you need to know, madame?"

The baroness had the good grace to flush, and the blood rushing to her face made more obvious the pockmarks she bore. "I beg your pardon, my lord. My duty is to gain as much information for the emperor as I can. I have overstepped the bounds of good manners, however, and I do apologize."

"It would be impossible for me not to forgive you, my dear Irina." He smiled, his eyes skimming over her ample bosom. Then he took her hand up and kissed it.

"You are very gallant in your manner, my lord," she told him, wondering as she withdrew her hand whether she might seduce him. He was not a young man, yet he had a young mistress who bore the look of a woman well satisfied. Her blue eyes studied him.

"I am flattered," he said, "but I am very much in love with the lady."

Again the baroness blushed. "Do you divine minds, then, my lord?" It was said angrily, for she was angry at herself for being so transparent.

Patrick laughed softly and said, "Do not be angry, my dear Irina. As I have previously said, I am flattered." Then, with a courtly bow, he left her. Slipping into his seat next to Rosamund, he leaned over and kissed her shoulder.

"She is offended," Rosamund said quietly. "What did you do?"

"I refused her," he replied just as softly.

"Was that wise?" Rosamund wondered.

"What? Would you have me seduce her?" He was surprised.

"Nay. But you might have given her reason to hope and kept her friendship, my lord," she told him.

"She asks too many questions," the earl replied.

"About me, I assume. Of course she does. She is friends with Lord Howard, I have learned. Or so he believes."

"Aye, he would believe it. But trust me when I tell you, Rosamund, that Irina does nothing without considering how it would effect the emperor and her own position. It is not in her best interests or those of Emperor Maximilian to seduce the English ambassador," Patrick said. And he chuckled. "She would make a right armful, however, my darling." And he laughed aloud when Rosamund shot him a furious look.

"Well, 'twas you who suggested I seduce her," he defended himself.

"I most certainly did not!" Rosamund responded indignantly.

He grinned. "MacDuff says his piper will play for us this evening, sweetheart."

"The maestro says my portrait is coming along nicely, but he will not let me see it until it is finished," she told him, changing the subject.

"What are you wearing?" he asked her.

"Lavender draperies," she purred sweetly. "I decided that as long as he has seen me as God fashioned me, and since Annie is with me, I would pose for him as he wanted. As the goddess of love."

He was uncertain whether he was angry or amused. "Are your breasts bare?" he queried her.

"Only the left one," she replied innocently.

"Not the right?" His eyes were now dancing with amusement.

"Nay. Only the left," she told him. "I am a modest goddess, my lord."

"I am relieved to know it. But what am I to do with a portrait of a bare-breasted goddess, lovey? I can hardly hang it at Glenkirk."

"Then why did you commission a portrait of me, my lord?" she wondered, and she reached for her goblet to sip at her wine.

"I wanted you to have it to remind you of our days here in San Lorenzo," he said softly, and he kissed her shoulder again.

"The maestro paints this portrait for himself," Rosamund said. "He will never let you have it. I have arranged, however, for him to paint your portrait so I may have a tangible memory of you when we are no longer together. I desire no reflection of my image, Patrick, and you could hardly hang a painting of me at Glenkirk, especially one with a bared breast." She chuckled. "From what you have told me of your daughter-in-law, the lady Anne, she would most definitely not approve."

He laughed. "Nay, poor Anne would be quite shocked," he agreed.

"So now, my lord, what are we to do? You have spoken with the baroness, and she has, I expect, told you that her emperor will not cooperate with King James," Rosamund said low.

"Aye, but if we are to complete the impression of two lovers who have run away for a time from their responsibilities, then we must remain here in San Lorenzo for another month or so," the earl said. "Besides, the maestro will need more time to complete his goddess of love," he teased her. "Will you mind remaining away from your beloved Friarsgate longer? I know how much you love your home."

"Where you are is my home, Patrick," she told him, tears in her eyes. "We will return eventually, and I must go with you to court, for I promised the queen I should come back. I cannot disappoint her. She has been a good friend. We will spend the summer at Friarsgate, and my daughters will come to know you. And you will meet my family, Patrick. They will like you."

"And you will come to Glenkirk with me in the autumn," he said.

Rosamund shook her head. "I think not, my darling, for I do not believe that your son would be pleased to know that you have found love. I would present a threat in his eyes, and I shall not be the cause of a rift between you and Adam."

"You cannot know that," he said.

"But I do," she answered him. "If I were in your son's position, I should feel threatened that my father brought home a beautiful young mistress. And mayhap not just a bit jealous given the wife I have chosen. Not this year, Patrick, but in time, when Adam has learned to accept I am no threat to him, or to Glenkirk, then I will come. I promise. For now we will enjoy the San Lorenzo sun and the warm days and nights. We shall swim together in the sea, and we shall have our portraits painted."

"And spend our nights making love, my darling," he said, his glance heated.

She smiled. "Aye, I shall live for the nights, Patrick," she told him.

"Have you spoken to your Annie?" he asked her.

She shook her head. "I have done something far more clever. I do not wish to broach that delicate subject with her. I thought it best that they come to us regarding the matter. Before I came down tonight, I left the drawing the maestro made upon the table in our dayroom where Annie will be certain to see it. I expect she and Dermid are even now setting the date. We have hardly set an exemplary example for our servants to follow, my lord."

"We are their betters," he said. "Our privileges are greater under such circumstances."

"Because we are their betters it is even more important we set them a pattern for good behavior," Rosamund responded.

"Yet you will not marry me," he replied quietly.

"Nay, I will not, for I am not of a mind to marry again. But I will also not bring your bastard into this world, my lord. Dermid cannot guarantee Annie that, can he? I should not be surprised if his seed has already taken root in the foolish girl's hidden garden. But when Annie sees that drawing she will know we know of their misdeeds. They will certainly come to us for permission to wed, and we will give it. Moreover, we will witness the deed, Patrick."

"You are certainly wickedly clever, my love," he told her admiringly.

"I have been managing my servants since I was barely out of leading strings," she answered him. "It is better in a case like this not to plunge head-on into accusations and recriminations, Patrick. It leads to resentment and bitterness. Though some will not admit to it, those who serve have feelings also. I wish Annie and her Dermid to continue to serve us happily, not angrily."

He nodded. "I think you are wise as well

as clever, Rosamund," he said.

And the following day he was hard put not to chuckle aloud when Dermid, serious of demeanor, came to solemnly request his master's permission to ask Lady Rosamund for Annie's hand in marriage. "You wish to take a wife?" he asked. "Aye, 'tis a good thing for a man to have a wife, Dermid. There is no lass at Glenkirk who takes your fancy? You would have this English girl? You may have to remain in England, then, you understand. Have you discussed this with the lass?"

"Annie says she'll go wherever I go, my lord," Dermid answered. "If we stays at this Friarsgate, she says, her lady will give me a place in her service and we will have a cottage of our own. My younger brother, Colm, would gladly serve you in my place, my lord. But if you desire it, we will come to Glenkirk. I know you would see Annie had a place in your household."

The earl nodded. "I would happily give her a place, though she will find my son's wife a harder mistress to serve, Dermid. That is not a decision you need make now, however. But answer me this, Dermid. What if war should break out between Scotland and England again? What will you do then?"

"Wars are fought, 'tis true, my lord, by men like me. But they is begun by men like you. I do not think our good King Jamie will begin a war. But Annie and me must take our chances if war comes. She says Friarsgate is as isolated as is Glenkirk. If there is war, perhaps both places will escape the chaos. It is the best we can hope for, my lord."

"Aye," Patrick agreed. "Go along, then, Dermid, for you have my permission to speak with Lady Rosamund."

"Thank you, my lord," Dermid said, and he hurried off.

Well, the earl considered, Dermid and Annie had obviously been thinking marriage all along. Their passions had just gotten the better of them. He understood, and he knew that Rosamund did, too, which was why she had not approached their servants angrily. Why, he thought, why had he not met her sooner? Why had fate waited until this moment in his life to bring him love such as few men ever know? Why was it that they both knew deep in their hearts that while their love for each other would never die, they would be parted sooner than later? He sighed deeply. His soul was too Celtic for him to rail at the fates. He realized that he was fortunate to have been given the gift of Rosamund Bolton at all. That such a young and lovely woman could so eagerly give him not just her body, but her heart as well, was a miracle. He wondered what life had in store for her once they were parted. Then he shook his head impatiently. He should not question. He should just accept and be grateful for whatever time they had left. He looked out into the ambassador's gardens where Dermid was even now engaged in earnest conversation with Rosamund. He wondered what was being said, but he could imagine.

Dermid had found Annie's lady by the fishpond, contemplating the golden fish darting back and forth among the lily pads and water hyacinths. He knew that she was aware of his presence, and so he waited patiently. Finally Rosamund looked up from the marble bench where she was seated.

"Yes, Dermid, what is it?"

He bowed very politely. "I have come, my lady, with my master's permission, to request your consent to wed with your Annie," he said in a breathless rush. Then he flushed beet red, and his eyes dropped to his leather-shod feet.

"And Annie is in agreement?" Rosamund responded seriously.

"She would give me no answer until you gave your permission, my lady, but I believe she will say yes," he said.

"Annie has always been a good girl, Dermid, and an obedient servant,"

Rosamund noted dryly, "although I think she has not been so careful of my admonitions of late. I will count upon you to see that she is in the future. If you decide to remain at Friarsgate, there is a place for you. If you decide to take Annie to Glenkirk, you will go with my blessings. You have my permission to ask her to wed. If she says yes, then the marriage shall be celebrated as quickly as possible. The earl and I will stand witness to your vows. I shall dower Annie as I would any of my personal servants. She will come with three changes of clothing, a warm winter cloak, a pair of leather shoes, an iron pot and an iron pan, two wooden bowls with pewter spoons, two pewter mugs, bedding, and five silver pennies. If you decide to remain at Friarsgate, I will eventually see you have a cottage, but for now you will be given a small room in my house."

His mouth had dropped open with surprise as Annie's dower portion was enumerated. "I had no idea Annie was so well propertied a lass," he said honestly.

"I do not stint those who serve me faithfully and well," Rosamund replied. "Now, go and find Annie. I am sure she is anxious. You will both return to me when all is settled, and we will consider the date together with his lordship."

"Yes, my lady!" Dermid bowed and almost ran from the garden.

Rosamund smiled, watching him go. If only all of life were that easy, she thought. If only . . . She sighed. *If* was the most difficult word in the English language. Then she heard footsteps on the gravel path, and looking up, smiled at Patrick. "They will be back shortly, and we will help them choose a date," she said as he sat down on the marble bench next to her. "Let us make it as soon as the church will allow. I would have them enjoy San Lorenzo without guilt, as we are, my lord."

"You have a romantic heart, sweetheart," he told her, taking her hand in his. He lifted it to his lips and kissed the back, then each finger in turn, and finally the palm.

She smiled at him. "I surely must, for I fell in love with you at first sight, Patrick."

"And I with you," he responded. "Ah, Rosamund, sometimes my heart aches at just the sight of you, for I love you so."

Quick tears rose in her amber eyes. She blinked them back. "I still sometimes fear to waken from this most marvelous of dreams to find Logan Hepburn pounding on my door and demanding that I sire a son for him," she half-laughed. "Still, I hope he is happy with his Jeannie. I think his family chose well for him."

"You think of him?" Patrick found he

was jealous, though he knew he had no reason to be.

"Not really," she answered quietly. Her tone bade him to leave the issue, for to question her loyalty to him would be unforgivable.

And before either of them might pursue it further, Annie and Dermid returned to stand before them. Both had rather foolish smiles upon their faces.

"It is settled, then," the earl said to them.

"Aye, my lord!" Dermid replied, grinning. "Annie has agreed to be my wife."

"The marriage must be celebrated as soon as the church will allow," Rosamund told them. "I shall speak with the bishop today."

"Oh, thank you, my lady!" Annie cried. "And Dermid has told me how generous you are being to me. I thank you again!" She caught up her mistress' hand and kissed it fervently. "We don't deserve it, either of us, after we was so bad. But I swear it was only that one time, and we couldn't help it!"

"The likeness, as caught by the maestro, was most remarkable," Rosamund murmured.

"He's a bad man, that one!" Annie said indignantly. "And speaking of the devil, he is awaiting you on the terrace, my lady. He says you should have been ready in your costume, for his time is valuable. The nerve of the fellow!"

Rosamund laughed at this, as did the earl. "I completely forgot he was coming," she admitted. "Annie, you and Dermid may have the rest of the day off to celebrate your betrothal. His lordship will keep us company while the artist works today."

"Thank you, my lady!" Annie said again. "I'll tell the bold fellow you will be with him shortly." Then she and Dermid hurried off, chattering as they went.

"I will enjoy watching the Venetian work," the earl said, amused. "I doubt he will be pleased to see me."

Rosamund laughed again. "Nay, he will not. He is always attempting to get Annie to leave me on one pretext or another. He has obviously not given up his intentions to seduce me. I am proving a great challenge to him." She arose from the bench. "Come along, Patrick. I should not keep him waiting any longer. While I change into my costume you must tell him you have decided to view him at his work today."

The earl chuckled. "The fool would never appreciate you, Rosamund, as I do. He just wants to crawl between your luscious thighs."

"I know," she responded. "I have to admit I enjoy teasing him about it, but today, my lord, with your presence in mind, I shall be a model of decorum."

They returned to the villa, and Rosamund hurried to their apartment to change. She found that Annie had laid out her costume. She looked at it critically for the first time. She had not considered that Patrick might actually see her in the garment. It was, the artist had told her, called a chiton. It was of sheer lavender-colored silk and fastened on one shoulder by means of a heart-shaped golden broach, leaving her left breast exposed to view. The garment fell in graceful folds, the waist girded by a delicate twisted golden rope. Still, every line of her body was visible, Rosamund now realized. She might as well be posing naked for the maestro, which was, she suddenly understood, just what he had wanted in the first place. The entire circumstance had amused her so that until now she hadn't been aware of what a fox Paolo Loredano truly was.

But to admit her naivety at this point would be a defeat, and she did not intend to suffer defeat at the hands of this wretched artist. Rosamund stepped out onto the terrace where the Earl of Glenkirk was even now seated, engaging Paolo Loredano in conversation. "My dear maestro, I do apologize for keeping you waiting," she cooed, and she saw Patrick's dark eyebrow quirk with his amusement. She realized that her lover knew her well enough to understand that she had become fully aware of the situation. There was still an innocence about Rosamund that delighted him.

"My darling," his voice boomed. "How charming you look. I congratulate you, maestro, in your choice of costume. But should her hair not be loose about her shoulders?"

"*Sì! Sì!*" Paolo Loredano exclaimed. "You have the artist's eye, my lord. I have not yet concentrated upon her hair, as I have been busy sketching in the delightful rest of her. When we are finished today I shall show you, but I shall not allow you, Madonna, to see the painting until it is complete."

"Of course, maestro," Rosamund replied. She had heard all this before. She took her place on a small platform that had been erected on the terrace and placed her right hand upon a faux column, turning slightly. "Is my position correct, maestro?" she asked him sweetly. "I am never certain that I remember."

"You are *perfecto*, Madonna," he assured her, and he began to work.

For some minutes he painted in silence while the earl and Rosamund exchanged passionate glances. Paola Loredano was more than aware of it, and he found himself jealous, though he had no right to be. He wanted this exquisite Englishwoman more than he had wanted any woman in a long time. He was also painting the voluptuous Baroness Von Kreutzenkampe now, and he was bedding her as well. She was proving a lusty tumble, but he still wanted Rosamund Bolton. He had discovered at an early age that he was a man of vast appetites.

After some time had passed, Rosamund protested. "The sunlight is beginning to burn my skin, maestro." Without another word, she stepped from the platform. "Come tomorrow," she said, "but you must come earlier. My flesh is delicate." Then she left him, returning to the apartment from which she had come.

"She is *magnifico!*" the artist said, forgetting the earl was in his company.

"If you touch her with disrespect," Patrick said, "I shall be forced to kill you, Venetian. You do understand that, do you not?"

"You have much passion in your soul for a Northman, for a man of your years, my lord," the artist said.

"I also have a skilled sword arm, especially for a man of my years," the earl answered him. "Your talent is great, Paolo Loredano. Do not waste it, or your life, over a woman. Any woman. But most especially my woman. You come from honorable folk. If you give me your word, I shall accept it."

The artist shook his head regretfully. "I cannot," he said with a sigh. "Alas, my lord, my cock more often than not overrules my head."

Patrick chuckled. "I was the same in my youth," he admitted. "But I love this woman as I have never loved another. Insult her, and you insult me."

"I understand, my lord, and I promise to try to behave, but I cannot guarantee it. Besides, the ladies have a tendency, indeed a weakness, where I am concerned. It is often not my fault. They seduce me," the artist said with an infectious grin.

"But Rosamund will not seduce you," the earl replied. "That much I can guarantee you. And if you make an attempt on her honor, she will probably retaliate in a manner not to your liking." The earl rose from his seat. "Now, let me see what you have done so far," he said, walking over to where the easel was set up. He looked, his eyes widening. "You are amazing, maestro," he complimented the artist. "Your skin tones are incredible! I can almost feel the softness of her beneath my fingertips."

"What is it that you possess, my lord, that has drawn this woman to you?" the artist asked the earl frankly. He understood that but for Rosamund he and Patrick Leslie might be friends.

"I am as surprised by my good fortune as you are, maestro," the earl answered honestly. "All I can tell you is that our eyes met, and we both knew."

"Knew what?" Paolo Loredano was puzzled.

"Knew that we were meant to be together," came the intriguing reply.

"Yet you do not marry," the Venetian remarked.

"That is not meant to be. Our love, yes. But naught else. We have both understood that from the beginning," the earl explained.

The artist nodded slowly, finally understanding. *"Tragico,"* he said. "To be loved by a woman like that, knowing you must one day be parted. How do you both bear it, my lord? I know that I could not."

"We are grateful for the time we are given, maestro. Surely you understand that nothing in our lives is permanent. Everything is in a continuous flux around us," Patrick said quietly.

"But to have no hope!" the artist cried dramatically.

The Earl of Glenkirk laughed. "But we do have hope, maestro. We hope that each day of bliss we share together will lead to

321

another. All things eventually come to an end. Most people refuse to accept that truth. Rosamund and I do. We may be together for years. We may not. When the time comes that we must be separated, we will part reluctantly, sadly, but we will be happy for what we have had together and for the memories we will both always carry with us no matter where our paths in life take us."

The artist sighed gustily. "You are a braver and nobler man than I, my lord. I could not accept the knowledge so sanguinely as you have. But that said, be warned I shall continue my attempts to seduce the *bella* Rosamund. Women do not resist Loredano for long." And he grinned his engaging grin at the Scotsman.

"You will undoubtedly come to a bad end, maestro, killed by an outraged father or husband," the earl chuckled. "I bid you good day, then." And he ushered the artist from the terrace, through the dayroom, down the stairs, and out into the courtyard. "When will you begin my portrait?" he asked.

"Tomorrow," the artist answered him. "I shall paint the beautiful lady early, and you afterwards." Then Paolo Loredano mounted the horse being held for him by a groom and rode off.

The earl turned to go back into the villa

only to be met by Rosamund on her way out. "Where are you going?" he asked her, for a moment suspicious and jealous.

"We are going to see the bishop," she replied. "I want Annie and Dermid wed quickly." She turned to the groom. "Fetch our horses, Giovanni," she told the man.

He felt foolish, but he kept his feelings to himself. "Aye, it is best we go together," he agreed. She was so beautiful. Today she wore a wonderful pale green silk gown, embroidered with darker green and gold threads. Her beautiful hair was covered by a dainty lace veil that had been dyed to match her gown. Had there ever been a lovelier woman than Rosamund Bolton?

The animals were brought, and they mounted them, riding through the embassy gates and down the hill to the main square of Arcobaleno, then to the cathedral. The bells in the old church began to toll the noon hour, and after tethering their horses they entered the stone edifice where the bishop would be celebrating the noon mass known as sext. They joined the other congregants, kneeling on the velvet cushions provided for the gentry as they prayed. A choir of boys sang sweetly, their young voices piercing the quiet atmosphere of the cathedral heights. The air was fragrant with frankincense and myrrh as the priest assisting the bishop wafted the censer about.

Tall pure white beeswax candles in ornate gold candlesticks decorated the altars, the delicate flames flickering in the afternoon light that streamed in through the stained-glass windows making multicolored patterns on the gray stone floors. Looking up at the windows about the cathedral Rosamund remembered the first time she had seen stained glass and her silent vow to one day have such glass at Friarsgate.

When the mass was over they approached the bishop, requesting a moment of his time. The elderly man was the same cleric who had performed Janet's betrothal ceremony to the duke's son years ago. He was quite frail now, and he looked at Patrick and said, "I should admonish you and the lady for your behavior, my lord, but I shall not. What is it I may do for you?"

"We would like you to waive the banns of marriage for our two servants, my lord bishop. It is best they marry soon," the earl said.

"Is there a child involved?" the bishop asked.

"Not that we are aware of yet, my lord bishop, but it is best they are married quickly. The air of San Lorenzo seems to be conducive to romance," Patrick responded.

The bishop chuckled. "I will waive the banns for them. Bring them to me tomorrow before sext, and I will marry them myself. Would that I might do the same for you and your lady, my lord."

"Would that you could," the earl replied.

The bishop turned and peered at Rosamund. "Have you run away from your husband, my child?" he inquired of her.

"I am widowed, my lord bishop," she answered him quietly.

"Then there are other reasons that cannot be overcome," the old man said, nodding. "Kneel before me, my children." They knelt, and the elderly bishop blessed them, making the sign of the cross over them.

Rosamund began to weep softly, and Patrick felt tears pricking his own eyes.

The bishop smiled softly as he stood over them, then bid them rise. Thanking him, they left the cathedral, riding silently up the hill back to the ambassador's villa.

"I will tell Annie," Rosamund said as they mounted the stairs back to their apartment. "There are preparations to be made. Annie should have a fine gown for her wedding day. Pietro," she called, and the majordomo was there.

"Madame?" he said.

"Send for Celestina. Annie is to wed Dermid tomorrow. The bishop is performing the ceremony in the cathedral. We need a gown for the bride," Rosamund told him, and she smiled.

"At once, madame!" Pietro replied, and he hurried off to find a servant to send to his daughter's shop.

"Annie! Annie, where are you?" Rosamund called, entering their apartments.

"Here, my lady," the girl said, coming into the dayroom.

"Tomorrow is your wedding day, Annie of Friarsgate! The bishop has waived the banns and will marry you to Dermid himself!"

"In the cathedral?" Annie was wide-eyed.

"In the cathedral," Rosamund replied, smiling. "I've sent for Celestina, for you must have a pretty dress."

"Oh, my lady!" Annie burst into fulsome tears. "You are too good to me, and I was so naughty." She lifted her apron to wipe at her eyes.

"I hardly have set you an example to follow, Annie, but follow it you did, and you should not have. Still, I know you and Dermid love each other or you should not have strayed from the path of virtue. Dry your eyes, lass. We have a few things to do before this is finished."

"Oh, my lady!" Annie's eyes were suddenly round with worry. "What if Dermid and I stop loving each other once we wed?"

"That is not likely to happen," Rosamund reassured her servant. "Women must wed, Annie, if they do not enter the church. Dermid is a good man. He was warned by his master to treat you with respect. But his heart became involved, I fear, and you are a very pretty girl. He will not stop loving you, lass. And you must be a good wife to him. But you will be, I know."

"You know all about love, my lady, don't you?" Annie said.

"Aye," Rosamund replied with a smile. "I do know all about love."

Celestina arrived in a flurry of excitement, her daughter Maria behind her, weighed down by several gowns. "A wedding!" she exclaimed, smiling. "Maria! Put the gowns on the chair!" She glared at Rosamund. "I could wish it were for you, *signora,* and not your serving girl. She is with *bambino?*"

"God's foot, I hope not!" Rosamund exclaimed, making an attempt to save Annie's reputation.

" 'Tis a miracle, then," Celestina said dryly. "Arcobaleno is a small place. Little can be kept secret. The lusty wench has been seen with her lover strolling in the square at night. They kiss and they kiss. We both know what much kissing can lead to, eh, *signora?*" And she laughed her hearty laugh, her several chins waggling up and down as she did. Then she became serious. "Come, girl, let us see what you will have."

"Oh, my lady, you choose," Annie said, suddenly overwhelmed by it all.

"Let us see what Celestina has brought you," Rosamund replied. She looked at the three gowns spread upon the table and chairs in the dayroom. "The pink is too deep and bold a color," she said. "What is it the Spanish say? It takes a brave woman to wear yellow. I think we are not that brave, and besides this lovely blue suits your coloring best, Annie. Do you like it?"

"I ain't never had anything this fine, my lady," Annie said softly. She stared at the gown of pale blue brocade. The garment had soft linen pleating about its low square neckline, a tightly fitted bodice, low tight sleeves with an embroidered cuff, and a matching embroidered hanging girdle.

"Let's try it on, then," Rosamund said.

Celestina and Maria helped the young servingwoman from her garments and into the blue gown. To their surprise, the fit was a perfect one. Annie fingered the silky skirt, a dreamy smile upon her face.

"It needs nothing," Celestina remarked, sounding not just a little pleased. "Her hair should be unbound despite her naughty behavior, for propriety's sake if nothing else. But a wreath of flowers in her hair would not be wrong, *signora*." She nodded. "She is a pretty bride, eh? And with the long sleeves she can wear the gown back home in your icy England."

"Do you like it, Annie? Will it suit?" Rosamund gently pressed her servant.

"Like it? Oh, my lady! In all my born days I did not think to have such a wonderful gown! I only hope I do not wake from this dream." She was smiling.

"Get out of the gown, girl!" Celestina said impatiently. "You will ruin it before your wedding. I can see you are preparing to weep. Tearstains are difficult to remove!" She and Maria hurried to remove the garment from Annie's slender frame.

"You may send the bill to the earl," Rosamund said. " 'Tis his man Annie is marrying tomorrow."

Celestina chortled. "Aye, he should pay for it since his servant could not behave himself. And I hope he'll see the bride and groom have a bit of wine drunk to their long life and many *bambini, signora*."

Rosamund nodded. "*Grazia,* Signora Celestina," she said. "We are in your debt again for your kindness."

"Hang the gown in a cupboard, girl," Celestina instructed Annie. "You don't want to have wrinkles come the morrow."

She nodded at Rosamund. *"Ciao, signora.* Your command of the Italian tongue grows quite good. San Lorenzo seems to agree with you, eh?" Then, signaling to Maria, who had packed up the other two gowns, she departed with a wave of her plump hand.

"You did not ask the price of the gown, my lady," Annie said softly.

"It is a simple garment, Annie, and Celestina will be fair," Rosamund responded. "To haggle the cost would have been insulting. Besides, I know his lordship would want you to look your best for Dermid. Now, do not tell him about your gown, for it would be bad fortune. And you will sleep with me tonight, Annie. Abstinence and anticipation will make for a far more exciting wedding night," Rosamund told her servant.

Annie nodded. "Yes, my lady," she replied meekly.

"Go and find Pietro for me now," Rosamund instructed the girl, who hurried off to do her mistress' bidding.

The old majordomo came, and bowing, asked, "How may I serve you, my lady?"

"Neither of the servants' chambers can contain a bed suitable for a husband and his wife, Pietro. Is there perhaps a small room that Annie and Dermid might have for themselves?" She smiled. "I indulge them, I know, but they are so in love."

"By chance," Pietro responded, his eyes twinkling, "there is a single bedchamber next to your apartment, my lady. It is unoccupied. The ambassador rarely has a houseful of guests, and we are expecting no one that I am aware of at the moment. The bed is quite commodious, and suitable to a newly wed couple. But your servants will also be easily available to you. Will that suit?"

"It will more than suit, Pietro, and I am grateful for your courtesy towards Annie and Dermid," Rosamund answered him.

"I shall have the housekeeper air out the chamber and prepare it for the bride and groom. After that, however, they must keep it clean and neat themselves," Pietro said.

"Annie is a good housekeeper," Rosamund promised.

The majordomo bowed and departed the apartment.

"What is this?" Patrick demanded as he reentered the dayroom. "Annie says she is to sleep with you tonight."

"I think it best," Rosamund said. "We must at least preserve the appearance of propriety, my lord. And Pietro is opening up the bedchamber next to our apartment so Annie and Dermid may have their privacy when they are not needed."

"And where am I to rest my head this

night?" the earl demanded.

"Why, in your own chamber, my lord," Rosamund replied with a mischievous smile. "I have told Annie that anticipation but stimulates desire. We shall see just how much, my lord, eh?" And she laughed softly.

His green eyes narrowed. "Madame, you try my patience with your indulgence of our servants. They are a lusty, naughty pair who do not deserve your kindness. But I, who adore you, do deserve it. Am I to be denied my rights because of our servants?"

"When," Rosamund teased him, "did the time of day ever matter to you, Patrick Leslie? You are a far lustier devil than your servingman, but perhaps I am beginning to tire you out." Her amber eyes were bright with anticipation.

"I think, madame," he said slowly, "that your behavior is in need of some correction." He made a move towards her.

Rosamund edged away from him, putting the table between them. "Is it?" she taunted. "And are you man enough to deliver me that correction, my lord?"

His eyes narrowed again at her challenge. "I am, madame. I think that your round little bottom must be spanked until you admit your fault to me." He leapt forward, turning the table aside as he did so.

With a little shriek of surprise Rosamund

fled him, now putting a chair between them. "You are slow, my lord."

"And you, madame, too confident." He strode towards her, backing her and the chair into a corner of the room. And when he had put her there he smiled wickedly and said, "Now what, madame? You have no route of escape from your punishment now."

Wide-eyed, she could but watch as he yanked the chair away. She attempted to dart beneath his arm and escape, but he caught her, and sitting down on that same chair, he pulled her down over his knees. "Now, madame," he said in menacing tones as he deliberately and carefully lifted her skirts up to bare her round little bottom, "you will be spanked." His hand came down on her buttocks with a satisfying smack.

"Ohhh!" Rosamund cried. A second blow descended, and she asked him, "Is that the best you can do, my lord?" Her ridicule, she quickly discovered, was a mistake, and her flesh was soon tingling and distinctly warm with his punishment.

"Say you are sorry for mocking me!" he growled.

"What will you give me if I do?" she asked from her rather ignominious position across his broad lap.

He laughed, and a hand slipped beneath

her to forage between her nether lips. She was very wet, and he smiled. "Your punishment, Rosamund, has been every bit as effective for me as it has been for you." His hand descended thrice more on her hapless bottom. "Are you sorry yet?" he inquired softly.

"Yes," she exclaimed. She was hungry to have him within her and amazed that the spanking he had given her had resulted in such white-hot lust.

He set her on his feet, fumbling with his clothing, and seeing his lover's lance free at last, Rosamund sat upon it, her back to him. He unlaced her bodice, then pushed aside the swath of her auburn hair from her neck. His hands cupped her breasts, and he pinched the nipples even as he fondled the twin globes of her bosom. His lips brushed her nape, and then his teeth sank into her graceful neck, and he groaned as she rode him with an expertise that always astounded him. "Witch," he whispered in her ear, his tongue licking at the curl of perfumed flesh.

"Devil!" she hissed back, her body arching as she strove to force him deeper into the heat of her eager body. She ground her buttocks, still hot with her punishment, into his body. He filled her full, and her head began to spin while she once again wondered why it was this man who could love her so completely, and none before him. She felt no disloyalty to Owein. They had loved each other and been loyal to each other; but no man until Patrick had ever given her the supreme pleasure she was now experiencing. "Oh, sweet Mother Mary!" she gasped. "Oh, Patrick! Don't stop! Please don't stop!" She shuddered with the pleasure coursing like boiling honey through her veins. "Ahhh! Ahhh!" She shuddered again, feeling his passionate tribute flooding her body. "Ahhh, Patrick!" And she collapsed against him.

"Rosamund! Rosamund!" he groaned in her ear, his breath hot and moist. "There has never been a woman like you, I'll vow! If I died in the next minute I should be content, my darling." He pressed a kiss against her nape, his warm lips lingering as he breathed in the familiar scent of her. "I love you. I shall always love you!"

Rosamund sighed, but she was not yet ready to open her eyes. She relaxed against his broad chest, his manhood still within her. "I shall never love another as I love you, Patrick," she told him.

His hand tenderly fondled her breast for a few moments, and then he said, "We cannot be found like this, my darling. Can you arise from me now?"

Rosamund stood on shaky legs and

breathed in several deep breaths. She drew her skirts down, brushing away the wrinkles. "You must rearrange yourself, my lord, if we are not to shock our two lusty servants." She smiled when she said it, noting that his manhood had not lessened greatly in size. "You are very randy today."

"And did you enjoy being spanked, sweetheart?" The green eyes twinkled.

"I did," she admitted. "It seemed to add a fillip of excitement to our passion." Then she blushed with the admission.

He chuckled. "I could not resist," he said softly. "Your taunts were most exciting, my darling."

"I should not like you to spank me often," she told him. "Your hand is hard, I fear. My poor bottom is still tingling."

"Lovers sometimes play games, Rosamund. But it is not necessary to play them all the time," he explained.

"Mayhap one day you will spank me again," she said with a sly smile.

"One day when the occasion calls for it," he agreed.

"I promise to be very good for now, my lord," she said sweetly.

"I am glad for it," he replied, grinning, "although I will admit you have the most fetchingly rounded little bottom, my darling."

"It compares well with other bottoms

you have spanked?" she asked innocently.

"Rosamund!" And then he laughed. "Extremely well," he admitted.

"I wish we never had to go home," she suddenly burst out.

Patrick took her into his arms. "But we do. Not for a while, but eventually, my darling. I know you want to be at Friarsgate again, and I promise I will take you there myself and remain with you for as long as I can. Now, be happy, my love, for we are together now, and no matter what happens we shall always love each other, Rosamund. Always!"

Chapter 9

Annie and Dermid were married on a warm and sunny March day. It was a tale, they both agreed, that they would one day tell their children, of how they were wed by a bishop in a great stone cathedral with stained-glass windows before the Lady's altar. It was an auspicious occasion for such a humble pair. And afterwards the Earl of Glenkirk and Rosamund escorted them to a small inn, where they shared wine with the newly wed couple. And when the toast had been made and the sweet vintage drunk, the earl told them that he had asked the innkeeper for his finest room. Dermid and Annie would remain the night. The innkeeper was paid for the room and for a good supper to be served in a private salon. Then Patrick and Rosamund left their two servants to enjoy their first day of married life together — alone.

When they returned to the villa, Lord MacDuff was waiting for them. "I have a message from his majesty, just arrived within the hour," he said. "You are instructed to leave San Lorenzo on the first of April, but you are to travel overland again to Paris, where you will have an audience with King Louis and reassure him in the strongest terms that Scotland will not break the auld alliance." He handed Patrick a sealed packet. "For you," he told the earl.

"Thank you," Patrick said, opening the message.

"So, your servants are successfully wed," MacDuff said to Rosamund.

"By the bishop himself," she replied with a smile. "And not a moment too soon, I suspect. They are both very young and filled with the juices of their youth."

"You are a very kind mistress," MacDuff said. "Many a woman would have beaten her servant for such behavior and sent her away."

"Annie and Dermid are both good servants, my lord," Rosamund responded. "They simply needed to be guided into the proper path."

"Will you go back to court?" the ambassador asked her candidly.

"I promised the queen I would," Rosamund said. "I do not break my word once given, my lord. While I miss Friarsgate and my daughters, I owe Margaret Tudor that small allegiance. She was a good friend to me when I was at her father's court as a young girl. She was responsible for my happy marriage. She is so desperate to give her husband a healthy son, and while I expect the child will be born by the time we return, I would congratulate her and encourage her in her motherhood. The king's *lang eey* saw that she would indeed have a healthy son, but until that wee laddie rests safely in his mother's arms, and she is certain of his health, she will fret. Queens have few friends, my lord, but I am Queen Margaret's true friend."

Ian MacDuff nodded. "Aye," he agreed. "Friendship is a rare commodity for those who rule, lassie. I admire your ethics as well as your good sense. They are not qualities a man usually admires in a woman." He grinned at her. "I also admire your beauty, however, and knowing you these past few weeks, I think I am now envious of my old friend Patrick Leslie."

"My lord, are you flirting with me?" Rosamund gently teased him.

"It has been a long time, lassie, but I believe I am," he admitted.

"Well, cease, you old dog," the earl said, slipping an arm about Rosamund's waist. "The lady is mine, and I will cede her to no one."

"What does the king say to you, or should you not share it?" Ian MacDuff asked.

" 'Tis little more than what you have told me," Patrick replied. "He wants me to tell King Louis of my attempts here in San Lorenzo. Is the messenger still here? I would send a communiqué with him. He is one of our people?"

"Aye, he's a Scot. He purports to be a factotum for an Edinburgh guild of merchants, but of course he is not. 'Tis just a pose he affects to divert attention from his travels. He's come here before," Ian MacDuff said. "He'll remain the night, as he usually does. Then we'll send him back mounted on a fresh horse."

The earl nodded. "Send him to my apartment and I will give him his instructions."

Patrick wrote to James Stewart in detail of what had transpired between him, Venice, and the Holy Roman Empire. He had previously sent pigeons with the simple words, Venice, nay. Max, nay. Now he filled in the details of his conversations with Paolo Loredano, the doge's representative, and Baroness Von Kreutzenkampe, who was Emperor Maximilian's emissary. The earl's memory was a flawless one, and always had been. He recalled his conversations with both the artist and the baroness. The king would see it all as if he had been there himself. The earl apologized for his inability to change what was happening, but at least, he wrote the king, he had put a strong suspicion of Henry Tudor in both Venice and the Holy Roman Empire's consciousness. They would now be suspicious of England, and act accordingly.

"You are to go directly to the king, wherever he may be when you arrive in Scotland," Patrick instructed the messenger. "And you are to deliver this message only into his hands. No secretary or page. The king's hands. Do you understand?"

"Yes, my lord," the messenger said.

"And you will tell his majesty that we will follow his instructions regarding our return. We should reach him by early June."

"Yes, my lord."

Patrick handed the messenger a second packet, along with a small bag of jingling coins. "And when you have seen the king, I would have you ride to Glenkirk for me and give my son, Adam Leslie, this. Tell him I am well."

"Yes, my lord, thank you. Glenkirk is in the northeast, is it not?"

"It is. You will find it," Patrick told the man. "And I thank you for your service."

"What did you write to Adam?" Rosamund asked her lover when the messenger had departed.

"That Glenkirk was to remain in his care

for a while longer, for I choose to visit a friend in England before I return home," the earl said.

"San Lorenzo has been like a marvelous dream, and now to know I am to see Paris," Rosamund replied. Then she laughed. "I have never before enjoyed travel or being away from Friarsgate, but when I am with you, my darling, I do not care."

He smiled down at her and bent his lips to brush hers. "The artist will be waiting for me, sweetheart," he said. "Your portrait is almost finished, but mine is not, and I would have it done before we leave so I may make arrangements to ship the paintings back to Scotland."

"The maestro will not give you my painting," Rosamund said. "He paints it for himself. I have told you before that he does."

"We will see," the earl said with a smile, and then he left her. He told the artist what Rosamund had said, and Paolo Loredano smiled.

"She is correct, and she is not," he told the Earl of Glenkirk. "Wait, my lord, and you will see. You will not be disappointed, and you will pay me well, I guarantee it." Then he laughed. "You are an excellent subject, my lord. Where will this painting hang when it is yours?" He peered around the large canvas.

"Over a fireplace in the Great Hall of Glenkirk Castle, opposite a painting done of my daughter. Rosamund has commissioned this portrait, but she has given it to me."

"*Si,* she told me that was what she wanted. I have done for her, however, a miniature of your head, my lord. She requested it."

He had not known that, and he was touched. A shadow passed over his face. How long? he wondered. How long until the fates would part them again?

"Do not look so serious, my lord," the artist said. "You have lost your happy expression. Think of the *bella* Rosamund, and be glad!"

Patrick laughed, his bleak mood dispelled.

"Ah, that is better!" Paolo Loredano cried.

San Lorenzo was abloom with spring now. Flowering vines climbed house walls, and the fields along the road were ablaze with color. The air was growing warmer each day. The sea was as warm as their bathwater. They rode out, passing vineyards now green with new growth. They swam and made love whenever and wherever the mood took them. March was coming to a close, and their April departure loomed. Annie and Dermid in a euphoria of newly wedded bliss had to be prodded to complete their daily tasks. Rosamund finally threatened to separate them at night if they did not do their duty.

They would not travel incognito on their return. It was unnecessary. There would be horses for them to ride and a traveling coach when they did not choose to ride. Their route was set, and the duke sent a rider ahead of them to book accommodations at the best inns along their route. They would travel to Paris under the duke's protection, and from there to the coast to take passage home to Scotland on a vessel that would be awaiting them.

Finally their trunks were packed, and they went to the palace for a farewell dinner with Duke Sebastian. And after the meal was over, Paolo Loredano and his servant brought three canvases into the hall.

"And now, Madonna," he said, looking directly at Rosamund, "your portrait." Slowly he drew the covering from the first canvas.

There was a delighted cry from the audience. There Rosamund stood, garbed as the goddess of love in her lavender draperies, her auburn hair blowing in the soft breeze, a single breast bared. She was surrounded by hills, and beyond her lay the blue sea.

"It is beautiful!" the painting's subject cried. "You have surely made me more than I am, maestro, and while I know you have painted this for yourself, I regret I cannot have it. I remember once telling Queen Margaret that country folk did not have their portraits painted, as did the noble folk. I never thought to see myself portrayed in a painting."

"Then," Paolo Loredano said with a delighted grin, "you will be happy with what else I have done, and your lover will pay well for it." He whipped the covering from the second canvas.

Rosamund gasped with surprise. The artist had done two paintings of her. In this one however, he portrayed her wearing her favorite green velvet gown. She stood proudly, holding a sword pointed downward, a stone edifice and a blazing sunset behind her. It was a truly magnificent portrait, and Rosamund was absolutely stunned.

"It is how I will always think of you, Madonna," the artist told her. "The mistress of your Friarsgate, defending your beloved home. I have heard your England is green, and you have said your land is surrounded by hills. It is how I have represented it. I hope it pleases you."

Rosamund rose from her place at the duke's table and walked over to Paolo Loredano to kiss him full upon his lips. "I have no words to thank you, maestro," she told him. "I could have never dreamed such a portrait of me. *Grazia! Mille grazia!*" Then she returned to her seat.

The Venetian put his fingers to his lips. "You have paid me more than my work is worth, Madonna," he told her gallantly. Then he moved to the third canvas and disclosed its subject, Patrick Leslie, the Earl of Glenkirk, standing tall and handsome as he stared from the painting. "And lastly, San Lorenzo's first ambassador from Scotland. I hope it pleases you, my lord." He bowed in the earl's direction.

"It more than pleases me," the earl said. "You have certainly earned yourself an excellent commission, maestro, and I gladly pay it. You will see the paintings are made safe for shipping?"

"I will, my lord. Yours shall be sent to Glenkirk, and I shall have the lady's sent to England." He came back now to his place at the duke's table, saying to Rosamund as he did, "The miniature has been packed by your servant and is with your possessions, Madonna."

When the evening had finally concluded and most of the guests departed, the duke said to the artist, "You have not forgotten you promised me the portrait of the goddess of love, Paolo, have you?"

"I have not forgotten, *signore*," the Venetian replied. "And you have not forgotten the price agreed upon, have you?"

The duke reached into his embroidered satin doublet and drew out a bag of coins, which he handed to the artist. "Count it if you will, but it is all there," he said.

"There is no need, *signore*, for I accept your word. The painting will remain with you, but I should not hang it until I am certain your friend the Earl of Glenkirk is gone."

"Were you able to seduce her?" the duke wondered.

"I am ashamed to admit I was not," the artist said. "She is an unusual woman." Then he bowed to the duke. "Good night, my lord," he said. He left the hall and returned to the villa he was renting.

A great grin suffused his features as he stood looking at the third portrait he had painted of Rosamund. It was somewhat similar to the one he had sold to the duke, but not quite. The beautiful goddess of love in this particular painting was entirely nude. Paolo Loredano chuckled to himself. The sheer draping he had chosen for her to wear had, in the proper lighting, provided him with an excellent view of her delicious body. He had sketched her first in charcoal, and once he returned to his studio he had copied the sketch onto the large canvas, completing this painting at his leisure in the evenings. Some nights he had slept as little as two hours, but it had been worth it. This goddess stood upon delicate gold-edged clouds, surrounded by small winged cupids, the deep blue sea below her, the paler blue sky above and around her. Her luxuriant auburn hair blew delicately about her lush body. Her head was topped by a wreath of spring flowers. He had perfectly captured her exquisite round breasts and the plump mound of her mons.

He sighed, regretting his inability to possess Rosamund Bolton. Her love for Patrick Leslie had rendered her impervious to Paolo Loredano. And that in itself made his loss all the worse, for he had never before failed to woo a woman he fixed his sights upon into his bed. Fortunately, they were far from Venice, and his reputation would be safe. Particularly when he returned with this magnificent rendition of love. It would be assumed that he had made this beauty his mistress during his winter sojourn in San Lorenzo. And when it was suggested he would neither confirm nor deny it. But this was a painting he would retain in his own possession for some time to come. He almost wished he might show her, and her alone, this secret rendition just to see her delightful outrage. But no. It was over, and Rosamund Bolton was now gone from his life.

Paolo Loredano sighed a final time before snuffing out the lamps in his studio and climbing the stairs to his empty bed. He slept well past the dawn, and when he finally awoke, Patrick Leslie and his beautiful mistress were many miles from Arcobaleno, on the road to Paris.

Lord Howard, the English ambassador, had not been invited to the previous evening's farewell. He arrived at the duke's palace the following morning to discuss his master, King Henry's dissatisfaction with the current trade agreement between England and San Lorenzo. Ushered into the Great Hall where the duke was overseeing the hanging of his new portrait of the goddess of love, Lord Howard stared hard at the other two paintings that awaited the artist's supervision for their transport. He looked at the young woman in the green gown with her sword and her almost defiant look, and he suddenly knew where he had seen her before! It had been at his master's court several years ago. She was a friend of Queen Katherine's. Now, what was a friend of the queen's doing with a Scottish nobleman? He was not certain the answer was of any import, but he would mention it in his next dispatch to his master, the king. He gazed again at the painting. She was very lovely. He wondered that his master had not been enchanted by her, but then, it was soon after that disgraceful episode with two of his female cousins who had been in the queen's service. The king would have been discreet in his wanderings at that point and would have looked farther afield for his amusement.

The duke turned to greet his visitor now. "Ah, Howard, what do you think of my painting? Does the Lady Rosamund not make a wonderful goddess of love?" He chuckled. "Of course, Lord Leslie believed the artist was keeping this painting for himself. I made a little arrangement with Loredano, for I found the lady quite lovely. What a pity she is so in love with her earl. I would have enjoyed having her in my own bed, and so would have the Venetian, I have not a doubt." He chuckled again.

"That is why there are two paintings?" Lord Howard thought he understood. "Was not Lord Leslie aware that his mistress was being painted with her breast bared?"

"He knew, but they both found it amusing for her to do so. She commissioned the portrait of him as a gift for her lover. Magnificent, isn't it?" The duke admired both paintings. "He is a great artist, Paolo Loredano. Every bit as worthy as Titian."

"Titian?" Lord Howard looked confused.

"Another Venetian artist," the duke said. "Now, let us get down to business, my lord. The day is warm, and there is a pretty flower seller in the market square I wish to visit this afternoon. She shows much promise," and he chortled wickedly, winking broadly at the English ambassador. "I remember Patrick Leslie in his younger days. He would have vied openly with me for such a lovely prize."

"Then, perhaps it is better he is now gone," Lord Howard replied dryly, and as he said it he wondered just where the Earl of Glenkirk and his mistress had gone. To France? To Venice or Rome? Back to Scotland? He could not ask the duke without seeming overly interested. Besides, did it really matter? Patrick Leslie was not important. He was a man in the twilight of his years, having a final fling with a beautiful young woman. He had no power or influence. He had obviously come to San Lorenzo for no other reason than to escape the Scots winter and impress his mistress with a minor accomplishment that he had held in his younger days. Still, Lord Howard considered, it would not harm him to err on the side of caution and put this in his next report to King Henry. Everything, even the most seemingly minor detail, was important to the king.

The two subjects of Lord Howard's interest now cantered along the coast road towards Toulouse. They stopped the first night in a town called Villerose, in another little duchy, Beaumont de Jaspre. The weather was fair and warm. And, as they gradually began to travel in a more northerly direction towards Paris, the sunny skies remained with them. They followed a road along the Rhône River as far as Lyon, turning west then to ride cross-country to Roanne on the Loire. The vineyards in the Loire Valley were green with new growth, but several weeks behind those of San Lorenzo. Their road led to Nevers and from there to Chateauneuf, where they picked up the main road to Paris. There was more traffic as they moved towards the capital. They saw more soldiers than they had previously seen. It was obvious that France was on a war footing and already fighting with the pope's league.

They finally reached Paris in late April. Rosamund was exhausted and glad for this respite from their travels. Annie was obviously already with child and equally relieved to stop. The duke had arranged for them to break their long journey at a small house he owned just outside the city. The concierge had been alerted to their coming. The house was freshly cleaned and aired. Two servants, a maid, and a stableman had been brought in for their visit. The morning after their arrival, Patrick left to seek out an audience with King Louis, if indeed the king was in Paris.

He was, and after waiting almost the entire day, he was finally admitted to King Louis XII's august presence. He bowed low and said quietly so that only the king might hear, "I come from James Stewart, but I must speak with you privately, monseigneur."

The king's eyes flickered, curious. He was a tall, handsome man with a warm smile. "Leave us!" he said to his attendants, and they immediately vacated the chamber. "Sit down, my lord," he invited the earl, "and tell me why you have come."

"*Merci,*" the earl replied, and he seated himself opposite the king. "I was called by my king several months ago to come from my northern home to Stirling, where he was holding his Christmas court. I had not been in his presence for eighteen years. Long ago I was King James' first ambassador to the duchy of San Lorenzo. The king wished me to return there, traveling secretly, although once I arrived it was no longer a secret." He smiled at King Louis.

"Though my king held out little hope of his plan succeeding, he still believed it necessary to try. I was to treat with representatives from the Emperor Maximilian and the doge in an effort to weaken the alliance they had made with Pope Julius, Spain, and Henry of England. As you know, the English king has been pressing my king to join with them. But James Stewart will not betray his alliance with France, my lord. I am here to reassure you he will keep his faith with you."

"I had no doubt he would," the French king responded. "Your mission, of course, failed."

"It did. However, I was able to plant within the minds of both emissaries a suspicion of King Henry," Patrick said.

"And how did you do that?" King Louis asked, smiling.

"I told them the truth of his personality and his ambitions," the Earl of Glenkirk replied with an answering smile. "You know, of course, the story of the Venerable Margaret's jewels."

"I do," King Louis said. " 'Twas shocking and most meanly done. I do not believe I should like this Henry Tudor if indeed I ever met him. I doubt I shall, but my son-in-law, Francois, will have to deal with him one day. I think, perhaps, they might get along, for they have similar characters. Francois, like Henry Tudor, is a large man with a large appetite and a great lust for all that life has to offer. Still, he is a good husband to my daughter Claude." Then King Louis arose from his chair, signaling that the interview was over. "Tell James Stewart that I thank him for his efforts on France's behalf. And I particularly thank him for his honorable stance. I know it will not be easy. His brother-in-law's reputation already grows."

The Earl of Glenkirk bowed politely. "I shall take your good wishes to my king, my lord, and I thank you for seeing me." Then Patrick backed from the French king's presence. He returned to the little house outside of Paris on the Seine.

Rosamund was awaiting him. "I began to fear for you when it grew dark," she told him. "You will not have eaten, I expect. Come. Dermid brought us a good supper from the nearby inn." He looked tired, she thought, leading him to the table and seating him. "Annie is not feeling particularly well, and so I insisted she rest. It is often this way with a first bairn." She lifted the cover from a tureen and ladled a good-smelling stew onto his plate. "These French know how to cook," she told him, setting the plate before him and tearing a hunk of bread off the loaf for him. "Eat, Patrick, and then tell me what transpired this day." She poured a dark red wine into his goblet and then waited while he ate. He was obviously hungry, she noted, as he quickly cleared his plate of food, mopping every bit of the gravy up with his bread. "More?" she asked, and he nodded. "You did not eat all day, did you, my lord? That is not good for a man of your years."

Patrick swallowed down a portion of his wine. "I had to wait for King Louis to see me," he said. "Or at least for one of his pompous secretaries to make an appointment for me. I was so persistent, they let me in at the last moment." He spooned the stew on his plate into his mouth, eating vigorously until he finally seemed satisfied. His wine cup was refilled twice. Now the Earl of Glenkirk sat back and took Rosamund's hand up to kiss it. "Thank you for taking such good care of me, sweetheart."

"We cannot always be roiling with passion, Patrick." She smiled back at him. "Now, tell me what King Louis said."

"He said he expected no less of Jamie Stewart than he had gotten in the past. That he knew Scotland would adhere to our auld alliance. He sends King James his good wishes. 'Twas a courtesy the king sought of me, and King Louis knows it. There is little need now for us to remain here."

"But I have never been to Paris," Rosamund said. "And when shall this country girl have the opportunity to come again, my lord? Can we not spend just a few days here? I should very much like to see the cathedral, and besides, Annie really could use a respite before we begin the last of our journey. A sea voyage is apt to play havoc with her belly."

"Two days," he said, "and we depart on the third. Will that satisfy you, madame?"

"It is more than generous, my lord," she assured him.

"I'll send one of the duke's men to Calais to see if our ship is awaiting us. He'll not have time to return to Paris, but he can meet us on the road. The English will be on the lookout for vessels sailing beneath the French or Scots flags."

The following day Patrick and Rosamund visited the great Cathedral of Notre Dame on the Ile de la Cité. Paris itself was a bustling and noisy city, and to Rosamund's surprise it was quite different from London, despite the similarity of having a river running through it. The French were colorful and vibrant. They saw gypsy performers in the streets. The taverns overflowed with revelers. No matter the war, Paris was always vibrant and alive.

"It is exhausting," Rosamund laughed as

they returned home the evening before they were to finally depart. "I do not think I could live here. Did you see the fabrics in some of the shops? They are marvelous, but they do not have a wool as fine as we raise at Friarsgate. The wools I saw were heavy and coarse. They were Scots, or Irish, or mayhap even English, some of them. But they were not of the quality of Friarsgate wool. I must speak with my agent in Carlisle and see what can be done about that. The French appreciate quality, and I can offer them that."

"I have never before seen this side of you," he marveled. "You are suddenly a woman of commerce."

"I have not the advantage of your birth, my lord. Friarsgate folk have always been simple people, but we are industrious. I see profit here, and to overlook it would be foolish," Rosamund told him.

"You are growing restless with this life you have been leading, aren't you?" he said, reaching out to tip her face up to him.

"Aye," she admitted, "I am. You have been busy, Patrick, on your mission of diplomacy for your king. I have been an ornament for your pleasure. And mine," she amended with a small smile. "But I am not used to being so idle."

"I will have you home by midsummer,"

he promised her, and he smiled back. She almost broke his heart with her loveliness, he thought to himself.

They departed Paris the following morning just before dawn. It was Rosamund's twenty-third birthday, and quite forgotten even by her. They met the duke's man along their path. A ship was awaiting them. It was a Scots vessel, but it would fly the flag of a Flemish merchant prince. At Calais they boarded their transport in a falling rain, but the seas were relatively calm. Two days out, as they made their way up the North Sea towards Leith, the weather cleared, giving them a brisk and unusual southeast wind. They saw other sails on the sea, but no one challenged them even as they neared the border between England and Scotland. They sailed closer to land now, and the captain pointed out the opening to the river Tyne.

"We're almost home, my lord," the captain said. "We'll be entering the Firth of Forth shortly. We dock at Leith in the early morning."

It was early May, and the mists partially obscured the land as they reached their destination. Their luggage was off-loaded and taken to the inn from where they had departed almost six months before. They were settled in a comfortable apartment with several fireplaces all now blazing warmth and taking the chill off the early morning.

"I will have to arrange for transport to Edinburgh, or wherever the king is now," Patrick told Rosamund.

"Inquire if the queen has been safely delivered," Rosamund said, and he nodded.

"Aye," the innkeeper replied to the question asked by the Earl of Glenkirk. "The wee queen did give birth to a fine healthy bairn on the tenth day of April. They say the king does wrap the laddie in a blanket and ride through Edinburgh town wi him so the people may see this next Jamie Stewart."

"And the queen is well?" the earl inquired.

"Och, aye, she is, my lord," the innkeeper answered with a smile. "She but needed a bit of seasoning to do it well."

"The king is in Edinburgh yet?" the earl queried.

"Aye, he be in the town," the innkeeper said.

"I'll ride in today," the earl said.

"I'll go with you," Rosamund responded. "I must see Meg, and I did promise to return. The sooner I see her, the sooner I can confess my deception, and then perhaps she will let me go home. It has been nearly five months since I've seen my lasses, Patrick."

"I'll send a message to Glenkirk," he said. "Adam will not be unhappy to remain master there for a while longer. I am anxious to see your Friarsgate, lovey."

"Annie and Dermid can follow tomorrow," she decided. "We can do without our servants for a night, and heaven only knows if there will even be room for us. Court life is not the most gracious for ordinary folk."

They rode the few miles between the port of Leith and the capital city of Edinburgh. Once at the castle, the Earl of Glenkirk sought out the king to give him his final report. Rosamund, however, went immediately to the queen's apartments. Margaret Tudor spied her friend immediately and shrieked a greeting.

"Rosamund! Oh, come and see my beautiful boy, Rosamund! I am so glad that you are back! How are your girls? Come! Come!"

Rosamund laughed and crossed the room to peer into the ornate cradle by the queen's side. The month-old boy stared up at her. He was plump and alert. Waving his little fists at her, he made small noises, and Rosamund laughed again. "Oh, Meg, he is a fine laddie! The king must be so pleased!" She curtsied and blushed slightly, realizing that she had slipped back into a familiarity she should not, but the queen waved her hand, dismissing the breach.

"Come and sit with me, and tell me all about Friarsgate," the queen said.

"We must speak privily about that," Rosamund said quietly.

Immediately the queen's curiosity was piqued. "Get out! All of you! I would speak confidentially with the lady of Friarsgate. You, also," she said to the cradle rocker. "My son will survive without being in constant motion." And when the queen's chamber had been emptied, she turned again to her childhood friend and said, "Tell me."

"I have not been at Friarsgate, Meg. I have been with the Earl of Glenkirk in the duchy of San Lorenzo." Then she went on to explain the mission the king had sent Patrick on, and of how he would not go without her, and of how she loved him so desperately that she had lied to Margaret Tudor and gone. "Will you forgive me?" she asked the queen as she concluded her tale.

"Of course I forgive you!" the queen said sincerely. "So, you love him. But does he love you? And if he does, why does he not offer marriage?"

"He does love me, but I choose not to marry again, Meg. At least not now. I have a duty to Friarsgate, and Patrick has his duty to Glenkirk, although his son is able to carry on in his absence. With your permission I am now going to go home to Friarsgate, and Patrick will come with me for a time."

"You must bide with me for a brief while," the queen pleaded prettily.

"Agreed," Rosamund said, laughing once more, "though you really do not need me. You have all your women to keep you company."

"They are not my friends," the queen replied. "You know that queens have few friends, Rosamund." Then a sly smile touched her lips, and she asked, "Is he a very good lover? My Jamie certainly is, despite the years that separate us, but the Earl of Glenkirk is really old. Can he still make love? Or is this the kind of love you bore for your second husband, Hugh Cabot?"

"He is a magnificent lover and frequently exhausts me, Meg," Rosamund replied candidly. "I love him, you know, and my passion for him is not in the least as it was for Hugh, who was more father to me than any."

"How strange that this love should come to you at this time and in this place," the queen noted. "I love the king, you know. And he is very good to me, although I suspect he believes I am not the cleverest of women. He often treats me as he would a favored animal. So he sent your earl to try to weaken this alliance the pope has now formed. He knew it would not work, of course." The queen's foot was absently rocking her son's cradle as she spoke, and the baby was now falling asleep.

"King James is an honorable man. He will not betray this old alliance that Scotland has with France. There is no need for him to do so," Rosamund said. "I think we both know that your brother, King Henry, seeks an excuse to make war on Scotland. He cannot be pleased that you have given your husband a son when poor Kate cannot give him one. It must frustrate him that Scotland holds the balance of power here. England cannot invade France with France's ally on his northern border. So he seeks to isolate Scotland from the rest of Europe. Your husband, Meg, is a man of peace. He sees what peace has brought Scotland. This country is prosperous and content, no matter your easily insulted earls and lairds." She smiled. "Now Scotland has an heir. There is even more at stake."

"Yet Jamie builds a navy," the queen noted.

"To protect Scotland, Meg. He seeks to defend his sea borders. His navy is a bulwark against foreigners," Rosamund explained. It had always been difficult for

Meg to see the large picture.

"Henry is jealous of Jamie's ships. He is now building a navy, too, Kate writes me," the queen responded.

"Kate is well?" It had been a long time since anyone had spoken to her of Katherine of Aragon, now England's queen.

"But that she cannot seem to give my brother a living heir," Meg said. "Henry will be patient just so long, and then who knows what he will do. The fault lies with Kate, I fear, for my brother has his share of bastards, and he has impregnated her several times. But her children die. I wonder if it is not God's judgment. Perhaps my father should have sent her back to Spain. Perhaps she should not have wed Arthur's younger brother. But, then, what is done is done. Have they found you a place to rest your head?"

"We arrived early this morning, and after settling at an inn in Leith we came directly here. Annie and Dermid will follow tomorrow. They are wed, and Annie is already expecting a bairn," Rosamund replied.

"It is always inconvenient when one's tiring woman finds herself with child. At least they are wed."

"They might not have been but for Paolo Loredano," and Rosamund went on to tell the story of how the artist had sketched

Annie with Dermid in a most compromising position.

The queen laughed. "I'll wager the naughty girl was surprised when you faced her with your knowledge."

"I said nothing. I just left the sketch for them to see. They came then and asked our permission to wed," Rosamund chuckled.

"Oh, I have gossip about your old suitor, Logan Hepburn," the queen said. "His little wife is big with child. It will be born sometime in October. They say he mounted her again and again until she proved fecund. Since then he has not been near her, although he treats her with kindness. They say he has a mistress somewhere in the borders. You are well rid of the fellow."

"Logan is not a bad man, Meg. I was simply not ready to marry again, and he needed a legitimate heir. I am relieved his family prevailed. Besides, Friarsgate is my home, and I could live nowhere else," Rosamund told the queen.

"So your earl will go with you over the border?"

"Aye. For a while," Rosamund answered.

"The castle is full, I fear," the queen announced. "You may sleep in my apartments, Rosamund, and Lord Leslie in the hall. He has done it before, I am certain."

"The distance between here and Leith is little. We can remain at the inn." The idea of being separated from Patrick for even a few nights made her unhappy.

"Nay, you will remain with me," the queen murmured sweetly. "We shall send for your cousin Lord Cambridge to come back to Scotland. He must be bored to death at Friarsgate by now."

"He will not come unless he has a place to lay his head in privacy," Rosamund said.

"I understand he leased a house in the Highgate in anticipation of your return. When he arrives I shall give you permission to live there," the queen said.

"I do not know how to thank you, Meg," Rosamund told Scotland's queen sharply.

The queen giggled. "You will find a way to be with your earl, Rosamund. Sometimes the king and I have made love in the oddest places just for the fun and excitement of it. You could not expect to lie to me and disappear for several months, and I would not punish you. Even if you were helping Lord Leslie complete his mission for my husband. Nay. This will be your chastisement."

When the Earl of Glenkirk learned of the queen's decree, he said, "I will speak with Jamie."

"Do not, lest you endanger my friendship with the queen, Patrick," Rosamund warned him. "Meg cannot remonstrate with her husband for the deception I played on her, and so she punishes me. I will accept it with good grace. We are both exhausted with our travels, and a few nights apart cannot harm us. She is sending to Friarsgate for my cousin, and tells me he has leased a house here in the town. Believe me that Tom will return with the messenger, for he will not wait a moment to rejoin this court given the opportunity. And I am anxious for news of home. He will invite us to join him, and we will be together once more."

" 'Tis you who should be the diplomat, sweetheart," he told her with a smile.

Rosamund was correct when she said that her cousin, once summoned, would come posthaste from Friarsgate. He did, and no sooner had he arrived than he sought her out, knowing he would find her in the queen's apartments. He had gained a bit of weight, enough to show, and she teased him.

"I see Maybel has taken good care of you, cousin," she greeted him, and patted the small silk-covered belly he attempted to hide beneath his ornate doublet.

"My dear Rosamund," he murmured, kissing both of her cheeks. "You are looking lean, yet strangely content, cousin." He glanced about the queen's antechamber. "Am I permitted to see the princely heir?"

"My lady, here is my cousin Lord Cambridge, who you will remember. He has returned at your invitation and is anxious to see the prince."

"You will go back to England this summer, my lord," the queen greeted Tom, "and you will tell my brother, Henry, what a fine laddie I have birthed the King of Scotland." She smiled and held out her hand to be kissed.

Lord Cambridge took the plump little hand and saluted it. Then he said, "Madame, it would be worth my life, and you surely must know I am not a brave man, for me to bring your kingly brother such a bold message. If I should see King Henry, I will say that you are looking well and that your son appears healthy for the moment."

The queen laughed. "My husband says this wee laddie of ours will reign as king one day, for his *lang eey* tells him that. You are welcome back to our court, my lord."

"I could not refuse so gracious an invitation, madame, but I regret that I cannot remain long. My cousin must return home, and I must go south to see to my own holding. I have been gone far too long."

"Aye, and Rosamund does long for her Friarsgate after her adventures abroad," the queen said mischievously. "Go along now and tell your cousin of what has transpired while she has been gone. I know she is anxious to speak with you."

The two Boltons bowed themselves from Queen Margaret's presence and found a secluded place in the castle's Great Hall where they might sit and speak.

"My lassies are well?" was her first question.

"They thrive, and Philippa grows more like you every day," he told her. "Bessie and Banon are charming little wenches, the wee one in particular. She has a way about her, and all who meet her love her. Maybel wants me to tell you that you are to cease your foolishness and return home immediately." His eyes twinkled as he said it.

"Patrick is coming with us," Rosamund said quietly.

"Will you wed him?" Lord Cambridge inquired.

She shook her head. "Nothing has changed, Tom. I still owe Friarsgate my loyalty first, and Patrick his to Glenkirk. We need no vows between us to prove our love for each other. He will come with me and remain until he feels it is time for him to go. His son is grown and capable of managing in his father's absence."

"Then you will be safe while I am gone. I go south only to sell my estate, Rosamund. I am purchasing Otterly from your uncle Henry. It is practically in ruins at this point. Mavis, his wife, has run off, and 'tis unlikely he'll ever see her again. Her sons, including your uncle's lad, have taken to robbery on the high road. They'll all be hung eventually. One already has been. The two daughters Mavis birthed are whoring in Carlisle, I am told. Henry Bolton is a broken man. I have promised him a cottage on the estate and a servant to look after his needs. I intend that Otterly be restored and made magnificent. It is for Banon one day, and I will see that Bessie is so well dowered that she will be considered quite the heiress. Philippa, of course, has Friarsgate after you, unless, of course, you give the earl a son."

"Patrick can no longer sire bairns, Tom. An illness rendered his seed dead. There is no chance of my having another child." Leaning over, she kissed her cousin on the cheek. "You are so good to my girls, Tom. Are you sure this is what you want to do?"

"Aye, I do, Rosamund. I am but a few generations out of Cumbria, and the land seems to catch at your heart. I never cared much for my house at Cambridge. I'll keep the London and Greenwich houses, however," he said. "You never know when we might want to trot south to court, although quite frankly, Queen Katherine's court is a bit too formal, dull, and staid for me. I far prefer this delightful court of King James."

"Here you are, sweetheart." Patrick had come upon them. "I understood you were back, my lord." He held out his hand to Tom. "Stay seated, my lord. I am going to join you." He looked at Rosamund. "You have asked him, I hope."

"Asked me what?" Tom wanted to know.

"There has been no time. I have been getting the news of home," she replied.

"You must ask him," the earl said, a desperate tone in his voice.

"Ask me what?" Lord Cambridge repeated.

"May we please stay at the house you have leased here in Edinburgh, Tom? The queen has had me sleeping in her antechamber, and poor Patrick has been in the hall. We so long for a comfortable bed to lay our heads in, dear cousin."

Tom laughed. "The Tudors have a rather wicked sense of humor, my dear Rosamund. I told the queen when I leased the Edinburgh house that when you returned she was to give you the key to it. This great hulking old castle is scarcely a place a guest of little importance, such as you and the earl, want to stay. She must have truly missed you, cousin, that she played this jest on you. Of course you may stay with me. The house is not large, but it is comfortable and clean. And it is an easy walk up the castle hill. You know how I dislike being late for social functions. I thought when I arrived yesterday that you had not returned yet, as you were not in residence and the housekeeper said no one had come. I assumed the queen had been sent word of your impending return, which was why she sent for me. What a wicked tease she is." And he laughed heartily.

Neither the Earl of Glenkirk nor Rosamund joined in his laughter. They were not amused.

"Can we go now?" the earl asked. "I need a bath and a soft bed."

"I will excuse myself from the queen's presence," Rosamund said. "Do not go without me, my lords. You will have to share your bath, Patrick."

"As we did in San Lorenzo," he replied softly, and he smiled into her eyes.

"Aye," she said slowly, her amber eyes never leaving his.

Lord Cambridge shook his head wonderingly. Nothing had changed, he thought. They were as deeply in love now as they had been at Christmas. Yet Rosamund would not marry the Earl of Glenkirk and had said quite frankly that one day they would be parted, as the fates meant them to be. He worried for his cousin. He had loved her as the sister he lost ever since they had met. But this love she bore for Patrick burned white-hot, and what would happen when they were separated he feared to learn.

The queen was gracious in her small victory over her friend. She released Rosamund from her company. "Go home, and be with your lasses," Margaret Tudor said. "Your earl has done us good service, and you should be together. I will ask you to come to me again one day. Godspeed, dear Rosamund."

Rosamund kissed the queen's hand, and after curtsying, immediately left her. Together she and Patrick took their leave of the king.

James Stewart's warm amber eyes surveyed the pair. "Twice you have come to my aid, Patrick. If I call you again, will you come?"

The Earl of Glenkirk nodded. "You are my king, Jamie Stewart, and though I lost my beloved daughter, Janet, in your service, I will answer your call. I think that you royal Stewarts are not fortunate for the Leslies of Glenkirk, but I will come should you need me."

"Had you not come this time, Patrick, you should not have met Rosamund Bolton," the king reminded the earl.

"Aye, that is to your credit," the earl agreed affably.

"Are you bound for Glenkirk, then?" the king asked.

"Nay. I have sent a messenger to my son asking him to maintain his position as sole keeper of our lands for a time longer. I am of a mind to see England. I shall go with Rosamund to Friarsgate."

"Claven's Carn is on your route," the king said mischievously.

"We will not be stopping," Rosamund replied tartly.

The two gentlemen laughed. Then the king and the Earl of Glenkirk embraced. James kissed Rosamund's hand, and she curtsied prettily.

"Go with God," the king told them as they left him.

Lord Cambridge was waiting for them, and together they walked down the castle hill to the house in the Highgate that he had leased. "I have come all the way to Edinburgh and am not to go to court," he grumbled. "It does not seem fair."

"You are welcome to remain," Rosamund told him sweetly.

"Without you? After all these months? I think not, cousin!" Lord Cambridge said firmly. "Ah, here we are." Drawing a key from his pocket, he unlocked the door of the gray stone house and led them inside. "Mistress MacGregor!" he shouted. "We are here!"

A small, thin woman came from the dark recesses of the long hall. "I am nae deef, yer lordship," she said, and seeing the earl and Rosamund, she curtsied.

"My cousin wants a bath," Lord Cambridge announced to the housekeeper.

"You'll have to take it in the kitchen, m'lady," Mistress MacGregor said. "The tub is there wi the hot water. There is nae one to lug it all upstairs."

"I shall be happy to bathe before a hot fire in your kitchen," Rosamund said. "My servants will be here shortly. Dermid will do any heavy work you require, and Annie, while expecting a child, is quite strong."

The housekeeper smiled broadly. "I'll be pleased for a wee bit of help, m'lady," she said.

"Annie is expecting a child?" Tom looked at her askance.

"She and Dermid wed in March," Rosamund quickly explained. "After Patrick and I have washed, are in warm, clean clothing, and are fed, I shall tell you all of our adventures in San Lorenzo, Tom. Oh, I wish you had been there! You would have simply adored it. The weather was warm. There were flowers everywhere in February. It was really a little bit of heaven on earth."

"I am so pleased to learn that," he replied dryly.

Annie and Dermid arrived with a cart carrying the luggage. They had been directed from the castle where they had first gone, having just come this day from Leith. Rosamund, with Annie's help, bathed in a sturdy oak tub before the kitchen fire. Afterwards, the earl, with Dermid's aid, bathed in the same water before it grew cold. Wrapped in chamber robes, they sat before the fire in the room that served as a hall, their feet turned to the fire taking the chill from the June night. Mrs. MacGregor served them a fine dinner of broiled salmon, duck with plum sauce, fresh green peas, bread, and cheese. There was good brown ale to drink. Finally sated and relaxed, they shared with Tom their adventures of the past few months. He laughed to learn of the nudes the artist, Loredano, had done of them unawares. He was interested to learn that a Howard was an ambassador from King Henry.

"I remember that particular Howard. A sly fellow with ambition not suited to his few talents. He recognized you?"

"Aye, but as I was never formally introduced to him, I claimed I knew him not," Rosamund said. "He looked like the sort of fellow who sees plots where there are none."

Tom nodded. Then he said, "I cannot wait to see the portrait he did of you, my dear girl. Is it marvelous? Is it too wonderful?"

"It is magnificent!" the Earl of Glenkirk enthused. "He pictured her among her hills, a flaming sunset behind her, defending Friarsgate. There are really no words to describe how wonderful this painting is, Tom. You will have to judge for yourself."

And afterwards, as Patrick and Rosamund lay together in the first bed they had shared in weeks, he held her close, stroking her long auburn hair. They had made long and sweet love earlier. Now they were both allowing the exhaustion of the past few weeks to claim them.

"Are you asleep yet?" he asked her.

"Almost," she murmured.

"Let us leave for your Friarsgate soon, Rosamund. I am weary of travel," he told her.

"Aye, in a day or two, after I have caught up with my sleep. It will give Tom a few days to play at court before we go," she said, and she yawned. "I am so tired, Patrick."

"A few days to sleep, aye, my love," he agreed, and then he began to snore softly, and curling up next to him, Rosamund joined him in his slumber.

Chapter 10

Three days later they departed Edinburgh for Friarsgate. Lord Cambridge promised to follow them in a few days' time, for the queen had asked him to remain at court for a short time.

"I have told her I have absolutely no news of her brother's court, but she insists I stay for a few weeks. I may go directly south to save time. I want this business with your uncle Henry settled as quickly as possible."

"You will make a far more congenial neighbor than he," Rosamund said.

"Pity him, cousin," came the reply. "His fall is quite sad, and he is a broken man. His wife destroyed him. He can be certain only that young Henry is his get, yet all Mavis' bastards bear the name of Bolton. Though her adultery was an open secret, your uncle was too proud to publicly expose her. Still" — and this was said cheerfully — "as I have previously said, those lads will all end their days on the hangman's rope."

"You find gossip where there should be none," Rosamund laughed. "Write to me, and let me know when you intend to return to us. You will have to stay at Friarsgate while Otterly is made fit for human habitation again."

"I intend to tear the place down and build a new house," Tom said.

"And will its interior match your houses in London and Greenwich, cousin?" Rosamund asked him, knowing as she spoke what he would say.

"Of course," Lord Cambridge answered her predictably. "You know, dear girl, how I despise change. And this way the servants can come north with me, as they come to Greenwich, and not be idle. I have been keeping them in London all these months while they do naught. Shocking!"

"Tom, I adore you!" Rosamund said, and she kissed him on both cheeks.

"I am relieved to know I have not been replaced entirely in your heart, dear girl," he said, returning her kiss. "Travel safely, and I will indeed write to you."

"I want to know all your adventures," she said, laughing.

"My adventures pale in comparison to yours, dear girl. And to think when I first met you, you were such a quiet little country mouse," he replied. Then, with a wave of his hand, he left her.

"He loves you very much," the earl noted.

"I love him back," Rosamund said. "He is like a big brother, and he has been wonderful to me from the moment we met."

Edinburgh behind them, they moved south and west through the borders, traveling only in the daylight hours, for even in the best of times the borderland between England and Scotland could be a rough place. They forded the Yarrow River at Yarrow and the Teviot at Hawick below Jedburgh. They followed the path along Liddel Water through the Cheviots. Rosamund was anxious to get past Claven's Carn, but as luck would have it, the summer twilight found them right where she did not want to be.

"I'd rather camp in a field with the cattle," she said to Glenkirk.

"I would not," he told her. "He's a married man now."

"You will see, Patrick. And I would not harm that sweet wife of his for the world, but you will see. He will glower at me and make cruel remarks. She is not stupid, and she will wonder what it is all about. And his roughneck brothers and their wives will tell her I am flirting with him to take the onus off of him."

"Is there anywhere else we might stop?" he asked her.

"No," she admitted glumly.

"Then we have no choice but to stop at Claven's Carn."

"I shall say I am weary and must go to my bed immediately," Rosamund decided.

"Aye," Glenkirk agreed, "that would be best. Slump in your saddle and feign great exhaustion, sweetheart. I will speak for our party. And we have Annie and her belly, too." He chuckled. " 'Tis a sad group we are."

The earl had hired a group of men-at-arms in Edinburgh to accompany them to Friarsgate. Now, Rosamund, Annie, and the others behind him, he hailed the closed gates at Claven's Carn. "Ho, the castle!" he shouted.

"Who goes there?" a voice from the heights demanded.

"Patrick Leslie, Earl of Glenkirk, the lady of Friarsgate, two servants, and twenty men-at-arms. We request shelter for the night. The lady and the servant girl who is with child are wearied and can travel no farther. We ask the hospitality of Logan Hepburn and his wife."

"Remain there while I seek my master," the voice from the darkened heights said.

They waited and they waited. The minutes passed while the wind began to come up, and there was the smell of rain in the air.

"He would refuse," Rosamund said, "but his wife prevails upon him to remember that courtesy must be rendered to a traveler who asks it."

"You seem to know him well," Glenkirk said dryly.

"He is not a complex man," Rosamund replied sharply. Then she laughed softly. "He will have to give in to Jeannie's pleas or seem quite mean-spirited. If he had not this young wife, he would refuse us. As it is, he will make us wait outside his gates like beggars, wondering. He knows we would not ask shelter of him had we any other choice."

"Tomorrow you shall be home," Glenkirk soothed her.

A light rain began to fall, yet they still waited. Finally, they heard the creak of the portcullis as it was slowly raised, and the double wooden entrance doors began to slowly open, but just enough to allow them entry, one by one, into the courtyard. There they found the master of the house awaiting them with his pretty wife, who was very great with child. Patrick dismounted and then lifted Rosamund down from her horse. She slumped against him as if she were barely able to stand.

"I appreciate your hospitality, Logan Hepburn, and yours also, my lady Jean," the earl said in gracious tones. "Is there somewhere my lady might lay her head, for she is spent with all our travels? We were too eager, I fear, to reach Friarsgate today, and the darkness caught us." He smiled.

"Oh, the poor lady!" Jeannie said sympathetically. Her blue eyes went past Rosamund to Annie. "Come lass, you and your mistress," she said. "I will see you are bedded down. Have you eaten?" She bustled about them clucking.

"I fear I must carry the lady," the earl said, as Rosamund began to crumble to the ground by his side. He caught her up, murmuring as he did so, "Vixen! If there are stairs, you will have to carry me."

Rosamund swallowed back her laughter, pushing her face into his big shoulder to muffle the sound of it. But her amusement was cut short when Logan spoke.

"Give her to me, my lord, for there are stairs, and the lady has not a child's weight." He took Rosamund from the earl and strode purposefully into his house with Annie and the others following in his wake.

"He is so thoughtful," Jeannie said, taking the earl's arm to bring him inside. "He will put her in the guest chamber. Follow after him, lassie," she told Annie.

Logan took the stairs to the second floor of his house two at a time. He stamped down a dim hallway, kicked open a door, and entered a chamber. Dumping her on the bed, he snarled, "Did you have to come here, lady? Did you have to torture me once more with your perfidy?"

"I would have sooner bedded in hell this night," Rosamund snapped back at him.

"So," he said, "you are not as weary as you pretended to be. Is there no end to your duplicitous nature?"

"Do not speak to me that way, my lord," she told him. "I simply wished to avoid the scene now ensuing between us. You have a good wife, and I actually like the lass. I would not have her learn of your deceitful nature, especially as you seem to have gotten her so quickly with child. When is the bairn due?"

"It should be our child, Rosamund," he said softly. "I love you, and I always have. They forced me into this marriage because you fell so publicly into bed with Lord Leslie. This child should be ours!"

"Villain!" she cried. "Get out! Get out! Oh, I pray the Holy Mother that your wife never learns how cruel you really are."

"I am never unkind to Jeannie," he quickly responded. "She is as much a victim as I am, though she knows it not. She is like a small helpless kitten. You cannot be cruel to such a creature. You love it, and you protect it."

"Then why do you speak to me so?" Rosamund demanded of him.

"Because I love you," he said.

"You wanted an heir, and any woman would do, my lord," she replied.

"Aye, I want an heir. 'Tis every man's right. But that was not why I wanted to wed you, Rosamund Bolton. I love you. Why can you not believe it?"

"Get out of my chamber, Logan Hepburn," Rosamund said. "They will be wondering in the hall where you are. Ah, here is Annie. Come in, lass, and let us prepare for bed now. Good night, my lord."

"Do you really love him?" the laird of Claven's Carn asked.

"Aye, I do," Rosamund answered him. "As I have never loved any other, or will."

He turned and departed without another word.

"Lady Jeanne says she will send us supper," Annie said, wide-eyed.

"How much did you hear?" Rosamund inquired of her servant.

"All of it, my lady. I was outside the door, but I feared to come in," Annie responded.

"You will forget all that you heard," Rosamund told her.

"Aye, I will," Annie agreed. "His lordship says to tell you he will sleep in the hall with Dermid."

Rosamund nodded.

"Lady Jean is very kind," Annie noted.

"She was most solicitous about my condition, her being in the same way but a few months farther along. Her bairn will come in September, she says."

"She is a sweet girl," Rosamund agreed. "We must pray she gives him a son, else he not be satisfied."

"I hopes it's a lad I carry," Annie said.

A maidservant came to light a fire to take the chill off the evening. Another servant girl brought a tray with two bowls of lamb stew, bread, cheese, and ale. A third carried in a basin of warm water for bathing and set it on the edge of the coals in the fireplace to keep warm. The lady of the keep knew how to see her guests were made comfortable. Rosamund and Annie ate their supper with a good appetite. They washed their faces and their hands, then stripped off their gowns and climbed into bed. The bed was fresh and smelled of lavender. They slept soundly until the dawn.

Hearing the early birdsong outside the chamber's window, Rosamund awoke. She slid from her bed and pulled the chamber pot from beneath it, peeing, then emptying the pot out the window afterwards. The day was warm, with a south wind. And there was something in that air that called to her. Home, she thought. A few hours more, and I am home again at Friarsgate.

Patrick is with me, and I will have my family about me. She sighed. I am happy, she thought. She pulled her clothes back on and drew her boots onto her feet. A bath! Tonight she would have a real bath for the first time in weeks.

"Annie." She gently shook her servant by her shoulder. "Wake up, Annie. We will be leaving soon, and we will be home by afternoon."

Annie groaned, but she dutifully arose.

"I'm going downstairs into the hall, Annie. Do not be far behind me, lass," her mistress instructed, and Rosamund hurried from the chamber. In the hall she found Patrick up already, and she ran to him and kissed him. "I missed you last night," she said softly.

"He did not come down right away," the earl said softly.

"He would quarrel with me. Did I not warn you?" Rosamund replied.

"He got drunk before his brothers put him to bed, but his lady wife appeared not to be disturbed by any of it. She was too busy chattering with me. She is lonely here, I think. Her sisters-in-law are both flighty lasses with little on their minds but ribbons, laces, and bed sport."

"Let us go as quickly as possible," Rosamund said. "It is but a few more hours to Friarsgate. I do not wish to have to face Logan Hepburn again."

"You will tell me later," Patrick said. "I think we must at least wait for the lady of the house before we go. Come, sweetheart, and eat some porridge. There is a freshly baked cottage loaf, too." He led her to the high board, and a servant at once placed a large trencher loaf filled with oat stirabout before them. There was honey and heavy golden cream, which Rosamund added liberally to the hot cereal. They ate, and their goblets were filled with wine. A small round cottage loaf had been set before them, and Rosamund tore pieces from it, dipping the bits in honey and feeding them to her lover. He returned the favor, and soon they were laughing as they licked the drizzles of honey from each other's mouths.

Then Patrick suddenly grew serious. "It is not just that I want you, Rosamund. I find, to my surprise, that I need you."

She smiled into his green eyes. "I feel the same way, my love," she told him.

The mistress of the keep entered the hall. "Oh, you are both already up," she said. "Have you been fed? Did you sleep well?" She hurried up to the high board, smiling.

"We have been treated very well, my lady Jean," the earl told her.

"You have been a gracious hostess,"

Rosamund added. "I am so grateful for the lovely supper you sent me last night. I was so tired. We only arrived home recently. It seems, but for our lovely sojourn, we have been traveling for weeks."

"I am so glad you broke your journey here," Jean said. "I did so want to see you again."

"You are welcome at Friarsgate anytime," Rosamund told her.

"Oh, once my bairn comes I shall be going nowhere," Jean said. "And I am certainly in no condition to travel now. One day I shall come and visit you, however, when my bairns, for Logan's brothers say I must have a houseful, are grown, and not before." She smiled. "You have daughters, do you not?"

"Three, and a son lost," Rosamund responded softly.

"Everyone says it is a lad I'm carrying, for I am so big," Jean said.

"You cannot know until the bairn is born," Rosamund warned her. "Lassies can appear large, too."

Jean shook her head. "Nay, this is a lad, for Logan wants a lad. I cannot disappoint him."

"I am sure there is nothing you could do that would disappoint him," Rosamund replied. She turned to her lover. "My lord, are we ready to depart?"

"Where are Annie and Dermid?" he queried.

"We're ready, my lord," Dermid said. Annie, looking slightly sleepy, was by his side. "Horses are in the courtyard, and everyone's been fed. My thanks, lady." He bowed neatly to Jean and then turned to depart the hall with his wife.

"Please let us know when you are safely delivered," Rosamund told her hostess. "I will have Father Mata pray for you, Jean Hepburn. Tell Logan I am sorry we did not see him before we left. He seemed unwell last night. I hope whatever was bothering him has now left him. Say I asked after him." She smiled and slipped a hand into the earl's big one.

"I will." Jean smiled. "Travel in safety, Lady Rosamund."

When they were out again in the courtyard of Claven's Carn and mounted, Patrick leaned over, speaking so only Rosamund might hear him. "You have sharp claws, madame," he said. "I take it his offense last night was suitably unforgivable that you would torture him so cruelly."

"He once again declared his love for me," Rosamund muttered angrily.

The Earl of Glenkirk nodded. "That was indeed unforgivable," he agreed, "and particularly so as that trusting little wife of his is big with his heir."

They rode from Claven's Carn, down the hill, and onto the track that led over the hills into England.

"It bothers me that Jean Hepburn should ever be harmed by believing that her husband is not true to her. She is striving so hard to be a good wife to him."

"Do you think she loves him?" the earl wondered.

"I know not," Rosamund answered, shaking her head. "But he owes her his loyalty, and to tell me within the walls of his own house, with his wife in the hall below, that he still loves me — I wish I had slapped him. I was astounded by his words, Patrick! He is what I always believed him to be. A rude and crude borderer."

"I feel sorry for him," the earl said, surprising her.

"Why on earth would you feel sorry for him?" Rosamund demanded, her tone aggrieved.

"I feel sorry for him because he truly does love you, Rosamund," the earl said quietly. "I know you always believed he courted you because he needed, and wanted, an heir. That may be true in part, but the man is also deeply in love with you. The sight of us together last night tortured him. When he returned to the hall he

393

said practically nothing, but he drank himself into a stupor. His brothers had to carry him to bed."

"I am sorry for that," Rosamund replied. "But, Patrick, I never said I would wed him. I said no. I always said no. I feel sorry for him, too, but I will not be put in the same position with sweet Jean Hepburn as I was with my own queen. I am not comfortable with guilt, my lord, particularly when those who are responsible for these situations feel no guilt at all. Logan feels sorry for himself. He does not think of his wife. But I do. Henry Tudor felt deprived when I returned to Friarsgate. He did not consider the hurt he would do the queen if she had learned a trusted friend had been in her husband's bed. But I did."

"It is unlikely that you will see him again for some time, if ever," the earl responded. "The very sight of you is painful. I believe he respects his wife, even if he does not love her. And there is his pride to consider, as well."

"Aye, Logan is a proud man," Rosamund noted.

They rode for several hours, and suddenly the landscape about them began to grow familiar. She knew the hills about them. Rosamund leaned forward eagerly.

"You sense Friarsgate," he said to her.

She nodded excitedly. "I do!" she said.

"Just one more hill, Patrick, and we will see my lake and my fields. Oh God! I cannot believe I stayed away so long! Yet I should not have been anywhere else but with you, my darling. You love your Glenkirk every bit as much as I love Friarsgate. I look forward to seeing it one day."

"And you will," he promised her.

They followed the faint track of the road down the hill and then began to climb up the next. At its crest it was as she had said, and she stopped to take it all in. Below them lay Friarsgate, its meadows green in the late spring sun. There were sheep and cattle grazing placidly. The fields were golden with grain, and the orchards, as they rode down the hill and past them, were full of blossoms. The lake beyond the stone house sparkled in the afternoon light. The bell in the church began to peal, and the people came from their work and cottages, running to greet their returning mistress and her party. They reached the house, and Maybel came out, smiling broadly, with Rosamund's daughters in tow.

The lady of Friarsgate jumped down from her horse and, kneeling, gathered her children into her arms. "Oh, my darling girls!" she cried, covering them with kisses. Bessie, the baby, now four, squirmed protesting, but Banon and Philippa were openly glad to see their mother again.

"I did not expect you to be gone from us so long, mama," Philippa, age eight, said. "Uncle Thomas is a fine companion, but we missed you." Her gaze turned to the Earl of Glenkirk, and she quirked an auburn eyebrow.

Rosamund stood. "Philippa, may I present you and your sisters to Patrick Leslie, the Earl of Glenkirk." She looked sharply at her daughters, and they curtsied politely. "The earl will be visiting with us for a time," Rosamund said.

"Do you have a castle, my lord?" Philippa asked boldly.

"I do," he answered her, smiling down on this smaller version of his love. "One day I hope your mother will come and bring you to see it."

"Well, and 'tis past time you got home!" Maybel said sternly. "Although from the look of this fine gentleman I can see why you remained in Edinburgh so long. Come into the house now." Then she stared hard at Annie. "What's this? What's this? Do you return home with shame in your belly?"

"I be a respectably married woman," Annie said, and she pulled Dermid forward. "Yon Scot is my man, Maybel. Mistress has promised us a cot eventually."

"You'll have to earn it, girl," Maybel said sharply. "And just where was you wed, my lass?"

Annie looked to her mistress, and when Rosamund nodded, she said, "In a great cathedral, and by a bishop hisself, Maybel! There isn't a lass at Friarsgate who ever had a finer wedding, I'll vow."

Maybel looked astounded, but Rosamund spoke up, saying, "We have a wonderful tale to tell you. But not here. We have been riding most of the day, and we need food and wine, and most of all, a hot bath! It has been weeks since either of us has had a decent bath. Edmund!" She greeted the gentleman who had just come from the house. "Patrick, this is my uncle, Edmund Bolton. Uncle, Patrick Leslie, the Earl of Glenkirk." She led them all into the house now.

The hall was pleasantly cool, and looking about it, Rosamund sighed with pleasure. She had enjoyed her adventures in San Lorenzo and Edinburgh, but by God's blessed body it was good to be home at last. She settled herself immediately in her favorite chair by the hearth. She saw a fire already laid for the evening and smiled. She could hear the servants bringing in the luggage, and Annie, full of self-importance, directing them as to where it would go. A little maidservant with whom she was not familiar brought a tray with wine and sugar wafers.

"Who are you, child?" Rosamund asked.

"I be Lucy, m'lady. Annie's sister," the girl chirped with a small smile.

"Thank you, Lucy," Rosamund said, and then she turned to the earl. "Shall I begin our tale?"

He nodded. "It is over and done with now, and I doubt it will travel from Cumbria to the ears of King Henry," he answered her with a smile. Bending down, he lifted Bessie, who was hanging on his leg, up into his lap. The little girl snuggled down in his arms contentedly. For a moment, the Earl of Glenkirk's face grew sad, but then he sighed and smiled at the child.

"You are thinking of your daughter," Rosamund said softly.

"Aye," he admitted. "She was just about this age and size when her brother was born and she came to Glenkirk Castle to live. But tell your tale, Rosamund."

Rosamund looked about her. Maybel and Edmund were leaning forward. Philippa and Banon had expectant looks upon their faces. Rosamund began. She explained how she had met the earl almost as soon as she had arrived in Edinburgh and how they had fallen in love at first sight. She told them briefly of Patrick's previous sojourn in San Lorenzo, of how his beloved daughter was taken by slavers and sold into bondage, never to be seen again. She then went on to tell them that King James had called the earl from Glenkirk and asked him to act secretly for him in a certain matter that would require him to go to San Lorenzo after an absence of eighteen years. At this point, the Friarsgate priest, Father Mata, entered the hall and silently took a seat.

"It is good to see you, Father," Rosamund said. "I am telling the hall of my adventures."

"What have I missed?" the priest asked, and Rosamund quickly recapped her tale for him before continuing on.

"King James is a man of peace," she told her listeners, explaining how their own king was attempting to force his brother-in-law into a dishonorable act by betraying old allies or becoming Pope Julius' enemy.

"He was willful even as lad," Maybel said, shaking her head. "But go on, lass!"

"King James hoped to weaken the alliance England and the pope were building up against France. By doing that, his refusal to join them would become a moot point. That is why Patrick was sent back secretly to San Lorenzo, to treat with Venice's and the Emperor Maximilian's representatives. King James believed this mission was doomed to failure, but he felt he must at least make an attempt to prevent the war that will surely ensue between our countries if King Henry's mischief is allowed to prevail. Patrick agreed to go as long as I could go with him."

"You went across the sea, mama?" Philippa asked.

"I did, my daughter. I have seen France and San Lorenzo," Rosamund told them. "San Lorenzo is so beautiful, and while it was snowy winter here, the winter in San Lorenzo was sunny and warm. There were flowers in bloom, and I swam in the sea."

"God have mercy!" Maybel exclaimed.

Rosamund laughed. "We lived in a house called a villa that overlooked the sea," she continued on. "I met the duke who rules that fair duchy and even danced with him. I had my portrait painted by a great artist who had come from Venice to winter in San Lorenzo. When the painting arrives, we will hang it here in the hall. I remember once telling Margaret Tudor that country folk didn't have such luxuries as their portraits painted." Rosamund smiled.

"And what of Mistress Meg who is now a queen?" Maybel inquired.

"She was far gone with child at Christmastide, and she delivered a fair son this April. He's a lovely, strong bonnie lad, Maybel, and the Queen of the Scots is at last a happy woman. She loves the king,

and she has done her duty by Scotland,"
Rosamund said. "I had to lie to her when I
went off with Patrick to San Lorenzo, but
she has forgiven me the untruth. That is
why I sent Tom back to watch over
Friarsgate in my absence. Did he tell you
that he is purchasing Otterly from Uncle
Henry?"

Her uncle Edmund now spoke up. "Aye.
Even I am reduced to feeling sorry for my
half-brother. That second wife of his was a
wicked bitch. I never thought to see Henry
Bolton brought so low, but he has been.
Tom will see him well fed, well cared for,
and well housed as long as he lives. The
monies he is paying for Otterly have been
put with a goldsmith in Carlisle. They
cannot be touched. When my half-brother
is rested once again in his mind and body
he will make a will. You would not recognize him, Rosamund. He is as thin as a rail
now."

"Uncle Henry? He who was always so
plump and dyspeptic? I am indeed surprised," Rosamund replied.

"That fat face he once had is now as
narrow as a hermit monk's," Maybel
chimed in. "But the eyes staring out at you
would give you a fright. They are both
hopeless and empty of emotion at the same
time. I think him no less dangerous for all
his bad luck."

"Wife, have mercy," Edmund said.

"Fat or thin, he's a bad one," Maybel responded firmly. "I'll not be unhappy to see Lord Tom back and in charge of Otterly. He says it is for Banon."

"I know," Rosamund said.

"Lord Leslie's mission, then, did fail," Father Mata said quietly.

"Aye," Patrick answered him. "We remained in San Lorenzo the rest of the winter, for we were thought to be lovers briefly escaping from the obligations of our lives. Finally, on April first we began our return home, stopping first in Paris to reassure King Louis of King James' fidelity."

"It is unfortunate you were not successful, for peace is better than what will now come," the priest said.

"Are you aware," Maybel asked, "that Logan Hepburn has a wife?"

"I am," Rosamund replied. "I was at his wedding to Mistress Jean, and we stopped last night at Claven's Carn."

"I wonder that you would not have him," Edmund said slowly, and then seeing the look in his niece's eye, he stopped.

"Where is Glenkirk?" Father Mata inquired politely of the earl.

"In the northeast Highlands. I am long a widower with a grown son and grandchildren," Patrick answered him, offering the information he knew all of those who loved

Rosamund sought from him.

"Patrick will remain with us as my guest for a time," Rosamund told them.

"They're lovers," Maybel said afterwards to her husband, Edmund. "I never thought that my lass would be such a woman."

"Leave her be, Maybel," Edmund said quietly. "She is really in love for the first time in her life, and she is content. Can you not see it? Does she not deserve some happiness? We have been with her since her birth. We know what she has suffered and what she has endured. Rosamund has always done her duty by Friarsgate. She is entitled to some personal happiness. She is no longer a child."

"She should marry again," Maybel said stubbornly.

"Mayhap she will one day," her spouse replied. "And mayhap not."

"You thought Logan Hepburn would be a suitable mate for her," Maybel persisted.

"I did, but Rosamund did not," came the answer.

"But he loved her!" Maybel said.

"But he made the mistake of not telling her that the depth of his passion was for her and her alone. He could not keep silent about his need for a son. Rosamund did not like the idea she was being pursued because she was proved fecund, Maybel. I like this Earl of Glenkirk she has brought home."

"He could be her father," Maybel said, outraged.

"I doubt the depth of his feelings are particularly parental where my niece is concerned," Edmund chuckled.

His wife swatted irritably at him. "He'll not wed her. He has no need for a wife."

"And Rosamund has no need for a husband," Edmund reminded his mate.

"But to flaunt her lover before her daughters," Maybel fussed.

"I am certain they will be discreet," Edmund assured her.

"Banon and Bessie are not apt to see or understand it, but Philippa is eight now, and she has a sharp eye," Maybel said.

"Remind her of that," Edmund suggested gently.

"I most certainly will!" Maybel replied indignantly. "She has had him put in the chamber next to hers, and there is a connecting door. What would the children think if they entered her room and found that earl in her bed?"

Edmund chuckled, but Maybel looked outraged. "You will not be content, old woman, until you have had your say. So go and have it now."

Throwing him an angry look, Maybel hurried off to find Rosamund. Her step was determined as she climbed the stairs. Reaching her mistress' chamber, she opened the door without knocking. Surprised, Rosamund, who was alone, turned.

"Ah, Maybel, it is so good to be back," she said, smiling, and then, seeing the look on the older woman's face, she asked, "What is it? What is troubling you?"

"That man should not be here," Maybel answered bluntly. "To display your lover to your innocent daughters! To expose them to your lechery is unforgivable. What are you thinking, child? Have you considered your lasses at all?"

Rosamund drew in a long breath and then exhaled. "Sit down," she invited Maybel, motioning her to the bed. She, however, remained standing. "Do you recall my age now?" she asked the older woman, who shook her head. "I am twenty-three, Maybel. I have outlived three husbands, and I have three daughters. For twenty years I have done what was best for Friarsgate and its people. I will continue to do so. What I will not do, however, is be criticized for taking a bit of happiness for myself. I love you dearly, for you are the mother who raised me after my own perished. But that does not allow you the right to censure me. No one is more aware of my daughters than I am. Neither Patrick nor I will expose them to what you term 'our lechery.' We are lovers, yes. We have been since the first night we met and our eyes found each other across the Great Hall at Stirling Castle. I cannot explain it, and neither can he. It is simply the way it is. But to put your mind at ease, he would wed me if I would have him. He knows I prefer not to remarry, and so he does not press me. There can be no bairns of our coupling, for his seed was rendered lifeless years ago by an illness. Now, that should satisfy your curiosity, and I will not discuss it further."

"Why won't you wed him?" Maybel demanded, satisfied, but still inquisitive.

"Because I will not leave Friarsgate, and his allegiance is to Glenkirk," Rosamund explained. "He will return to Scotland this autumn. Perhaps he will come back to Friarsgate again, and perhaps I shall never see him again. Neither of us knows what will happen, but we know we are not meant by the fates to be together always. Now, Maybel, that is an end to it. I shall say no more, and you will be your dear self to Patrick."

"A woman who doesn't want to be a wife," Maybel opined. "I do not understand it at all!"

Rosamund laughed. "I know," she said. "It will ever be a puzzle to you, dear Maybel. I do apologize for flummoxing you so."

Maybel stood up. "Well, at least it is settled between us, child. Your earl seems a nice enough fellow. I can see you love him as you have never loved another. I'll go back to the hall now and see that the supper is ready. Where is that lazy Annie?"

"I have seen she and her husband have a comfortable room. I want her to rest for a few days. She has traveled all the way from San Lorenzo with a bairn in her belly. She is very tired."

"You spoil the wench," Maybel grumbled. "After dinner I'll have your bathwater brought so you may bathe." Then she departed Rosamund's chamber, closing the door firmly behind her.

"She loves you very much," Patrick said, stepping through the door connecting their two chambers.

"You heard it all?" Reaching up, she stroked his handsome face with her fingers.

"I was about to come through when she burst in," he replied. "She is right, you know. We must not set a bad example before your daughters. They are charming, by the way. I am particularly enamored of your youngest."

"When we retire to our chambers we will lock both doors to the hallway," Rosamund said. "There will be no interruptions, my lord. And you will share my bath tonight. I have a delightfully commodious tub for two. Owein always liked bathing with me," she told him with a mischievous smile.

"He was obviously a man of good taste and discernment," the earl said.

"Come and lie with me," Rosamund begged.

"It is almost the supper hour, and it would not do if we did not appear, or worse, appeared flushed and rumpled," he advised.

"We will just lie together and talk," she promised him.

They stretched out upon her bed together.

"Your lands are fair," he told her, "and very different from mine. Glenkirk stands amid the hills, though I have a loch, too. We can grow only what we need to sustain ourselves. Your fields, however, are bounteous enough to feed your vast flocks as well as your people. I look forward to riding out with you tomorrow."

"We are indeed blessed," Rosamund agreed. "Why must you leave me, Patrick? Can your son not manage your lands? Are you really needed at Glenkirk?"

"Until King James made me the Earl of Glenkirk, Rosamund, I was the laird of Glenkirk. I still am to my folk. I am their lord and the source of all that is good for them. I will be as long as I live," Patrick said quietly. "My son will not be accepted until I am dead. He will be respected as my authority in my absence, but he will not be accepted as their master, Rosamund. I know why you do not leave Friarsgate. It is for the same reason. And your girls are too young to manage on their own."

"I was managing at their age, but it was difficult, and I very much resented my uncle Henry, who coveted Friarsgate for himself. I will not put my daughters in that position. Maybel, Edmund, and my uncle Richard, who is the prior of St. Cuthbert's, protected me from harm, but it was hard on them, and they are older now."

"So we are at the same impasse as we have ever been," he said softly.

Tears rolled down her cheeks. "I know," she admitted, "and I hate it!"

He kissed the tears from her face. "We must be grateful for what we have," he told her quietly.

She nodded, but beneath her acquiescence anger was beginning to burn. She loved this man, and she always would. She didn't want to be separated from him. Ever.

At the evening meal the Earl of Glenkirk was seated on the lady of Friarsgate's right hand. And on his right hand was Philippa Meredith, the heiress to Friarsgate. Banon and Bessie had been fed earlier and were abed now, but at eight Philippa came to table with the adults.

"You are very handsome for an old man," Philippa observed.

"And you, I think, look like your mother," he replied, restraining his laughter.

"Maybel says I am my mother, too," Philippa responded. "Are you going to live here forever, my lord?"

"Nay," he told the child. "I have come to visit, as your mama and I became friends at King James' court. I shall depart for Glenkirk in the autumn."

"Will you ever come back?" Philippa asked. "I think my mother would be very sad if you did not come back."

"I will try to come back, Philippa," the Earl of Glenkirk said. "I know I will want to come back, but sometimes what you want and what must be are not the same."

"I thought grown-ups always got what they wanted," was the reply.

Patrick laughed softly. "Would that it were so, my pretty maid, but it is not. Grown-ups must do their duty, and more often than not that duty conflicts with what they want. Still, a duty should always come first. You must remember that, for one day you will be the Lady of Friarsgate."

The child nodded. "I think you have

given me good advice, my lord. I will remember it."

She was a serious little girl, he thought. His own lost daughter, Janet, was so different at that age. Janet, the half-wild Highland child who rode her pony at breakneck speed and protected her little brother from any who would tease him or otherwise seek to do him mischief. His Janet was as proud of her heritage as was this solemn little girl who was already gaining a sense of duty to Friarsgate. He had hated losing her to the heir of San Lorenzo, but better Rudolpho di San Lorenzo than the fate that had claimed her. Adam said that one day he would find his big sister, but Patrick doubted it.

The Earl of Glenkirk found that Friarsgate possessed the same isolation that his own Highland home did. The only news was brought by travelers, mostly peddlers coming over the border from Scotland. They learned that King James' shipbuilding was progressing apace and that the heir to Scotland's throne remained healthy and strong. Both the English and the Scots were strengthening their border garrisons. King James had signed a renewal of the alliance with France. In Europe war raged. Spain marched into Navarre, and Henry Tudor into Bayonne, awaiting their aid to win his French crown back. Disappointed, his fleet pounded the Breton coast as they made their way home to England once again.

The spring melded into a summer that seemed to move slowly one day and quickly the next. Now that Rosamund could swim, she insisted that Patrick teach her girls as he had taught her. Together they splashed about in her lake as Philippa, Banon, and Bessie giggled and sloshed each other with water in their efforts to learn.

"The water is certainly a lot colder than the sea in San Lorenzo," Rosamund remarked the first time they swam.

" 'Tis not as cold as Glenkirk's loch," he swore.

"Do you break the ice before you enter it, then?" she teased him back.

"Only in May," he assured her. "You'll see one day."

"Aye, I'll come to Glenkirk if you do not come back to me," she threatened with a grin. "Not this year, but next, I shall take my girls and we will winter in your Highlands as long as you will come back to Friarsgate with us the rest of the year."

" 'Tis fair, and a good idea, sweetheart," he agreed. "That way neither of us shirks our responsibilities to our holdings," he said.

They sat upon the lakeshore, watching the children.

"Oh, Patrick!" Rosamund said, and her voice was filled with hope. "Could we? It would be a perfect solution to the problem that besets us."

"Aye," he agreed slowly, "and then perhaps you would agree to marry me, Rosamund, and we shall never be parted again."

"Let us see how your son likes me first, darling," she advised. "I will drive no wedge between you two. Return to me in the springtime, Patrick, and if we are both of the same mind then, I shall come back with you to Glenkirk next winter with my girls."

"And we can be wed then," he told her.

She nodded. "But we must say naught to any right now, my lord. It will be our secret. There can be no marriage between us unless your son approves. Let Adam know me before you speak with him. Please."

"Very well, my darling. It shall be as you desire, for I cannot refuse you anything, it would seem."

In early September a carter arrived requesting payment for the great crate that he had transported from the port of Newcastle-on-Tyne to Friarsgate. Going into her strongbox, Rosamund counted out the coins, but she said, "Open the crate for me first that I may make certain your cargo is not damaged. Be careful!" she warned as the carter and his helper began to pull the crate apart.

Shortly, the painting as done by Maestro Loredano was revealed. The two carters lifted it from its packaging and held it up for all to see. There were great *oohs* from those gathered in the hall.

" 'Tis beautiful, lass," Edmund said. "I have never seen the like before."

"It would have traveled easier had he just sent the canvas," Rosamund noted dryly, "but I suspect that the maestro would trust no one but himself to see to the framing." Her eyes met the earl's. "I wonder what happened to the other painting."

Patrick laughed. "I suspect we shall never know, Madonna." Then he explained to Edmund and Maybel about the two paintings.

"He don't sound very respectable to me, this painter fellow," Maybel said.

"He was not respectable as we would have it," the earl answered her, "but you will agree that the fellow is talented. His rendition of Rosamund is masterful."

"Aye," Edmund agreed. "He has her so lifelike that I would expect her to step from the painting, my lord."

The harvest was now gathered in, and Friarsgate began to prepare for the winter to come. The anniversary of Sir Owein Meredith's death was celebrated in the little estate church. It was now three years since he had fallen from a tree in the orchard and broken his neck. The days were growing noticeably shorter, and the nights were now cold. Both Rosamund and Patrick were avoiding the inevitable.

"I can remain no longer or I shall have to spend the winter here," he told her one evening as they lay abed.

"Do not leave me," she begged him. "I am so fearful that if we break the spell that has surrounded us these past months I shall never see you again."

"Then come with me," he said, and he caressed her beautiful auburn hair.

She shook her head. "You know I cannot, Patrick. I am amazed at all I have done in this past year and the places I have been in that time, thanks to you. Promise me that you will return in the spring when the snows have left your Highlands. Oh, I wish you could at least remain until your birthday!"

"December is too late a time for me to travel. It is already October, and I should have gone two weeks ago," he said. "Rosamund, I am leaving tomorrow."

She cried out as if he had struck her, but then, turning a brave face to him, she said, "Then you must love me tonight, Patrick, as if you will not love me ever again!" She pulled his head to hers, and their lips met in a fierce kiss, each of them drawing from the other. She ran her tongue over his mouth, tasting him hungrily. His hands cupped her bottom, drawing her closer. "I love you!" she sobbed.

"And I love you as I have never loved another, Rosamund Bolton!" he declared. He caressed her, meaning it to be tender, but instead his touch aroused her passions. His mouth closed over a nipple, and he drew upon it even as he fondled the round soft flesh of her breasts. His fingers played between her thighs, and then she surprised him by turning herself about so she might take his manhood between her hands and suckle upon it. Her facile little tongue ran up and down the length of him. It encircled the ruby knob, and he moaned with pleasure as he experienced a delight he had not imagined her capable of giving. But before she unmanned him, he forced her away and onto her back once more. He mounted her and pushed into her welcoming heat, taking her face between his two big hands as he did, watching the subtle play of passion upon her lovely face as he thrust slowly back and forth until she was half-sobbing with her own pleasure. He bent his body now and gave her a long, slow kiss. "How is it that you make me young again, my sweet border lover? In what time and what place have we been before? I have never understood, Rosamund, but I do not care any longer, as long as I have your love for now and always!" His movements on her became more demanding.

The taste of him had been the most stimulating aphrodisiac she had ever known. She had not wanted to release him from between her lips, but she had also been developing a terrible need for him between her thighs, which he had quickly filled. Rosamund reveled in the feel of his manhood, thick and hard inside her. He taunted and teased her with his prowess as he moved back and forth, back and forth. For a long moment she believed that nothing would give her release, and then the delicious tingling began, and she was dizzy with the pleasure Patrick offered. "I love you!" she cried, and his lips met hers as her body began to experience spasms of passionate fulfillment as he released his love juices within her.

Rosamund wept afterwards. "I cannot bear it that we will be parted these next months," she sobbed.

He said nothing, for there was nothing left for him to say. Instead, he held her within the shelter of his arms and stroked her auburn head tenderly. Eventually,

Rosamund fell asleep, but Patrick remained awake for some time. Was this the last time they would be together? Nay, he did not feel that at all. He would return in the springtime, and they would love again. His instincts had proven correct so far. He had no reason to doubt them now, and he would not. Still, he regretted that he must go. The winter would seem very long without his Rosamund.

In the morning he bid them all farewell. Bessie, who had become the earl's special pet, cried to see him go. Dermid would accompany his master, but he would return in time for the birth of his first child in December. Edmund and Maybel were genuinely sorry to see Patrick depart. Rosamund put on a brave face, but Annie howled and cried until Maybel threatened to smack her.

"He'll be back, you foolish lass," she told the girl. "Were you not wed by a bishop in a cathedral? And is it not his child you carry?"

"Be brave, lass," Dermid said. "I have to go home and tell my ma, now, don't I?"

The two men mounted their horses, and Rosamund, standing by the earl's stirrup, looked up with a tearstained face and whispered, "Remember I love you, Patrick."

He leaned down, lifted her up enough to

kiss her lips, and replied, "And remember that I love you, Rosamund Bolton." Then he set her down again.

The others dispersed, returning to their duties, but Rosamund remained, watching until nothing of Patrick Leslie, Earl of Glenkirk, was visible but a faint cloud of golden dust. Returning to her bedchamber, she flung herself on the bed they had shared and wept wildly. The scent of him was yet on the pillows. *I cannot bear it,* she thought desperately. *I cannot live without him for six months. Oh, God! Why did I not have Mata marry us now? Why did I not at least go with him?* But she knew the answers to her questions even as she silently voiced them. The earl's son must approve a match between his long-widowed father and the lady of Friarsgate. Nor could she leave her girls again. Since their father's tragic death she had spent too much time away from them. Rosamund wished her cousin Tom were here now to comfort her. Then she sighed, and rising from her bed, she washed the tears from her face. She had duties to complete, and if she did not return to the hall soon, her daughters would be frightened. Taking a deep breath, the lady of Friarsgate walked from her bedchamber and down the staircase to where they all awaited her anxiously.

Chapter 11

A peddler, making his way back into England, stopped at Friarsgate in late October. He had spent the previous night at Claven's Carn. The lady of the house, he informed those assembled in Rosamund's hall, had a fine new son born earlier in the month. The lord was very pleased and was eager to show his heir to all who entered Claven's Carn.

"He got her with child quick enough," Rosamund said dryly. "She must have conceived on her wedding night, or shortly thereafter."

"It might have been your laddie," Maybel murmured softly.

Rosamund shot her a hard look. "I had no desire to wed with the lord of Claven's Carn, and well you know it. Patrick and I will marry next year if his son does not disapprove. It is what I want. It is what he wants."

"And if his son should not be content to see his father remarried, what then?" Maybel demanded, ever protective of Rosamund.

"Then we will continue on as we have," came the answer. "Adam Leslie may want to meet me before he gives his father a blessing on this match. If he does, I should certainly understand."

Maybel sighed. "Another old husband! I do not know why you would prefer Lord Leslie to Logan Hepburn."

Rosamund laughed. "I cannot explain it to you, dearest. I simply did not love Logan, but from the moment our eyes met, I knew Patrick Leslie was my destiny."

"A bitter destiny, I'm thinking," Maybel muttered.

"But it is mine to choose," Rosamund replied quietly. "No longer will I be told what I must do and whom I must wed. Those days are over."

"I never thought to hear you speak like this," Maybel responded. "That you would throw away your responsibilities astounds me."

"I am not eschewing my obligations, Maybel. I will always fulfill my duties where Friarsgate and my family are concerned. But why must I be unhappy by doing so?"

Maybel sighed. "I do want you happy, but I don't understand why you could not be happy with the lord of Claven's Carn."

"Well, I couldn't," Rosamund said, her patience wearing thin. "And he is wed now to a good lass who has given him the desired son and heir."

Maybel opened her mouth to speak again, but her husband leaned from his chair and put a warning hand on her shoulder. With a sigh of frustration, Maybel grew silent at last.

"Will Uncle Patrick return to us soon?" Philippa asked her mother.

Rosamund shook her head. "We shall not see him until next spring," she said.

"I want him to come home!" Bessie wailed, large tears rolling down her rosy little cheeks.

"So do I, baby," Rosamund replied, "but we must winter alone before we see the Earl of Glenkirk again."

"I want Uncle Tom back," Banon spoke up. "When will he return, mama?"

"Now, your uncle Thomas may well be back in time for the feast of Christ's Mass," Rosamund told her daughters with a smile. "I am certain he will bring you all lovely presents. He will soon be our neighbor, and won't that be fun?"

The three little girls all agreed it would indeed be grand to have Uncle Thomas as their neighbor.

"What will happen to your uncle Henry when Uncle Tom comes to live in his house?" Philippa queried her mother.

"It will no longer be Henry Bolton's

house," Rosamund answered her daughter, surprised that she even knew of the man. She had not seen him in several years, and while Philippa might have seen him once, she would have been very young. How had she remembered this relation? "Who has spoken to you of my uncle Henry?" she asked.

"I have," Edmund replied. "She is the heiress to Friarsgate, and it is important that she know her family's history, niece. It is better that it comes from me. I am more objective in the matter."

"And I do not understand why," Rosamund answered him. "Henry Bolton was never kind to you."

"But even given that I was born on the wrong side of the blanket," Edmund responded, "Henry could not take away the plain fact that I was the eldest and that our father loved me every bit as much as he loved Richard, Guy, and Henry. Because he was the youngest of us, he always felt it necessary to try harder. That trait developed into a foolish superiority as he grew older and comprehended that Richard and I were not legitimate while he and Guy were. Yet our father showed no preference among us. It has been quite frustrating for him, Rosamund. He has lived his entire life being haughty and arrogant because he was legitimate, and what has it gained him? His dismissive and overbearing attitude did not bring him happiness or love. It brought him two legitimate sons, one who died young and the other who is a thief. It brought him a second wife who whored with any and all, spawning a passel of bairns your uncle dared not deny for fear of being made a fool. And yet everyone knew. It gained him naught but your scorn. And now he is brought low. Only the kindness of Thomas Bolton will allow him to live out his days in comfort."

"He doesn't deserve it," Rosamund said bitterly.

"Nay, he does not," Edmund agreed. "Yet your cousin Tom will keep his word. He is a truly good Christian, Rosamund, whatever else he may be. And you have found your own happiness at last, so be generous of heart, niece, and forgive Henry Bolton. I have, and Richard did long ago."

Rosamund was thoughtful for a long moment, and then she said, "If Tom returns for Christ's Mass and the feast days following it, perhaps I shall invite my uncle Henry to be with us."

"More you the fool," Maybel said low.

"He is a toothless dog, wife," Edmund answered her.

"Even a toothless dog may be dangerous if he is rabid," she snapped sharply.

"If it would make you uncomfortable

then I shall not ask him," Rosamund said soothingly to her old nursemaid.

"Nay," Maybel replied. "I'll not be responsible for preventing you from making your peace with the old devil, if you will make it. He'll be dead soon enough."

In early December a letter came to Friarsgate from Glenkirk, brought by one of the Leslie clansmen. He was given shelter for the night and a hot meal. Dermid returned with him just in time for his son's birth. Rosamund sat down to read what her lover had written. She would give the messenger a letter to return to Glenkirk. Patrick wrote that his trip home had been uneventful. His son had taken fine care of Glenkirk in his absence. He had already spoken to Adam in confidence regarding their marriage. His daughter-in-law, Anne, was not told.

Adam was agreeable to this match between his father, particularly understanding that there would be no offspring due to his father's condition. He would, however, come with his father to Edinburgh in the spring to meet Rosamund. The earl wrote to Rosamund that because the winter was setting in, he did not know if he might communicate with her again. They would meet at an inn in Edinburgh called the Unicorn and Crown on the first day of

April. They would visit the king at court and ask his permission to be wed in his own chapel by the young archbishop of St. Andrew's, Alexander Stewart. They would then return to Friarsgate while Adam Leslie rode north with the news of his father's marriage. In the autumn, Patrick and Rosamund would travel to Glenkirk for the winter months. The earl spoke of his love for her and of how he missed Rosamund. His nights, he wrote, were long, cold, and dreary without her, his days gray and gloomy. He missed the sound of her voice, her laughter. He wished nothing more than to have her within his arms once again. "I will never love anyone as I love you, sweetheart," he concluded.

Rosamund read the missive, smiling with her happiness. She turned to the clansman who had brought it. "Have you been in the castle's Great Hall, lad?"

"Aye, m'lady," he replied.

"And has the painting of the earl been delivered and hung?"

"It came in the summer when the earl be away. Lady Anne were very surprised to see it. It was nae hung until the master returned. It be a fine painting. So lifelike, m'lady. All who see it say so."

Rosamund nodded. "The painting of me in this hall was painted by the same artist," she said.

"Aye," the clansman said. "I can see 'tis similar."

"I will be sending you home with a message for the earl," Rosamund told him.

"Thank ye, m'lady," the messenger said, and he went off with a servant to be given a sleeping space.

"I must be in Edinburgh on April first," Rosamund said.

"Oh, mama, must you go away again?" Philippa protested.

"Would you like to come with me?" her mother inquired.

"Me?" Philippa squealed excitedly. "Go with you to Edinburgh? Oh, mama! Aye, I should very much like to go with you. I have never been anywhere in all of my life."

"I did not go to King Henry's court until I was thirteen," her mother replied.

"Will I meet King James, mama? And Queen Margaret? Will we go to the Scots court?" Philippa demanded.

"Yes," her mother said, smiling. "We may even celebrate your ninth birthday there. Would you like that, Philippa?"

Philippa's face shone with her approval.

"You spoil her," Maybel said. "You must not spoil her."

"Children should be spoiled. Lord knows you did your best to spoil me, though you forget it now," Rosamund teased the older woman gently.

"I tried only to make up for Henry Bolton when you were a wee thing," Maybel defended herself. "I had no opportunity to spoil you once you were in Hugh Cabot's charge, for he enjoyed spoiling you himself, God assoil his good soul!"

"Aye, God bless both Hugh Cabot and Owein Meredith," Rosamund responded.

The Leslie clansman departed the following morning with a letter to his master from the lady of Friarsgate. Her correspondence to him was much as his to her had been. She had written of her loneliness without him, a loneliness such as she had never known in all her life until now. She had written of her daughters and of her estate, of their preparations for winter and how they were waiting eagerly for Tom's return. She told him that Claven's Carn had an heir at last. And she closed by sending him her undying love and telling him how eager she was for their reunion on the first of April, that she would bring Philippa to Edinburgh so both his only son and her eldest daughter could witness their marriage vows. She put a drop of her white heather scent upon the parchment, smiling as she did so.

On the twenty-first of December, St. Thomas' Day, Tom appeared back at Friarsgate, bringing with him her uncle

Henry. The children swarmed about this favorite relation hardly noticing their great-uncle. Rosamund, however, was shocked. Henry Bolton had indeed changed for the worse. He was gaunt, and his face wore a death's-head.

"You are welcome at Friarsgate, uncle," Rosamund greeted him.

His almost colorless eyes fastened upon her. "Am I?" he asked with just a touch of his old spirit. He leaned heavily upon a carved cane. "Lord Cambridge would insist I come, niece. He has purchased Otterly from me."

"Tom was right to bring you, uncle," Rosamund replied. "I am told you are alone now, and these festive December days should not be spent alone, without family. I was waiting only for Tom to send to Otterly for you."

Henry smiled cynically, the facial expression almost a grimace. He nodded. "I thank you for your welcome, niece."

"Come, uncle, and sit by the fire," Rosamund said. "Lucy, fetch Master Bolton a goblet of spiced hot cider." She led him to his place, seating him in a high-back chair with a tapestry cushion. "Your ride was cold, and the dampness threatens snow, I fear." She took the goblet her serving girl brought and put it in his gnarled hand.

"I thank you," he said, and he sipped gratefully at the hot cider. Slightly revived, his glance swept the hall. "Your daughters are healthy," he noted.

"They are," she agreed.

"The tallest one is your heiress?" he asked.

"Philippa, aye. She will be nine in April," Rosamund responded.

He nodded once more, then fell silent, the gnarled hand reaching out to stroke one of the hall dogs, a greyhound, which had come to his side.

Rosamund moved away from her uncle. She had thought that Maybel exaggerated Henry Bolton's state, but the older woman had not. Her uncle was pitiful, though she still sensed he could be dangerous if permitted. They would see he did not have any opportunity to cause difficulty.

Tom now hugged his cousin. "My dear, dear girl!" he exclaimed. "It is so good to see you once again and to return to Friarsgate. My business in the south is concluded. My Cambridge estate is sold to a newly knighted gentleman who paid quite a premium to gain it. Otterly is now mine. I did stop at court to pay my respects to his majesty. The queen strives for another child now that Scotland's queen is delivered of a fine laddie. King Henry is not pleased by his sister's successful accom-

430

plishment. He speaks of her as if she had betrayed him personally, and worse, as treasonous to England."

"When Queen Katherine gives him a son, he will consider differently," Rosamund said. "Remember, Hal never enjoyed being beaten at nursery games."

Tom chuckled. "Too true, cousin. But he would have Spain to marry when many advised against it. They have been wed several years now, and no living heir or heiress to show for it. A stillborn daughter, and wee Henry of Cornwall, born and died in the same year. There has been no sign of a child in two years. And there is his brother-in-law, Scotland, with six healthy bastards and a legitimate fair son for his heir. Nay, our King Henry is not a happy fellow."

"How fortunate, then, that we do not have to have anything to do with his court," Rosamund said.

Tom nodded. "Now, dear girl, what of your handsome Scots earl?" he asked.

"Patrick has returned to Glenkirk, but we are to meet in Edinburgh on the first day of April, Tom. We have decided that we will wed. We will spend part of the spring, the summer, and the autumn here at Friarsgate, and the winters at Glenkirk. That way neither of us deserts our responsibilities," Rosamund explained. "Patrick was most pleased with the way his son, Adam, managed Glenkirk in his absence. I can hardly wait until the spring, cousin. And I shall bring Philippa with me."

"With us, dear girl. I do not intend you wed again without me in attendance," he told her with a smile. "And what news from Claven's Carn? Has Lady Jean done what was expected of her?" And Tom grinned wickedly at his cousin.

"She birthed a healthy son in early October," Rosamund answered him. "A peddler returning to England brought word some weeks ago."

"But Logan Hepburn has not communicated with you," Tom noted.

"I would not expect Logan to do so," Rosamund replied. "We did not part on the best of terms, Tom. The night Patrick and I were forced to seek shelter at Claven's Carn, he fought with me and then drank himself into a stupor. We did not see him the following morning before we left, for which I was most grateful."

"Uncle Tom! Uncle Tom!" Rosamund's three daughters were surrounding him. "What have you brought us?" Their small faces were eager with anticipation.

Tom swept Banon up into his arms and kissed her rosy cheek. She giggled happily, glad to know she was still a favorite. "Now, my little lasses," he said. "I have one gift for each of the Twelve Days of Christmas for each of you."

"But uncle," Philippa responded, "Christ's Mass is not for another four days."

"I know," he replied, eyes twinkling, "and so my little poppets, you will have to possess your wee souls of great patience until then."

" 'Tis not fair," Banon, who was six, protested.

"Shame on you all," Rosamund scolded her daughters. "I cannot believe you are so greedy. Run along, now, and have your suppers. Philippa, you will remain."

Tom put Banon down, but not before giving her another kiss. Then he watched fondly as the two younger girls made their way from the hall. "They have grown even in the few months I was away," he said.

Rosamund nodded. "I know," she said. "In the months I was away, the same thing happened. I don't ever want to leave my lasses again."

He took her hand, and they sat together on a settle by the fire. Opposite them, Henry Bolton dozed, the greyhound now lying across his feet. "Your uncle has found a friend," Tom observed. "God help the man, for he has no others."

Rosamund sighed. "I must forgive him his treatment of me as a child," she said.

"He is to be pitied. I have not feared him since I was six and Hugh took my care upon himself. Poor Uncle Henry. Arranging my marriage to Hugh Cabot was his downfall."

"More your salvation," Tom chuckled, and Rosamund smiled.

"Aye," she agreed.

"So you are to be the Countess of Glenkirk, dear girl. He loves you deeply, but you know that, for you love him every bit as much," Tom said.

"It seems so strange," Rosamund replied, "to have found such love as I have found with Patrick. How I wish he were here now, Tom! God's blood, I miss him more with each passing day. I do not know if I can wait until April to see him again, to marry him, and be his wife. His title I care naught for, but I know I have never loved anyone as much as I love him."

Tom shook his head. "I will admit that I have never seen such passion as I saw between you two. I am glad you changed your mind, cousin, and decided to wed him. You would never again be happy otherwise."

"He will not live forever," Rosamund noted. "I will one day have to be without him, but I care not! I can think only of the months we have had together and the years we will have together. We met just a year ago on the eve of Christ's Mass, Tom."

"Even as poor Logan Hepburn was contemplating a marriage to you," her cousin said.

"Why must everyone speak of Logan Hepburn?" Rosamund asked him. "I do not love him. I did not give him my promise to wed him. I wanted no other husband in my life a year ago. Logan sought only a broodmare, and the swift results of his eager couplings with Mistress Jean prove my point."

"Indeed they do," her cousin agreed calmly. "I suppose we all speak of him because we expected that you would wed him eventually. We thought you desired a bit of courting, Rosamund, nothing more. That when he had softened your heart, you would agree to marry him. Did you feel nothing at all for the man?"

"At first he fascinated me," she admitted, "but then his constant nattering about an heir began to seriously irritate me. He never wanted me for myself, Tom."

"I think, mayhap, he did," her cousin said softly. "But he is a rough borderer and knew not how to express himself properly to you."

" 'Tis water beneath the bridge now," Rosamund said. "He has his son, and I have my love. We should both be content and happy, Tom. I know I am."

Henry Bolton listened to their conversation, eyes closed, his breathing shallow. So that damned Hepburn from over the border had been so bold as to seek Rosamund's hand at long last. Perhaps he had made a fatal error years back when the then lord of Claven's Carn had asked for the wench for his eldest son. They would have taken her away from Friarsgate, and he would have been left with it. He might even have offered the old lord a gold dowry in exchange for the estate. He could have borrowed on the land to raise it. But as his niece said, 'twas water beneath the bridge. And she, bold creature, had somehow attracted the attentions of a Scots earl. She would be a countess, and her small daughter would be left at Friarsgate when her mother went north. If only he could find a way to contact his son Henry. If he could kidnap this new heiress and wed her to his son, all should not be lost. If he did not woo his son away from the wicked life he was now leading, the lad would eventually end up at the end of the hangman's rope. He must think on this, Henry Bolton considered as he sat in his niece's hall eavesdropping.

Rosamund kept a good Christmas. Yule logs burned in the hall's fireplaces. The chamber was decorated with pine, box-wood, ivy, and holly. Fine beeswax candles burned about the room for the entire twelve days, and there were feasts each afternoon. Mummers from her estate came into the hall to entertain them. There were roasted apples and gingerbread men to eat, mulled cider and wine to drink. There was a side of beef that had been packed in rock salt and roasted. The Friarsgate folk were invited into the hall each day, and on the feast of St. Stephen Rosamund gave every one of her people gifts of fabric, small coins, sugar creatures, and in certain cases, fishing and hunting rights, to help them survive the winter months. No one was overlooked in the celebrations, especially Annie and Dermid. Their son had been born on the fourth day of December, and Rosamund's gift to them was the promised cottage.

Tom was as good as his word. He gave Rosamund's small daughters gifts on each of the Twelve Days of Christmas. And so none of the trio be jealous of the others, each day's gifts were almost identical. There were new leather boots one morning and new blue velvet gowns another. There were fine leather gloves sewn with seed pearls. Gold chains one day, jeweled ear bobs another. Pearl necklaces were tendered on the sixth day, a packet of silk ribbons on the seventh. There were small woolen cloaks trimmed with rabbits' fur on the eighth day, carved wooden balls and painted hoops on the ninth. The tenth day brought little red leather saddles, the eleventh day red leather and brass bridles. And on the Twelfth Day of Christmas each of Rosamund's daughters was gifted with an animal for riding. Bessie and Banon had white ponies. Banon's beastie had a single black hoof and Bessie's had a black star on its forehead. Philippa was given a pure white mare just fourteen and a half hands high.

"You are so very, very generous to them," Rosamund said, truly touched by his great kindness.

"Nonsense," he protested. "What is my wealth for if not to purchase small fripperies to give pleasure to my girls?"

"You can hardly call your gifts fripperies," Rosamund laughed.

"When you wed with your earl," Tom told her, "it is not likely we shall have another Christmas together again, particularly if you winter in Scotland."

"You will come to Glenkirk at Christmas," she said quickly.

"What?" he exclaimed, looking quite horrified, "I think not, dear girl. You may enjoy a winter in your lover's Highland eyrie, but I should not." He shuddered.

"The very thought of it is most distressing."

"That is just an excuse to avoid coming," she teased him. "I will wager you will ride over the border most eagerly to Stirling and King James' Christmas revels, Tom."

"The Scots king keeps a most merry holiday," he admitted with a grin. Then his look sobered. "God's blood, cousin! I have forgotten to tell you. When I stopped to see King Henry in the autumn I met a fellow named Richard Howard. He asked if I knew you. I told him, of course, that you were my most beloved cousin."

Rosamund paled. "He was the English ambassador to San Lorenzo," she replied. "I saw him at court after Owein died, but we were never introduced. He thought he knew me when we met at the duke's palace in San Lorenzo. While I most assuredly knew who he was, I was able to tell him honestly that we had never before met. Did he ask you any questions, Tom? Please think back, I beg you!"

"He asked if you had been to court, and I admitted you had indeed and that in fact you were a friend of the queen's, having been with her in your girlhoods and later after your husband died. But he was too inquisitive, and so I answered no more of his questions. Why are you concerned?"

"I did not want him to mention it to the king. Hal would consider it a fault that I visited San Lorenzo in the company of a Scots earl, I fear. I hoped he would not learn of it, especially now that I am to marry Patrick Leslie. I need no interference from our lusty king," Rosamund answered him. "Nothing happened in San Lorenzo that would have been of real interest to any king, let alone Henry Tudor. I think, however, Lord Howard felt the need to report something, lest he be considered useless to his master."

"The king said nothing to me," Tom responded. "If the purpose of Lord Leslie's mission was not public, then I believe you have no cause to fear."

"I hope not," Rosamund replied. "You know how jealous Hal can be."

Tom changed the subject, smiling at his cousin and saying, "I have a proposal to make to you, dear girl. While I have inherited great wealth, there is still my grandfather's enterprise, which supplies me with more funds each year. You have said since your return that you would like to market your fine woolen cloth in France. I believe we should go even farther than France."

"I have not the wool for a larger market, Tom," she answered him.

"That is true. But we can increase your flocks over the next few years while building a demand for the wool, and particularly the Friarsgate Blue cloth," he told her. "I cannot sit idle once Otterly is rebuilt, dear girl. I need an amusement. I think we should own a ship in which to transport the cloth abroad. What do you think? We could have a new vessel built in the shipyards in Leith while we prepare. It will take at least two years for us to make ready on all fronts, my dear Rosamund."

"Build our own ship?" She was thoughtful. "I have not the means for it, Tom."

"Of course you don't, but I do," he said calmly. "We shall be partners in this venture, cousin. I shall supply the vessel and any funding necessary. You shall supply the wool and the labor."

"It would appear that you are putting up more than I am," Rosamund answered him. "And we will need more sheep. You must be the senior partner in such an undertaking, Tom."

"We shall be equal partners," he told her. "Think on it, Rosamund. While the initial outlay is mine, afterwards most of the responsibility will fall on your shoulders. Besides, you and your daughters are my heirs. Why should you have to wait until I am dead and gone to benefit from my largesse? Especially when we can build something together."

"It is such a generous offer," Rosamund said.

"It is my Twelfth Night gift to you, dear girl," he told her with a broad smile. "Until you came along, cousin, I was but marking time. My life was dull and seemingly endless. After my sister died I had no one, but then you entered my life. I began to enjoy myself again. I found new meaning. I have a family once more. We shall build this little enterprise of ours together, Rosamund. Now say thank you, Tom, and agree with me."

Rosamund burst out laughing. "Thank you, Tom," she responded. "I do agree with you. Friarsgate wool is finer than much of what I saw in France. I do believe there is a market for it. We shall make a market for it!"

"And by keeping the supply low at first, we may keep the price high," he chuckled. "God's blood! There speaks the merchant in me. The king and his court would be most horrified to hear Lord Cambridge speaking thusly." He was wearing a most satisfied grin. "But then, I never really was of noble blood," he chuckled again.

"I am amazed at you coming to settle back in Cumbria," Rosamund said. "Once I remember you telling me that it was beautiful, but you wondered how I bore the lack of civilized company. Yet now you are willing to do so."

"That was before my family reappeared," he defended himself. "And I did keep the houses in London and Greenwich. We will go sometimes, and the girls must one day visit the court. We cannot have them growing up thinking Friarsgate is the world, even if it is the best part of it."

"When are you beginning your reconstruction of Otterly?" she asked him.

"The house is being torn down now," he said, "and the site will be cleared, but we cannot begin building until the spring. I shall start after your wedding to the earl."

"What are we to do with Uncle Henry in the meantime?" she said.

"I had a small but comfortable house constructed for him this autumn past. He has been living there with Mistress Dodger, the housekeeper I hired to look after him. Twelfth Night is almost over, cousin. Tomorrow we shall send Uncle Henry back to his own little nest. It is time. He is beginning to look too comfortable here at Friarsgate, and I find he asks too many questions. I suspect for all his tale of woe he is yet in contact with his son Henry the younger. He has said to me that he wishes he might save this lad from a bad life and a worse end."

Rosamund nodded. "I don't want him getting the idea that he might marry his son to one of my girls," she said. "I would put Friarsgate to the torch before I allowed that."

"We will see his dreams have no basis in reality," Tom replied.

"And yet I cannot help but feel sorry for him," she answered. "Still, I am not quite able yet to forgive him my youth. I do not really recall my parents, but from the time they died and Henry Bolton came into my life, I was miserable. Only when Hugh came was I safe. I want to be generous of nature to him, Tom, but I just cannot be."

"Then do not," he advised her. "Edmund and Richard have been almost saintly in their forgiveness, but they did not suffer the brunt of Henry Bolton. You did. Perhaps one day you will be able to forgive him, but now is not the time."

Rosamund took her cousin's hand in her own and kissed it tenderly. "You are so wise, Tom. If you are grateful for me, I am doubly grateful for you."

The following day Henry was transported in a comfortable covered cart back to his own home. Before he left he looked about the hall a final time. Seeing Philippa, he remarked, "Your eldest is nine, niece?"

"In April," Rosamund said. "Why?"

"My Henry is fifteen now. A good age for marriage."

"My cousin has become a thief. Hardly a match for an heiress," Rosamund said tartly. She led him from the hall, and a servant helped him into the cart.

" 'Tis only that he has no home any longer, and his mam's behavior broke his heart, niece. With a bit of good fortune he could become an upstanding man once again," Henry reasoned.

"I wish him good luck, then," Rosamund replied. Then she added, "But put from your mind any thought of a marriage between your son and my child. My girls will marry with men of higher station. Their wealth will bring them that."

"You would put Friarsgate into the hands of strangers?" he demanded, his color suddenly high. "This has always been Bolton land."

"As long as there were Bolton sons, it was Bolton land," Rosamund reasoned with him. "But there are no more Bolton sons, uncle."

"There is my son," he told her in a hard voice.

"And he will never wed with my daughter," Rosamund told him firmly. She patted her uncle's hand. "I am glad you came for the Twelve Days of Christmas, uncle. I believe your visit has done you good. You seem stronger than when you arrived. Farewell now, and God go with you." She turned, and hurried back into the house. She could feel her anger rising. Damn Henry Bolton and his spawn! Would the man never give up his quest for Friarsgate? No, she thought. Not as long as he lived.

The winter set in about them. The hills were white with the snows. The lake froze for a short time. Rosamund, Tom, and the girls, bundled in their warmest capes and furs, amused themselves sliding upon the icy surface of the water. They celebrated Candlemas on the second of February, and at midmonth the ewes began lambing. The shepherds watched over their flocks carefully. There had been a rumor of a wolf in the district, and the new lambs were an easy target.

"Put them in the barns at night," Rosamund ordered. "I will lose not a one."

"We will purchase some of those Shropshires you've wanted, come spring," Tom said.

She nodded with her agreement. "Aye, I should like a flock of them, Tom."

The shortest month was quickly over, and the hills began to show signs of life again, greening slowly as the month progressed. She had heard nothing more from Patrick but then he had warned her it would be nigh impossible to get another message through to her.

It would take two days to reach Edinburgh from Friarsgate. Annie, of course, would not be able to come with her mistress. Her younger sister, Lucy, had been being trained all winter to temporarily take her place and in future act as Annie's helper. Annie was disappointed, but every time she looked at her infant son she realized she was more content to have her wee Harry than to go with her mistress.

They had all been sewing throughout the winter so that Philippa might have two new gowns to take with her when she accompanied her mother. The young girl had her mother's coloring. One of Philippa's gowns was a medium blue velvet, and the other was a rich brown. Philippa was so excited she could hardly remain still at the fittings. She was also to have new chemises and caps. The Friarsgate cobbler made the young girl a pair of square-toed shoes with round enamel buckles decorated with colorful paste jewels.

"I have never had shoes like this!" she exclaimed excitedly when she was presented with them.

"They are for Edinburgh," Rosamund said. "You'll be wearing your boots until we get there. These shoes must last you a good long while, unless, of course, your feet grow too quickly. Try not to let your feet grow, Philippa," her mother cautioned.

Spring now took hold at Friarsgate with the ice gone from the lake and the white sheep dotting the green hillsides. Midmorning of the twenty-eighth, Rosamund and her little party departed for Edinburgh. She had resigned herself to spending the night at Claven's Carn. There was simply no way they could bypass it and reach decent shelter. She sent a messenger ahead with her request for shelter, and in late afternoon they reached their destination.

"Do try and behave, dear girl," Tom teased her wickedly.

Rosamund shot her cousin a fierce look. "I will, if he will," she replied, and Tom cackled with laughter.

They passed through into Claven's Carn's courtyard to be met by a Hepburn clansman who helped them from their horses and escorted them into the Great Hall.

Jeannie came forward, smiling, to greet them. "Rosamund Bolton, it is good to see you once again. Lord Cambridge. And who is this lovely lassie? Your daughter, from the look of her." She took Rosamund's two hands in hers and kissed her on both cheeks. Then she gave her hand to Tom who kissed it gallantly.

"My dear lady," he said, "you positively

bloom, I am pleased to see."

"Come sit by the fire and warm yourself," Jeannie invited them. "The spring is trying to gain hold here in the borders, but it was still, I will wager, a cold ride."

She signaled to a servant, and he brought a tray of mulled wine forth for her guests.

"This is my daughter Philippa Meredith," Rosamund introduced her child to the lady of Claven's Carn.

Philippa curtsied beautifully. "Madame," she said.

"Your eldest?" was the polite query.

"Aye," Rosamund answered her. "And your bairn?"

Jeannie nodded to a cradle by her side. "He sleeps," she said. "He is such a fine laddie! He shall have a brother come the autumn." And her hand went to her belly proudly.

"Or a sister," Logan said, coming into his hall. "Lord Cambridge. Madame." He came to stand behind his wife.

"Nay, Logan, 'tis another wee laddie I carry," Jeannie insisted.

"This is my daughter Philippa," Rosamund introduced her eldest.

"You have grown somewhat since the last time I saw you, Mistress Philippa," Logan said quietly.

"There was nowhere else where we could

break our journey, my lord," Rosamund quickly said.

"You are welcome," he replied. "To where do you travel?"

"Edinburgh," Rosamund said briefly.

"Mama is being married to the Earl of Glenkirk, and I am to be her witness!" Philippa said excitedly. "I have two new gowns and a pair of shoes with buckles!"

"How marvelous!" Jeannie said. "What color are your gowns, Mistress Philippa? And shoes with buckles, too!"

"One gown is blue, and the other is a fine golden brown, madame," Philippa replied.

"What a lucky girl you are!" the lady of Claven's Carn responded, smiling. Then she turned to Rosamund. "The earl is the gentleman who traveled with you last summer?"

"Aye," Rosamund answered her.

"He's a fine-looking man. You'll be a countess, won't you?" Jeannie smiled again, but her husband's look was dark.

"Aye, I will be, but I do not wed him for his title," Rosamund said.

"So you will desert Friarsgate," Logan growled.

"Nay, I will not. Nor will Patrick desert his Glenkirk. We will spend part of the year in England and part of the year in Scotland. It is no different than others, even the king, with many estates. And my daughters will be with me."

"I have bought Otterly from Henry Bolton," Tom quickly interjected before the conversation took a dangerous turn. "I tore the old house down and am just now beginning to build a new one."

"Which will be identical to his houses in London and Greenwich," Rosamund said, and she laughed. "My cousin dislikes change or discommoding his servants. The same people serve him wherever he goes. They, however, have spent the winter in the south without their master."

"They have been quite busy," Tom defended himself.

"Doing what?" Jeannie asked.

"I have a passion for beautiful things," Tom explained. "Consequently, I have too many possessions for two houses. I sent a list of what I wanted transported north to Otterly, and my servants have spent these last months collecting the items, cleaning them, and preparing them for their journey."

"Ah, I see," the lady of Claven's Carn replied. Then a servant came to her side and murmured in her ear. "The meal is ready now," their hostess said. "Let us to the high board. Lady Rosamund, please sit on my husband's right. Lord Cambridge, you will sit on my right, and Mistress

451

Philippa will be on my left." She led them from their places before the fireplace to the great oaken table where the food was now being brought.

The meal was a simple but well-prepared one. There was trout sautéed in butter and served with watercress; a fat capon stuffed with bread, apples, and sage; half a ham; and a lovely game pie with a flaky crust. The bread was fresh and warm. There was cheese and butter. To drink they were served an excellent brown ale. And when the meal had been consumed, a tartlet of winter pears in a wine sauce was brought forth.

"You keep a fine table, lady," Rosamund praised Jeannie.

The young woman smiled. "I was well taught. Logan does enjoy a good meal, as do his brothers."

"I notice them missing," Rosamund said softly.

"They are often late to table these nights," the laird of Claven's Carn said.

"Their wives are jealous that I have such a fine son, and even though they have bairns of their own, now that I am again with child, they seek to birth more bairns themselves," Jeannie giggled. "They are also not pleased that I have taken over the management of my household. They were most lazy. They flout my authority when they can, but it is unforgivable they are not here to greet our guests, Logan."

"The authority is yours, and they will eventually bow to it," Rosamund said. "You have simply to hold your ground, lady."

"My wife does not need advice from you," the laird growled.

"Logan!" his wife cried, blushing for him. "The lady of Friarsgate but meant to support me with her advice, which is good advice, I might add. I tell you little of the rudeness and disrespect your brothers' wives give me, but be assured that if it were possible for them to have their own homes, I should not be unhappy!"

"I did not realize, Jeannie," he quickly excused himself. "I will correct the situation as soon as I may."

"Nay, you did not know, for I do not complain. Now, ask the lady of Friarsgate's pardon, my lord," his wife instructed him.

"Nay! Nay!" Rosamund quickly spoke up. "I realized the laird meant no harm. He is but protective of his wife. I understand. My Patrick would be the same way."

"Your pardon, madame," he said nonetheless, and their eyes met.

Rosamund nodded. Then she leaned forward to say to the lady of the keep, "We must leave you early in the morning, madame. Might we be shown to our sleeping places now?"

Jeannie jumped up. "Of course, lady! Please follow me."

"I think I shall remain in the hall a while longer," Tom called after them.

"So," Logan said, after the women were out of earshot, "she is going to marry her earl."

"Aye," Tom responded.

"Do you like him?" the laird asked.

"Aye, I do," came the answer. "He loves her deeply. I have never before seen such passion between two people, Logan Hepburn. It is the right thing for both of them."

"If you say it, my lord," the laird replied gloomily. "I shall always love her."

Tom nodded. "I know that," he said. "But fate has given you a good wife, and God knows she is doing her duty by you. Two bairns in two years. You can ask no more of the lass. She is a gracious hostess, and she is devoted to you. I have never seen your hall look so fine. Be content. None of us ever gets all that we want in this life."

"Haven't you?" came the query.

Tom laughed. "Nay, not until recently," he admitted.

"You mean to live at Otterly?"

"I do, indeed. I sold my home in Cambridge. Finding my family here has made a new man of me, Logan Hepburn."

The laird nodded glumly. "Family is important," he agreed. "When is the wedding?"

"We will meet the earl and his son on the first of April at the Unicorn and Crown. Rosamund and Patrick are hoping that the king will allow their marriage to be performed in his chapel by the bishop of St. Andrews. The ceremony should be celebrated sometime in April. When is your new bairn due?"

"In early autumn," came the reply.

"Yon laddie is a fine boy," Tom noted.

For the first time Logan's face grew cheerful. "Aye, he is!" he replied enthusiastically. "He is very strong, my lord. Why, when he grips my finger I fear he will bend it. And he smiles all the time. He has obviously gotten his mother's sweet nature."

"You are fortunate," Tom said quietly. Then he arose. "Where am I to lay my head, Logan Hepburn?"

The laird arose. " 'Tis a small chamber, but one wall is against the chimney. You'll not be cold this night, my lord." And when he had settled his guest, Logan returned to the hall to sit before the fire. His son was gone from his cradle. A servant had obviously carried the lad to his mother for nursing. He sighed deeply. What the hell was the matter with him? There was peace. His lands prospered. He had a sweet wife who was as fertile as a rabbit and already one son to follow him. Why could he not be content with his life? But he knew the answer to his unspoken question.

He loved Rosamund Bolton. He had always loved her and always would. Nothing else mattered to him. It was a secret he must take to his grave, for he would not hurt Jeannie with his perfidy. She was a good lass. She was not the problem. He was. He asked himself again why it was he had not understood Rosamund enough to know she needed to hear the words "I really love you." Pressed by his family, he had babbled about heirs instead of telling her that the very sight of her set his pulses racing. That he could not sleep for the yearning he had for her. And now she would wed once again. Yet she had told him once that she would never wed again. What had changed her mind? There could be only one answer, and he knew it. She really did love Patrick Leslie, the Earl of Glenkirk. Loved him enough to leave Friarsgate for part of each year. The knowledge felt like a great weight on his heart. Why was it that she had loved Patrick Leslie at first sight, but she would not love Logan Hepburn? He had no answers to that question.

In the morning Rosamund and her party departed Claven's Carn after breaking their fast and thanking their hostess.

"Let us know when you are returning, and break your journey with us," Jeannie said graciously. "I shall look forward to seeing that handsome earl of yours again, lady."

"We will," Rosamund promised. She could do nothing else. She smiled and waved as they rode down the hill back onto the Edinburgh road.

"I do like the lady of Claven's Carn," Philippa said. "She was so nice to me. She said when we come back I may hold the baby."

Rosamund smiled at her daughter. Everything was so new and exciting for Philippa. "I like the lady of Claven's Carn, too," she told her child.

"The laird is very solemn, isn't he?" Philippa remarked. "I don't remember him very well, mama. Was he always so grave?"

"I would not know, Philippa," her mother said. "I do not know Logan Hepburn that well."

"I can't wait to see Uncle Patrick, mama. I am so glad he is going to be our new father. Banon and Bessie are, too, you know," Philippa confided.

"You have discussed it amongst yourselves?" Rosamund was surprised.

"We are young, mama, but who you wed affects us, as well," Philippa said wisely.

"Her mother's daughter," Tom murmured with a chuckle.

"When will we get to Edinburgh, mama? Will we get there today?" Philippa shifted in her saddle.

"Nay, tomorrow. Tonight we will shelter at Lord Grey's home. He lives near the city, but not quite near enough," Rosamund told her daughter.

"Scotland doesn't look much different from England," Philippa noted, looking about them as they rode. "I'm glad we are not fighting them, mama. But what will happen if King Henry does fight King James?"

"We will pray that that does not happen, my child," Rosamund said, but a shiver ran down her back. She shook it off. "Come on, Philippa! I'll race you to the top of the next hill!" And kicking her mount, Rosamund raced off, her daughter in hot pursuit.

Chapter 12

They reached Edinburgh on a chilly spring day. Philippa was wide-eyed with this sight of her first city, as was Lucy, who had traveled with them. Philippa's mouth fell open as a boy with a tray of buns on his head raced past them. There were women selling the first of the spring flowers and herbs. There were women selling milk, cream, and eggs as well as freshly churned butter, which was cut into chunks as their patrons desired. There was a man offering cups of water for sale, a poulterer with his crates of chickens, a fishmonger pushing his barrow as he shouted his wares. Philippa Meredith had never seen their like, and she didn't know where to look next. Rosamund watched her daughter, smiling at the child's amazement.

"Oh, mistress, look there!" Lucy pointed at a group of gypsies who were performing acrobatics on the street for whatever coins they might garner or steal.

They rode past the gypsies, turning into Barley Lane, where the Unicorn and

Crown Inn was located. In the courtyard, stablemen ran forth to take their horses, and Tom paid the armed escort that had escorted them from Friarsgate, counting out the coins each man was to have and then buying them all a round of ale. The men-at-arms thanked him, then clattered out of the inn's stone courtyard. There were less expensive inns where they might spend their earnings.

Rosamund's heart was racing. Was he here? God's boots! She was like a virgin with her first lovelorn swain, but the truth was she longed for the sight of his handsome face. They entered the Unicorn and Crown to be greeted by the innkeeper, a tall, thin man with a dignified stance.

"Welcome, my lord, and my ladies!" he greeted them, bowing as he spoke.

"Has the Earl of Glenkirk's party arrived yet?" Lord Cambridge asked.

"They are waiting for you, my lord. Allow me to escort you," the innkeeper said, his face impassive. He led them down a narrow hallway, opening the door at the end of it and ushering them inside. "I will fetch Lord Leslie at once," he told them. "There is wine on the sideboard. Would the ladies desire anything special now?"

"Please escort my daughter and my servant to our apartment, Master Innkeeper," Rosamund said quietly. She knelt a moment, putting her arms about Philippa. "I would greet Patrick alone, sweeting," she told the child. "You understand."

"Yes, mama," Philippa said dutifully, following Lucy and the innkeeper from the chamber.

"I need some wine," Tom said. "It becomes chilly as the afternoon wanes." He walked to the sideboard and poured himself a goblet from the pewter pitcher. Sipping it, he noted, "Why, 'tis not half-bad, dear girl. Will you have some?"

"And greet Patrick with wine on my breath?" she said. "I think not, cousin."

She arose and seated herself by the fireplace where a good fire was burning. "I shall warm myself this way."

For some minutes they waited in silence, and then the door to the room opened and a gentleman stepped inside. He went immediately to Rosamund, taking her two hands in his and kissing them. "I am Adam Leslie," he said, "and you are my father's Rosamund." He was tall and big, as his father was. His hair was a dark russet brown where Patrick's was a deep auburn. But he had not his father's deep green eyes. Adam Leslie was blue-eyed. "You are every bit as lovely as he claimed, madame." Then he turned to greet Tom. "You will be Lord Cambridge," he said, bowing.

Tom bowed back, his facile mind already

461

asking the question he saw forming on Rosamund's lips.

"Where is your father, Adam Leslie? Why is he not here to greet me?" she asked.

"He is here, madame," came the reply, "and you must be brave now for his sake."

"What has happened?" Her voice was shaking as she spoke.

Adam sat down heavily in the chair opposite Rosamund. "We arrived late yesterday," he began. "I have never seen my father so eager to get to Edinburgh. He was like a lad. We might have stayed the night several miles from the city, yet nothing would do but my father reach the Unicorn and Crown so if you arrived early today you would not think he had not come. The landlord served us an excellent dinner, and then we retired for the night. This morning my father awakened complaining of a sharp pain in his head. He arose from his bed, gave a loud cry, and collapsed. The physician is with him now."

Rosamund jumped from her chair. "Where is he? I must go to him! Take me at once, Adam Leslie!" She was pale and trembling with fear.

Adam did not argue with her. He stood and took her by the arm, saying to Lord Cambridge, "Will you come with us, too, my lord?"

Tom nodded, following as Adam Leslie led them from the chamber where they had been seated, down the corridor, and up a flight of stairs. Opening the door to one of the inn's guest apartments, he ushered them inside. Almost immediately a very tall, dark-skinned gentleman in long white robes came forth from another room.

"Ah, my lord, you have returned." He looked curiously at Rosamund and Tom. "This is the lady?" he queried.

"Aye, this is my father's betrothed wife, Master Achmet," Adam replied. "This physician was sent by the king," he explained to Rosamund and Tom.

"How is the earl?" Rosamund asked anxiously. She was still very pale and could not contain the trembling that continued to afflict her.

Seeing it, the physician took her by the arm and seated her near the fire, sitting next to her. He took her hand in his, his fingers wrapped lightly about her wrist, his gaze thoughtful. "Calm yourself, madame," he said in a quiet voice. "What has happened has happened. Your heart is racing too quickly, and that is not good for you. My lord, would you pour the lady some of that wine? When you have drunk a bit of it, madame, we will speak on the earl's condition."

Adam quickly filled a goblet and handed

it to Rosamund, who drank deeply and then, as she felt calmer, turned her amber gaze to Master Achmet.

"The earl," the physician said, "has suffered a seizure of the brain. He is yet unconscious. He may awaken with no ill affects at all. There seems to be no harm done to his limbs, for they are quite supple. He may awaken, the ability to speak gone from him. I have seen that in many cases. He may awaken with his memory impaired. Or he may not awaken at all. This is my prognosis, madame."

"Have you bled him yet?" she asked.

"Bleeding would not be advisable in this particular case, madame," the physician said. "The earl will need all his strength to recover."

Rosamund nodded. "When do you think he will awaken?" she asked.

"I do not know, madame," was the honest answer.

"I will nurse him myself," Rosamund said.

"That would be best for his lordship. The quality of women who purport to do nursing in this city is not at all good," the physician agreed.

"Tom, send a message to Friarsgate. Maybel must come!" Rosamund decided. "And we cannot remain here at the inn. You have a house in Edinburgh, don't you?"

"I sent ahead to have it opened and aired," Lord Cambridge replied. "I thought to let you and Patrick have a few days to yourselves there after your marriage, while I took young Philippa to court and showed her the sights of the city."

"When can the earl be moved?" Rosamund asked Master Achmet.

"I think it best he regain consciousness first," the physician responded.

"Adam" — Rosamund turned to Patrick's son — "forgive me for giving orders without consulting you. I am not yet your father's wife. Will these arrangements suit you?"

Adam came and knelt down next to Rosamund. "I know how much he loves you, madame, and I am content in the knowledge that you will take the best of care of him." He took her small, cold hand and kissed it gently.

"Thank you," Rosamund said simply. She turned back to the physician. "What am I to do?" she asked him.

"You must keep him comfortable and quiet. Moisten his lips regularly with water or wine. If he is able to swallow, give him wine to drink. I will come twice daily to check on my patient, madame. If there is an emergency, I can be reached either at the castle or at my house in the High Street." Master Achmet arose from his

465

place by her side. "I will leave you now," he said, bowing before he departed.

Rosamund was still wearing her cloak. She stood and unfastened it, laying it aside. "I want to see him now," she said and walked past them into the earl's bed-chamber.

Patrick lay upon the bed. His eyes were closed, his breathing shallow, his skin pale. Yet he looked no different than when they had parted last October.

"Oh, my love," Rosamund whispered softly as she sat upon the edge of the bed and took his hand into hers. His hand was clammy, and the limp fingers did not squeeze hers back. "Patrick, can you hear me?" she begged him. "Oh, God, this cannot be! Do not take him from me. From his son. From Glenkirk."

The man on the bed lay still and silent.

Rosamund did not hear her cousin until he spoke to her.

"What am I to do about Philippa? Will you tell her, or shall I?" he asked.

Rosamund looked up at him, her face stricken with her grief. "You must tell her, Tom, if you will, for I cannot. I will not leave him now."

"Shall I send her home with Lucy?" he wondered.

"Nay. Poor lass, she was so looking forward to this trip. We are here now. You heard what the physician said. Patrick could awaken and be absolutely fine. If I send her back she could miss the wedding and would not be able to visit the court. You must take her to court, Tom. And how did the king know of Patrick's illness to send a physician? I would ask Adam that."

"He has already explained that to me," Tom said. "The earl had corresponded with King James in order that your marriage be celebrated in the Chapel Royal. As soon as they got here last night, Patrick sent a message to the castle. This morning, when his father fell ill, Adam sent to the king for aid."

"He is a good son," Rosamund remarked.

"He is like his father," Tom responded.

"It is too late to dispatch a messenger today," Rosamund said. "I will write to Maybel myself, but you must see my correspondence sent in the morning by the fastest means possible, Tom. And we will move Patrick as soon as the physician says we may. He was an odd fellow, wasn't he? He is not a Scot."

"He's a Moor," Tom told her. "Another bit of information I gleaned from Adam Leslie. His family was driven out of Spain by King Ferdinand and Queen Isabella. They resettled themselves across the Strait of Gibraltar. The physician has been visiting King James' court. He is a skilled doctor, and a surgeon, as well. You know the king has begun a college for medicine here in Edinburgh. He feels a physician should be educated and that surgeons should not be barbers as well. Master Achmet is skilled in diagnosing disorders of the brain. He is famous for his knowledge. King James hopes to convince him to lecture to the Scots students. It was fortunate he was here."

"How do you obtain all this knowledge in so short a time?" she demanded of him.

Tom grinned. "I have my own skills, cousin," he told her. Then he said, "Come out into the dayroom now with Adam. Your earl is comfortable for the moment. You need not sit by his side constantly."

"His lips are dry," Rosamund replied. "Let me moisten them. I will join you shortly." She went across the bedchamber and dipped a clean cloth she found into the pitcher of fresh water sitting on the table beneath the window that looked out over the inn's back garden. The garden below was showing signs of green in many places. After returning to Patrick's side, Rosamund wiped the cloth gently over his mouth several times. He made no movement or sound at all. Rosamund felt tears beginning to fill her eyes. She blinked, and they ran down her cheeks. Impatiently she brushed them away as she bent and kissed his cold lips. Then she replaced the cloth by the pitcher and went out into the next room.

"He is so still," she said to Adam. "His lips were beginning to dry. I have moistened them." Looking about, she saw her cousin was no longer there.

"He went to seek out your little daughter," Adam said.

"Poor Philippa," Rosamund responded. "She will be very distressed to learn her beloved Uncle Patrick is ill. My girls love him very much."

"He was always wonderful with my sister, although she tried his patience greatly," Adam said.

"You never found her," Rosamund answered him. "I am sorry."

"I haven't given up hope, madame," he told her. "I will seek her until I find her. One day I shall. Then I shall bring her home."

"She is fortunate having you for a brother, Adam Leslie," Rosamund said. "My brother died when I was three. I do not remember him or my parents."

"My father has told me your history and of how you met," he replied.

"Does your wife know about me yet?" Rosamund inquired.

A small smile touched Adam's lips. "My father has told you of Anne?"

Rosamund nodded but said nothing, for she did not think it would be polite to say she had heard Adam Leslie's wife was a shrew.

He laughed a short laugh. "She is difficult," he admitted, "but it is just because she wants everything right. I have a fair mistress who keeps me happy. But Anne keeps Glenkirk in perfect order, and she has given me three children. I will ask no more of her. Nay, she does not know of you, madame, for my father was not of a mind to spend a winter locked up with her carping at him about his age and the foolishness of a man of his years thinking he was in love like some green youth. And of how a young woman would be interested only in his small wealth and title. And how if he managed to give her a child, another child would but lessen her children's inheritance. My father is, as you know, madame, a wise man. Better my wife learn of you after the marriage is celebrated."

Rosamund could not help but giggle at his recitation. "Aye, Patrick is a wise man, Adam, and I am certain he would want you to call me by my Christian name. Will you please do so?"

"I will, Rosamund, and gladly," he told her.

Tom had told Philippa of Lord Leslie's tragedy, and nothing would do but that Philippa come to her mother. The little girl could not refrain from weeping, but Rosamund calmed her daughter.

"Will you remain in Edinburgh with me, child?" she asked her daughter. "Your company will be a great comfort to me."

"Oh, yes, mama!" Philippa cried. "I shall not leave your side."

Rosamund smiled softly. "Nay. I will nurse the earl alone, Philippa. But Uncle Tom would take you to court to meet the king and the queen. It is important that you make that connection, for one day Queen Margaret could aid you. She is my oldest friend. Friarsgate needs friends on both sides of the border, given its location. You are my heiress. It is your duty to make the most of this first visit to Edinburgh. I will be content by Lord Leslie's bedside, helping him regain his health. When he is able, child, we will move to your uncle Tom's house here in town."

Philippa nodded. "Mayhap we will be there for my birthday," she said.

"I think we will," Rosamund agreed. "We are sending to Friarsgate for Maybel."

"She will not be happy to have to travel, mama," Philippa remarked.

Rosamund laughed. "Nay, she will not

be. But she will come because I call her."

"I hope Uncle Patrick gets well soon, mama," Philippa said.

"So do I, my angel," her mother concurred.

But Patrick Leslie, the Earl of Glenkirk, lay in a stupor for three days. The crisis would come sooner than later, the physician told Rosamund. In his unconscious state he was unable to swallow, and his body was drying out for lack of liquid. Halfway through the fourth day, the earl began to stir restlessly. Rosamund held a cup of water to his lips, and while his eyes did not open and he did not give any other sign of consciousness, he drank greedily until he fell back upon his pillows.

"He will live," Master Achmet pronounced upon learning of this new development.

"But he is not awake," Rosamund said.

"He is attempting to wake himself, madame. It may take another few days. Keep him comfortable and feed him watered wine."

Rosamund followed the physician's instructions. With Adam's help, she kept the earl's large body bathed and clean. She saw that he was put in a freshly laundered linen shirt each morning and again each evening. She changed his bedding daily. Patiently she held the pewter cup to his lips and coaxed him to drink a dozen times a day. She slept by his side at night in case he should awaken or otherwise need her. Her devotion was commendable. Adam began to see what kind of woman his father had fallen in love with and desired to wed. He found himself admiring Rosamund.

At first Adam had been concerned when his father had confided to him that he had fallen in love. Patrick had arrived home to celebrate his fifty-second birthday. Adam was more concerned when he learned that Rosamund was only twenty-three. It was true that marriages between many people of their class had a disparity of age between the bride and the groom. But his father had been widowed for twenty-nine years. While he certainly had a healthy appetite for female flesh, he had never evinced the slightest desire to marry again. But now his father's face lit up each time he spoke to his son of Rosamund. Each day during the winter Adam's father had written to his beloved. These letters were now in a leather pouch that the earl had brought with them. He wanted to share his winter's loneliness with this woman he adored. Adam was finally convinced that his father was not in his dotage and that spending the remainder of his life with Rosamund Bolton was the right thing for the Earl of Glenkirk to do. Now he gave her the packet of letters, but Rosamund, concerned with Patrick's health, put them aside to read another time.

When Adam met Rosamund he knew instantly that his instincts had been sound. She loved his father every bit as much as he loved her. Her concern for the earl and her tender care of him were real. Not once did she complain. Not once did she whine that now her wedding was to be delayed. Her sole reason for being, it seemed to Adam, was his father's well-being and eventual recovery. And then Master Achmet said they might move the earl to Lord Cambridge's house. While he was not fully conscious yet, he did appear stronger and able to make the short journey.

Tom had purchased a house off the High Street with a large garden in the rear that was now beginning to come into bloom. The earl was carried in a litter from the bedchamber in which he had been residing into a covered cart. Rosamund was by his side and rode in the cart with him. At Lord Cambridge's house, servingmen hurried forth to carry the litter inside and upstairs to the bedchamber where the earl would now rest. He seemed none the worse for the transfer between the inn and the house. Rosamund was beginning to show her exhaustion, but they could not convince her to leave Patrick's side.

And then Maybel arrived from Friarsgate. "As if my poor child hasn't had enough difficulty in life," she announced as she entered the house. "Where is she?"

Tom chuckled, and even Adam was forced to smile at the older woman's words. His sister's grandmother, Mary MacKay, had been much like Maybel.

"What, Maybel, no greeting for me?" Lord Cambridge teased her.

"Good day to you, Thomas Bolton," Maybel said. "And this fine fellow, from the look of him, is the earl's son." She curtsied. "My lord. Now, where is Rosamund?"

"She is upstairs, and we are both glad you are here, Maybel," Tom said. "Come, before you see her, and let us tell you what has transpired. Will you have a bit of ale?"

"I might, if it's good ale," Maybel considered as he led her into the house's small hall and settled her. "Ah, at last a seat that does not rock back and forth. I am not a good traveler, my lords," she told them. "Now, tell me all."

Adam Leslie explained what had happened though Rosamund had given Maybel some idea in her message to Friarsgate. Maybel listened and nodded as the tale unfolded.

"Has there been any improvement?" she asked when Adam had finished.

"He hasn't opened his eyes yet," Adam said, "but he is awakening. You can tell it. And he is able to drink. Rosamund has been feeding him like an infant. She makes him a drink with wine, eggs, a bit of cream, sugar, and a bit of grated cinnamon stick or vanilla bean. He seems to enjoy it, for he drinks it all each time she gives it to him. She also makes him egg custard, and she gives him milk toast."

"He is growing stronger?" Maybel said.

"Every day," came the hopeful reply.

Maybel nodded. "Is the physician bleeding him?"

"Nay. He said it is not necessary and would but weaken my father," Adam responded.

"I never heard of not bleeding a patient," Maybel remarked. "Is this a good physician? Have you consulted others?"

"He is the king's physician," Tom said. "And so you are not taken unawares, he is a Moor."

"What is that?" Maybel demanded suspiciously. "Some foreigner, I'll vow."

"Aye, he comes from Spain, and the king brought him to lecture at his college," Adam explained.

"A Jew?" Maybel queried.

"A Mussulman," Tom answered her, grinning. "An infidel, Maybel."

"God have mercy on us all," the old

woman said, crossing herself. "Are you absolutely certain he is not out to murder the earl?"

To Maybel's consternation, both men laughed. "Nay," they told her with one voice.

"He is the king's most trusted man, Maybel. I swear it," Tom said.

"Well," Maybel allowed, draining the mug of ale a servant had brought her while they talked, "if you says so, my lord, I must believe it." She stood up. "Now, take me to my child."

They both escorted her upstairs to the earl's bedchamber where Rosamund sat. She jumped up when Maybel entered the room, wordlessly hugging her old nursemaid.

"Thank God you have come!" she cried.

"Thank God and his Blessed Mother Mary, indeed!" Maybel agreed. "I have never seen you so pale, so worn. You are to go to bed at once, Rosamund Bolton, and I'll hear no nonsense about it! I am here now, and I will watch over Lord Leslie myself. You will be no use to the man when he awakens if you continue on as you have. Where is Lucy?"

"With Philippa," Adam said.

"Have you a servant girl who can help me, my lord?" Maybel asked Tom. "Not one of those flighty lasses with little more wit than a post, but a lass who can follow orders." She looked at Rosamund. "Are you still here, my lady?"

"I sleep by his side at night in case he should waken," Rosamund said.

"Well, for now you will sleep in another chamber," Maybel said firmly.

"Next door," Tom quickly said to his cousin before she might protest. "And I will find a lass among the servants to help you, Maybel. Come, Rosamund," he coaxed her, taking her by the arm and leading her from the bedchamber.

"Well, my lord" — Maybel looked straight at Adam — "what think you of this?"

Adam shook his head. "I do not know," he admitted. "I had hoped he would regain his full faculties by now. The physician says, however, that it is not unusual and that he is making a little progress each day. He believes he will open his eyes shortly."

"And what think you of my lady, Adam Leslie?" Maybel asked directly.

"I think she loves him desperately, Maybel. I pray my father recovers so that they may marry and live their lives together," Adam answered honestly.

Maybel nodded. "You are, I can see, like him. At first I was not certain it was right. I have been with Rosamund since her birth. Her sweet mother was not strong. I have protected her as best I could from those who would harm her. She has been fortunate in her men. Both Hugh and Owein adored her and she them. But her feelings for them were nothing like those for your father. I have never seen the like of such a love. I doubt few have. To see them together was to see magic," she concluded.

"I know only that I have never known my father to be so happy in all of my life," Adam told her. "My mother died birthing me, but it was said he had a fondness for her. He has never remarried, yet when he speaks of your mistress, Maybel, his whole face is alight and shines with his love for her. His happiness is palpable."

Maybel smiled at Adam. "Aye, you are like him," she repeated. "Now, get you gone, and I will watch over your father while my mistress gets a well-deserved rest."

He smiled back at her, and after bowing, he left her alone with his father.

Well, Maybel thought to herself, and isn't this a pretty mess? Patrick Leslie appeared to be sleeping, his breathing even and quiet. Maybel shook her head. The earl had been in an unconscious state for more than a full week. Was it indeed possible he would recover? She had full intentions of questioning the doctor thoroughly when he came in the evening. Maybel sat down by the earl's bed. Poor man, she thought.

Rosamund lay down in her gown, fully expecting to wake in a few hours' time. Instead, she did not open her eyes for almost twenty-four hours. When she did, Lucy was in her bedchamber preparing a bath. The tub had been set before the fireplace, and tendrils of steam arose from the scented water.

"What time is it?" Rosamund asked her sleepily.

"Why 'tis just shortly past the noon hour, my lady," Lucy replied politely.

"How long have I been sleeping?" Rosamund demanded.

"Practically a full day, I believe, my lady. Maybel said to prepare you a bath and wake you now." Lucy curtsied.

"Where is Philippa?"

"Lord Tom has taken her to the castle, my lady. He said it was past time the lass met the queen." Lucy was most chatty.

Rosamund arose quickly, crossing the floor to open the door between her chamber and the sick chamber. Maybel was sitting by the earl's bed, knitting. "Why did you allow me to sleep so long?" Rosamund said half-angrily as she moved into the room. She went to Patrick's bed and felt his forehead. It was perfectly cool to the touch. "I'll sit with him now," she told Maybel.

"Nay. You'll bathe yourself, Rosamund Bolton, for never have I known you to stink, and you do. Wash your hair, too. When you are clean, put on fresh garments, and then you will eat something. After that, you may come and sit by your beloved, but not until then, my lass."

For a moment Rosamund considered arguing with Maybel, but then she saw the futility in it. There was no emergency. Patrick was comfortable. He had no fever; nor was he restless. He had already survived a day without her. An hour more would not matter. "Yes, Maybel," she said meekly.

Maybel barked a sharp laugh. "Well, I am glad to see you still know how to bow to the proper authority," she teased.

Rosamund returned through the door connecting the chambers. With Lucy's aid, she divested herself of the clothing she had been wearing for almost ten days. She had never in her life, she realized, taken so little care of herself and her person. She was surprised that Tom had said nothing, for he was the most fastidious person she had ever known in all her life. She climbed into the oak tub, and the sweet water surrounded her, easing aches she hadn't even realized she had. She sighed.

"Warm the drying sheets by the fire, Lucy," she instructed the girl, and then she began washing her long auburn hair with the perfumed soap. Lucy rinsed her mistress' tresses after each washing, and then wrung the water from the hair and pinned it up for her mistress. Rosamund now began a serious cleansing of her person. She was shocked to see how much dirt she had collected, but then she realized that, from the moment she had arrived, there had been no time to remove the dust of her travels. She climbed from the tub at last, Lucy wrapping her in a drying sheet. Then, sitting by the fire, she let the girl wipe the water from her arms, her legs, and her shoulders. "Give me my hairbrush, Lucy."

"It's here, my lady," Lucy answered her, handing the brush to her mistress.

Rosamund unpinned her hair and began to brush her long locks free of the remaining water, her head turned to the fire to aid in the drying process. And when her hair was dry again, with Lucy's help she dressed in clean garments, almost embarrassed at how she had let herself go. What if Patrick had awakened and seen her looking no better than some dirty slut from the streets? Her fingers smoothed the orange tawny velvet of her gown. She braided her hair up and tucked it beneath a matching cap with a pretty gold trim, then adjusted her tapestried girdle about her waist.

"Mistress Maybel says you are to eat now, my lady," Lucy said. "I've already instructed the kitchen for you. I have but to pull this bell cord, and the meal will be delivered." She yanked on the cord. " 'Tis a marvelous invention, my lady, ain't it?"

"Indeed it is, Lucy," Rosamund agreed. "Perhaps we should see if we can install such a device at Friarsgate. Then perhaps you wouldn't linger in the kitchens so long."

"Oh, my lady!" Lucy blushed.

A servingman knocked upon the chamber door and entered with a tray. After handing it to Lucy, he moved the tub away from before the fire, drawing forth a small table from its place against the wall. Setting it before the chair, he took the tray back from Lucy and put it down upon the table. Then, with a short bow, he exited the room.

Rosamund sat at the table and began to eat. She was not surprised by her good appetite, for she had scarcely eaten since they had arrived in Edinburgh. The cook had sent her up a dish of four fat prawns that had been steamed in white wine. She devoured them before they cooled. On her plate was a thick slice of beef, a slice of rabbit pie with a wonderfully flaky crust, a breast of roasted capon, a slice of ham, an artichoke, and some new peas. Rosamund ate it all, mopping the gravy and juices on her plate with pieces of freshly baked bread that she tore from the small loaf on the tray. She finished the bread, smearing it with butter as she did. Lucy watched wide-eyed, and when her mistress had eaten everything on the tray, she removed it to the sideboard, and refilled her lady's cup with more wine.

Rosamund sat silently for several minutes, and then she arose. "I am going to the earl now," she said, and she crossed her chamber to enter his room.

Maybel looked up. "Ah," she said with a smile. "You do look rested and clean now. He has been restless today, but he seems well otherwise." She arose. "I will now take a bit of ease for myself. I am not as young as I once was, my child."

Rosamund put her arms about Maybel and embraced her. "Thank you," she said.

"For what?" Maybel demanded. "You are my lady, my child. You needed me, and I came. I will always come, Rosamund."

"But I know how you dislike travel even as I once did," Rosamund responded.

Maybel chuckled. " 'Tis true, lass, but this trip was not as bad as going down to

London. And I've always wanted to see this city." Then she patted the younger woman.

Rosamund moved to the earl's bedside and leaned over to feel his forehead. He had no fever. She caressed his dark hair lovingly, and as she did, his nose began to twitch. He sniffed quite distinctly several times. He had never before done that. Then, suddenly, his eyes opened. They were not at first focused, but they were open. His hand reached up to fasten about her wrist. Rosamund gave a little cry of surprise. Then she said, "Maybel! Get Adam Leslie! The earl is awakening!"

Maybel rushed from the bedchamber calling to Adam as she went. "My lord! My lord! Your father is awakening! Come quickly!"

Adam had been in the hall below. He took the stairs two at a time, almost knocking over the older woman as he dashed into the bedchamber to join Rosamund at his father's side.

The Earl of Glenkirk's eyes were beginning to focus, and seeing his son, he said, "Adam! What has happened?"

"You have been ill, father," the young man answered him. "I think now you will get well, thanks to Rosamund. She has barely left your side these ten days."

"Rosamund?" The earl looked confused.

"Yes, Patrick, my love, it is I," Rosamund said, almost weeping with her joy.

The confusion on Patrick's face deepened. Finally he said, "Do I know you, madame?"

It was as if an icy hand had plunged into her chest and gripped her heart. Unable to help herself, she let the tears roll down her cheeks. She pulled free, moving away from the bed, for she could not bear the sight of the confusion on his handsome face. "He does not know me," she whispered softly to no one in particular.

Maybel grasped her hand. "The Moor said his memory would come back slowly when he regained his senses, my baby. He has just woken up. Lord Adam is his son. He would remember his son first. Be brave!"

"I cannot bear it if he doesn't remember me!" Rosamund cried.

"You will bear what you must!" Maybel replied. "You cannot run from this, my child. And you have never been a coward. Now, the earl had just opened his eyes. Give him a chance to assemble his memories. Surely the ones he made with you are so precious that he will not have forgotten them."

Rosamund drew a long, deep breath. Then she said, "We must send for Master Achmet."

"I agree," Adam said, coming to her side. "He's tired and yet confused. Let him rest a bit now that his consciousness is restored to him. It will be all right, Rosamund." He took her in his arms to comfort her.

The feel of those strong arms about her broke her control. Rosamund began to weep as if she would never stop. "I shall die if he does not remember me," she sobbed.

Adam said nothing. There was nothing he could say that would possibly comfort Rosamund. He recalled what Master Achmet had said that first day. That his father might regain all of his memory, part of it, or none of it, if he did not die. He was himself anxious to know how much his father recalled, but at least his father had remembered him. Adam knew he would himself have been devastated had his father not remembered him. He could feel Rosamund's anguish in not being recognized. His arms tightened about her. Certainly his father would eventually remember this woman he loved.

For a brief moment it was, she thought, like being in Patrick's arms again. She sighed softly, thinking if she but raised her head it would be he, and he would smile down into her eyes and kiss her. "Patrick," she murmured.

"You must cease this caterwauling at once!" Maybel's strong voice said.

Rosamund was immediately yanked back to reality. She was not in Patrick Leslie's arms. She was in Adam's. He was doing his best to comfort her. She was to be his stepmother. She sniffled several times and was able at last to bring about an end to her weeping. She straightened herself, moving gently from his embrace. "I am sorry," she said quietly. "I did not mean to cause such a fuss, Adam." Reaching up, she patted his cheek. "Thank you for your kindness." Then pivoting, she went back through the connecting door into her chamber. She turned before closing the door. "Will you let me know when the physician arrives?"

Wordlessly he nodded. He found himself a bit shocked by the reaction he had experienced when holding her in his arms. Had Maybel not been in the chamber, he realized, he would have been tempted to raise her lovely tearstained face and kiss it.

"It is a natural reaction, my lord," Maybel said. "How can a man not want to comfort a beautiful woman when she cries so piteously?"

"I wanted to kiss her," he said quietly.

"Well, of course you did!" Maybel answered him. " 'Twas the most natural thing in the world. A pretty woman in distress. What man wouldn't want to kiss away her sorrow?" Maybel patted his arm.

"She is to marry my father!" he groaned.

"All the more reason to want to comfort her," Maybel reasoned. "Now, Adam Leslie, send for the physician and put this innocent lapse from your mind." She pushed him from the room and went back to sit by the Earl of Glenkirk's bedside. He lay sleeping a most natural sleep now. Pray God he remembered Rosamund when he next awoke. Had the lass not had enough misery in her life?

The physician came, and the earl was awakened. "He is still weak," Master Achmet said, "but he is most assuredly past the worst of it. The king will be well pleased when I tell him."

"And his memory?" Adam asked. "He does not seem to recall everything."

"It may come, or not," the Moor said inscrutably.

"He does not remember me!" Rosamund said, desperation in her voice.

Master Achmet's dark eyes were sympathetic as he spoke with her. "I cannot imagine forgetting a lady such as yourself, madame, but it is possible he will not remember. Still, he has just now awakened. Give him a little time." Then he turned to Adam. "I believe, my lord, that I can confine my visits to this house now to once daily." He bowed himself from the room as he said it.

When Tom returned from his visit to court with Philippa, the young girl was filled with excitement for what she had seen and whom she had met.

"The queen says I look like you when she first knew you, mama!" Philippa said.

Rosamund smiled wanly. "Indeed, my daughter," she replied spiritlessly.

"Run along now, poppet, and tell Lucy of your adventures," Tom said. He had seen at once his cousin's malaise. When Philippa had skipped off, he said, "What has happened, dear girl? You look positively half-dead."

"Patrick has awakened," she told him.

"That is wonderful news!" he exclaimed.

"He does not remember me," Rosamund said.

"That is not wonderful news," Lord Cambridge said.

"What am I to do, Tom? I cannot marry a man who does not know me!" Rosamund was positively distraught.

"I saw the physician departing as we returned," Lord Cambridge said. "What has he to say about the matter?"

"He says that Patrick may or may not regain all of his memories, Tom. God in heaven, I cannot bear it if he has forgotten me! I will die! I will die without him!"

Tom sighed. He remembered that both Rosamund and Patrick had said when they had first met that while their love would endure, they would eventually be separated. He had thought at the time that Rosamund was being rather dramatic, but now he considered that they both might have had a premonition. Still, their passion for each other had led them to believe they might remain together. And now this. It was eerie, and there was nothing he might do to comfort her. "The queen wants to see you," he said.

"I cannot see her now!" Rosamund cried.

"You cannot leave Edinburgh without paying your respects. She has been patient with you because of Patrick's illness, but the physician will tell the king that the earl is now awake. The queen will therefore decide you must come to her soon, and you must, cousin. Philippa charmed them both. She sat on the floor of the queen's privy chamber and played with the little prince, who has begun to toddle. Today was his first birthday. Your daughter, when she was told it, immediately took off the little gold chain she was wearing and placed it about Prince James' neck. It was a gracious gesture and much appreciated by both their majesties. Philippa has all the right instincts to please the high and the mighty. I think we may have to take her to Henry Tudor's court in another few years. I do believe, dear girl, we may snag a noble husband for her."

Rosamund looked at him bleakly. "He does not know me," she said again.

"Be patient," Tom counseled her gently. He could almost feel the pain she was experiencing. "Be brave. You have always been."

"I know," Rosamund answered him, "but I love him, Tom. I have never before really loved anyone like this. I do not expect to love again, if ever, like this. If he does not remember me, remember us, what am I to do?"

"We will cross that water when we come to it, cousin," he replied. "It is all we can do in this situation."

She nodded slowly.

At first Rosamund was unable to go back to nursing the earl. But then Tom and Adam convinced her that if Patrick's memory was to be jogged, she must be with him as much as she could. It was difficult, however, for he treated her like a complete stranger. He was polite, but distant.

"You had us all quite frightened," she told him one afternoon in late April. "I wonder what made you finally open your eyes, my lord. We had almost given up hope."

"I smelled white heather," he told her.

And Rosamund remembered that she had bathed and washed her hair that day with her scented oils and soaps, which were all perfumed with white heather. "Did you?"

"You wear it," he noted.

"Aye, I do," she said. Remembering how he had always loved the scent, even bathing in it when they were in San Lorenzo.

"But that afternoon it was particularly strong," he replied.

"I had just bathed," she responded.

"My son tells me we are to marry," he told her.

"We were," she said.

"You do not wish to marry me now, madame?" His look was curious.

"How can I marry a man who does not remember who I am?" Rosamund asked him. "If your memory does not revive itself, my lord, there will be no marriage."

"You do not wish to be a countess?" he asked.

Rosamund laughed almost bitterly. "I was not marrying you to become a countess, my lord. And before you ask it, I was not marrying you for wealth. I have wealth of my own. Nor were you wedding me for my wealth."

"Then why were we marrying? I have a grown heir and two grandsons. I need no other bairns," he said.

"You cannot have any more bairns, my lord. A fever burned your seed lifeless many years ago." So there were other things he did not recall of his past. "We were wedding because we loved each other," she told him.

"I had fallen in love at my age?" he laughed, but then he saw the stricken look upon her lovely face, and he said, "Forgive me, madame. It seems so odd to me that a man of my years should fall in love with so beautiful a young woman. And you returned my love?"

"I did. We spent last winter together, and you came back with me to Friarsgate in early summer. It was there we decided to wed. We would spend the spring and summer and early autumn there. In late autumn and winter we would live at Glenkirk," she explained. "You believed that Adam had done so fine a job managing your lands in your absence that you might trust him completely now."

"Though you say it is so, and I believe you, I can recall none of it," he said to her.

"And you do not remember going to San Lorenzo last winter for the king?" she said.

"Nay, I do not," he replied. "I would never have gone back to San Lorenzo. 'Twas there that my darling daughter, Janet, was taken from me. Nay. I would not go to San Lorenzo."

"And yet you did because the king needed your help, and you are his loyal servant," Rosamund said. "We spent a wonderful winter and early spring there. Our servants, Dermid and Annie, wed there with our blessing."

"Dermid More is married?" He was genuinely surprised. Then he asked her, "What did Jamie Stewart want of me that he sent me back to San Lorenzo?"

"My king was harassing your king into joining what is called the Holy League," Rosamund began. "Since the purpose of this alliance is against the French, your king would not join. He sent you to San Lorenzo in hopes you might weaken the alliance once you had spoken with the representatives of Venice and the Holy Roman Empire."

"Did I succeed?" the earl asked.

"Nay. But while King James suspected you would not, he felt he had to try. We stopped in Paris on our way home to reassure King Louis of Scotland's fidelity," Rosamund finished. "You recall none of this?"

He shook his head. "Nothing, madame. I

495

cannot believe I went back there."

"You were reluctant," she told him, "but we did go. And we were happy together in San Lorenzo."

There was a long, awkward silence, and then he said, "I am sorry, madame, that my memory seems to have fled me."

"What is the last thing you recall, my lord?" she questioned him.

Again he shook his head. "I was, I think, at Glenkirk," he told her. Then he asked, "What year is this, madame?"

"It is April in the year of our Lord, fifteen hundred and thirteen, my lord," Rosamund told him. "And we are in Edinburgh."

He looked genuinely surprised. "Fifteen hundred and thirteen," he repeated. "I thought it was the year fifteen hundred and eleven, madame. I seem to have lost two years of my life. But I believe I remember most of the rest of it."

"I am glad for that, my lord," Rosamund said softly. She blinked back the tears she felt pricking at her eyelids. Weeping would change nothing.

"When," he asked her, "do you think I shall be well enough to return to Glenkirk?"

"I believe we must ask Master Achmet," Rosamund responded.

"I do not like these dark-skinned

496

Moors," he noted. "A dark-skinned slave betrayed my daughter."

"He is highly thought of by the king," Rosamund answered him. "The king sent him to you when you fell ill, my lord. His care of you and advice have been excellent." She arose from her seat by his bedside. "I think, my lord, you had best take your rest now. I shall leave you."

"I am being treated like an old man," he grumbled. "I think you are well rid of me, madame. When shall I be able to leave this bed of mine?"

"We shall ask Master Achmet that, too, when he comes today," Rosamund repeated as she slipped from the room. Outside in the hallway, she sighed. His memory of the last two years was not returning, and her hopes for their reunion were slowly fading. She felt hollow and more alone than she had ever felt in her entire life. And the casual words he had spoken, saying she was well rid of him, had been like a blow to her heart.

Philippa Meredith turned nine years old on the twenty-ninth of April. The Earl of Glenkirk was allowed into the hall for her birthday dinner. He had been walking about his bedchamber for several days now, and his physical strength seemed to be returning. The little girl was shy of the earl now, for he considered her a stranger. It was difficult for her to understand, but her manners were impeccable. In the stress of the situation everyone forgot Rosamund's twenty-fourth birthday on the thirtieth of the month.

Plans were now being made for the Leslies to return to Glenkirk, and for Rosamund and her family to go home to Friarsgate. Lord Cambridge escorted his cousin to see the queen. Margaret Tudor had been advised of the state of affairs. She held out her two hands to Rosamund as her old friend entered her privy chamber. There was nothing even she could say, she knew, that could help the situation. The two women embraced.

"I pray you never know such sorrow and pain as I do now," Rosamund told her.

"He remembers not at all?" the queen said.

"Almost everything up until two years ago. Master Achmet says it may all come back eventually. It is the best I can hope for, Meg." They were alone.

"I will pray for it, and for you, dear Rosamund," the queen said.

Prince James was brought and displayed for the lady of Friarsgate. He was a healthy- and ruddy-looking little boy, but Rosamund saw little of the Tudors in him. Finally, her visit at an end, Rosamund took her leave of the queen.

"There will be war soon," Meg said. "Keep safe, dear Rosamund."

"Do you really think so?" Rosamund replied.

The queen nodded. "My brother will not listen to reason. He is as ever stubborn. He is forcing Scotland to the wall over this damned Holy League." She sighed. "You should be safe, but keep watch." She pulled a ring from her finger. "If Scots invade your lands, show them this ring and say the Queen of Scotland gave it to you and says you are to be free of harassment."

Rosamund felt tears fill her eyes. "Thank you, your highness," she said, addressing Margaret Tudor, Queen of Scotland, formally. Damn! She cried so easily these days. The two women embraced a final time, and then Rosamund backed from the queen's privy chamber and departed the royal residence.

Chapter 13

Rosamund returned to her cousin's house. It was the second day of May, and preparations were now well under way for their departure on the morrow. Both parties would be leaving in the morning. The Leslies would be going northeast to Glenkirk. The Boltons would travel southwest to Friarsgate. Adam knew how devastated Rosamund was and how she strove to hide it from them all, especially her little daughter. He sat together with her in the hall after everyone else had gone to bed.

"If he remembers, I will send to you," Adam promised her.

"My instincts tell me he will not remember," Rosamund replied. "When your father and I met it was as if lightning had struck us. From that first moment our gazes joined, we knew that whatever had been between us in another time and place must once again be between us. But we also had a knowing, a foreboding if you will, that we would not be allowed to remain together in this life. As our love for each other grew even greater, however, we pushed that shared premonition into the back of our minds. We pretended that it was simply we did not know how to do our duty to both Glenkirk and Friarsgate if we wed. And then we resolved this difficulty, which allowed us to plan our marriage. But fate will not be denied, Adam Leslie. Patrick and I were not meant to be forever more. And fate has once again taken a hand in the matter." She sighed. "Your father will live out the rest of his life without ever remembering those glorious months we had together or how passionately we loved each other. I, on the other hand, will never forget. That is my punishment for attempting to defy fate," Rosamund concluded sorrowfully.

"He could remember," Adam insisted.

She smiled sadly. "How like your father you are," she told him. Then she rose from her place and left him alone in the hall.

The morning came. Once again they gathered in the hall to break their fast. And afterwards both parties found themselves ready to depart. It was an awkward moment. Finally Rosamund walked over to the Leslies. She held out her hand to Adam, who kissed it.

The earl gave Rosamund a brief smile. "I thank you for your care of me, madame," he said, as he, too, kissed her gloved hand.

Reaching up, she touched Patrick's handsome face. "Farewell, my love," she whispered, her eyes scanning his face a final time for something. Anything. There was nothing. Rosamund's hand fell to her side, and she turned and walked through the front door to where her horse was waiting, mounting it without assistance. She heard Tom and Philippa behind her offering their good-byes. They joined her finally, and their party moved off down the lane and into the High Street.

Adam Leslie watched them go. Watched as they turned into the High Street. "You remember nothing, father? Nothing?"

"Nothing," Patrick Leslie, Earl of Glenkirk said. "I wish I did, for she is lovely, but I do not. I should have been cheating her had I pretended otherwise." Then he walked from the house and mounted his horse. "Let us go home, Adam. It seems I have been away from Glenkirk forever."

Tom had hired two dozen men-at-arms to escort them home. Once on the road, Rosamund became more visibly anxious to reach Friarsgate. The first day she forced the pace, refusing to stop until the sun had set and the land was enshrouded in twilight. She had passed the comfortable inn

502

Tom had meant them to stay in, and now they bedded down in a farmer's barn with no supper.

"You cannot treat the men this way," he told her half-angrily.

"I must get home," she insisted. "I will die now if I do not get home!"

"Philippa should not be sleeping in a hayloft, Rosamund," he said. "And we have had nothing to eat, dammit!"

"Give the farmer's wife something, and she will feed you," Rosamund replied.

Tom swore a long string of rather colorful oaths beneath his breath.

Rosamund laughed. "Why, cousin," she said, "I did not think you knew such wicked language." The laugh had been hard.

In the morning Tom paid the farmer's wife more coin than she had ever seen to feed them all. She willingly complied, though the fare was simple. Rosamund barely ate at all, and she demanded that they all hurry.

"We have a long day's ride ahead of us," she said, and she mounted her animal and rode off ahead of them.

Without being told, two of the men-at-arms leapt upon their own mounts and hurried after her while the rest of them finished their meal before departing.

"What the hell is the matter with her?" Tom asked Maybel as they rode.

"Friarsgate is where she gains her strength," Maybel answered. "Her strength is almost gone with her anguish. She will ride her horse into the ground to reach home before her will dies on her."

"Neither Philippa nor Lucy nor you can keep such a pace," he said.

"I will do what I have to. Philippa and Lucy are young. We will all survive just knowing that Friarsgate is awaiting us," Maybel told him.

They rode on. At the noon hour he insisted that they stop at a comfortable inn, to rest the horses, he told her. Then he ordered a large meal for them all, including the men-at-arms, for he knew she would ride until they could no longer see the track ahead of them. He also knew that they were approaching the border.

"We can stay the night at Claven's Carn," he told Rosamund.

She looked coldly at him. "No," she said. "I will not stop at Claven's Carn."

"Then break our journey here today. You almost rode us into the ground yesterday," Tom pleaded.

"No," she said again. "We can get past Claven's Carn, and then by noon tomorrow we will reach Friarsgate, Tom."

"There is no place between Friarsgate and Claven's Carn where we may stay!" he shouted at her.

"We can bed down in a field," she replied.

"You would ask Maybel, Lucy, and Philippa to sleep in a pasture?" His face was flushed with his anger.

"If you hadn't made us stop to indulge everyone with food and drink we might have gotten even closer to home today," Rosamund said, ignoring his outburst.

"You have gone mad!" he accused her.

"I want to go home, Tom! What the hell is the matter with that?"

"Nothing! As long as you don't kill us all getting there, Rosamund! We will stay at Claven's Carn tonight, and that is final!"

"You may stay at Claven's Carn. I will not," she told him implacably.

The day, which had begun fair, now clouded up with typical springlike contrariness. By sunset, a light rain was falling, and Claven's Carn loomed ahead, its two towers piercing the graying twilit sky.

"Ahead is where we will overnight," Tom told the captain of his men-at-arms. "Send a man ahead to beg shelter for the lady of Friarsgate before they close the gates."

"Yes, my lord!" the captain said, signaling to one of his men to go.

"The laird will not refuse us hospitality," Tom murmured to Maybel.

"Nay, nor will his wife," Maybel said.

"But I warn you now that your cousin will fight you in this matter. I have known Rosamund all her life, and when she sets her mind to something, nothing will prevent her from enacting her will. Still, I have never seen her quite like this before. I think if there were a border moon she would travel on this night."

"The horses will not stand the pace," he said.

"Then try and reason with her," Maybel told him.

Tom spurred his mount ahead in order to ride apace with his cousin. "Rosamund, be reasonable, I beg of you," he began.

She stared straight ahead.

"If you will not have mercy on those who travel with you, consider the horses. They cannot be ridden without rest."

"We can rest when we are past Claven's Carn and over the border," she said stonily. "It is not dark yet, Tom. We can make several more miles before the darkness sets in and obscures the track."

He grit his teeth, struggling to maintain an even tone with her. "I should not disagree if the weather would cooperate, but with every moment the rain grows heavier. It will be one of those all-night spring rains, cousin. You cannot ask Maybel, Lucy, and your daughter to ride through the night in the pouring rain. And again, I beg you to consider the animals. How will we see the road when the darkness falls? There is no moon on a rainy night. If we do not shelter at Claven's Carn, we will be forced to spend the night out in this weather. If any of us catches an ague, it could kill us."

"We will have men with torches light the path for us," she said implacably.

"I know you mourn, Rosamund," he began, but she waved him away.

"Stop at Claven's Carn if you must, Tom, but I have to go on," she told him.

"What does it matter if we stop?" he demanded, his voice now showing his anger and impatience with her. "We will still not reach Friarsgate until tomorrow."

"I will reach it earlier if I travel farther today."

"You have truly gone mad!" he said, and after turning his horse about, he rode back to where Maybel plodded along in the line.

"She says we may stop, but she will go on," he reported. His face was red with his frustration.

Maybel could not help but laugh. "Do not trouble yourself over it, my lord. Let her believe she is going on tonight. We will ask the lord of the keep to ride after her and convince her to return and seek shelter. He will do it. He has never stopped loving her, despite his good wife."

"She hates Logan Hepburn!" Tom exclaimed. "If he said come, she would go. If he said turn right, she would turn left."

"True, true," Maybel agreed. "But I suspect that because he loves her, he will not allow her to remain in the storm even if she insists she will. He will bring her to shelter, never fear."

And Maybel chuckled again.

"You are a most devious old woman," Tom said admiringly. "And I never until now realized it."

"I know my child," Maybel told him.

They had reached the path that turned off up the hill to the border keep of Claven's Carn. Rosamund brought their party to a halt as the man-at-arms they had sent ahead came riding down the hill.

"The laird and his wife bid you welcome," he told them.

Rosamund turned to the captain of the men-at-arms. "All but two may go with my cousin, daughter, and the women," she told him. "I will want torches to light the path for me, as I must go on as long as I can tonight."

The captain shook his head. "Lady," he told her, "we were hired to escort you home, and that we will do. But I will not expose my horses to certain death if you ride them through the night without proper shelter, food, and rest."

"I will give you new horses," Rosamund told him.

"You will kill my men," he replied. "The answer is nay! Look about you! The hills are already shrouded in mist that will turn to fog before long. You will not be able to make enough headway to matter before you cannot even see the path before you with a light. Take shelter here."

"I will not stop now," Rosamund said. "Give me a torch, and I will travel on by myself."

Tom thought his head was going to explode, but remembering what Maybel had advised, he said to the captain, "Let her have a damned torch!"

"My lord!" the man protested, but then he grew silent at Lord Cambridge's look. "Yes, my lord," he said, and then he handed Rosamund his own torch. "Lady," he pleaded, "take shelter, I beg you."

Ignoring him, Rosamund moved slowly forward, passing them and disappearing into the mist until only a pinpoint of light from her torch could be seen.

Tom led them up the hillside to the keep. In the courtyard Logan was there to greet them despite the rain. He quickly scanned the group, and the disappointment in his eyes was evident when he did not see Rosamund. Lord Cambridge saw it, and dismounting heavily from his horse, he said, "We must speak now, quickly and privily, Logan Hepburn."

The laird did not argue, instead beckoning his guest into the keep with the rest of their party. Inside, Logan's wife was waiting to greet the guests, and she led them into her hall while Logan moved off with Tom. In a small room the laird called his library they spoke without sitting. "What has happened?"

"I will try and make this tale as brief as I may," Tom began. "When we reached Edinburgh we discovered that the Earl of Glenkirk had suffered a seizure of the brain. He was lying near death at the inn. The king sent a skilled Moorish physician of his own, and between this doctor and Rosamund the earl was saved. But, alas, his memory was impaired. He could not remember the last two years of his life at all. Do you understand, Logan Hepburn, what I am saying?"

"He did not remember Rosamund," the laird said, his voice a mixture of both regret and joy.

"She nursed him faithfully for a month until he was strong enough to return home, but under the circumstances there could be no marriage," Tom concluded. "She is filled with sorrow and anger. And tonight, as we seek shelter here at your home, she rides on alone for Friarsgate in the storm."

"Jesu! Mary!" The strong oath exploded from his mouth.

Tom restrained the smile threatening him. Maybel had been right.

"Are you telling me she is out there in the rain? Alone? Are you mad to allow her to do such a thing?" the laird of Claven's Carn roared.

"We could not stop her, I fear," Tom said mildly. "She is a determined woman, and Friarsgate is her strength. She needs to get home."

"But she does not need an ague. It could kill her!" he exclaimed.

"Perhaps you might reason with her, Logan Hepburn," Tom said.

"I would sooner reason with a she wolf," he growled, "but she cannot be allowed to endanger her life, even in her grief. I will fetch her. You will go into the hall and explain all of this to my lady wife that she may be prepared for your cousin's arrival, which will not be a peaceful one, I fear."

"Thank you, Logan Hepburn," Lord Cambridge said quietly.

Logan laughed a short laugh. "You knew I would go after her."

"Maybel knew," he replied.

They returned to the hall where their party was already warming themselves by the fireplaces. Logan went to his wife, murmured something in her ear, and then departed the company, leaving Tom behind to explain. He called to a servant to bring his cloak, and outside in the courtyard his horse was brought. After mounting it, he took up a torch and cantered through his gates out into the stormy night. At the bottom of the hill he turned onto the track leading over the border and into England. The fog was beginning to thicken now, and he was forced to move slowly. It was growing dark, as well. She had the advantage of a quarter of an hour on him, but he would catch up with her and return her to Claven's Carn.

His horse moved cautiously but steadily forward, and where the fog and mist lifted in certain places the animal moved a bit more quickly. Finally Logan saw the faint glow of her torch ahead of him. For a time he seemed to gain no momentum as he moved towards it, but then the fog lifted briefly where he rode and he hurried his horse along. The distance between them grew smaller. He had been following after her close to an hour now. He could almost see her horse now. He kept moving until once again he was given the advantage of a clear track. Rosamund was directly ahead of him in the rain, but she did not hear him for the thunder now beginning to rumble. He rode up abreast of her, but she was concentrating so hard on the road beneath her mount's feet that she didn't see him at first.

"So, madame, you are as stubborn as ever," Logan said even as he reached out to half-lift, half-pull her from her horse, placing her before him on his. His arm tightened about her waist like a vise as she immediately began to struggle.

Rosamund had shrieked with surprise, not just a little frightened at the sound of a male voice and then her removal from her horse to her captor's. She quickly realized in whose company she was. "Let me go, you damned villain!" she yelled.

"You have led me a merry chase, madame, but you will return with me to Claven's Carn."

"I will not!" She punched at him in an effort to release his hold on her person.

Logan Hepburn sighed. "I know what happened, you virago. I am sorry! If you had married me in the first place, none of it would have happened."

"I didn't want to marry you!" she told him furiously. "Why could you not understand that I wasn't ready to remarry? All you could do was babble on like some damned brook about needing an heir. You made me sound like breeding stock!"

"I didn't mean it that way. I thought you understood I loved you, still love you! I assumed because you had children you would welcome the opportunity to give me an heir as you gave Owein Meredith heirs for Friarsgate," he yelled back at her. He turned his mount and was relieved to see hers turn and follow him.

"You assumed? No, you damned borderer! You presumed! You did not ask. You told me what you would do. What you wanted. You never said you loved me and hoped that I would be the mother of your children. Nay! You told me that you would come and wed me on St. Stephen's Day and that I would give you heirs. You never asked me what I wanted, Logan Hepburn! Now, put me down and let me be on my way!"

"Nay, madame. You will return to Claven's Carn with me if it takes us all night to get there. You will eat a hot meal, and you will sleep in a dry bed. And your horse will get his rest, dammit," he told her.

"Bah! You have learned nothing, have you? There you go, once again telling me what I will do!" she shouted. "Well, I won't! You aren't my lord and master!"

"Rosamund, shut up!" he roared, and then unable to help himself, he kissed her mouth hard. His head spun as the familiar white heather fragrance she wore rose up to envelop him with its subtle but powerful scent.

Rosamund yanked her head away from his, slapping him with her free hand as she did. But she was finally stunned into silence. She had not been kissed since Patrick Leslie had kissed her. Why was it that men she didn't want were always kissing her?

They rode slowly on. It seemed forever, and then the horses turned from the road onto the path leading up to the Claven's Carn keep. In the courtyard he put her down from the horse and slid from his saddle. Rosamund turned about and hit him a blow with her fist. It was a hard blow, and it actually staggered him. Unable to help himself, he burst out laughing as she turned away and stamped into his house. Rubbing his jaw, he followed her.

In the hall, Jeannie came forward clucking sympathetically as she saw Rosamund enter. "Oh, you poor dear!" she cried. "Come to the fire and warm yourself. I can only imagine how desperately you desire to get home, but you must not wear yourself out, Rosamund. You need your rest. Oh, I hope you have not caught a chill or an ague. These spring rains can be so treacherous." She took her guest's soaking cloak from her and gently pressed her into a chair. "Tam, wine for the lady!" she called to a servant. "Logan, take her boots off and warm her poor feet the way

515

you do mine when they are cold," Jeannie instructed her husband.

"Madame, please," Rosamund said, "I am not used to being fussed over in such a manner. I will be fine. Well-meaning though the Hepburns may be, I was quite capable of getting home by morning by myself."

"You were no more than a mile or two from here," the laird said as he knelt and pulled her boots off.

Jeannie took the footwear and set it by the fire to dry. "Her feet, Logan," she repeated, smiling at Rosamund. "Logan will have your poor little feet warm in no time at all. You must be ravenous. I will fetch you a plate myself." She bustled off.

Her belly was even more evident now than it had been at the end of March, Rosamund thought glumly. Then she started as she felt his big hands enclosing one of her feet. "What are you doing?" she demanded, attempting to free her foot from his grasp.

"Warming your feet as my lady wife has instructed me, madame," he said in bland tones, but the eyes looking up at her were filled with mischief.

He wanted her to argue with him, Rosamund realized. It would be useless, she knew, and so instead she said, "Very well, but be quick about it, Logan Hepburn. I am indeed frozen. Where is my family?"

"I assume they have eaten and gone to their beds, madame. It is late." One big hand cupped her small foot while the other rubbed it gently. He couldn't help but stare down at that foot as it nestled in his palm. It was a dainty foot, the skin soft and smooth. He had the most incredible longing to kiss it, which he forced back.

"I think you are actually beginning to succeed," she remarked.

"Logan is the best foot warmer!" Jeannie said enthusiastically as she returned with a plate of food for her guest.

Rosamund took the plate and began to eat, but her appetite was not what it had once been. In fact, since she had arrived in Edinburgh to find Patrick so ill she had hardly eaten at all. Food had the tendency now to repel her rather than appeal to her. Still, for Jeannie's sake she made the attempt.

Finally Jeannie reached over and took the plate from her. "I understand," she said softly. "At least you got something down."

Rosamund looked into the young woman's face, seeing genuine sympathy and kindness. She felt the ever-present tears beginning to well in her eyes. She nodded at her hostess, but said nothing.

"Are her feet nicely warmed now?" Jeannie asked her husband.

"Aye," he said, standing up again.

"Then fetch Rosamund some wine, Logan," she commanded, and when he had gone off, she said, "I could see you wanted to cry, but would not before a man. I cannot even begin to imagine the sorrow you are suffering, Rosamund. I am truly sorry for it."

Again Rosamund nodded, wordless. Then she turned away, gazing into the fire.

When Logan returned a few moments later with the requested goblet of wine, his wife stopped him with a hand, putting a finger to her lips.

"She has fallen asleep," Jeannie said.

"I'll carry her to her bed," he replied.

"Nay," Jeannie said. "You will wake her if you do, and then she will not sleep at all, Logan. Leave her by the fire. Her cloak is dry now. Cover her with it. She will sleep the night, I think. Let us to bed, husband."

He nodded. "You go ahead, lass," he told her. "I must be certain all is locked and barred."

"Of course," Jeannie answered him, and she left the hall.

Logan moved through his keep as he did every night before he retired. He checked the outer doors to make certain they were barred. He saw that the lamps were doused, the fires banked. Finally returning to the hall, he sat down opposite Rosamund. Her face was so familiar to him, for it was the face that haunted his dreams. He remembered the child he had first seen at that cattle fair in Drumfie those long years back. He had fallen in love with her then and there. Why was it that fate had conspired to keep them apart? He shook his head. Then, realizing his wife would wonder where he was, he arose and left her sleeping in his hall.

Rosamund was awake when he reentered the hall early the next morning. Awake and arguing with her hired captain-at-arms. "We still have another day's ride!" he heard her say as he came upon them.

"Yer a madwoman, lady, and I'll not go another step in yer company," the captain said implacably. "You have almost killed my men and my horses with yer pace these past two days. Pay us what you owe us, and we will be on our way."

" 'Tis but another day's travel," Rosamund said. "You cannot expect three women and a single gentleman to travel these last miles without the company of men-at-arms. Today is the most dangerous part of our journey, for we are prey to both the Scots and the English as we go. You were hired to take us to Friarsgate!"

"Not another mile in yer company, lady," the captain said. "Pay us now."

"Pay him," Logan said. "You can trust him no longer, madame. If you force the issue, he will wait until he is out of sight of Claven's Carn, take his monies forcibly, and leave you stranded. My clansmen and I will escort you the rest of the way."

For once Rosamund did not argue with Logan. She might have been grief-stricken, but she was no fool. His words made perfect sense to her. Reaching into her gown, she drew forth a leather bag of coins. Opening it, she emptied a third of the coins into her hand, stuffing them into a pocket. Then, drawing the bag shut, she tossed it to the captain. "You were hired to take me to Friarsgate, not Claven's Carn. I have paid you for the distance you traveled with me. Now, take your men and get out of my sight!"

With a curt nod to the laird, the captain walked quickly from the hall.

"I do not like being indebted to you, Logan Hepburn," Rosamund said.

"You are not," he replied. "You are my nearest neighbor for all you are English. I would be a bad neighbor if I did not escort you to Friarsgate under the circumstances."

"I would not waste the day here," she said sharply.

"As soon as your party is ready, lady, we will go," he told her.

"How is your son?" she asked politely.

His craggy face lit up. "He's a braw wee laddie, he is. They say he is my image, and it may be true, but he has his mother's disposition."

Rosamund couldn't help but smile at his words. "Then you are indeed fortunate, Logan Hepburn," she told him.

Now he laughed. "Meaning?" he teased her.

"I think we need not go into it, my lord," she answered him.

He nodded. "Aye," he said, "for you and I will never agree on anything, will we, Rosamund?"

"I cannot predict the future, Logan Hepburn," she told him wearily. "Once I thought I could, but it has been proved otherwise this spring."

Tom came into the hall, followed by Maybel, Philippa, and Lucy. "Ah, you are up already," he greeted her jovially.

"Do not speak to me, you traitor!" she told him. Then she said, "Our men-at-arms have taken their monies and decamped. The captain would not take us farther. The laird has kindly offered to escort us home today."

"Gracious! Everyone is already up," Jeannie said, coming into the hall. "I am a poor hostess, I fear." She bustled about, speaking with her servants, seeing that the morning meal was quickly served.

"The lady of Friarsgate's escort has run off," Logan told his wife. "My men and I will be their protection on the final leg of their journey home today. We should be back by dark, lass." He kissed the top of Jeannie's head.

"Of course you must accompany Rosamund and her party," Jeannie said. "It is the most dangerous part of their trek. Take enough men so that the robbers lurking in the hills will be deterred from attacking." She turned and smiled at Rosamund. "Borderers, I have discovered, be they Scots or English, can be difficult and rash in their actions."

Rosamund found herself smiling back briefly. "Aye, they can," she agreed.

The meal was served, and they sat themselves at the hall's high board. Lucy had gone to the kitchens to be fed, but Maybel was considered an honored guest by virtue of her long service and her marriage to a Bolton. There was hot oat stirabout served with pitchers of heavy golden cream and equally golden sweet honey. Loaves of fresh bread were placed upon the table along with two bowls of hard-boiled eggs, a crock of newly churned sweet butter, and strawberry conserves. Both watered wine and ale were offered.

"Philippa!" her mother cautioned as the young girl signaled a servant to pour some ale into her goblet. "You will drink watered wine or plain water."

"Mama!" Philippa protested. "I am nine now!"

"You will not have ale at breakfast until you are twelve," her mother said.

"Your mam certainly never did," Maybel enforced Rosamund's ruling.

"Oh, pooh!" Philippa complained, but then she nodded at the servant with the wine pitcher to serve her.

"I remember being her age," Jeannie said with a small smile. "Nine is neither fish nor fowl. It is a hard age for a girl."

When the meal was finished Logan announced that he would assemble his men, and they would depart shortly. He hurried from the hall.

They attended to their needs, and then Rosamund thanked their hostess for her kind hospitality. No mention was made of the lady of Friarsgate's reluctance to shelter at Claven's Carn the previous evening.

The two women embraced, and then Jeannie said, "Rosamund, I have a favor to ask of you. Will you be this new baby's godmother?"

"Surely you have someone else who

would suit better," Rosamund protested.

"Nay, I do not. Logan's sisters-in-law do not like me since I made Logan give his brothers their own cottages. They attempted to undermine my authority in my own hall because they thought I was young and to be taken advantage of, but I was not so innocent that I did not see. So when Logan asked me what I would have as a reward for giving him a son, I told him I would think on it. After their rudeness to you earlier this spring, I told my husband I wanted his brothers and their families in their own homes. He did not protest my request, but in return his brothers and their wives became my son's godparents. His brothers were satisfied, but their wives were not."

"But surely your own family —" Rosamund began, but Jeannie stopped her with a wave of her hand.

"My family comes from the far north. I am but a memory to them. Please, Rosamund, say you will be my new baby's godmother. You are the only friend I have."

The girl's words touched her, and with a small smile Rosamund said, "If your husband, the laird, will agree, then I should be honored to be your baby's godmother, Jeannie Hepburn." Jesu! Would she never be free of the Hepburns? She kissed

Jeannie's cheek, then turned and left the hall.

In the courtyard the laird, his men, and her party were already mounted, waiting on her. Rosamund climbed into her saddle, moved her animal up next to Logan's, and nodded. They moved off through the courtyard and down the path to the road below. The day was a sunny one although the blue sky was filled with clouds of all hues, scudding back and forth in the wind. About them, the hills were a May green, and here and there were grazing sheep. They saw parties of men twice on distant hillsides, but their party being larger, the two bands turned away.

Seeing the second group, Rosamund said to the laird, "I thank you, Logan Hepburn, for your escort this day."

He turned and grinned. "I suspect you would have been a match for any borderer intent on robbing you, lass, but better cautious than sorry." He moved his horse ahead.

Tom rode up next to her. "Well, cousin, you seem calmer this day than you have been since we departed Edinburgh. I am relieved to see it."

"You were right," she told him, "about last night."

"I know," he answered her calmly.

She swatted at him affectionately. Then

she grew serious once more. "I do not ever remember being so miserable, Tom," Rosamund told him. "I shall never get over what has happened. I cannot believe it is over and Patrick is gone from my life."

"He may in time regain his memories of you, cousin," Tom began, but she waved an impatient hand at him.

"Nay, he will not. Do not ask me how I know, but I do. It is the same way I knew when we first met that we should not be together forever," Rosamund responded.

"Then what will you do, cousin?" he asked her.

"I will not marry again," she said. "Friarsgate is my responsibility. I have my daughters. Philippa is half-grown, and I must begin considering families to approach with an eye to making her a match. And you and I have a new enterprise to consider. I shall fill my days." But not my nights or my heart, she thought silently.

They had departed just as the sun was creeping over the horizon. By late morning Rosamund began recognizing landmarks and knew they were almost home. Finally they topped a hill rise, and there below lay the lake. Her meadows were heavily dotted with sheep and lambs. Her pastures were well tenanted by her cattle. The fields were green with the new growth of grain. They could see the Friarsgate folk going about their workday. Coming down the hill, Rosamund called out greetings to those she saw. A boy ran ahead of them announcing the mistress' return. Rosamund briefly wondered if they had been told of her unfortunate adventure, but she knew Edmund would not have left her people in the dark lest they ask questions. She smiled at some children waving in the orchards now in bloom. It had been a day like this when she had come home to Friarsgate with Patrick a year ago.

Her uncle came to greet them as they arrived at the house. Father Mata was with him, and he greeted the Hepburn of Claven's Carn, as well. He was Logan's kinsman, and they were friends. Rosamund slid down from her horse as Edmund helped Maybel dismount. Philippa and Lucy were already heading inside.

"I am sorry, niece, for your misfortune," Edmund said.

"Thank you," she said. "Will you see that the laird and his men are fed, Edmund? They intend to travel back to Claven's Carn today. I am tired and would retire to my own rooms." She turned to Logan. "Thank you, my lord," she said to him, and then she was gone.

"Well," Tom said with some humor, "at least she didn't hit you this time. You have just the slightest bruise on your chin, dear boy." They walked together into the house.

"What is this?" Edmund asked his wife as they followed the two men.

"Don't ask me, old man," Maybel said. "I was abed long before they dragged her in from the rain and her own folly. Tom will know every detail, and you will obtain it from him. Ah, I thank our Lord Jesu and his Blessed Mother that I am once again safe at home! Annie watched over you all?"

"Annie did a fine job," Edmund assured Maybel.

They entered the house.

"You look troubled, husband," Maybel said. "What is it?"

"A message came from the king while Rosamund was away. It arrived on the very day of your departure. Because it had the royal seal, I opened it. Inside was the terse message: 'The lady of Friarsgate is commanded to attend on his majesty, King Henry, at Greenwich.' Because she had gone off to wed, and I knew she would not be back quickly, I sent a reply back to the king saying Rosamund was not at Friarsgate but the message would be given to her upon her return. I sent it with the royal messenger who brought the king's missive. I have heard naught since."

"You must tell her at once," Maybel said.

"Tomorrow," Edmund decided. "I can

tell she is weary and heartsore. Let her have a peaceful night before we burden her again, wife."

"Aye, you are right, old man," Maybel agreed.

The Hepburn of Claven's Carn and his men stayed long enough to eat a good meal while their horses were rested and fed. They departed in early afternoon, Tom seeing them off.

Rosamund watched from an upper window. She saw Logan turn once as they rode from her courtyard, but she knew he had not seen her, for she was shrouded in shadow. Why had he turned back? she wondered to herself. Then, shrugging, she put herself to bed and slept until first light the following morning. When she woke she did not at first realize she was home. Then a small ripple of contentment slipped over her, and she knew exactly where she was. Rosamund arose and dressed herself. Leaving her chambers, she walked slowly down the stairs. Even the servants were only just beginning to stir. Unbarring the front door of the house, she walked outside into the dawn.

About her the air was sweet and fresh with the new grass in her meadows. She could hear the faint lowing of the cattle and the baaing of the sheep. The birds sang brightly as they did only in the fullness of spring. Above her the sky was clear and bright blue. She looked east and watched as the stain of gold on the horizon deepened and the bright crimson ball of the sun began to creep upwards. The horizon exploded with color: gold, lavender, scarlet, and orange. It was so unbelievably beautiful that she began to weep. She was home at Friarsgate. Safe at Friarsgate. But Patrick Leslie, the Earl of Glenkirk, was lost to her forever. I do not know if I can go on without him, Rosamund thought to herself, wiping the tears from her face. He should be with me now, seeing the sunrise, smelling the sweetness, knowing my love.

But it would not be that way between them ever again. "How can I bear it?" she whispered aloud. "How can I live my life without you, Patrick?" But she would. She would live her life without the Earl of Glenkirk because she had no other choice. She had responsibilities. She had Friarsgate. She had Philippa, Banon, and Bessie to consider. She might grieve in the privacy of her own chambers, but she must live her life for Friarsgate and for her daughters now. Turning away from the sunrise, Rosamund walked back into her house, where she found Edmund awaiting her in the hall.

"It will be a good day," she told him.

"Have you eaten yet?"

"Nay," he answered her.

"Then, let us break our fast together," she said.

"Do you not wish to go to mass first?" he asked.

"Not today," she replied. "Sit, uncle."

He accepted her offer, saying, "A message came for you while you were gone. I answered it for you." He handed her the packet.

Rosamund opened it, scanning the contents. Then she said, "I have no time to attend the king right now."

"I do not think, niece, that it was an invitation. It seems more a command to me."

"I will go in a few months," Rosamund responded. "If another royal messenger arrives, I shall say I am too ill to travel."

"You cannot ignore the king's command," he counseled her.

"I know," Rosamund replied. "I will go after the harvest and return before the wintertime. I have no desire to be away from Friarsgate again, Edmund."

"I wonder what King Henry wants of a simple countrywoman?" Edmund said.

"I wonder, too," she said. He did not want her out of lust, she knew. There were more than enough women at court willing, nay eager, to satisfy his desires. Why had he sent for her? And then she knew. Lord Howard had probably put two and two together, especially after Tom said she was his cousin, and had been at court as a girl. Well, Henry Tudor would have to wait until she was ready and strong enough to travel. Rosamund did not think she was able to do battle with her king at this moment in time.

A month passed, and it was June. Word filtered up from the south that King Henry had departed for France with a great army sixteen thousand strong. With them went horses and much ordnance for the battles to come. The king was boyishly eager for the encounter. His advisers were nervous. Henry Tudor had no heir. What if he were killed? Would England be plunged once again into civil war?

At Friarsgate the summer passed peacefully. Tom spent much of his time at Otterly overseeing the construction of his new house. He came from time to time with amusing reports of its progress. New Otterly would be ready for habitation by late autumn, and his servants were up from London and already in residence in the half-built house. They brought with them several cartloads of furnishings. Lord Cambridge arrived bursting with all sorts of information. On the king's orders, the goldsmiths of London had fashioned a magnificent harness and trappings for King Henry's warhorse. The monies expended would have purchased at least twenty brass field ordnances. Another thousand pounds was given over to the purchase of solid gold buttons, aglets, branches, and elegant chains so that when his armor and crusader's tunic was laid aside, the royal doublet would glitter like a sunburst. Emperor Maximilian had sent his fellow monarch a solid silver crossbow in a silver gild case. The royal arms and weapons were equally magnificent.

"I am devastated I was not there to see it," Tom lamented.

"Hal was always one for his appearance. He will surely spend his father's treasury," Rosamund noted.

"There is more, dear girl. Brew houses were constructed in Portsmith so that beer could be made for the armies and the navies. They brewed a hundred tons of beer a day. I do not know how many brewers, millers, and coopers were there, making their barrels as fast as they could. The beer was put in its barrels in deep trenches covered with boards and atop the boards' turf. But despite this royal generosity, the soldiers complained the Portsmouth beer was too sour and demanded the barley malt beer of London. But it, too, proved sour. I suspect the damp of the coast is responsible. At any rate, the fleet sailed, the ships' holes filled with men, horses, and sour beer. And all arrived safely in France."

"Then Hal has his amusement and will not notice that I did not answer his summons," Rosamund said.

"You will have to go eventually," Tom told her. "I will travel with you, dear girl. I dare not trust you to the king's care, now, do I?" He chuckled dryly.

Word began drifting into the north. The king had arrived safely at his possession of Calais. He had been warmly welcomed by the cheering citizenry. But suddenly England found itself practically the sole supporter of the Holy League. Henry Tudor's father-in-law claimed he believed himself near death and was reluctant to leave Spain. He was, he said, "too old and too crazy to endure war." But Ferdinand, had the truth been known, was a skinflint who did not choose to expend monies in a war someone else could fight for him. Venice sent no troops, and in that city it was said the pope himself had become neutral, for the papal offensive that had been planned to come through Provence or Dauphine never materialized. The Holy Roman Emperor sent few troops, but those sent were paid by the English. His daughter, Margaret of Savoy, however, continued to defy

France loudly, daring the French to do their worst, for she, she claimed, would be protected beneath English arrows.

In late July the English departed Calais and moved into the French territories. A successful skirmish near St. Omer left them eager for more. On August first the English arrived before the walls of Therouanne. After ten days of siege, a herald arrived bringing a message from Henry Tudor's brother-in-law, France's old ally, King James of Scotland. The English were to leave Therouanne. They were to depart the territories of France. They were, in fact, to return home. James Stewart was warning the young English king that war would shortly break out between them if he did not cease his hostilities in France.

Henry's reply was a strong and clear one. "It becometh ill a Scot to summon a King of England. Tell him there shall never Scot cause me to return my face." Henry continued by pretending outrage that James had threatened his ally by marriage. He grew more publicly indignant as his audience grew. "Recommend me to your master," he told the herald as he sent him off, "and tell him if he be so hardy to invade my realm or cause to enter one foot of my ground, I shall make him as weary of his part as ever was a man that began any such business."

The Tudor king knew his wife, acting as his regent, and his captains at home would handle any situation with Scotland should it arise. The King of England was free to pursue his war on the continent.

On the sixteenth of August, near the town of Guinegate, the English and the French in almost equal numbers met. Surprising the French, who were not expecting them so soon, the English charged. The charge sent one group of French soldiery careening into another. Panic ensued. The French turned and galloped off in a retreat, leaving behind their standards and weapons, and most oddly, many of their spurs. The English followed, gaining a great victory that became known as the Battle of the Spurs. Afterwards the English took Therouanne, and Henry, with his army in tow, went on to Lille, where he paid a social call on Margaret of Savoy. He was royally feted and charmed everyone, playing any instrument offered him, proving his prowess with his silver crossbow and dancing in his stockinged feet until dawn lit the skies about Lille.

Well rested, the English king moved on to capture the great walled city of Tournai with its double-thick walls and ninety-nine towers. And after that, he captured five more walled towns, seven in total. By autumn, when England's king left for home, he was no longer considered an untried boy king by his contemporaries. He had become Great Harry, and the news of his victories spread back to England and as far to the east as the sultan's capital of Istanbul. Henry VIII was now considered a man to be reckoned with by the world about him.

At Friarsgate, before all of this was known, Rosamund received a message from her old friend, the Queen of Scotland. Margaret saw what was coming. She knew her husband's plans and how her arrogant, clever brother had driven him into a corner from which he had but one way of emerging: by means of war. There could be no escape from what was happening around them.

"Gather your harvest in, and keep close to Friarsgate," she wrote. "I do not believe either of the armies will come your way, but beware of those on both sides of the border, especially the deserters. God keep you, dear friend, and those you love safe from this storm that is upon us. I am again with child. When it is possible I will write to you again." The letter was signed simply, "Meg." Not "Margaret R," but "Meg."

Rosamund shared her knowledge with her family and all the Friarsgate folk. "We must keep watch on the hills for invaders or other troublemakers," she said. She turned to her uncle. "Make it so, Edmund. There must be a watch kept round the clock."

"Do you wish to send her highness a reply?" the young messenger asked.

Rosamund nodded. "Remain the night, lad. I will write the queen. You will depart at first light. And on your return, stop at Claven's Carn. Tell the laird, Logan Hepburn, that war is coming between Scotland and England."

"Are you softening your stance towards the Hepburn?" Tom asked her.

"I send him warning for his good wife's sake. She is near her time, Tom. Whatever these kings do, Logan Hepburn is my neighbor. We borderers are a different breed from those others of our nationality."

He nodded. "I will remain here with you, dear girl. If the queen is right, and war is upon us, it is likely the invasion will come from the southeast. We shall probably see nothing here, but you have the queen's ring, which should protect us from the Scots if they come over the border in this region."

"Aye, I would feel easier if you remained, Tom. I pray that Meg is wrong. The Scots do not fare well when they go to war with England. And we both know Hal.

If his brother-in-law is fortunate enough to overcome him, England will not rest until the insult has been avenged. We will be at war forever, and Friarsgate cannot escape if that is so. Damn! Why could not Hal have been a man like his father? Oh, Tom, do you think that Patrick will answer King James' call?"

"I think that Adam will see his father, newly recovered from his seizure, not be allowed to join the king's ranks, though he may do so himself," Lord Cambridge said, and he shook his head. "And what is it really all about, Rosamund?" he sighed.

"I do not know, Tom," she answered him. "I think most wars are begun from nothing."

Chapter 14

Logan Hepburn stared down at the new grave in his family's burial ground. He could almost hear Jeannie's voice, pleading with him not to leave her. But he wasn't leaving her. Not really. He was simply answering his country's call. The queen's own messenger, bound for Edinburgh from Friarsgate, had stopped some weeks before to pass on Rosamund's warning of the strife to come. And then the head of his entire family, Patrick Hepburn, the Earl of Bothwell, had sent word of the king's call to arms. A man didn't ignore such a message if he were loyal, especially if he were kin to one of the king's best friends and longtime supporters.

He had gathered twenty-five men, not including his two brothers, Colin and Ian. But when Jeannie learned he was planning to depart she grew hysterical, and nothing he did could calm her. As she was near her time, he decided to give her a few days to grow used to the idea that he was leaving. But he sent his brothers ahead with twenty of his troop, delegating Colin, the elder, captain in his absence. It was almost a week before he could calm his wife and make her understand that this is what a man did when his king required it.

"Your own father and brothers will have answered the royal summons," he told her. "I have no choice but to go, else I be branded a traitor and shame our earl."

"They did not teach me this in the convent," she wept.

"We have been fortunate in having had peace between our two countries for many years," Logan explained. "But in our country's history, Jeannie, when the king has called, his subjects have answered. England is our most ancient and bitter enemy."

"But they have not attacked us!" she cried. "Why must the king attack them? What do we want with English soil, Logan? Explain it to me. Make me understand why you must leave us now!"

"I do not believe the king means to take any of England for his own, wife," he began. "I think this is a means of forcing Henry Tudor to come home and cease his war against King Louis. If his own realm is in danger, certainly he will leave France and hurry home to defend it. King James will probably withdraw at that point. They will argue over reparations, and peace will come again. There is little danger, I promise you."

"No war can be fought without casualties, Logan," Jeannie said. "Even if there is no English army in the north of that land, its citizens will fight the Scots, and men will die. I fear for you, for our children growing up without their father."

"I have to go," he said finally. He could waste no more time cosseting her.

"I know," she told him, resigned, "but still I do not want you to leave me."

"My brothers and our men are already a week ahead of me, Jeannie," he said. "I am ashamed that I am not with them. Is this the lesson you wish me to teach Johnnie? That a man should be a laggard in war, in his duty?"

"No! No!" she cried. "Of course not, Logan."

"Then I must leave you, lass, lest I bring shame upon the family. It is difficult to erase such shame. It lingers for years," Logan told her.

"Go, but go before I grow frightened again, Logan," she told him. "Go now!"

"Maggie and Katie will be coming with their bairns. I promised my brothers," he said to her.

"Aye," she replied. "They should be here for safety's sake."

He hurried from his hall. He hadn't even

kissed her in farewell. He had just gone, relieved to escape, anxious to catch up with Colin and Ian, and eager to join in the fun of an invasion. After gathering up his five remaining men, they set out unaware of what lay ahead of them.

James Stewart had sold off much of his personal wealth in order to purchase the seven great guns he planned to use to chastise the English and make them fully aware of his strength. They were called the Seven Sisters. His brother-in-law, Henry of England, would continue to fight alone, for the pope had received word that the Ottoman ruler was even now planning a large campaign into Western Europe. He sent to James asking him to mediate between the Holy See and King Louis of France. James Stewart chortled with satisfaction, but the English refused to allow his ambassadors through their territory. They would gladly receive his ambassador in London, but he could go no farther, thus rendering him useless. Henry Tudor considered his war against France a holy war, even if the pope no longer saw it that way. Henry Tudor knew what was right, and besides, the pope had written to him saying that he had changed his mind about Scotland acting as an intermediary between him and France. Having been offered no proof of this, James Stewart and his advisers did not believe it.

No more was heard from the pope, and the Scots knew that this was due to the English cardinal who now had his ear. The English were all but at war with the Scots upon the high seas. James Stewart, after many years of devoted service to Christendom, was shunted aside by the pope in favor of a younger man with a great deal of gold, which Henry Tudor was using to buy as much influence as he might. The Venetians were now busy preparing to defend themselves from the Turks, should it prove necessary. King Ferdinand, that wily and dishonest ruler, did nothing but mouth platitudes. France was busy fighting England, and Scotland was alone to fend for itself.

The Earl of Hume went forth to clear the Northumbrian border forts. He did so, but he lost a third of his men to English arrows due to his own neglect in clearing the gorse and bracken from the field where they fought. The English had hidden in this thick undergrowth, rising to ambush the too-confident Scots. Yet despite this, just about every man in Scotland between sixteen and sixty had rallied to the king's banner. Clansmen from the Isles, clansmen who normally would have fought each other, artisans, merchants, felons who volunteered to serve the king, the sons of the poor, and the sons of the well-to-do all marched side by side with their beloved king.

The king had been visited before he marched down into England by an old crone who demanded to see him and would not be satisfied until she did. Like the king, she had the *lang eey*.

"Dinna go down into England, Jamie," she warned him. "Dinna go, for ye shall nae come hame again!" Her glance pierced him. Her finger waggled at him.

But James Stewart knew it. His own second sight had told him this long ago.

The old woman continued with her warning. She grasped his sword hand so tightly he thought she had crushed it at first. His bones, she said, would not return home. And then she made reference to his heirs, who would be desperate to live in a green land, not Scotland, and how two gold rings would make one. That he did not understand, but he thanked her and gave her his royal blessing. At that she stared but a moment into his eyes, and then shaking her head, darted off, leaving the king to ponder what he had not comprehended. Two rings making one? But when the morning came, James IV of Scotland began his final march into history. It was his destiny, and he knew it.

Logan Hepburn was aware of none of this as he rode from his holding in the southwest of Scotland to meet with the king's forces. The journey was an odd one, for the land seemed to be deserted. Here and there he met up with other men both young and old, and they joined his little band, for their destination was the same. So they traveled through the early autumn rains, moving west and south. They crossed the Tweed River moving into England now, the evidence of the army ahead of them plain to see. They found Ford Castle and its lands about it untouched. The lady of the castle, alone, had been cooperative, and James Stewart had spared her holding, though he had burned her house down as he departed. He remained a few days before moving on to Flodden. And it was there Logan and the men with him found the Scots forces on the ninth day of September.

The mist, the smoke and the heat of battle rose from the field below the hill known as Flodden Edge. On the west side of the hill they found the trees had been cut down and a fort constructed. And it was before that fortress that Logan stood, watching in horror as the battle was coming to its dreadful end. He could see the king's banner in the mud, which meant the king was dead, for while he lived that banner would remain flying no matter what. His gaze moved over the field, but he saw no Hepburn flag aloft either. The ground was muddy, and many of the men had fought in their stocking feet because leather boots would have slipped easily on the treacherous ground. The Scots had lost the battle now coming to its close. That was painfully clear to Logan and his companions. The stench of death was everywhere. The laird of Claven's Carn put his horn to his lips and blew it. The distinctive note the horn sounded would tell any of his own people still alive to follow the sound and come to him. He waited and then blew his horn twice more. Finally, three of his clansmen struggled from Flodden Field and up the hill to where he waited.

"Any more?" he asked curtly. The smell of death surrounded them.

They shook their heads.

"My brothers?"

"Slain, my lord, with the Earl of Bothwell," one of the men reported, adding, "The English forces are also to the west, my lord."

"We'll go north and east then," Logan said grimly. "Quickly now, lads, before the English start looking about for living prisoners. Take whatever horses and boots you can find for yourselves." He waited briefly while the trio found mounts and footwear. Then, with a wave of his hand, they cantered off, leaving the battlefield behind. They rode straight for the border. It was imperative they not be caught in England. Their timely exit gave them more chance at survival than those left alive behind them had had. They rode until there was no more light left to see the ground beneath their horses' feet.

That first night, they made camp beneath the overhanging rocks in a narrow ravine. They lit a small fire beneath the rocks where it was unlikely to be seen. The formation where they sheltered was almost a cave. They had eighteen oatcakes among them. Broken in two, one cake could serve as a day's rations. Thirty-six pieces divided among the nine men would last them four days. They would be well into Scotland by then and might beg a meal from a local clansman. They would be welcome into any hall with the news they brought. That night, those with whiskey left in their flasks shared it with their companions. They would refill those flasks with water come the morrow.

Around their little fire that first night the three Hepburn clansmen told their laird the story of the battle. Their spokesman was Claven's Carn's blacksmith. His name was Alan Hepburn, and he stood six feet, six inches in his stocking feet. His brow furrowed as he remembered.

"The king were a brave laddie," he began. "He led us all himself, although the Earl of Hume did give a lot of orders. At one point our own earl said loudly that he saw no crown on Hume's head and he should shut his mouth and let the king command us, for he did it better than any."

The men listening laughed quietly, those who had not been there picturing it, for they knew their earl very well.

"The battle was fierce," Alan Hepburn continued. "The English were led by the Earl of Surrey, I was told. The king did not mean to fight in the field. He meant the English to have to come to us on the height, but their wily old commander sent troops around us to the west. The king feared they might get over the border, and none left to defend the farms but old men, women, and very young laddies. Ah, he were a good man, our Jamie was!" Alan Hepburn said, and he wiped the tears forming in his gray eyes. " 'Twas he who told us to remove our boots, for the ground was slick with mud and we would be in less danger of sliding and falling in our stocking feet."

"What happened?" the laird asked his blacksmith. "We were well matched, and we should have won the day. Something had to have happened. Did any of the earls withdraw their men?"

The blacksmith shook his head. "Nay. Half the men were down the hill, and then the phalanx was broken, my lord. They began to slip and slide. One grouping fell or tumbled into the other. The mud was treacherous, and many could not arise. The English swooped in on them, and it was slaughter. Your brothers, however, were already with our earl in the midst of the field with the young archbishop of St. Andrews, who was fighting with his father, the king. Much of the clergy avoided direct combat, instead firing the canons, for then they could be said not to have been fighting."

"You saw my brothers go down?"

"Colm, Finn, and I were battling nearby. The Earl of Bothwell was surrounded, and your brothers rushed to his defense. They were slaughtered," Alan said. "Hume, the young archbishop, and the king were then slain. The word began to spread that the king had been killed. It took the heart out of the men, my lord, and then we heard your horn. At first we were not certain it was you, but the call came twice again, and so we fought our way from the battlefield to find you," Alan finished.

"I am ashamed I was not with you," Logan said.

"Thank God you were not, my lord, for

this day we have lost our good king and the flower of Scottish nobility," Alan told him. "Claven's Carn needs you, especially as your lad is so young."

"The new king is not much older," Logan replied. "God help Scotland now. What of the Earl of Angus? Was he also killed?"

"Nay, my lord," Alan said excitedly. "The king left old 'Bell-the-Cat' Douglas behind, for the queen begged it. She and Bishop Elpinstone do not get along it is said."

Logan nodded. It had been a wise thing to do.

They had ridden for the next few days, making their way back to Claven's Carn. When their oatcakes had run out they stopped at a farm, begging a night's shelter in the warm, dry barn. Both the men and the horses were grateful.

"Can you feed us?" Logan asked the farmer. "We have eaten the last of our oat-cakes last night and have had naught this day. I can give you news of the king."

The farmer nodded. "We've not much, but we'll share," he said.

"When my men are cared for I will come in and tell you everything I know," the laird of Claven's Carn said.

The farmer's wife delegated Alan, who was the largest of the laird's men, to carry a cauldron of rabbit stew into the barn. She followed, her apron filled with several loaves of bread. The men called their thanks to her as she returned to her cottage and then set about tearing chunks of bread off the loaves, and dipping them into the stew to eat. Their knives speared what tender pieces of meat they could find. Inside the farmer's dwelling, the laird of Claven's Carn told of the disaster at Flodden while he ate a bowl of the stew, thinking it was the best he had ever tasted. The farmer placed a small mug of beer before him, and he nodded his thanks.

"So, our Jamie is dead," the farmer said. "God assoil his good soul." He crossed himself, as did his wife. "The battle was terrible, then. I could not go. My bairns are not old enough to help, and my wife is again with child." He hung his head.

" 'Twas better you remained than became canon fodder," the laird replied. "My wife is also with child and grew frightened when she knew I must go. I sent my brothers, now slain, and twenty men with the king. When I had calmed Jeannie, I followed, only to reach Flodden at the end. I saw no fighting. Three of my clansmen survived the battle. The others were with me. I am ashamed, for I knew the king. The Earl of Bothwell, the Hepburn of Hailes, was my kinsman. I was married in the royal chapel at Stirling."

"What was meant to be has come to pass," the farmer's wife said softly. "If it was meant that you die at Flodden, you would have. It was not."

"You have the *lang eey*, mistress?" Logan asked her.

"Sometimes I see things," the farmer's wife said quietly.

He nodded. "The king had the *lang eey*."

"I know," she answered him. And then she said, "I will feed you and your men again in the morning, my lord of Claven's Carn. And I will give you what oatcakes I can spare. The harvest was good despite the rains, and I can make more for the winter."

Logan thanked the woman and left the cottage, joining his men in the warm barn. Most were already sleeping soundly in the sweet-smelling hay. Dry for the first time in days, he joined them. Two days later they arrived at Claven's Carn, where Logan learned that his wife, Jeannie, had died in childbirth, his second son with her. They had already been buried in the family grave site on the hillside. His sisters-in-law sat gossiping in his hall, oblivious and uninterested in Flodden.

"Do you not wish to know of your husbands?" he asked them.

"Had they survived," Katie, his brother

Ian's wife, said, "they would be with you."

"Will you not at least weep for them, then?" he inquired of the pair.

"Would it bring them back?" Colin's wife, Maggie said.

Astounded by their hard hearts, the laird sought out his old nursemaid, who lived in his keep and knew everything that happened within. He found her in her chamber at her loom, weaving and humming as she worked. "What happened, Flora?" he asked her as he sat down on a stool by her side. "How did my wife die and the lad with her?"

Flora turned her face to him, her hazel eyes sorrowful. "The bairn was just a wee bit early according to my calculations, but bairns will come when they will, Logan laddie. The young mistress was frightened with your going. She wept all the time after you left us. She was certain you would be killed and voiced her fears to any and all who would listen. You would die, and she would be left a widow with two children to manage Claven's Carn for your son, John. She would be the prey of wicked men and robbers who would know she was alone and helpless."

"Jesu!" he swore softly. "I did not realize she was that frightened."

"You had to go, Logan laddie," Flora said. "The lass was convent bred and afraid of her own shadow, though she hid it well from you. She did not wish to shame you. The wee bairn came feet first, but in his struggle to escape his mother's womb, he became entangled in the cord and strangled. I could not turn him, though I might have been able to if either of your sisters-in-law had helped me. I needed them to aid me, but they would not. They said you would blame them if anything happened, and they could not afford your ill will for they had their own bairns to consider. The women servants were all in their own cottages, as their men were gone. I had no one. The lad was stillborn, and I am sorry. He was a big bairn for all he came early. As for your poor wife, she bled to death. There was nothing I could do, Logan laddie. You know I would have saved her if I could. I am so sorry," Flora concluded.

He nodded slowly. "Who buried her?"

"Several of the old men dug the grave. I bathed her and sewed her into her shroud," Flora told him. There were tears in her eyes as she spoke.

"And Maggie and Katie?" he asked.

"They are bad wenches, both of them," Flora said in a hard voice. "They would not even accompany your wife to her last resting place. It was raining that day, and they said they did not want to get wet, but all those others left here did follow the bier. Your lady was well liked for all she came from the north," Flora finished.

Logan stood up. Then, bending slightly, he kissed the old lady's soft cheek. "Thank you, Flora," was all he said, and he departed her little chamber. In the hall again, he went to where his sisters-in-law sat together. "Get up! Pack your belongings. You will leave here with your children first thing in the morning," he told them. "I do not want to ever see either of you again."

"You have been talking to the old woman," Maggie said. "She hates us."

"When I sent you to your own cottages you told me Jeannie hated you," he said scathingly. "My brothers are dead in the defense of our land, yet you shed not a single tear. You wantonly let my young wife perish for you would not help Flora, who might have at least saved Jeannie if she could not save my son."

"It was Maggie's idea!" Katie cried to him. "She said we would have our own back on Jeannie for sending us to those poky cottages, Logan. I wanted to help."

"I think you lie," he returned. "If you had wanted to help her, you would have helped no matter what Maggie said to you. Now, hear me, both of you. The cottages in which you reside are yours. I shall see you and your bairns fed and clothed. I will train the three lads you have between you in the use of arms. I will dower your two lassies one day, and I shall make matches for them. But I do not ever want to see your faces in my hall again. What I do, I do for my brothers' sakes. They were good brothers, and their children will not suffer because their mothers are hard-hearted trulls. You will not be permitted to remarry, for if you do I will send you from Claven's Carn without a moment's hesitation."

Katie began to weep, but Maggie said boldly, "I cannot believe you mean to do this to us, Logan. We were good wives to Colin and Ian."

"Which is why I do not take your bairns from you and put you out upon the high road," he told her in a hard voice. "Now, get out of my sight, both of you!"

"You never loved her!" Maggie said. "And she knew it, Logan."

"Nay, I did not love her," he admitted freely. "But I liked her well, and I respected her position as my wife and the chatelaine of this household. Aye, she knew I did not love her, but I might have, given time."

Maggie laughed bitterly. "How could you love anyone when it is Rosamund Bolton who has always filled your heart, Logan?" Then, turning, the sniveling Katie behind her, Maggie departed the hall.

He poured himself a large goblet of wine, draining the goblet where he stood. Then, turning, he went outside and up the hill to where his wife and son lay buried. He stared down at the fresh earth mound, just beginning to green over. "Jeannie," he said, "I am sorry, but I thank you for wee Johnnie. And whatever happens, he will know you were his mam and that you loved him. He will know you were a good wife to me and that I respected you. But still, I am sorry that I didn't love you." He remained where he was for many minutes, while the sun set and the stars began to come out above him. Finally he swung about and returned to his hall, where the servants, so well trained by his wife, had his supper waiting. And after he had eaten, he went to the nursery where his son and heir lay sleeping, his thumb in his mouth. Poor bairn, Logan thought, without a mother. And the little king without a father. What was going to happen to Scotland with an infant king whose powerful uncle, namely Henry Tudor, was now just beginning to flex his muscles?

James V was crowned at Stirling on the twenty-first of October in the year 1513 by James Beaton, the Archbishop of Glasgow. He was seventeen months old and surrounded by what remained of the Scottish nobility, who wept loudly as the great crown of office was held over his little red head. It was a cheerless coronation. The country's main concern was England. A peace must be made, and Henry Tudor could not have anything to do with his nephew's upbringing, although he should surely desire it and would attempt to influence his sister.

The English queen had been hurrying northward with her own army when Surrey had defeated and killed James IV at Flodden. She was again with child, but in imitation of her late mother, Isabella of Spain, she had been quite prepared to go into battle. She sent Henry the good news of Scotland's defeat, even going so far as to enclose the bloodstained plaid tunic that James Stewart had been wearing when he was killed. With the influence of both England and Spain, James had been excommunicated by Pope Julius. His body was therefore denied a Christian burial and disappeared. Gone to hell, the English said. Not so, the Scots defended their beloved deceased monarch. James IV, like King Arthur, had disappeared, but he would return — *Rex Quondam, Rexque Futurus* — the Once and Future King — when Scotland needed him the most. It was small comfort.

Henry Tudor returned in October from his French adventures. Katherine made certain he was greeted like the hero he believed himself to be. Henry was no longer the second son of that upstart Tudor family that had usurped a throne. He was Great Harry. The English king was flushed with his own victories even though they were now overshadowed by the victory at Flodden.

"It is your victory as well, my lord," his queen told him, and the Earl of Surrey, the actual victor, nodded in agreement. "Scotland is crushed." She carefully omitted the fact that while James IV was now dead, Scotland still had a king — her husband's nephew, James V. But Henry's pride in his military accomplishments was short-lived, for in December of that year his wife was delivered of a stillborn son.

"An eye for an eye," Margaret, Queen of Scotland, said grimly upon hearing the news. She was not of a mind to be charitable now. Full with her second child, she was also filled with sorrow at James' death and angry to have been left with all the responsibility of Scotland, its infant king, and the child soon to be born. Her husband's will had named her tutrix, or guardian of the young king. Margaret Tudor was in effect the ruler of Scotland. Her regency was approved by the king's council. But as the sister of England's king, she would not be trusted entirely by the Scottish nobility. It mattered not that as James Stewart's wife and queen her loyalties had always been to Scotland. She was a woman. She was English. Scotland's nobles looked to France to John Stuart, the Duke of Albany. The duke was James III's nephew and the king's nearest legitimate male kinsman. In an age of political intrigue, dishonesty, and backbiting, John Stuart was known as an honest man. His ethics were above reproach.

The queen's council consisted of Archbishop Beaton as her chancellor and the Earls of Angus, Huntley, and Home, who were appointed to aid the queen, but it was noted that the queen would be served by a rota of nobles who would function on her council, in turn, advising her in the daily affairs of her government. It was agreed that the queen would make no decision without first consulting six gentlemen, three of whom would be temporal and three who would belong to the clergy. Margaret was not quite the featherhead her husband had believed. That was a role she had played because that was the kind of woman James desired in his queen. She was, her council quickly discovered, hardheaded and shrewd when she put her mind to a problem.

Stirling Castle was chosen as the king's

chief residence. Lord Borthwick would be the castle's commander with the title of captain. The arms that had been sent to James IV by King Louis were now brought to Stirling, which made it impregnable. The queen held the treasury, making her even more powerful. She sent out a call for parliament to meet come spring. The government secure, peace would be the next item on the agenda.

England suggested the peace first, and Queen Katherine sent one of her favorite priests to Queen Margaret to comfort her. But in the borders, Lord Dacre, on the king's instructions, was still raiding the Scots, burning and looting. Scotland was now a land of widows and motherless children. Proclamations were issued in the new king's name, forbidding their abuse or the abuse of their children. Still, rape, robbery, and other violence was being done to those widows and their offspring, and there were not enough men left to keep the peace, so many suffered though the queen and her council did their best to prevent it.

But many of the young men now come into their lordships were eager to continue a war against England. Eager for revenge, they saw no use in a peace with their ancient enemy. They wanted a strong military leader to confront Lord Dacre. They appealed to King Louis to send them the

Duke of Albany. But the French king could not be cajoled into any actions that would threaten Margaret's regency. He corresponded with the young widowed queen, assuring her that he would not send the Duke of Albany to her until she requested it. He would not make peace with England without her permission, for France was ever Scotland's oldest and most faithful ally. He asked if he might send to her Le Chevalier Blanc, one Monsieur La Bastie, his most trusted diplomat, to help her. And, too, the Scottish ships that James IV had lent him were still in France. Would she like him to return them along with the king's cousin the Earl of Arran and Lord Fleming?

The full Scottish council met in Perth in November. It was agreed that the queen's regency of the young king would not be interfered with in any manner. The auld alliance with France was confirmed once more, and the Duke of Albany was requested of King Louis for the defense of Scotland. Bell-the-Cat Douglas, the Earl of Angus who favored an English alliance, was absent. Grieving the loss of his two sons, he had gone home to die.

In England, King Henry was furious and worried by turns. As the young king's uncle, he saw himself as the boy's natural guardian. He wrote to his sister telling her she must stop Albany from coming. He feared the strong duke might supplant Margaret by virtue of his sex and possibly spirit the little king to where he might be eliminated. Then he wrote to Louis asking him to delay Albany's departure for Scotland until England had made its peace with its northern neighbor. Margaret did not like her loyalties being torn or compromised by any. Her sole duty, she said, was to her bairns.

Both Friarsgate and Claven's Carn, by virtue of their locations, had been spared any border raids. Adam Leslie wrote to say the Leslies of Glenkirk had ignored the summons to war and had undoubtedly been overlooked in the resulting confusion that followed King James' death at Flodden. Patrick's health remained strong, but his memory of the past two years had not returned. Rosamund read the letter stone-faced. She had buried her grief deep in her heart now, allowing it to surface only in the darkest of night when she was alone in her bed. There had been no word from Claven's Carn regarding Jeannie's new child. Rosamund assumed that Logan had put his foot down firmly when his wife asked if his neighbor might be the child's godmother. She was not disappointed. It would have been a very awkward situation, but then, sweet Jeannie did not know the relationship that her husband had attempted to forge between himself and the lady of Friarsgate.

The harvest had long been gathered in, and the St. Martin's goose eaten. December was upon them. A messenger arrived from Margaret Tudor early in the month, even as it had two years previously. This was not an invitation, however. Meg wrote to tell her old friend of the great battle at Flodden in September at which her husband had been slain. Little Jamie was now Scotland's king, she was enceinte with her late lord's child to be born in the spring, and she was regent of Scotland according to her husband's last will and testament.

"I am weary with all I must do," she wrote, "but those lords not slain at Flodden with my husband have been most sympathetic and helpful to me. We will survive. My brother, Henry, the cause of my unhappiness, is of course blustering and blowing that he should be the guardian of my bairns. I should never allow such a thing, but if I even considered it, the ghosts of all the Stewart kings before my son would rise up to haunt me, and rightly so."

"Aye, I imagine Hal would enjoy having Scotland in his custody," Tom said when he learned the news. Then he chuckled. "He cannot get his own son so he would have James Stewart's lad to father."

Rosamund could not help but laugh herself. "Living in the north has caused you to become careless in your speech, cousin," she said. "You should not dare say such a thing in London."

"You never did answer the king's summons, did you?" he said.

"Edmund answered it for me," she replied. "Besides Henry Tudor has more important things to consider than a widow in Cumbria whom he once knew. He is a player now upon the world's stage, Tom. Whatever he imagines I was doing with the Earl of Glenkirk has now been overlooked because of the great and terrible victory at Flodden."

"What news from Claven's Carn? Did the sweet Jeannie deliver her lord a second son, or a daughter?" Tom asked her.

Rosamund shook her head. "I have no idea. I have heard naught, but then, given the times, I am not in the least surprised. Besides, I can hardly believe that Logan Hepburn would have wanted me for that child's godmother. Do you?"

"Perhaps I shall take a few of my men and ride over the border," Tom said. "I am curious, and whatever you may say, cousin, so are you."

"Go, then," she told him. "The weather will hold for another few days. But beware of getting caught at Claven's Carn for the winter, Tom. I do not believe that you would like it at all. Jeannie has certainly done her best, but it is still an uncivilized place."

He laughed. "I remember you once said you should never get to wear your fine gowns if you inhabited such a place."

"And it is still so," Rosamund noted dryly.

The next morning being dry and mild for December, Lord Cambridge departed his cousin's house with the half-dozen men-at-arms he now traveled with when he left Otterly. They reached Claven's Carn in late afternoon, riding through its gate easily as they were recognized by the clansmen guarding the little castle's entry. Tom dismounted, and upon entering the house, went directly to its hall. It was empty but for a servant girl rocking the cradle by the fire. Lord Cambridge walked over and looked into it, surprised to find not a new infant, but the laird's fourteen-month-old heir.

"Where is your mistress?" he asked the servant.

The girl's eyes grew large with her fright. Nervously, she arose from her place. "The mistress be dead, good sir."

"And the bairn she carried?" he inquired, surprised and not just a little saddened by the news.

"With its mam, sir," the girl said.

"Go and fetch your master, lass. Your charge is sleeping and does not need you."

The girl ran off, leaving Tom to ponder the knowledge he had just obtained. So little Jeannie had died and her child with her. It was a tragedy, yet Logan still had one son to follow him. Widowed, would he now seek out Rosamund again? And would she have him in her grief over Patrick? The winter to come might be dull, he thought, but certainly not the spring and summer to follow. A small smile touched his lips. Already this little journey had provided him with enough information to give him several months' amusement teasing his cousin.

"Tom!" Logan entered his hall. "What brings you to Claven's Carn? We are supposed to be enemies again, England and Scotland." But he smiled.

"I rarely pay heed to the politics of kings and queens, dear boy," Tom answered. "And particularly when the church is involved. I have only just learned from your son's little nursemaid of your great tragedy. What happened?"

A shadow passed over Logan's handsome

face. "You have, if I remember, a fondness for my whiskey. Sit down, Tom Bolton, and I will tell you what happened to my poor little wife." He poured them two pewter dram cups of an amber liquid from a carafe on the sideboard. Bringing them to his guest, he offered him one, and they sat before the fire, the cradle holding Johnnie Hepburn between them. "I got the call to arms. She did not want me to go. I had to send my brothers and most of my men on ahead while I calmed her. When I caught up with them the battle was almost over. Its outcome obvious, and the king dead. When I reached Claven's Carn again I learned she had died in childbed with the bairn, another son. She was already buried, of course, poor lass. 'Twas just as well. I later learned her father and brothers had all perished in the battle. Her mother has entered the convent where Jeannie was educated to live out her life in prayer and mourning. I sent to her regarding her daughter."

Tom nodded sympathetically. " 'Twas a great tragedy for Scotland, but, then, the history between our countries has never been peaceful for long."

A long silence ensued, and then Logan said, "How is Rosamund?"

Lord Cambridge's face was impassive as he answered, but he thought immediately,

Ah, he still wants her. "She yet mourns her own tragedy, Logan."

"Did the Leslies go to Flodden?" he wondered.

"I do not know, but I do know that Adam would not let his father answer the call. I suspect he never even told him of the summons. And he wisely remained put at Glenkirk himself. He may have sent a troop, but I know not. He wrote to Rosamund that it was not likely they were missed. He is right, I think. The first earl, like you, was but the laird of his people before he became James IV's ambassador years ago."

"Did you like him?" Logan asked.

"Aye, I did. He was a good man, and he loved Rosamund deeply. The misfortune that befell him last spring was indeed tragic. Yet he knows it not, as his memories of the last two years have vanished for good, it would appear."

"Is her heart broken?" Logan queried Lord Cambridge.

"Aye, it is. But hearts can be mended, or so I am told," was the reply.

"I have been given another chance with her," Logan said softly.

"Perhaps," Tom answered him. "But go slowly, Logan Hepburn. Do not attempt to overwhelm my cousin this time by being forceful with her. She needs a strong man, but that man must also respect that she is a strong woman. You need not break her spirit to bend her to your will."

The laird of Claven's Carn nodded, understanding. "You will tell her of my wife's demise?"

"I will. But do not come courting until midsummer. She liked Jeannie and would not approve of any disrespect shown towards her. And in the name of all that is holy, Logan Hepburn, do not mention the bairns you desire of her! If you can coax her to the altar, the bairns will come as a natural result of your passions for each other. Now, tell me, what is for dinner, dear boy, for I am absolutely ravenous?"

The laird laughed aloud. He had forgotten how amusing Tom Bolton could be. Laughing felt good. It had been a long time since he had laughed. Hearing a small noise coming from the cradle, he saw his son was awake. Lifting the lad from his bed, he displayed him to his guest. "Is this not a fine lad, Tom Bolton? Do I not have a fine son?"

"Indeed, Logan Hepburn, you do!" Lord Cambridge agreed.

The boy squirmed in his father's arms, anxious to get down. The laird set him upon the floor, and the little fellow toddled over to one of the great wolfhounds in the hall, climbing upon its back and crowing with delight. The two men laughed as the dog turned its massive head and licked the child's face lovingly.

"I'll have him on his first pony come the spring," the laird boasted. "He's a braw little laddie, Tom Bolton."

"Aye," Tom agreed. "I can see that he is." *And I can see you are a good and doting father, which will not harm you in my cousin's eyes.*

"You'll stay the night?" the laird said.

"I will," Lord Cambridge responded. "Will your brothers be joining us?"

"They were lost at Flodden," Logan replied.

"Ah, your sorrow is great, my lord. A winter of mourning will ease your heart, I am sure," came the reply.

In the morning Tom returned to Friarsgate, eager to impart all that he knew to Rosamund.

She wept learning of Jeannie and her child. "And the wee laddie she bore last year motherless. Ah, cousin, these are hard times for us all."

"They are," he agreed.

Afterwards, when she had gone from the hall, Edmund asked Tom, "Will he come courting, do you think?"

"Perhaps, but I have advised him not to appear until at least midsummer," Tom replied. "She liked Jeannie."

"Aye, she did," Edmund agreed.

"You must tell Maybel to hold her peace," Tom said.

"Aye," Edmund agreed. "I will remind my well-meaning spouse that if she natters on at Rosamund about Logan Hepburn being a bachelor once more, it could drive the lass away. Of course, Logan may do that himself if he goes on about bairns," Edmund chuckled.

"I've warned him about that, too," Tom responded, chuckling himself.

They celebrated the festive holidays, which concluded with Twelfth Night in early January. Tom was once again generous with Rosamund's daughters. She was amazed that he had managed to find gifts for them all under the circumstances.

"Perhaps in the spring," he told her, "I may travel into Scotland and see about that ship we want to build. It has been a year now since I first suggested it, dear girl."

"We have lost no time," she assured him. "The new flocks we bought last summer are doing very well. We'll have quite a birthing of lambs next month."

"I have never understood why sheep insist on having their offspring in February," he said. "The weather is foul, and the wolves are hunting vigorously."

"No one has ever understood sheep," Rosamund told him, laughing. "It is their own way, and they will have it, I fear. At least I have the flocks all gathered in now that the snows are covering the grazing on the hillsides."

The winter had now set in about them. Tom returned to Otterly to husband his own estate and attend to his business affairs. The days were beginning to grow visibly longer again by Candlemas on February second. Father Mata was teaching Rosamund's daughters six mornings a week. The three girls sat at the high board and studied diligently, for both their mother and their uncles had said it was important, no matter what others might say. All of them could read and write now. The young priest taught them Latin, not simply the church Latin needed for the mass but the Latin that was spoken within the civilized nations. Rosamund taught them French even as their father had taught her when they first met. They already knew their numbers and simple arithmetic. Rosamund and Edmund schooled Philippa in how to keep Friarsgate's accounts, as the responsibility would one day be hers.

"Great lords have others to do this for them," Rosamund said, "but a wise woman knows how to manage her monies herself, lest those others attempt to cheat her because she is a woman or make mistakes. It is not easy to manage Friarsgate, but if you would keep it safe you must learn, Philippa. Do you understand me, my child?"

Philippa nodded. "Aye, mama, I do. But when I marry one day, will my husband not take on this task for me?"

"Friarsgate will belong to you, Philippa, not your husband. You are the heiress to Friarsgate, my daughter. It will be yours until you pass it on to your eldest-born son or daughter," Rosamund explained. "It will never be your husband's property. I am the last Bolton of Friarsgate. You will be the Meredith of Friarsgate, but your heir, and I do hope it is a son, will be the next lord or lady of this manor. My unfortunate uncle Henry could never live with this knowledge. For him Friarsgate is the Boltons', but our sons are now all gone."

"What about Uncle Henry's son, mama?" Philippa asked innocently.

"He could never be the heir unless your sisters and I were gone from this earth," she said. "I have not seen him since he was a child. He was an obnoxious little boy, strutting and making pronouncements."

"They say he is a robber chief now," Philippa said.

"So I am told," Rosamund replied.

"Who told you that?"

"Maybel did. She said Uncle Henry's son is even worse than his strumpet mother," Philippa repeated.

"I suspect Maybel is right," Rosamund answered her daughter, "but she should not have said it to you, Philippa. Put my wicked uncle and his offspring from your mind. They will have nothing to do with your life."

"Yes, mama," the little girl said dutifully.

Rosamund sought out her old nursemaid. "Do not speak to the girls about my uncle's son. You will frighten them, Maybel."

"Very little frightens that trio," Maybel answered pithily.

"That is because they are young and sheltered. They have not lived as I did as a child. I don't want them to be afraid of the Boltons."

"You keep them too close, Rosamund," Maybel said. "Philippa has been to Queen Margaret's court. I think you should take her to her own king's court to meet our good queen. She was once your friend. Perhaps she will favor Philippa if she knows her. Philippa will be ten in April. It is time you begin seeking out a worthy husband for her."

"Not yet," Rosamund said. "Perhaps when she is twelve."

"All the good matches will be taken if you wait too long," Maybel replied, outraged by Rosamund's attitude. "Why, you had two husbands by the time you were her age, and a third two years after you were twelve."

"Which is precisely why I shall wait until Philippa is older. I don't want her marrying some graybeard. I want her to fall in love and marry a man closer to her in age, who will hopefully be her one and only husband," Rosamund said.

"Romantic twaddle!" Maybel huffed.

"But she is my child," Rosamund said, "and I will plan her life, as it is my right to do. I mean to plan wisely for Philippa and her sisters."

"They may have their own plans," Maybel said sharply.

The hillside now began to grow green with the coming of spring. The ewes proudly shepherded their new offspring into the meadows beneath the warm spring sun. The fields were plowed and the grain sown in those being used this year. The orchards came into full bloom. Rosamund's second daughter, Banon, celebrated her eighth birthday on the fifteenth day of March. Philippa turned ten at the end of April, and Bessie was six by the end of May. Tom came from Otterly, as he had for the two previous birthday celebrations. He brought Bessie a small terrier pup as a present. She squealed with delight upon opening the basket in which he had placed it, and then she hugged him. The squirming puppy jumped from its basket and scampered across the garden with Bessie in hot pursuit, causing them all to laugh. It was at that moment uninvited guests arrived, ushered into the gardens by a house servant.

"Such gaiety," Henry Bolton said. He was accompanied by a tall young man whom Rosamund immediately recognized as her cousin Henry the younger.

She arose. "Uncle, this is a surprise, but you are, of course, welcome." She deliberately ignored her cousin.

"I have brought my son with me today. He has been living with me," Henry said.

"I had heard he has taken to robbery, uncle," Rosamund replied.

"Nay, nay, niece. He is a reformed man. Aren't you, my son?" Henry said.

"Yes, father," the young man responded. His gaze had fastened upon Philippa. "Is that the heiress to Friarsgate?" he asked his sire.

"You have never been noted for your subtlety, cousin," Rosamund told him. "But if you think to wed my daughter, put it from your mind. I told your father this in December." She glared at her relations.

"The little wench has to marry someone, cousin," the young man replied.

"There are two criteria for her husband. She must love the man she marries, and he must be of a high social station. You fit neither of those standards, cousin. If that is the purpose of your visit, then you have wasted your time."

"Is this the kind of hospitality you offer me?" Henry demanded, outraged.

"You come into our midst unannounced, uncle, bringing my cousin, who has spent his last years in robbery and mayhem. Your purpose is to make a match between my innocent child and this ruffian, something I previously told you was not possible. And you wonder I do not welcome you with open arms? You have dedicated your life, uncle, to stealing Friarsgate from me. You have failed. Now you hope you may yet gain it through my daughter. It will not happen, I tell you! Now, get out! Take your wicked spawn with you and know that you shall never darken my door again!" Rosamund stood as tall as she could, her index finger pointing out of the garden. About her, her family was very, very quiet. Her daughters had never seen her this angry.

"You were always a difficult girl," Henry said. His face was red with his outrage.

"This is Bolton land, you stupid bitch! It must remain Bolton land! I will kill you before I allow Friarsgate to be given to a stranger!" He lunged at her furiously, but Rosamund was quicker and stepped back.

"Get out!" she told him again in a hard voice.

Henry's face now turned from red to deep red to purple. "Why could you have not died with your brother and your parents? You have ever been a thorn in my side, you damned bitch! This should all be mine!" He was foaming about his lips, and then with a loud cry, he collapsed at her feet and was very still.

"I think you have finally killed the old devil off," Henry the younger said as Edmund knelt, seeking a pulse from his half-brother.

Edmund looked up. "He is dead, Rosamund."

"Good!" she replied vehemently.

Father Mata stepped forward. "Have mercy, lady," he counseled her gently.

"He had none on me," Rosamund said softly. Henry Bolton was dead. She could scarce believe it, but it was true. Then she said, "I will give him in death what I would not give him in life, Mata. He may be buried here at Friarsgate."

The priest nodded approvingly.

"His cottage?" Henry the younger said.

"Is it now mine?"

"Nay," Tom quickly said. "I built it for your father to live out his life in, but it is part of Otterly, and Otterly is mine. I know your father had a will, young Henry, and you are his sole heir. Meet me at Otterly in a week's time, and we will see what it is you have inherited."

The young man nodded. Then he turned to Rosamund and bowed. "I will not say it has been pleasurable seeing you again, cousin," he told her wryly. "And I should far rather wed and bed you than the little wench who is your heiress. I am old enough now by far, and it is said that I am skilled in passion."

"Get out!" Rosamund said once more. "The sight of you sickens me, and your lack of grief is shameful."

"I do not grieve for him," her cousin said. "He was wretched to my mother. I hated him for it. Had I gotten my hands on Friarsgate, I should have exiled him from it even as you did. And I would not have allowed his bones to be interred in its soil." He bowed to her once more. "Perhaps I shall return, cousin."

"Do not," Rosamund said in a hard, cold voice.

Chapter 15

The morning after Bessie's natal day they laid Henry Bolton to rest in the family burial site next to his mother. Rosamund's parents and brother were interred next to her grandfather. His son had not returned for his burial. Rosamund was very concerned that Henry the younger was in the vicinity and that he had seen Philippa. "Did you know," she asked Tom, "that my cousin was with his father this winter past?"

Tom shook his head. "If I had, I should have called the sheriff," he said. "God's blood, dear girl, I could have been murdered in my bed, and none the wiser!" He looked distinctly pale at the thought. "I wonder that Mistress Dodger did not tell me, but then I saw little of her during the winter. I shall certainly speak with her when I return to Otterly in a few days' time."

"If they cozened her, or threatened her, you can no longer trust her," Rosamund noted, "especially as my cousin is about. God! What am I to do, Tom? If only Patrick and I had been wed."

"Do you still think of him?" Lord Cambridge wondered.

"He is never far from my thoughts," Rosamund said softly, sadly.

"You will never forget him, cousin," Tom said, "but you must get on with your life, for he will never be with you again, and you know that."

She nodded. "I do, and yet I cannot help but grieve. But that grief I will keep to myself, Tom. My problem remains if Henry the younger still lurks about. What am I to do to protect Philippa? I cannot have her constantly dogged by men-at-arms, and I would not frighten her."

Rosamund's answer to her problem came several days later when a messenger arrived from Queen Katherine commanding her to court. She was astounded, for she could not imagine that someone as unimportant as she indeed was had been remembered. Certainly the queen had more important matters to consider. Henry Tudor's adventures in France the year before and England's great victory at Flodden had placed England clearly in the world's spotlight. Even here in the north it was known that representatives from all the countries of Europe were arriving in London to present their ambassadorial credentials to the king. How had she been recalled in light of all of that?

"Does it matter, dear girl?" Tom asked. "This is the solution you sought. We shall go to court, and take Philippa with us. She has met Queen Margaret and her late lamented spouse. Now let her greet her own king and queen. Who knows what may come of it, Rosamund? I shall send word to have both the London and Greenwich houses opened and made ready for us. The trip will serve another purpose, for I would have you meet with my goldsmiths, and we must choose a factor to serve us in London. Our ship will be ready to be launched by next year, and by withholding our cloth this year we will build up our stock and increase the demand for it."

"I will set the men to work building a stone storage house for us while we are gone," Rosamund said.

"Then, you will go?" he asked.

"Of course I will go. I was not here last year when the summons came, and then the war came, making it unsafe for travel. I cannot afford to offend the queen or her husband. Aye, I will go, and taking Philippa with us is the best way to keep her safe from Henry the younger. But will Banon and Bessie be safe from him?"

"Philippa is your heiress, and it is she he wants," Tom assured her. "If she is not here, then there is nothing here for him. Still, I would make certain Friarsgate is well guarded in your absence. I hesitate to suggest it, but I shall nonetheless. Why not send to the laird, your neighbor, and ask if you may hire some of his clansmen for the purpose of guarding Friarsgate, and your younger daughters? You may not like Logan Hepburn, but he is honest and brave."

"I do not dislike the laird," Rosamund said slowly, "and what you have proposed makes strange sense to me, Tom. But I would have you send to him."

"I think it would be preferable if Edmund made the overture, as he is your bailiff," Tom said.

"Aye. You're right," Rosamund agreed. "I should not like Logan Hepburn to get the wrong idea." ▪

Tom hid his smile, nodding solemnly.

Edmund sent to the laird of Claven's Carn, asking that he come to discuss a matter of business to both of their best interests. To Edmund and Tom's amusement, the laird returned with the Friarsgate messenger. They kept their humor from Rosamund, who had decided to allow her uncle to manage the negotiation. The three men sat in the hall of the house while the servants brought them ale, bread, and cheese.

"What is it I can do for you, Edmund Bolton?" the laird asked the older man. His eyes quickly scanned the room.

"Old Henry Bolton came with his ruffian son on our Bessie's natal day. He interrupted the celebration. He wanted to make a match between Henry the younger and Philippa, something Rosamund had already told him was impossible. She told him again, and the old man fell into a terrible temper tantrum, which to our surprise, killed him on the spot. We buried him several days ago. Henry the younger, however, remains a danger to Philippa. Having been commanded to court, Rosamund will leave shortly with Tom, taking Philippa with her in order to protect her heiress. She means her daughter for better things, and being introduced into court is the first step."

Logan nodded. "Aye, she is wise where the lassie is concerned. Friarsgate is no small inheritance. I see you have added Shropshires to your flocks."

"We have," Edmund replied.

"What do you seek of me, then?" the laird of Claven's Carn asked his companions.

"We wish to hire some of your clansmen who might otherwise be idle, to serve us as men-at-arms in the event that Henry Bolton the younger and his friends decide to take matters into their own hands while Rosamund is in the south," Edmund explained.

Logan nodded. "Aye, 'tis a wise precaution, Edmund Bolton. Now, allow me to make another suggestion. If Rosamund's younger daughters are not at Friarsgate while she is away, they will be safer. I would gladly keep those two lassies secure from harm at Claven's Carn. Henry the younger will never know or even consider the girls are so near, just over the border with me. And I will also lend you two dozen of my own people to serve you as men-at-arms. That should certainly deter the lady's cousin from his mischief."

" 'Tis a brilliant suggestion, my dear boy!" Tom enthused, speaking for the first time in the matter. "Of course, we would send a lass or two with the girls to attend them, you understand."

"Of course," the laird replied, "but Jeannie, God assoil her sweet soul, trained me a fine housekeeper who keeps the servants in good order. Mistress Elton has granddaughters of her own. My house is well fortified. It has never fallen in a siege because our well is within our courtyard, as is our granary. I think the lady's lasses would enjoy my wee son, Johnnie, and he them."

"We must, of course, speak with Rosamund, Logan Hepburn," Edmund said.

"I have not seen her since I arrived," the laird responded, attempting to sound casual, but his tone gave him away. "I have news of the queen for her."

"Go gently, lad," Tom warned him softly.

"I am certain Rosamund will join us at table this evening," Edmund answered. "We will discuss the matter further then, Logan Hepburn. It is a generous offer, and a clever one, too. It is unlikely Henry the younger would think to look to Claven's Carn."

"I do not know if I can sit at the high board with him," Rosamund said when her uncle told her that the laird was with them.

"You must," Edmund responded. "He has agreed to hire out his clansmen to us at a most reasonable rate, but it is his offer to shelter Banon and Bessie that pleases me greatly. They will be far safer from my nephew Henry at Claven's Carn than here. At Friarsgate they could be kidnapped as they walked to the church, or played in a meadow or by the lake. If they are constantly guarded by men-at-arms it will frighten them, niece. Now, tell me why you will not face Logan Hepburn." He took her hand and looked into her lovely face.

Rosamund blushed. "Now he is a widower, I fear he will begin again to importune me to marry him," she said. "If I offend him, he could withdraw his offer of support."

Edmund smiled. "Would it be so dreadful, niece, if a handsome man sought to pay you court? Forgive me, but Patrick Leslie is as dead to you now as Owein Meredith. You are fortunate in your memories, but you are yet young. Philippa is ten, and in a few years, too few I might add, she will be ready for marriage. You were willing to spend part of your year at Glenkirk as the earl's wife. Would it be any different should you wed Logan Hepburn one day, Rosamund? At least he has an heir, and you know he has no designs on Friarsgate," Edmund concluded.

She was silent for a long moment, and then she said, "I will come to the high board, uncle. More than that, however, I will not promise you."

"Try not to fight with him, niece," Edmund said with some humor.

Rosamund laughed. She could not help herself. "Very well, uncle," she promised him.

Logan tried not to stare when she came into the hall. She wore a gown that matched her amber eyes. It was a simple dress that fell in graceful folds. Its neckline was low and square, but made modest by its soft linen pleating. The tight sleeves had little fur cuffs. The bodice was close-fitting as well. An embroidered girdle hung from her waist. Her auburn head was bare, and she wore her hair in two simple plaits.

"Good evening, Logan Hepburn," she greeted him. "Thank you for coming to our aid once again."

"Henry the younger is ever a trial to Friarsgate, isn't he?" the laird teased her.

She smiled. "I can but hope I do not have to spend my life quarreling with him as I did his father," Rosamund said. "Please sit down, here on my right hand," she invited.

He obliged her, seating her first before taking his own place.

"I am sorry about your wife," Rosamund told him. "And to lose a bairn, as well. If I had but known she was alone, I should have gone to her aid, Logan. I liked Jeannie muchly. How is your little Johnnie?"

"He thrives," the laird answered. "She was a good wife, Rosamund, and I respected her greatly." Then, after a pause, he said, "I am sorry for your loss, as well, lass."

A spasm passed over her visage, but then she said, "Thank you." Nothing more.

"I bring you happy news," Logan told her. "Queen Margaret was delivered of a fine son, Alexander, Duke of Ross, on the thirtieth day of April."

"How wonderful for her, and yet how sad," Rosamund said.

"That is your birthday, isn't it, lady?" he inquired.

"Aye," she said softly, wondering how he had known it.

The meal was served. Of Rosamund's three daughters, only Philippa sat at table.

"I am to go to court to meet the queen," Philippa said. "I am now ten."

"A perfect age to meet a queen," he said with a small smile. She was a charming miniature of Rosamund, he thought.

"I was nine when I met Queen Margaret and King James, he who was slain at Flodden," Philippa replied. "My mother says he was a good king."

"God's blood!" Tom swore, and then he said to Philippa, "You must not say that when we visit the English court, dear child. Speak of the king's sister, the Regent of Scotland, if you must, but say naught about Jamie Stewart."

"Why not?" Philippa demanded to know.

"Because," her mother said, "these two kings were enemies. It is ill-advised to praise a man's enemy before him, Philippa. Do you understand?"

"Why were they enemies?" Philippa answered her mother with another question.

"England and Scotland have been enemies since time immemorial," Rosamund responded.

"Why?" Philippa persisted.

"I am not really certain," Rosamund said honestly.

"But you visited King James' court, and I know you did not think him your enemy. And if the Scots are our enemies, why is the lord of Claven's Carn at our table this night, mama? And why is he protecting Banon and Bessie when we are away if he is our enemy?"

Tom chuckled.

"Your daughter is no fool, madame," the laird of Claven's Carn noted.

"Sometimes I think Philippa too wise for her own good," Rosamund said quietly. Then she turned back to her child. "The English and the Scots in the borders sometimes have a different relationship than others of our race, Philippa. I cannot really give you a good explanation for it. Queen Margaret was my friend at her father's court when I was growing up, but you know that. My friend asked me to visit her, and as there was no war between our countries then, I went. I should go again if she asked me. As for the Hepburns of Claven's Carn, they have been our neighbors forever. I do not believe we have ever fought each other. Uncle Tom will be with us at court. Edmund is too old to mount a strong defense of Friarsgate, although I know he would try if asked, but I will not ask it of him. The laird has kindly offered to protect your sisters, and I am grateful for his offer. I will accept it gladly. The only thing separating England and Scotland in this particular matter is an invisible border, Philippa. But if it is invisible, then we cannot see it and so it is not there. The Hepburns are our neighbors. They are good neighbors."

"Thank you, madame," Logan said.

She nodded in reply, and for a moment she grew breathless. She had forgotten that his eyes were so blue-blue.

"Am I to understand that your lasses will come to me?" he said carefully, not wanting to press her in any manner. Tom had warned him to go gently.

"Did I not make myself clear in the matter, my lord?" she asked him, a trifle irritated.

"I would not presume, madame, which is why I query you," he told her, and his eyes were dancing.

Rosamund felt her cheeks growing warm with a memory. Once she had indeed accused him of presuming when he had said he but assumed. She looked directly at him, and to her surprise, her heart began to hammer again. What the hell was the matter with her? "Yes," she said, "I should like you to keep Banon and Bessie at Claven's Carn while I am away, my lord. And I thank you for your kindness in offering my daughters your protection."

Still seated, he bowed from the waist. "I am glad to be of some service to you, madame," he told her, his face impassive, his tone mild. "I think it might be best if I took them back with me tomorrow. It is not likely your unpleasant cousin has gotten his thoughts or his men together yet. I realize it is short notice, but your daughters' safety must be our first consideration. And in addition to the men-at-arms I shall loan you, I shall also send my men to escort you south. With Henry the younger skulking about, you cannot be certain any men-at-arms you hire will not be subverted by false promises. They will not wear their plaids, and to an untrained ear, a Scots borderer and an English borderer sound much alike. They will claim to be your own Friarsgate folk."

"That is very generous of you, Logan Hepburn," Rosamund exclaimed.

"It is brilliant!" Thomas enthused.

"Indeed it is," Edmund agreed.

"With your permission, madame, I can make it so," he said.

Rosamund looked closely at Logan. There was absolutely no mockery in his tone or his attitude. She nodded. "Aye, I would be glad to have your men protecting me. I will pay them the usual rate for hired men-at-arms, of course."

"Of course," he replied. "They will all be grateful for the coin, madame, for it is not often they can come by a bit of silver."

The meal over, Rosamund arose from the table. "I must go and see that Banon and Bessie's belongings are packed for the morrow." She hurried from the hall.

When she had gone, Philippa said, "You like my mother, don't you, Logan Hepburn?"

He turned his blue eyes to meet her gaze. "Aye, I have always liked your mother, lass."

Philippa was very curious. "When did you first meet her?"

"I first saw your mother when she was Bessie's age," he answered her.

"She was married to Hugh Cabot, then, was she not?"

"Not the summer I first saw her, but soon afterwards," he told the girl, looking to Edmund and Tom for guidance, but they said nothing, nor gave any indication that he should cease his tale. "Then, when your mother was widowed, I came courting, but she had gone to court. And when she returned she was betrothed and about to wed with your good sire, Owein Meredith. And sadly, she was widowed again."

"Why didn't you come courting then, my lord?" Philippa pressed him.

"I did, but I did not approach your mother properly. She turned me away and went up to Edinburgh," he explained.

"And she fell in love with Uncle Patrick. But he has forgotten her now. She is always very sad, my lord. Do you wish to court her again?"

Logan heard his two male companions chuckle softly. He swallowed hard, not quite certain what he should say, but Philippa was not going to be denied an answer. She stared directly at him, her head cocked to one side questioningly. "Aye," he told the little girl. "I should very much like to court your mother and marry her, lass, but she is a prickly creature, and I must move carefully this time, for I do not want to lose her again. You must not tell her this, Philippa. Do you understand why?"

Philippa nodded. "I will try to see she contracts no involvements while we are visiting King Henry, my lord. My sisters and I are in agreement that mama is happier with a good husband than without one. We think that you should do very well as our stepfather, if, of course, you are in agreement."

Astounded, he nodded slowly. "Aye," he said.

"Then, it is settled," Philippa told him, and she arose from the high board. "Mama will need my help. I shall leave you gentlemen now." And she glided from the hall with far more elegance than most girls her age had.

Tom and Edmund burst out laughing, and the two men laughed until their eyes watered, and their sides ached.

"She has far more presence at ten than my own poor Jeannie did at eighteen," the laird of Claven's Carn said when his companions finally ceased their laughter. "God's blood! I hope she will not tell Rosamund of our conversation."

"She won't," Edmund assured him. "She is much like her great-grandmother. My father's wife was a woman of much good sense who liked to have her life and the lives of those about her well ordered. Philippa is the same. She may look like her mother, but she is nothing like her in character. She will keep this conversation that you have had to herself until she feels the time is right to reveal it. If indeed she ever does."

"She is an unusual little lass," Logan said.

Edmund arose from the table. "Come with me, Logan Hepburn, and I will show you where you are to sleep this night. Good night, Tom."

Lord Cambridge stood up. "Good night, Edmund. Logan," he said, and he strolled off to find his own bed.

In her rooms, Rosamund had gathered her two younger daughters to her and explained that they would be going to Claven's Carn for a visit. "The poor laird is very lonely without his wife, and you will have his little lad to play with, my darlings."

They nodded, not objecting, but they knew the truth, for Philippa had told it to them earlier. She had also told them not to say anything to their mother, for it would but distress her to learn that they knew. "She thinks we are still babies," Philippa had said.

When she had tucked her daughters into their beds, Rosamund went to help with the packing. Maybel was already gathering what Banon and Bessie would need.

"I am frankly surprised at your good sense in allowing Logan Hepburn to watch over the lasses," she said bluntly to Rosamund.

"I had to put aside my own feelings and think of what is best for my daughters," Rosamund answered her.

"So," Maybel pounced, "you have feelings for the laird!"

"He still irritates me, if that is what you mean," Rosamund said shortly, "but not so much tonight, perhaps. He was thoughtful and careful in his speech with me. I could not fault him at all."

"Mayhap he has changed," Maybel suggested.

"Men rarely change after a certain age," Rosamund said dryly.

"But that young wife of his, God assoil her soul," Maybel said, crossing herself, "may have taught him better. He did not love her, but it is said he liked her well enough."

"You are getting as bad as Tom with all your gossip," Rosamund laughed, teasing her old companion.

"I cannot believe that you are going away again," Maybel replied. "You never relished all this traveling about before. Now suddenly you are home but a short time and then you are off again. I like it not!"

"I should have been perfectly content to spend the rest of my life at Friarsgate, Maybel. I have had more than enough of adventuring, but I cannot ignore a royal summons, can I?"

"But why has Queen Katherine summoned you? The friendship between you is nowhere near that of your friendship with Queen Margaret," Maybel noted. "Queen Katherine does not need you as she once did when you were girls."

"The summons may have the queen's signature, but it comes from the king, I am most certain," Rosamund said. "The English ambassador in San Lorenzo thought he recognized me. We had never met, but he had indeed seen me at court when I last visited. Tom tells me he has returned to England. He probably remembered who I was and told the king. Henry Tudor would have certainly been curious as to what I was doing in San Lorenzo last winter with a Scottish lord. His curiosity is such that he will not be satisfied until he knows the answer to that question."

"But he is a mighty king," Maybel said. "All of Europe is at his feet right now. He has won great victories in France and broken Scotland's spirit at Flodden. Why should he care about the answer to such a question, Rosamund?"

"Because we were once friends, Maybel. He will want to assure himself that I have not betrayed him in any way. Everything like that matters to him. The smallest detail or fact consumes him. It is his way."

"Will you tell him of the Earl of Glenkirk?" she asked.

"I have no choice, for Lord Howard will have certainly told him," Rosamund answered her.

"Could you not send him a message explaining?" Maybel queried.

Rosamund laughed. "I wish I could," she said. "But the king will want to look into my face, into my eyes, as I relate my tale. It is the only way he can be certain that I am still loyal to him. Henry Tudor is a jealous man, Maybel."

"It seems to me," Maybel muttered, "that he has changed little from that boy who attempted to seduce you beneath his own grandmother's nose."

"Oh, he has indeed changed, Maybel. Power and wealth have brought about that change. He wields both mightily, even if beneath the surface he is still that bad boy," Rosamund said quietly.

Maybel sighed. "I don't like your going," she said.

"Nor do I, but to disobey a royal summons would bring dire consequences upon Friarsgate, and I have spent my entire life watching over my lands. I do not want to be forced into another arranged marriage with one of the king's men; nor do I want Philippa endangered. I will go. Besides, Tom will be with me, and you know how much he can amuse the king and queen. I will be all right."

In the morning the laird of Claven's Carn prepared to take Rosamund's daughters with him over the border into Scotland. They met unexpectedly in the Great

Hall before the others had assembled. She had just come from the mass.

"I am glad we are alone," he said. "I wanted to assure you that I will guard the lasses as if they were my own, Rosamund."

"I know you will," she said. Her insides were melting at the sight of those blue-blue eyes as he looked at her.

"When will you return?" he asked softly.

"I do not know," she responded honestly. "I do not really enjoy King Henry's court, but I cannot refuse my own queen's call. I suspect the king has learned of my sojourn in San Lorenzo and wants an explanation. Henry Tudor is a suspicious man, always seeing demons where there are none to be found."

Logan nodded, understanding. Then he said, "Rosamund, I do not always speak with delicacy, but might I humbly request that you contract no alliances while you are away. I should like, nay, I should enjoy, the opportunity to become your friend when you return."

"My friend?" She looked at him askance.

He flushed, realizing what he had said might easily be misconstrued. "Your friend," he repeated. "And perhaps a friendship between us could lead to a . . ." he hesitated, afraid to say the word lest he frighten her off for good.

"You wish to court me with an eye towards marriage?" she asked frankly.

"Aye!" And his look was one of such relief that she laughed.

"Then I will contract no unions while I am away, Logan, but other than that I make you no promises. Do you understand me? I am still not certain that I will marry again." The smile she gave him was tremulous and brief.

He wanted to say that she had shown no hesitation with Lord Leslie, but he did not. He remembered seeing them together at Stirling. He had never in his life beheld such raw and unbounded love as they had exhibited for each other. He had never imagined love like that existed. But even if she never loved him like that, he knew he wanted her as he had always wanted her. He would accept what she had to give, if indeed there was anything left in her heart. "I understand," he told her. "I ask nothing, and you render me no promise. We shall begin anew, and perhaps something good may come of it, Rosamund."

The hall began to be peopled now with servants, and the children came, eager and excited, running to Logan and bidding him a good morning. Rosamund was touched by the sight of it. Her daughters obviously liked the Scotsman, and that was to the good.

"My lord! My lord!" Bessie was tugging

at his sleeve. She was the daughter most like Owein Meredith with her soft blond hair and gray-blue eyes.

"Yes, Bessie," he asked her, "what is it, lass?"

"May I take my puppy with me, my lord? The terrier that Uncle Tom gave me for my natal day celebration?" She was holding a small black and tan pup in her arms.

Logan leaned down, saying as he did, "He doesn't look very big, Bessie. I suspect he won't take up a great deal of room, and he would be very lonely without you. Aye, we must take him. Does he have a name yet?" His big hand stroked the pup's head, and the puppy's tongue licked at his fingers.

"He is Tam for my Uncle Tom," Bessie answered.

"We'll put him in a small basket, lass, and you will carry him yourself on your pony," the laird told her with a smile.

"He is a very kind man, mama," Philippa murmured, coming to her mother's side. "I do believe Banon and Bessie will have a fine time with him."

"Yes," her mother said. Nothing more. She was suddenly seeing Logan in a new light. Perhaps Jeannie, God assoil her soul, had indeed civilized him.

After the morning meal they prepared for the laird's departure. In the courtyard, the girls already mounted upon their ponies, Logan said to Rosamund, "I will return tomorrow with the men I intend to watch over Friarsgate, as well as those I choose to escort you south."

"I would leave tomorrow, but I will travel only as far as my uncle's monastery."

" 'Tis a good plan. Young Mistress Philippa should not be tired her first day on the road," he answered.

She nodded in agreement and, looking about, said, "I see no one upon the hills spying on us yet."

"Nay. I sent my men early to see what was happening, and as we suspected, your cousin hasn't gotten himself together yet. I think we may both make our getaways before he is aware you and your daughters are gone," Logan said. "I thank you for your hospitality, Rosamund Bolton." Then he mounted his stallion and moved to the front of his men, and they moved off, Rosamund's daughters in their midst, the cart with the children's belongings and two servant girls following.

Rosamund waved to Banon and Bessie, but after a cursory salute the two little girls were more intent on what they perceived as the adventure ahead than their mother behind. Rosamund felt tears coming. "Oh dear," she said, brushing them impatiently away.

"They are only going to Claven's Carn, mama," Philippa said. "You are not losing them forever, you know."

Rosamund laughed a watery laugh. "Philippa, you have such common sense. I do not know where you got it from, but I am glad."

"Edmund says I am like my great-grandmother," Philippa told her mother.

They spent the day completing the arrangements for their journey. Several of Rosamund's gowns had been altered and remade at Tom's direction, so she would not appear unfashionable at court. Philippa's gowns from the previous year at the Scots court were also remade, and a third gown was added to her wardrobe. The proper accoutrements and jewelry were chosen and packed.

"I wish I could go with you this time, my lady," Annie said wistfully. She was again with child, and her son was not yet weaned.

"Lucy suits me," Rosamund told her tiring woman. "You have trained her well, and you can be proud of your little sister."

"But she gets to go to court," Annie bemoaned her fate. "I should like to go again."

Rosamund laughed. "There is no pleasure in all that traveling, as you well know, Annie, or have you forgotten so quickly?"

her mistress teased her.

"Aye, I've forgotten the trial of travel, but I remember San Lorenzo in the winter sunlight, my lady," Annie said wistfully.

"You have had the best of it, Annie. San Lorenzo and King Henry's court, and King James' court, God assoil his good soul," Rosamund told her

Annie nodded. "I have," she agreed. "Still, I should like to see Great Harry in all his glory. Will you remain long?"

"No longer than I must," Rosamund said.

Annie closed the trunk holding her mistress' gowns, which she had packed very carefully. "They say the lord of Claven's Carn would court you if you would allow it."

Rosamund shook her head. Why was it the servants always knew what you did not want them to know? "I am on my way to London, Annie. I have scarce time for a lovelorn Scot now, do I?"

Annie grinned at her mistress. "You was always one for keeping secrets," she said.

"No one can keep anything secret at Friarsgate," Rosamund replied with a laugh.

Logan returned the following morning bringing with him thirty men. "The younglings will remain at Friarsgate to

607

keep it safe. The more experienced men I am sending with you," he said.

"How are Banon and Bessie?" she asked him anxiously.

"Tired after their ride yesterday, but God's blood, Rosamund! You have bonnie daughters. They've charmed my house-keeper already, and Johnnie is enchanted with them. He's never had playmates before."

"Is he like you?" she asked him.

"It's like your Bessie. He looks like me, but he is his mother's son, with Jeannie's sweet manner about him. He may change as he grows older, but having never raised a lad myself, I don't know."

"If the girls become too much, send for Maybel. She will keep them in order. I thought it better she remain here, as her absence would be more quickly noted than my younger daughters'," Rosamund told him. Then she said, "I thank you again, Logan Hepburn, for the hire of your men and your care of my girls."

"I will anxiously await your return," he said.

"I think I may miss your arrogance just a little," Rosamund said to him. "You are so polite with me, it is if you are walking on eggs, Logan Hepburn."

"I am," he replied. "I am attempting to prove to you that I am not a rough borderer, a Scots scoundrel, as you once called me, Rosamund, that I am indeed worthy of your hand. If I allowed myself to revert to my former self, I should seriously consider preventing your going. I should sweep you into my arms and kiss you until you were weak. Then I should carry you to the church and have Mata marry us." He smiled just a trifle wolfishly. "But you prefer a more civilized lover, so if I am to have any chance of winning you, I must be the man you desire. When we are at last wed — if you will have me," he amended, "then I shall become the man you need, Rosamund Bolton." He bowed, then bent, cupping his hands together to boost her into her saddle.

Rosamund settled herself, but her heart was hammering nervously. Yet when she looked down at him, her amber eyes were grave. "Yes," she considered, "I do miss the arrogance." And she smiled wickedly at him, gathering her reins in her gloved hand.

"Golden brown velvet suits you," he murmured, taking her other hand and kissing it. "Give my regards to your uncle Richard, madame."

"Be assured, I will," she responded, and then she kicked her mount, moving away.

They traveled as far as St. Cuthbert's Monastery, where Rosamund's other uncle,

Richard Bolton, was prior. They were welcomed into St. Cuthbert's and settled into the guesthouse for the night. Prior Richard invited them to dine with him in his private dining chamber. She had not seen this uncle, Edmund's younger brother, in well over a year.

"So, niece, while my brother has kept me well informed, I am surprised to see you once again journeying down to court. I did not consider you particularly interested in that sort of life," the prior said.

"I am not, but the queen has summoned me, and I thought it an opportunity for Philippa to be introduced to her and presented to the king. In too few years, uncle, I must find a good match for my daughter."

The prior nodded. "Yes," he agreed. "Philippa is indeed growing up." He turned to the little girl. "You have no desire to serve Holy Mother Church, my child?"

"Only in the capacity of a wife and mother, my lord prior," Philippa answered him politely.

Richard chuckled. "You have done well with her," he said.

"Edmund says she reminds him of her great-grandmother," Rosamund answered him with a smile.

"Yes," the prior replied thoughtfully. "Our father's wife was a woman of good sense and good heart. She treated all her husband's sons equally, though it surely must have been difficult, as Edmund and I were bastards. Still, she loved us the same, and she chastised us the same. Now, why has Queen Katherine called an unimportant northern landowner to court?"

Rosamund explained to her uncle why, she believed, she had been summoned.

"You must be very careful," the prior advised her. Then he smiled at Philippa. "My child, go with Brother Robert. He will show you about my little realm before it is too dark. You will not have time in the morning."

"If you wished to speak with my mother privily," Philippa said, "you had but to ask, my lord prior."

"I am asking," he responded, not in the least ruffled by her boldness.

When the young girl had gone, the prior spoke seriously to his niece. "You were the king's lover. He is bound to be jealous of your relationship with the Earl of Glenkirk. You must deal with him most skillfully if you are to escape his wrath, Rosamund."

"Uncle! The king does not care about me. He simply wished to accomplish what he had earlier set out to do. But nonetheless, I know he will be curious as to why I was with Patrick. He will not be satisfied until he knows the entire story."

"You had some feelings for the king, I am certain," the prior persisted. "You have not the nature of a trollop or a courtesan. And he would have had feelings for you, for this king never does anything he cannot justify. Therefore, he will have convinced himself that he was in love with you, even if it was for only a brief time. The fact that you did not remain in love with him when you parted will be your greatest sin in his eyes, niece. You must be careful how you present your relationship with your earl to him. Edmund said to see you with Patrick Leslie was something magical. He said he had never seen such love between two people. I am sorry for what has happened. And there is no sign of his memories returning?"

"The Moorish physician said if after a year or more nothing had changed, it was very unlikely it would. At least Patrick remembered everything prior to his return to court. He did not lose everything," Rosamund told her uncle.

Richard leaned back in his chair. "But you did," he said.

"It broke my heart," Rosamund admitted. "But life must go on, uncle, mustn't it?" She smiled a small smile at him.

"The laird is after her again," Lord Cambridge volunteered cheerfully.

"Tom!" She was blushing.

Richard laughed. "I am happy to hear it. Now, niece, all you must do is convince Henry Tudor that you are his most loyal subject and escape his clutches so you may come back to Friarsgate. I shall pray for you."

"Your prayers, uncle, will be my shield against the king," she told him.

In the morning they began their journey in earnest, traveling south deep into England. It was even more exciting a journey than her travels into Scotland, Philippa thought as they went. There were neat little villages and charming towns the likes of which she had certainly never seen. As she rode through England, Philippa began to realize just what being heiress to Friarsgate entailed. She suddenly understood the talk of a proper marriage. She was not some simple village maiden. She was the daughter of a knight who had been the loyalist of the king's men. Her parents had been wed at a king's command. And now she was going to court to be presented to their majesties, to be shown off by her mother and to attract a family with an eligible son. She might be only ten years old, but she was the heiress to Friarsgate, and in a few more years she would be ready to marry. Philippa sat her white mare proudly.

After many long days of travel they arrived in London and went directly to Lord Cambridge's house on the river. Built of weathered brick, it was covered in green ivy and stood four stories high from its entrance to its gray slate roof. Watching them pass through the iron gates, the gatekeeper doffed his cap at them. They rode up the raked gravel driveway through the green park. The first week of June had already passed, and the air was warm.

The front door to the house opened as they approached it. Servingmen hurried out to unload the luggage cart as the majordomo, bowing, greeted them and ushered them into the house.

"My lord, we are relieved you have finally arrived," he said.

"You received my messenger yesterday," Tom said. "Did you send to the queen to say the lady of Friarsgate would arrive sometime today?"

"I did, my lord. The royal messenger came with a message not an hour ago. I have it here, my lord." He handed Lord Cambridge a parchment.

"The men-at-arms are ours and must be housed and fed. Please see to it. And show Lucy where her mistress and her mistress' daughter are to reside. The child is next to her mother?"

"Yes, my lord," the majordomo said.

"Everything is as you would wish it." He bowed neatly.

"Come, dear girl, and let us show Philippa the hall," Tom said.

"If it is the same as Otterly's hall, uncle, I know where it is," Philippa said excitedly, running ahead of them.

"You may know where it is, my adorable one, but the view! The London view is magnificent. Tell me if you do not agree," he said with a chuckle as they entered the room.

The chamber ran the length of the house. It was paneled, and at one end there was a large fireplace with iron mastiffs for firedogs. The lead-paned windows running across one wall of the hall overlooked the Thames River. The ceiling was coffered, and multicolored carpets covered the wide floorboards. Enthralled, Philippa ran to the windows, staring openmouthed at the river with its busy traffic below. Rosamund found a chair and sat down, looking to her cousin who was even now opening the message from the palace.

"What does it say?" she asked him.

He scanned the parchment rapidly, then looking up, said, "Her majesty welcomes you back to London. You are called to court tomorrow before the noonday meal. It is not particularly informative, dear girl."

"At least it doesn't tell me to report to

the Tower, Tom," she teased him.

He laughed. "A bath! That is what I need. A bath. An excellent meal prepared by my own chef, and blessedly, my own bed tonight."

"Mama, there are two boats at a dockage at the water's edge," Philippa said.

"They are barges, my daughter. The one with the blue velvet trappings is mine. They are made fast at a quay, which is pronounced *key*. London's streets are narrow, and the traffic can sometimes be difficult. We find traveling by river to the palace far easier, quicker, and much more preferable."

"Oh, mama, there is so much I don't know," Philippa said nervously. "Do you really think I am ready to go to court?"

"You are," Rosamund assured her child, "but perhaps not tomorrow. Tomorrow mama must go and see what it is the queen wants of her. After I have done my duty, Philippa, then I shall bring you to see what court life is all about."

"And once I have had a day there myself," Tom chimed in, "I shall have all the latest gossip for you, my little one."

Rosamund shook her head, grinning. Then she said, "Very well, cousin. Let us get down to business. Will you bathe before or after the meal? The poor servingmen will be run ragged bringing us both hot water."

"Before!" he said. "I do not want the stink of the road interfering with my palate, dear girl. You, on the other hand, eat like the countrywoman you are."

"I do not consider food a holy experience, cousin," Rosamund told him.

They separated, Rosamund taking Philippa upstairs to her apartment. Lucy was awaiting them, and her enthusiasm at their quarters reminded Rosamund of Annie's very reaction when she had come to court after Owein's death.

"The majordomo said this little room is for me," Lucy told them.

"Where am I to lay my head?" Philippa asked.

"Why, Mistress Philippa, you have your very own room. Come, and I'll show you. It's right next to your mama's." She led them into Rosamund's bedchamber, and after going to a paneled wall, pressed a hidden lock allowing a door to spring open. "See! It's your very own bedchamber, and you can see the river from the windows. And," she continued, looking at Rosamund, "there is no other entrance into this room but through your mother's chamber. You will be as snug as a birdling in its nest."

Rosamund realized she had not seen this door before or even known it was there. There had been a tapestry covering the door. She wondered if there was such a room at the Greenwich house or at Otterly. Still, it was the perfect chamber for her young daughter to sleep in, and its decor matched the rose velvet of her bed-chamber.

Several hours later, as the twilight deepened, they sat down to dinner in Lord Cambridge's hall overlooking the river. The cook had outdone himself. There were large prawns in a mustard sauce and pickled eel. There was a capon stuffed with apples, raisins, bread, and sage; a leg of lamb; a game pie made with venison and another filled with pieces of duck in a red wine gravy. There was a small country ham and a platter of asparagus in white wine, along with bowls of peas and small whole beets. There was fresh bread, sweet butter in a stone crock, and several cheeses. And when the remains of the meal had been cleared from the table, a basket of fresh strawberries and a large bowl of thick Devonshire clotted cream was placed upon the board. Philippa was permitted just a small goblet of wine, not watered. She nursed it carefully.

Sated, Tom pushed himself back from his table. "An excellent meal," he told his majordomo. "Tell Cook I said so."

"Indeed, my lord, I will." The major-domo looked to Rosamund. "Your bath will be ready in half an hour, my lady," he told her.

"Thank the men," Rosamund answered him. "I know the work involved in bringing the water upstairs, and I appreciate their effort."

"Yes, my lady," the majordomo said. From the beginning, the lady of Friarsgate had always been thoughtful of her cousin's servants. She was a most unusual woman.

"I am so tired, mama," Philippa said, yawning.

"Then you shall bathe first, my poppet," her mother replied, "but bathe you will, for you have not had a bath since we departed Friarsgate. While many in the court do not bathe regularly, you will find the king has a most sensitive nose and is most put out when a courtier stinks."

"What shall I do tomorrow when you go to see the queen?" Philippa asked.

"You shall stay in your bed, resting from our journey, and then you may walk in your uncle's gardens. The river is a most fascinating sight, and you will enjoy it. Especially as it is summertime," Rosamund told her daughter.

Finally the majordomo came to tell the lady of Friarsgate and her daughter that the tub was now filled and awaiting them.

"Good night, dear Tom," Rosamund said to her cousin as she excused herself.

"Good night," he called as they departed the hall. "Sleep well, cousin, for tomorrow you must be at your best."

Upstairs, Lucy had scented the bath with her mistress' white heather, and the room was perfumed with the smell.

"Help Philippa first," Rosamund instructed her young tiring woman. Then she went into her bedchamber and sat in the window seat looking out over her cousin's gardens and the river. Night had fallen, and she could but see the lanterns in the boat traffic on the water. She remembered the rather suggestive statues in the garden and smiled to herself. It was unlikely that Philippa would understand the nature of them, and she would be able to observe well the male anatomy, which would serve her in good stead one day.

Tomorrow, she thought. Would she see the king tomorrow? They had parted on good terms. She must assume that while he would be curious, and perhaps even angry about her involvement with the Earl of Glenkirk, he would forgive her if she asked him nicely. Nicely. Would it involve surrendering herself to him again, to prove not just her loyalty to him, but her devotion? It was disquieting to even consider such a thing, but she must look at her situation from all sides in order to be prepared for whatever was to come.

Finally Lucy came to her saying, "Mistress Philippa is tucked snugly into her bed, my lady. Will you bathe now?"

Rosamund arose from her place by the windows. "Aye, but first let me bid my daughter sweet dreams," she said. She had not heard Lucy and Philippa come into her bedchamber to enter the child's room. Now she clicked the small latch and went into the little bedchamber herself. The lock was most silent. "Good night, my darling," she said to Philippa. "Dream only of good things, and may the angels guard you."

"I will, mama. This is the most wonderful bed. Uncle Tom always has the nicest things about him."

"Aye, he does," Rosamund agreed. She bent and kissed her daughter.

"Mama? The king will be kind to you, won't he? He won't put you in the Tower?" Philippa's little face looked anxious.

"No, poppet," Rosamund assured her. "The king has always been most kind to your mama. I'm sure he will be again." Then, blowing out the candle on the little nightstand by her daughter's bed, she exited the room, leaving the door ajar in case Philippa would need her in the night.

Lucy helped her to disrobe, gathering her mistress' traveling garments up carefully. "Some will need washing, others a

621

good brushing, my lady. What will you wear tomorrow?"

"I cannot think," Rosamund said. "Just hang my gowns in the garderobe. You pick for me, Lucy, and have the gown ready when I awake."

"Yes, my lady," the young tiring woman said. Then she helped her mistress into her tub. "We'll have to do your hair tonight, my lady. It's full of dust, and won't show to its best advantage unless it is clean. You'll want to make a good impression when you return to court. 'Tis said the king likes a pretty woman."

"It is the truth, Lucy," Rosamund told the girl. "But remember that such thoughts are not voiced for fear of offending the queen. Queen Katherine is a most genteel lady who expects decorum from the women around her. Long ago the king became involved with one of her ladies, but which of a pair of sisters no one was certain. Both were wed, and their husbands were important men with family connections. Both ladies were exiled from the court in disgrace, and the queen was most distressed. But worse, their husbands were embarrassed before their king. Pretty women must be most circumspect around his majesty." Then Rosamund settled back to let Lucy wash her long auburn hair.

And when it was done and pinned atop

her head, Rosamund washed herself quickly, for the water was beginning to cool. Finished, she stepped from her tub, and Lucy wrapped a warmed bathing sheet about her and then dried her with another towel. Still wrapped in the sheet, Rosamund sat down by the fire, unpinned her hair, and brushed it until it was dry. Then, after slipping on a clean lace-trimmed chemise, she left her dayroom where the tub had been set up and climbed into her own bed.

"Will that be all tonight, my lady?" Lucy inquired politely.

"Aye. Find your own bed, Lucy. You are no less tired than the rest of us. Good night," Rosamund said. And then she closed her eyes. She was in London again. Something she had never considered. Tomorrow she would go to court and face the king.

Tomorrow. What would tomorrow bring? And why was Rosamund Bolton of such interest to Henry Tudor? Well, perhaps tomorrow would bring her the answers she needed. Despite her exhaustion she was restless for some time before she finally fell asleep.

Chapter 16

Rosamund awoke to hear the birds singing in Tom's garden. A warm breeze blew through the windows. She yawned and stretched her limbs. Turning her head, she looked through the half-open door in the paneled wall. Philippa was still sleeping. Poor child, Rosamund thought. It had been a long and hard trip for her, but she had never once complained. The return home was always easier, Rosamund considered. She threw back the coverlet on her bed and arose, then pulled the chamber pot from beneath her bed, used it, leaving it for Lucy to empty. Then she went to the windows and leaned out, sniffing the air, which smelled so different from country air. There was more traffic on the river than she had remembered. The two barges made fast to the quay bobbed in the morning sunlight. She turned back into her bedchamber, went to the door of her daughter's room, and closed it softly.

"Good morning, my lady," Lucy said, coming in with a tray for her mistress. She set the tray down on the table near the fireplace.

"Good morning," Rosamund responded. "Philippa is still sleeping. Let her be until she awakens naturally."

"Yes, my lady," Lucy responded. "Now, come and eat. It is past eight o'clock, and you have not much time if you are to be at Westminster on time."

Rosamund sat down at the table. "Nay," she agreed. "It would not do for me to be late. Is Lord Cambridge up yet?"

"Oh, yes, my lady. And he is already driving his man to distraction with all his fussing about what he will wear today. He wished to know what you will wear."

"What did you choose, Lucy?" Rosamund asked her tiring woman.

"Well, my lady, considering your position right now, I thought it best to err on the side of flattery when you go to reacquaint yourself with the queen. I chose a gown of Tudor green for you," Lucy said. "It is a simple garment, modest in its design, for you do not wish to appear ostentatious."

"I was not aware I had a gown of Tudor green," Rosamund said slowly.

"It is one that was made for you in San Lorenzo. I remade it with a more suitable neckline and sleeves," Lucy informed her mistress. "Let me show you." The tiring woman hurried from the bedchamber to return a moment later with the gown. She spread it out for her mistress to view.

Rosamund would not have recognized it for one of the dresses that Celestina had made her but for the paneled underskirt with its delicate windflower and butterfly embroidery in silver matte threads. Gone was the bodice with the deeply scooped neckline, and billowy sheer silk sleeves. In its place was a bodice with a square-cut neckline, the sleeves now tight at the wrist with silver embroidery and covered by wide new sleeves of the same silk brocade as the gown, with large turned-back cuffs. It was a gown made to suit the height of fashion.

"You did this?" Rosamund was very surprised.

"Yes, my lady," Lucy said, blushing with pride.

"You are extraordinarily skilled with your needle, Lucy," her mistress said. "Thank you, for you have rendered a gown otherwise unsuitable for England most suitable. Go and tell Lord Cambridge's man that I shall be wearing Tudor green."

Lucy colored, pleased by her mistress' compliments. "I'll be but a moment, my lady, and then we must get you dressed," she said.

Rosamund sat down at her breakfast table. The cook had sent her a dish of eggs poached in a cream sauce flavored with nutmeg; fresh bread; butter; jam; and a mug of cold, sharp ale. Finding she was hungry, Rosamund ate it all and drained her mug. Lucy was already back, moving about her bedchamber and laying out petticoats and stockings, shoes and jewelry. She brought her mistress a bowl of warm water and a small cloth. Rosamund washed her face and hands. Then she scrubbed her teeth with the cloth and a mixture of pumice and ground mint. She was proud of her teeth, for unlike many others, she had them all, and they were white and even. She donned her stockings, petticoats, and chemise. Next came her bodice with its beautiful sleeves. Now Rosamund sat down so Lucy might dress her hair properly.

The tiring woman brushed her mistress' long auburn hair free of tangles. It shone with rich color. Lucy thought it a shame that Rosamund's hair must be hidden beneath a cap and a veil, but that was the custom of the court. She parted the hair in the middle, gave it a final brush, and then set a green silk French hood trimmed with pearls on Rosamund's head back just enough so that some of her beautiful hair would show. A sheer white silk veil was attached to the French hood. "I don't like these caps and veils," Lucy said. "You have such beautiful hair, my lady."

" 'Tis the fashion, and we must follow it," Rosamund replied.

Lucy set a shakefold on the floor for her mistress to step into and then drew the hooplike contraption up. She then carefully lowered Rosamund's brocade skirts over her head, careful not to jostle the French hood. They settled over the hooplike shakefold, giving the garment a graceful look. The tiring woman quickly fastened the skirts. "There," she said. "You look most proper, my lady. Let me get your jewelry case."

Rosamund chose a heavy gold chain of square links from which hung a gold and pearl crucifix. She also slipped a long rope of pearls about her slender neck and several rings upon the fingers of both hands. Thanks to her cousin she had a fine collection of jewelry now. She was no longer the little girl who had first come to court. She was the lady of Friarsgate, a woman of property and some small wealth.

"You'll need no cape, my lady," Lucy informed her. "The day promises to be warm and fair."

"Mama?" Philippa stood in the doorway to her little chamber. "Are you going to court now? Oh, how beautiful you look! I have never seen you in so fine a gown."

"I was going to wake you before I left,"

Rosamund told the little girl. "You slept most soundly."

"Aye. I was tired. I did not know London was so very far from Friarsgate. Edinburgh is not as far," Philippa said.

Rosamund laughed. "I remember making the trip the first time when I was thirteen. I thought we would never get here. Your father had been sent to escort me, and he was very entertaining, so I did not get discouraged or bored. Especially as it was the first time I had ever been away from my home overnight."

"Papa was always a great deal of fun," Philippa agreed. "I do miss him."

Rosamund nodded, thinking how much more simple her life would have been if Owein had not died. But then she should never have known her cousin Tom, or Patrick Leslie. Everything, she was beginning to realize, happened for a reason. "Although the queen has sent word that I am welcome and she wishes to see me, Philippa, her day is always a busy one. I may not be recognized until late in the day, and so I might not be home until long after dark. Lucy will be with you, and you know your uncle's servants, as they have come from Otterly," Rosamund explained to her daughter. "I want you to rest and enjoy the garden."

"Yes, mama," Philippa said dutifully.

Rosamund bent and kissed her daughter's brow. "Tomorrow I hope to bring you to court to meet the queen and mayhap even the king." Then she turned and hurried from the room and downstairs, where she found her cousin awaiting her.

"Come, dear girl, or we shall be late!" he admonished her.

"Shall we each take our own barge?" she asked him.

"Of course," he agreed. "We are back at court, and who knows when either of us shall be willing to come home." Then he chuckled mischievously as he escorted her from the house and down to where the two little vessels waited, bobbing in the morning sun.

"Wait for me if you get there first," she implored him. "I would go in on your arm, cousin."

"Of course, dear girl!" he assured her, helping her down into her own watercraft.

Rosamund settled herself, bidding her two rowers a good morning. They returned her greeting and then, loosing the little vessel from the quay, they maneuvered out into the broad channel of the river and began their trip downstream to Westminster Palace. Both barges moved in tandem so that they arrived at the king's current residence together. Lord Cambridge was on the royal quay in time to help his cousin from her transport. Together they entered the palace, and as both had been there before, there was no need to ask for directions to the queen's apartments.

Upon reaching it, Lord Cambridge said to one of the guardsmen at the door, "Lady Rosamund Bolton is expected by the queen." Then, kissing his cousin on the cheek, he told her, "I'm off to find some of my former playmates, dear girl. You can seek me if you truly desire to find me." Then, with a wink, he was gone.

The guardsman opened one of the tall double doors for Rosamund, and she stepped through into the queen's apartments. It was, as usual, filled with chattering women. At first Rosamund saw no one with whom she was familiar. Then a woman servant of the queen, a Mistress Drum, hurried over to her.

"Lady Rosamund of Friarsgate, is it?" she said.

"Yes," Rosamund replied. "How nice to see you once again, Mistress Drum. Will you tell the queen I have come?"

"Yes, my lady. You may wait here among the magpies." Mistress Drum bustled off across the chamber.

Rosamund chuckled. It was an apt description for all the women gathered in the queen's antechamber. She waited for some minutes and then Mistress Drum returned.

"Her highness cannot see you now, my lady, but she says you are to remain here awaiting her pleasure," Mistress Drum reported.

"Here in the palace?" Rosamund queried politely.

"Nay. Here in her antechamber," Mistress Drum said apologetically. She glanced about the room. "Ah," she said, "I see a comfortable chair there for you, my lady," and she led Rosamund over to it. Then, with a sympathetic smile, she hurried off.

Rosamund sat down. She had no other choice. And then she waited. And she waited. The hour for the main meal of the day came, and the queen and her ladies glided through the antechamber on their way to the Great Hall. Rosamund stood up as the queen came into the room, but passing her by, Katherine of Aragon gave no indication that she even saw her old friend waiting. She exited her apartments. Rosamund sat back down. She had not been invited to the meal and therefore could not go. The antechamber was empty now even of maidservants, and it remained empty for the next few hours while Rosamund continued to wait. Once, she got up and went to the necessary, returning quickly lest she be found gone. She could see the progress of the day into early evening through the windows of the queen's antechamber. The long twilight deepened into night, and Rosamund remained seated. Finally the door to the room opened, and Mistress Drum came back in, the look on her face a surprised one, for she had not expected to see Rosamund still there.

"You are still here, my lady?"

"I think perhaps the queen has forgotten me," Rosamund replied quietly.

"I shall find her at once and tell her you are still here," the servant said, obviously distressed that Rosamund had waited all day. She departed the chamber, and when she returned she wore an even more distressed look upon her face. "I am sorry, my lady. The queen says you are to go home and return tomorrow."

"Thank you, Mistress Drum. Please tell her highness that I shall return and wait upon her pleasure tomorrow," Rosamund said, rising, shaking her skirts, and leaving the antechamber of the queen's apartments. She could feel her anger rising, and she needed to leave the palace as quickly as possible. What was the matter with Kate that she had been treated in such an unkind fashion? She had been sitting all day, alone most of the time. No one had spoken to her. She had been offered no refreshment, and then she had been summarily dismissed. Well, tomorrow she would find out what it was all about.

But when Rosamund returned the next day, and the next, she was treated in the same fashion. She was made to wait the day alone, without so much as a cup of water. Then she was sent home without any apology.

On the fourth morning when she arrived at Westminster, Mistress Drum greeted her with an encouraging smile. "She has said she will see you today, my lady," the servant informed Rosamund.

Then she lowered her voice. "I've been with her for years, and I've never seen her be so unkind to an old friend."

"It's all right, Mistress Drum," Rosamund replied softly. "It isn't always easy being a queen."

Mistress Drum nodded her head in agreement. " 'Tis the lack of a child that troubles her muchly. And her so devout and faithful, too."

"God will work his miracles in his own time," Rosamund said.

"Amen!" The servant crossed herself, then she said, "You'll have to wait again, but it will be sometime today. I promise."

So Rosamund sat down in her chair to wonder again why the queen was being so rude. It was not like Kate. As loyal as she was to her queen, Rosamund considered that she could be home now doing many other things. It was a long and arduous journey from Friarsgate. And then, too, there was Logan whom she had promised to allow to court her. Did she really want him do so? Why was everyone so determined she remarry? How could she give herself to any man after Patrick Leslie? She let her mind wander back to their sojourn in San Lorenzo. It had been the most perfect time in her life, and she doubted anything could ever be as wonderful as those months she had had with him there and at Friarsgate. It had been a perfect dream.

The morning passed. The queen and her ladies departed for the main meal of the day. Rosamund continued to wait. And then, in late afternoon, the door to the queen's antechamber opened, and Katherine of Aragon entered the room. She looked directly at Rosamund and said, "Come!" Rosamund jumped up and followed her old friend into her privy chamber.

The queen whirled about and said in a cold voice, "How dare you ignore my summons of a year ago, Rosamund Bolton!"

"I did not, your highness," Rosamund protested. "I was not at Friarsgate when your invitation came. I was in Edinburgh, where I had gone to be married."

"And did you marry?" the queen asked. Her dark eyes were unreadable.

"Nay," Rosamund said softly.

"Why not?" The question was snapped like a whip crack.

"When I arrived, Lord Leslie had suffered a seizure of the brain. I spent over a month nursing him, but his memory only partly returned. He recalled nothing of the past two years. He did not remember me. We could hardly wed under the circumstances."

"Perhaps he had just changed his mind, and the illness was his excuse to avoid marriage with you," the queen said cruelly. It seemed she wanted to hurt Rosamund.

Tears, unbidden, slid down Rosamund's pale cheeks. "If you had seen him, Kate, if you knew him, you would understand why such a thing was not possible."

"I have not given you permission to use my Christian name," the queen said.

"I beg your highness' pardon," Rosamund responded.

"Was this the same man with whom you whored in San Lorenzo?" the queen queried.

"Yes," Rosamund said without hesitation. There could be no convincing the queen of their love. Katherine was too devout a woman to comprehend that kind of passion.

"You have no shame, do you?" the queen said. "I should have never thought

636

that you had the soul of a born whore when we knew each other as girls, Rosamund Bolton."

Rosamund did not answer. Even though they were alone, it would do no good. She quietly accepted the insult. The queen would not remain angry forever.

"Did you enjoy whoring with my husband?" the queen suddenly demanded.

"What?" Rosamund was staggered by the queen's accusation, but no matter what happened she would never admit to Katherine of Aragon of her brief affair with the king. It had been a private matter, and few knew of it.

"Do you deny that you were my husband's whore when you last came to court?" the queen said furiously.

"Yes!" Rosamund cried. "I most certainly do deny it! How could you even think such a thing of me, K— your highness?"

"I have it on the best authority," the queen replied stonily.

"Whoever has told you this lied," Rosamund declared indignantly. But she knew who had told the queen, and the bitch would regret it.

"Why would a friend to me since my childhood, a countrywoman, lie to me, Rosamund Bolton?" Katherine said.

There was nothing for it, Rosamund thought. She must take the bull by its horns now and reassure the queen, regain her friendship for Philippa's sake. "I think I know who has told you this terrible untruth, your highness. I know she believed what she thought she saw, and though I swore on the Blessed Virgin it was not so, she said she would tell you. I begged her not to, for your sake, your highness."

"Inez would not lie to me," the queen responded, now sounding a bit unsure. Inez was an old friend, but then Rosamund had helped her in her darkest hour. "Why would she lie to me?"

"Because Inez thought it was the king with me that night. It wasn't. It was Charles Brandon. We had had a harmless little flirtation, and I was departing the next day. We met to kiss and cuddle. That was all. There was nothing more serious than that, your highness. In the darkness of the hallway Inez mistook Charles Brandon for the king. I could not convince her otherwise, though I certainly tried. You know yourself that they are often mistaken for each other at a distance. I begged Inez not to distress you with her groundless suspicions. She was insulting to me and now attempts to embarrass me publicly with her evil and slanderous tongue!" Rosamund sounded properly indignant.

"I want to believe you," Katherine said slowly.

"Madame, I would have you believe me, but whether you do or not, my conscience is clear," Rosamund swore, thinking as she did, *I am surely damned now.*

"I thought you ignored my summons last year because you were ashamed to face me," the queen told her.

"I returned from Edinburgh broken-hearted, your highness. I threw myself back into Friarsgate and its care. I nurtured my daughters and oversaw their education. I prayed for Lord Leslie. I could not face the world. And then the Scots marched into England, and we were at war. I dared not leave Friarsgate then. I had to remain to defend my home from the ravages of the intruders. But we were, thank the Blessed Mother, kept safe." She crossed herself.

The queen sighed. "Inez can be impetuous, and she is very stubborn when she takes a position," Katherine reasoned.

"I remember," Rosamund said, and she smiled a small smile.

"I am of a mind to believe you, Rosamund Bolton," the queen told her.

"I would be most grateful if you did, your highness. If you remain angry at me you will not receive my eldest daughter, Philippa. I have brought her with me to meet you. She is ten years old, and in another two years I must seek a good husband for her. I thought it was time she gained a bit of polish."

"Oh!" the queen exclaimed excitedly. "I remember when your daughter was born. Is it really that long ago? It must be if you say it is. What is she like, Rosamund?"

"She looks like me," Rosamund answered the queen. "But I am told she is very much like her great-grandmother, a practical woman of strong common sense. She is very excited about meeting you and perhaps even meeting his majesty."

Katherine of Aragon held out her hand to Rosamund. "Kiss my ring, Rosamund Bolton. I will forgive you," she said. And when Rosamund obeyed, the queen kissed her on both cheeks. "We are friends again," the queen said. "Bring your daughter with you tomorrow. I will tell Inez that she was indeed mistaken. I have treated you harshly, Rosamund, and I now regret it."

"Your highness is a busy woman. I was content to wait for your notice," Rosamund murmured, curtsying. She was amazed that she had not been struck down in the good queen's presence by her great lie. Still, she had lied to protect the queen's heart as much as to protect her own reputation. Perhaps it was not so terrible a lie, and for some reason the memory of the king's grandmother, the Venerable Margaret, as she had been

640

known, popped into her head. Rosamund knew that that good lady would not have approved her affair, but she would have thoroughly approved the lie to protect Katherine, the queen. In order to produce an heir, the queen must be happy with her spouse. And she must be content with her life and those around her.

"You may join your cousin in the Great Hall now," the queen said. "We shall be here at Westminster for only another couple of days. The weather grows too warm for London, and plague does tend to arise here in the summer months. We are decamping for Windsor. The king does enjoy Windsor in the summertime. You will remain with us, of course."

"I am honored to be asked," Rosamund said. "But, dear highness, remember that I am necessary to Friarsgate. My bailiff uncle grows old, and all my daughters need me. I would hope when you prepare to move on from Windsor I may be permitted to return home again."

"Should we choose a husband for you, Rosamund Bolton, while you are with us?" the queen wondered aloud. "You should have a husband."

"I do not disagree, madame, but remember that the Venerable Margaret said a woman must wed first for her family and then was permitted to marry for herself. A nearby neighbor has expressed an interest in courting me. We have been known to each other since I was six years old. When I was widowed before, he sought my hand, but I had already been promised to Owein Meredith," Rosamund explained smoothly. The one thing she did not need, or want, was another husband chosen for her. And there was no need for the queen to know her "neighbor" was a Scot.

"Oh, how exciting!" trilled the queen, smiling. "Is he handsome?"

"I suppose some would say it, but his best feature is very, very blue eyes," Rosamund answered, returning the smile.

The queen nodded. "A man with blue eyes is difficult to resist," she agreed. "The king has blue eyes."

"Yes, I recall," Rosamund murmured, not wanting to get any further into a conversation regarding Henry Tudor. She curtsied again, saying as she did, "With your highness' permission, I will go and seek out my cousin now."

"Of course," Katherine replied graciously. "You may give him my regards. I have seen him in the Great Hall these past nights but have had no opportunity to speak with him. A most amusing gentleman. Did I hear he had sold his estates in the south and moved north to Cumbria to be near your family?"

"Indeed, madame, he did," Rosamund replied. "It is comforting to have him nearby. Family is so important."

The queen nodded in agreement, and taking this as her cue, Rosamund curtsied once again, backing out through the door between the queen's privy chamber and the anteroom. That room was once again filled with chattering women, and as she crossed it, her eye caught that of Inez de Salinas. Rosamund smiled sweetly at her, nodding in a friendly fashion, restraining the laughter that threatened to burst forth from her at the look of surprise on the Spanish woman's face. Then she hurried to the Great Hall, where she found Tom dicing with some gentlemen. Seeing her, he murmured something to his companions, gathered his winnings, and joined her. Together they sought a secluded spot where they might talk without being overheard.

"She has seen you." It was a statement, not a question. "What excuse did she give for keeping you waiting for four days after demanding you come down from Friarsgate?" he asked.

"Inez," was all Rosamund said.

"What?" For a moment he looked puzzled, but then, as she explained, it all became clear to Lord Cambridge again.

"Remember the night we left the

summer progress several years ago to return home to Cumbria? Remember what she saw, and how I denied it, naming another gentleman? She did not believe me, but I did think I had prevailed upon her to be silent. She was not. She ran rumormongering to the queen," Rosamund said.

"And what did you do?" he asked her.

"I denied it, of course. I will always deny it, Tom. I was vulnerable. He was all-powerful. I could not refuse. It was a supreme moment of weakness, and I not only regret it, but I am ashamed it ever happened, though at the time it was exciting even if it was forbidden. I will always deny it, for I should never deliberately harm Kate. She is too important to England. And he will certainly never admit to it, even to his confessor, I suspect. He believes too strongly in his divine right." Rosamund smiled mischievously.

"And she believed you?" He was anxious for her.

"She wants to believe me," Rosamund replied, "but she will always be suspicious, for that is her nature and Inez has played on it. But I have been no less duplicitous, for I have played on her desire to retain our long-standing friendship. She can never forget what Owein and I did for her when she was in such dire straits."

"We must help her believe you over

644

Inez," Lord Cambridge said.

"We must leave the issue alone," Rosamund said. "She has agreed to receive Philippa tomorrow."

"Nay. It will but take one small thing to make your lie more palatable to accept than Inez de Salinas' truth," he told her. "Trust me in this matter, cousin."

"I am told the court is moving to Windsor shortly," Rosamund said, attempting to turn the subject. "Did you know? Do you perchance have a house in Windsor, cousin?" she teased him.

He laughed. "Nay, but I knew, and so I have reserved an entire floor of one of the town's finer inns for us. We shall not be sleeping in a hayrick, my dear girl."

The day moved into the summer twilight, and the Great Hall began to fill with courtiers. The women Rosamund had known casually during her last stay at court now approached her and greeted her as if it were her first day back with them. Rosamund was gracious, but amused. It was obvious that her censure had now been officially lifted. Inez de Salinas was not among these women.

And then suddenly Charles Brandon approached her, smiling toothily. "My dear Rosamund," he purred like a large tomcat anticipating a meal of finch, "how delightful to see you returned to court." He lifted her hand, his gaze meeting her own startled one, and kissed it, retaining it afterwards and tucking it through his arm. "Come, my lovely, and let us speak of old times." And he led her off, murmuring as he did, "Try not to look so surprised, my pet. After all, am I not an old lover?"

Rosamund looked up into the handsome face, and her laugh tinkled loudly enough for the ladies left behind to hear it. But then she said, "My lord, please explain yourself."

"Your little prevarication must be made real to those who would gossip unkindly, should it not, Rosamund Bolton?" His dark eyes scanned her face. "Aye, you are very lovely. What a pity you insist on sequestering yourself in the north."

"I still do not understand, my lord," she told him.

"I knew years ago, just after you had gone," he said. "The king's Walter told me what had happened and requested that if ever asked, I confirm your lie. But no one ever asked until tonight, when Walter once again approached me. He said this little charade would be necessary to convince a certain lady."

"But she was nowhere near us," Rosamund replied.

"Trust me, dear lady," he told her. "The little incident is already being reported to her as we speak together. You were surrounded by her minions, were you not?"

"I owe you a debt of gratitude, then, Charles Brandon," Rosamund said quietly.

"Nay, madame, 'twas I who owed you. But now my debt is paid in full, I believe," he said to her.

"How is it you owe me a debt?" Rosamund asked.

"When you were a girl first at court in the Venerable Margaret's care, God assoil her good soul" — he crossed himself — "there was a plot devised that Prince Henry seduce you. Perhaps you will remember it. Though I did advise against it, I held the wagers."

"I remember," Rosamund told him. "And I agree that we are now even, my lord." She chuckled softly. "I remember that my husband insisted you turn over the wagers to the king's mother for charitable purposes. Richard Neville was very angry."

"Did you tell his father, as you had threatened?" Brandon asked her.

"Nay, but I refused to sell him warhorses after that," she said with a grin. "The horses Owein raised and trained were most prized."

He laughed. "You may be a country lass, madame, but you were always a very clever one. I believe we have now satisfied whatever curiosity there was about the gossip

bruited about by Senora de Salinas." He
raised Rosamund's hand to his lips once
more. "Good evening, madame," he said,
and with a bow, he permitted her to move
away from him first before he turned to
find and rejoin his own friends.

In an instant, Lord Cambridge was at
her side. "My dear girl, what was that all
about?"

"You spoke to the king's man Walter,
did you not, Tom?" Rosamund queried
him. "I am very much in your debt,
cousin, for it."

"I thought it the best way to stem any
gossip and defeat Inez de Salinas' wicked
tongue," he told her. "I know you like
fighting your own battles, Rosamund, but
this was one engagement I felt must be
won immediately for Philippa's sake."

Rosamund leaned over and kissed her
cousin on the cheek. "Aye, Tom, you were
right," Rosamund agreed. Then she sighed.
"May we go home now? I want to tell
Philippa that she is to meet the queen tomorrow."

"First you must pay your respects to his
majesty," Tom advised her. "Now that you
have the queen's forgiveness and friendship
again, he will know it and expect you to
come to him."

Rosamund sighed again. "Very well. But
come with me, Tom. I cannot face Hal by

myself. Especially after what has transpired in the last few hours."

"I watched Brandon," he told her. "I thought he played his part quite nicely, my dear girl. A former lover, hopeful of rekindling an old friendship. And you were perfect. Surprised he would approach you, but charming even as you rejected his advances. It was well played out, cousin."

"I have taken part in enough court masques to know how to act my part, Tom," she told him with a wicked smile. "Come along, now, and let us greet the king."

They made their way through the Great Hall arm in arm. Reaching the foot of the dais upon which the king's throne was set, Rosamund curtsied deeply and her cousin bowed with his usual elegant flourish.

Henry Tudor viewed them through his small blue eyes. She was lovelier than ever, he thought. He considered another liaison with her, but then recalled that they had barely escaped exposure the last time. Only her quick wit had saved them. But Inez de Salinas had attempted to make difficulties with Rosamund's return. She was foiled again by the lady of Friarsgate, and he had seen Charles Brandon play his part in the charade. The queen was now fully convinced Inez had been mistaken, but Inez was too stubborn, or proud, to admit to her error. The woman would have to go back to Spain shortly with her merchant husband. He could not have Katherine distressed.

"You are welcome back to our court, Lady Rosamund," he said.

"I thank you, your majesty," she replied. Then Rosamund curtsied again and backed away from the foot of the throne with her cousin.

The king turned to speak with the queen as the lady of Friarsgate and her cousin disappeared into the crowd. "My dear wife," he said quietly, "I think Maria's sister must leave us soon."

The queen nodded. "As much as I regret losing another old friend, my dear husband, I believe you are correct. Inez has grown troublesome as she has grown older."

"You will see to it, then, Kate?" he asked.

"I will, Henry," she promised. Then she said, "Rosamund has brought her heiress to court. The little girl is ten now, and Rosamund would have her presented to us. I have invited them for tomorrow, Henry. Will you receive the child, too?"

"Of course, Kate," he told her with a smile.

Having paid their respects to the king and the queen, Rosamund and Tom departed Westminster in their separate barges to return home to Bolton House. The night had already fallen, but the moon silvered the Thames River as they went. Philippa was already abed when they arrived, and Rosamund let her daughter sleep. She knew the girl would not be able to go back to sleep on learning she was to go to court the following day to meet Great Harry and Spanish Kate. The morning would be time enough. Philippa was more than ready, and so was her wardrobe.

Rosamund prepared for bed; then after dismissing Lucy, she sat down in the window seat in her bedchamber that overlooked the gardens and the river below. Contemplating her day, she realized again that the court was a dangerous place. I should far rather face a pack of rampaging borderers, she thought, than have to spend my life dealing with those people. Life at Friarsgate was far simpler. Everything was as it seemed. Poor Inez de Salinas would suffer the deceptions that had been played upon her this night because they all sought to protect Katherine of Aragon from heartbreak. Inez had once been her friend. But in a moment's time that all changed.

Inez would be disgraced. Rosamund knew that wasn't fair, but if she had admitted to her indiscretion with the king several years back, Rosamund would have suffered far greater difficulties. Inez, in her great desire to protect her mistress, would be penalized only for allowing her imagination to get away from her and persisting in it. It was no great crime, but it was an annoyance neither the king nor the queen wanted to be bothered by any longer. Inez had outlived her usefulness. Had it been known, however, that Henry Tudor and Rosamund Bolton had indulged their passionate natures in a brief affair, Rosamund would have not only lost the queen's friendship and patronage, but the king's, as well. Henry did not want to flaunt his mistresses. Discretion was the key to success with England's king. And Rosamund had not fought so long and so hard to protect Friarsgate, impeded by her very sex, to lose it and the king's friendship, which was in the end more valuable than the queen's.

No, she thought to herself. I do not like court. Nor do I like the person I become when I visit the court. Everything I do is controlled of necessity by others. I have always hated other people running my life. We will go home as soon as we can. Perhaps we will not even wait for the summer to end. Once Philippa has met the king and the queen, is there any reason for us to stay? There was, and she knew it. Rosamund had made her peace with

Queen Katherine, but she had yet to make it with the king. He had not cajoled his wife into asking Rosamund to court simply for social reasons. Lord Howard had obviously said something to the king. She thought she had seen him briefly tonight in the Great Hall, but she was not certain of it, and if it was he, he had not noticed her.

The river outside lay quiet in the time between the two tides. The water looked like a sheet of beaten silver. There was no traffic to mar its surface now, for it was very late. There was the scent of roses and honeysuckle from Tom's garden. It wafted into her bedchamber on the faintest of breezes. It was a night for lovers, Rosamund thought to herself. Patrick. She closed her eyes for a brief moment, but the tears still pushed from beneath her lashes and slipped down her cheeks. She sighed, resigned, and brushed the tears away with her hand. The last time she remembered a night like this, he had been with her. He would never be with her again. She knew it. But still her heart had great difficulty accepting the knowledge. *But I have to accept it. When I return home, Logan Hepburn will come courting, and this time I must either accept him or send him away forever. I am not certain I want to lose Logan's friendship, but I am also not certain I want another husband.* Rosamund arose from her place by the window and found her bed. She knew she would be awake all night if she didn't quiet her mind.

In the morning Philippa came from her little bedchamber and climbed into her mother's bed. "Good morrow, mama," she greeted her parent.

Rosamund opened her eyes, and drawing her daughter near, kissed her cheek. "You are going to court today, Mistress Philippa," she said, laughing aloud at the look of delight that suddenly appeared on her daughter's face.

"Today?" Philippa squealed excitedly. "You spoke with the queen yesterday? Oh, mama, why did you not wake me last night when you came home?"

"Because, my darling, you would have never gone back to sleep," her mother said.

"What am I to wear?" Philippa asked. "What time are we due? Will I meet the king, too, mama?"

"We will arrive before the main meal of the day so you may eat in the Great Hall," Rosamund said with a smile. "You will wear what you choose from among your gowns, my child, although I do think the lavender silk is very flattering with your hair and your skin."

Philippa jumped from the bed. "I must have a bath!" she exclaimed. "You have said the king's nose is a sensitive one, mama. Lucy!" she called. "Lucy!"

"Gracious, Mistress Philippa," the tiring woman said, entering Rosamund's bedchamber, "what is the matter?"

"I am going to court today, Lucy! I shall wear the lavender silk, and I want a bath!" Philippa cried.

"My lady?" Lucy asked politely.

"I think the violet brocade gown, Lucy. It will blend nicely with my daughter's wardrobe," she finished with a smile.

"Yes, my lady," Lucy chirped. "I'll see to the bath right away."

Philippa scampered back into her bedchamber and began riffling through her little trunk. "Jewelry, mama! I have no jewelry! How can I meet the king and the queen without jewelry?"

"But you do have jewelry, my poppet," her mother replied. "When you were born the king's grandmother sent you a broach of emeralds and pearls. I brought it with me for you to wear. And you will have a rope of pearls from my own jewels. It shall be yours to keep, Philippa. You will always remember that I gave it to you on the day you met King Henry and Queen Katherine."

"Oh, thank you, mama!" Philippa cried.

The bath was drawn, and the young girl bathed, washing her hair again and drying it in the open air as she sat in the window seat of her mother's chamber, brushing her long auburn tresses. Rosamund used the bathwater after her daughter, and while she bathed her cousin came to speak with her.

"Philippa will need adornment," he said.

"She has the broach the Venerable Margaret sent at her birth, and I am giving her a rope of my pearls, but she could use some pretty rings, Tom. Do you have something that would suit her?"

He nodded. "I'll give them to her before we leave. What are you both wearing? I would match my clothes to yours, dear girl. We should not clash on such a momentous occasion."

"Philippa will wear her lavender silk gown and I my violet brocade," Rosamund said. "Do you still possess that burgundy short coat with the pleated back, Tom? It would be quite marvelous, you know."

"My dear girl, I have indeed taught you good taste over the years, haven't I? It is the perfect suggestion. I shall go and have my man prepare it now." Blowing a kiss at her with his fingers, he left her to complete her ablutions.

When she finished bathing Rosamund dried herself, for Lucy was busy helping Philippa. Then she managed to don her own undergarments, but Lucy was necessary for getting into her gown, a beautiful creation of violet silk brocade with a silver-embroidered and quilted underskirt of a lilac-colored velvet. The low square neckline of the dress was also embroidered in silver thread. False undersleeves with slashings and frilled linen cuffs showed from beneath her wide violet brocade cuffs. Rosamund wore a violet silk French hood edged in pearls with a pale lilac-colored silk veil flowing behind, allowing the fine color of her hair to show. Her square-toed shoes were covered in purple silk.

Little Philippa was now brought forth in her lavender silk gown with its plain quilted underskirt of satin. The long, tight sleeves of the gown had small cuffs embroidered with tiny pearls. The square neckline of her bodice was also embroidered in pearls. About her waist was a twisted gold rope with a long tassel, and her shoes matched her gown. Her hair was left long, bound only by a lavender ribbon.

Rosamund put a rope of pearls over her daughter's head, letting it fall on the girl's flat bodice, where she pinned the emerald and pearl broach in the center. "There," she said. "You are quite elegant, my child." Then she reached into her jewelry box and drew out the gold chain with its gold-and-pearl crucifix and a second rope of pearls and put them on. On her fingers she affixed several rings. Satisfied they were both ready, she said, "Lucy, put on a clean cap. Today you will come to court with us."

The young tiring woman's mouth fell open in surprise. "I must change my gown," she gasped. "Is there time?"

Rosamund nodded, and Lucy ran off. "A lady should generally travel with her maid-servant," she explained to her daughter. "I have left Lucy behind these last few days to watch over you, as we have traveled simply from Friarsgate, without a large retinue. Today, however, she comes with us."

Lucy quickly returned wearing a gown Rosamund had not known her servant possessed. "Annie gave it to me, my lady. She thought I might need something better than my everyday." The dress was a silk one Rosamund had given Annie once. It was dark blue with a plain bodice and single skirt. The neckline was square, as was the fashion. It was edged in pleated linen. Lucy also wore a lace-edged lawn apron and a matching cap. She looked every inch an upper servant.

The three women descended into the hallway below, where Lord Cambridge was now impatiently awaiting them. He nodded with approval, then said, "Cousin, you must take my barge with Philippa and Lucy. It is larger and will accommodate you better. I will follow in your little vessel. Come. We will be late if we do not hurry."

Philippa was almost sick with her excitement as they entered the spacious barge and began their journey downriver to Westminster Palace. The river traffic had been interesting from the gardens of her uncle Tom's house, but out upon the water it was even more exciting and fascinating. She didn't know where to look next, and she was joined in her enthusiasm by Lucy.

Rosamund pointed out interesting sights as they traveled, but the tide was with them this morning, and they were quickly at the Westminster quay. A manservant helped the women from their vessel onto the stone dock. Lord Cambridge was right behind them.

"Philippa," he said, "there was something I meant to give you back at the house." He opened his hand to reveal several small rings. "There is a pearl, an emerald, a fine green agate, and an amethyst to match your gown. Put them on, my child. All the fashionable court ladies wear a multitude of rings."

With a delighted smile, Philippa took the rings offered and put them on her hands, holding them out to admire. "Thank you so much, uncle," she said to him, kissing his cheek. "Do you think I should wear two on each hand?"

"I think three on your right hand — the pearl, the emerald, and the agate — and on your left hand wear the amethyst to display it to its best advantage. Put the pearl between the two green stones, my child," he advised her.

They entered the palace, going to the Great Hall where the court would now be assembled to watch the king and the queen break their fast after the first mass of the day. As they walked, they were greeted, bowed to, and nodded to by many of the courtiers. The lady of Friarsgate was back in favor with the queen, and the child with her was her heiress. Fathers with second sons eyed Philippa and nodded. The girl looked strong of limb and with all her wits. She would, it was rumored, not only inherit from her mother, but from her uncle, as well. The Boltons were not a particularly noble family, but they were landed gentry with a goodly estate. And the queen favored them.

"Why do they all stare at me, mama?" Philippa asked, noticing the interest in her small person.

"You are my heiress," her mother said softly. "You are already being appraised as a marriage possibility."

"I know I must marry well one day," Philippa noted, "but I would hope to love my husband as you and my father loved

660

each other. I know I shall not find the kind of love you found with Lord Leslie, but I remember my father well. He had a great care and respect of you, mama."

"Aye, he did," Rosamund said, remembering Owein Meredith, her third husband and the father of her three daughters and deceased son. He had been a good man, and he had loved her as much as he was capable of it. Until they had been matched, Owein had spent all of his life but six years in the service of the Tudors. "I shall not give you to just anyone, Philippa. I will have to be satisfied that the man you wed does indeed care for you. Do not fear, my daughter. You and your sisters will go to good husbands. I promise."

They were now in the Great Hall. About them the courtiers milled, waiting. Rosamund moved through the crowd until they were before the high board. There she stopped, waiting for the king and queen to enter the hall. The trumpets sounded a flourish. The people in the hall drew back, opening an aisle down which Great Harry and his queen traveled, smiling and nodding to those in the hall, their attendants following them.

Seeing Rosamund and her daughter, the queen stopped. "This is Philippa, isn't it?" she said with a warm smile. "Welcome to our court, my dear child."

Philippa curtsied deeply, replying a bit breathlessly, "Thank you, your highness."

"Henry, here is the lady of Friarsgate, and she has brought her child to greet us," the queen said softly to her husband.

Henry Tudor took Rosamund's hand in his and kissed it. "We are happy to greet you again, madame, and your child." Then he turned his attention to Philippa, and he was all charm, smiling down from his great height at the little girl. "Why, poppet, you quite resemble your mama. I see nothing of Owein Meredith in you, but for your gentle manner. You are most welcome to our court, Philippa Meredith. Your sire was a fine man and a good servant to the House of Tudor. I believe he would be proud to have such a beautiful little daughter. I know I would be."

"We all pray for your majesty's wish to be fulfilled," Philippa said tactfully.

The king lifted the little girl up so they were face-to-face, and then he kissed her cheek. "Thank you, my child," he said as he set her down, and then he moved on.

Philippa almost swooned with her excitement. "He kissed me, mama!" she trilled. "The king kissed my cheek!"

"The king can be kind, Philippa, and he likes children. You said the right thing to him, and he will remember it. You have his favor, and that is important."

"Wait until I tell Banon and Bessie that the king kissed me," Philippa said. "They will be so jealous. They were jealous when you decided to take me to court, mama."

"Of course they were," Lord Cambridge chuckled. "All little girls want to come to court. It is every girl's dream, Philippa. But you must not boast and brag when we return to Friarsgate."

"But I can tell them that the king kissed me, can't I, Uncle Tom?"

"Of course, my child," he told her. Then he turned to Rosamund. "My friend Lord Cranston has a young son from a second marriage who is two years older than Philippa. I see him across the hall, and I would like to introduce Philippa to him."

"She is too young for a match, Tom," Rosamund said.

"Of course she is," he agreed. "But Cranston's family is very well off, and it cannot hurt for Philippa to meet them. When she is older and ready to wed, can she not love a rich man's son as well as a poor man's son?" he teased her.

Rosamund laughed, but then she grew serious. "I hope to obtain a title for her," she said. "There must be some poor earl whose heir could be matched with Philippa, provided they were suited to each other."

"Ah, cousin, you are more ambitious

than I thought. I am not unpleased. But let me introduce Philippa to Lord Cranston, anyway. He may be of help to us one way or another," Lord Cambridge said. "And I do know an earl with a son who might do."

"My lady?" A young page stood at her side.

"Yes?" Rosamund replied. The boy wore the king's livery.

"His majesty would see you immediately. I will escort you," the page responded.

"And I will take Philippa off to be introduced about," Tom said. "Keep your temper in check, dear girl. Philippa, my angel, walk with your uncle. I shall be the envy of every man here today."

Philippa giggled and moved off with her uncle as Rosamund turned and followed the boy in the Tudor livery from the Great Hall.

Chapter 17

The little page led her from the Great Hall down one long corridor and into a narrower, dimmer one. Finally he stopped before a paneled door, and opening it, ushered her inside. "I will wait outside to escort you back," he said politely, closing the door behind him.

Rosamund looked about her. It was a small chamber with a corner fireplace in which a fire was now burning, warming the damp room. The walls were of linen-fold paneling. The well-worn floor of wide boards was darkened with age. There was a single lead-paned casement window looking out on an empty courtyard, above which she could see the blue sky of the late June day. The small courtyard itself was seasonless. Had she been a prisoner in this room she would have had absolutely no idea of the day, the month, or the time of year. There were but three pieces of furniture: a small square oak table and two chairs with high carved backs, each containing a single tired tapestry cushion of an indeterminate color and design. Rosamund sat down and waited. By now she was well used to waiting for Tudor monarchs, she thought to herself with a wry smile.

Finally a door she had not even noticed, for it was so well constructed and concealed, opened in one of the walls, and Henry Tudor stepped into the room. Had he gotten bigger? she wondered, until she realized that the design of his costume was meant to convey that very impression. Still, a man who stood well over six feet needed little else to make an impression. He looked straight at her with his small blue eyes as she came to her feet and made a deep curtsy.

"Well, madame, and what have you to say for yourself?" he opened the conversation forcefully.

"What would your majesty have me say?" Rosamund replied.

"Do not attempt to fence with me, madame!" he thundered. "You have not the skill for it."

"I am also not gifted with the long eye, sire, and so you must be more specific in your queries of me," Rosamund told him. She was not afraid. She should have been, but she was not. What was happening to her? What would happen if the king's anger could not be stemmed?

Henry Tudor drew a deep breath and

seated himself in one of the chairs. "Stand before me, Rosamund," he said.

She moved to face him.

"Now kneel," he commanded her.

Rosamund swallowed back her outrage and knelt before him.

"Now, madame, why did you go to Scotland?" he said.

"Because your majesty's sister invited me, and as your majesty well knows, Queen Margaret and I are friends from our youth," Rosamund responded.

"And why did you go to San Lorenzo, madame? It was my understanding that you disliked travel," the king replied.

"I went because the Earl of Glenkirk asked me to go," Rosamund said.

"He was your lover." It was not a question.

"Aye, he was my lover," Rosamund told the king quietly.

"I would not have expected such behavior from you," Henry Tudor said primly.

"I was to confine my whoring, then, only to your majesty?" Rosamund snapped at him. The floor beneath her knees was hard, and she was becoming angry. For all he was her king, he was still a spoiled lad.

Henry Tudor jumped to his feet, towering over her as his big hand gripped her arm, yanking her up. "Do not try my patience, madame. You well know how dangerous I can become when provoked." The blue eyes met her amber ones.

Rosamund pulled away from him. "Then, Hal, let us both sit down. I will freely answer any question you have of me, but this charade you attempt to play with me is both childish and hardly worthy of Great Harry." Her gaze did not waver beneath his.

He motioned her impatiently to one of the chairs, seating himself in the other. "Do not forget I am your king," he growled.

"I have never forgotten it, Hal." He had not reprimanded her use of his name, and so she continued it.

"Richard Howard, my ambassador, saw you in San Lorenzo," the king told her.

"I know," Rosamund answered. "San Lorenzo is a tiny place, my lord, and there are no secrets there that can be kept for long. Lord Howard recognized my face and was told my name. He knew he had seen me before."

"He said you lied to him when he asked if you knew him," the king noted.

"Nay, Hal, I did not lie. He had seen me at court long ago, and I had seen him. But we had never been introduced, so we could hardly know each other, now, could we?"

The king emitted a short burst of

laughter, then grew serious once again. "What was Lord Leslie doing in San Lorenzo? He had been my brother-in-law's first ambassador there years ago. Why did he go back, madame?"

"When the earl and I first met at Stirling, Hal, something odd happened to us. We fell in love, if indeed you believe in love, but whatever happened between us happened. We could not bear to be parted. The Scots court, however, was hardly the place for us to carry on our liaison, any more than your court would have been the right place. It was cold and snowy that winter. The earl conceived the idea of taking me to San Lorenzo, where we might enjoy the warmth of the south and pursue our passion for each other."

"You lived in the ambassador's residence," the king said suspiciously, still not convinced that her tale was completely innocent of deception.

"Aye, we did. It had been Patrick's home once, and Lord MacDuff insisted that we make it our home. I saw no harm in it. Our apartments looked out over the town, a charming place whose buildings are all the many colors of the rainbow, Hal. We could view the blue sea from our terrace. We had a large bath set out upon the tiled terrace, and we bathed daily in the fresh air, beneath the warm sun. There were flowers in bloom in February! It was a paradise!" Rosamund's face was alight with the memory.

"You were introduced to the duke," the king said.

"He was an old friend of Patrick's. His court is very informal, Hal. We visited several times, meeting a famed artist from Venice, a German countess, your own Lord Howard, and many others. Our servants fell in love there and were wed in a chapel within the cathedral by San Lorenzo's bishop himself."

"Lord Howard says this artist, a relation of the Venetian doge, painted you without garments," the king accused, looking shocked.

"The portrait that hangs in my hall, Hal, is fully clothed. The maestro painted me as the lady defender of Friarsgate. He made my home a castle, which of course it is not. I am surrounded by a sunset. It is quite colorful," Rosamund said, but then, because she realized the king was very well informed, added, "but he also painted me as a goddess. I wore a Greek chiton that left a shoulder and my arms bare. He vowed he wished to keep that painting for himself, which is why he also painted the other."

"That portrait now hangs in the Great Hall of the Duke of San Lorenzo, madame!

670

Lord Howard informs me that your naked limbs can be easily seen through the diaphanous draperies you have called a costume and that one of your breasts was quite bare!" Henry Tudor sounded outraged.

"What?" The surprise on Rosamund's face convinced the king that her own tale was true, as far as she knew. "The maestro sold the goddess painting to the duke?" Then she burst out laughing. "The duke, Hal, is a man of vast appetites where women are concerned. He would have enjoyed seducing me but that I would not have it. And the artist, as well. These men from the south are quite different from us, I fear. It took all my wits about me to prevent a disaster," she concluded. Then she said, "My cousin tells me that Lord Howard is back in England. He is not a good ambassador, Hal. He is much too abrasive and rude. He quite irritated the duke."

"When you returned in late spring you went back to my sister, did you not?" He ignored her remark about Richard Howard. It was not necessary Rosamund know that Duke Sebastian had sent him home to England for the very qualities Rosamund mentioned. It had been most embarrassing, especially as the duke had sent a message with Lord Howard saying he wanted no further English ambassador in San Lorenzo.

"Aye. I had promised Meg I would. She had been delivered then of her son," Rosamund answered him. Let him ask what he would. She would volunteer nothing unless asked.

"The boy? He is truly healthy?" the king inquired.

Rosamund nodded. "He is strong of limb and heart and mind, Hal. Your nephew is what the Scots would call a 'braw laddie.' "

"And after you had paid your compliments to my sister, you returned home alone?"

"I returned home with Lord Leslie," Rosamund said. "We decided that we would wed even though both of us had estates that must be husbanded. We thought we could spend part of each year at Friarsgate and part of the year at Glenkirk. Do the high and the mighty not travel between their lands?"

"Yet he left you," the king said.

"In the autumn, to return to Glenkirk. He wanted his son and heir, Adam Leslie, to know what it was he intended doing. He wanted Adam's approval, for he had been widowed since his son's birth."

"If he was a capable bed partner, and I must assume he was, madame, then I am certain his son would not have been pleased by the thought of having to share his inheritance with another child of his father's making," the king remarked.

"Patrick's seed was no longer potent due to an illness years before," Rosamund explained. "There was no danger of another child to supplant his grown son."

"And yet he was a passionate lover, for I know none but could satisfy you, Rosamund," the king noted.

Rosamund flushed, continuing with her story. "We were to meet in Edinburgh in the spring. I arrived to discover he had suffered a seizure of the brain. Though I nursed him until he was able to travel, not all of his memory returned. He had completely forgotten the last two years of his life. He did not know me at all. There was no possibility, under such circumstances, of our wedding." Her amber eyes glistened with tears as she spoke now. "His son keeps me informed as to his health, however."

"You are yet in touch with my sister?" the king asked.

"She sent to me warning of the war to come," Rosamund said. "You should not have encouraged King James to war, Hal."

"I?" Henry Tudor sounded outraged with her accusation.

"James Stewart was a good king, Hal. He was a good husband to your sister, and she loved him dearly. You forced his hand because you were jealous of him."

"Do you seek to visit the Tower, madame?" the king said coldly.

"I say to you the things that no others dare," she agreed, "but you need to hear them, Hal. James Stewart marched into England hoping to lure you home from France, but instead you sent Suffolk to engage him in battle. But for an accident of fate, Scotland would have beaten you."

"What accident?" No one had told him this. They had only trumpeted victory.

"The Scots phalanx broke on a slippery, muddy hill," she said, knowing he would understand the rest.

"It was obviously God's will that we prevail against the Scots," the king said piously, and he crossed himself. "God is on my side, Rosamund! He always will be."

"If your majesty says so," she murmured, her head bowing.

"But now, madame, what am I to do with you?" he wondered.

"I came to court for two reasons, Hal," she said. "Because I was summoned and because I wished to introduce my heiress to your majesties. I would return home now."

"Nay, not quite yet," he told her. "I am not satisfied that your conduct in the matter of this Scot was not treasonous, madame."

"God's wounds!" Rosamund swore.

"You know very well it was nothing more than I have told you, Hal. When have I ever been duplicitous with you? With your queen, aye, but only to protect her, but never with you!"

"I think you should accompany the court to Windsor," he said, smiling suddenly.

"No!" Her look was angry.

"You do not believe that we may have certain unfinished business between us, madame?" he demanded of her.

"Nay, I do not!" Her color was high now.

Reaching out, the king pulled her from her chair and onto his lap. His big hand caressed her heart-shaped face, and then he kissed her a passionate kiss. His mouth demanded far more than she would ever again give him.

Rosamund jumped from his embrace like a creature afire. "Hal! Are you mad? I have but only convinced the queen I was not your mistress, but rather Charles Brandon's lover, and you would attempt seduction? Do you know how fortunate we were in our brief encounter that we were not found out, given the example of the ladies FitzWalter and Hastings? If Inez de Salinas had not seen us parting that night we might have escaped detection altogether, but we did not. And I have had to weave a tapestry of lies to protect Kate, who is my friend. Do not do this to me! I will not have it!"

"I am your king, madame," he thundered at her.

"And I am your majesty's most loyal servant," Rosamund said, curtsying, "but I will not again be your majesty's whore. Imprison me if you will for it. But I will not yield what is left of my virtue and my dignity. How can you even ask it of me, Hal? Especially when I strove so hard to protect your reputation with your good queen."

She saw the look blooming upon his face. He would want to put his bad behavior on her, for in his own eyes Henry Tudor did no wrong. "Madame —" he began, but she stopped him, making it easy.

"If I have misled your majesty in any way, I humbly apologize for it. It was not my intention at all to be provocative or lewd," Rosamund said, stepping back from him and curtsying once more. "I beg your majesty's pardon."

He was silent for a long moment, and she knew he was considering the situation from all possible angles. How could he keep his sweets and yet eat them all up? It obviously proved too much of a conundrum even for him. "You are forgiven, madame. Nonetheless, I would have you come to Windsor. For Kate's sake, of course. Inez de Salinas has been sent away at last.

Your return gave me the opportunity to rid us of her, and for that we thank you. I know you will want to return home to Friarsgate from Windsor, and you have our permission. But bide a few weeks with us. Who knows when you will come to court again?"

"Perhaps never, Hal, but my Philippa will certainly come," Rosamund said.

He nodded. "Your daughters will always be welcome at our court," he told her.

"Thank you, your majesty," she replied.

"You may return to the Great Hall now, madame," he said.

Rosamund curtsied again and began to back from the room.

"You should really have another husband," the king suddenly remarked.

"Do not attempt to shackle me to anyone, Hal. Any bridegroom foisted upon me will not live to see the morning after the wedding," she warned him.

"I am your king, madame! I have the right to choose for you if I would."

"I have wed thrice for the pleasure of others, Hal," Rosamund replied. "It was your own grandmother, God assoil her good soul, who said that after a woman had done her duty, she had the right to marry for love."

"Will you find love again, Rosamund?" he asked.

"Perhaps, Hal, I will be fortunate," she said, and then she opened the door and slipped into the hallway, where the little page awaited her, rubbing the sleep from his eyes, for he had been dozing on his feet. She smiled and patted his blond head. "Take me back to the hall, lad," she told him, and she followed in his wake as he went.

She had scarcely arrived back at her destination than Tom was at her side. Philippa was not with him. "Where is Philippa?" she asked.

"I have introduced her to several young ladies, all close to her in age," he said. "A young girl should not be shackled at court to an older relation. Now, tell me at once, dear girl, what has happened?" He led her to an alcove where there was a bench, and together they sat.

"There is little to tell," Rosamund began. "He demanded to know why I had gone to Scotland and San Lorenzo. Lord Howard had indeed reported my presence there with Patrick. I explained all, but I will admit to keeping it as simple as possible. Then he thought perhaps we might take up where we had left off."

"No!" Lord Cambridge actually looked shocked, though he should not have been surprised.

"I have dissuaded him, of course, Tom,

but he would have us come to Windsor. He says we may return home from there, but we must bide a while," Rosamund explained.

"Actually," her cousin replied, "if you departed now it could cause gossip to arise, especially as Inez de Salinas has been sent publicly from court. They say she and her husband will leave for Spain soon, ostensibly to visit her elderly parents. And a few weeks of the court's amusements will not harm Philippa. She can make some valuable connections, Rosamund. Just recall your own stay as a girl. There are few who can claim a friendship with two queens."

"But I have no friends at the court," Rosamund said.

"It is time, then, that you made some," he said.

"I don't intend returning if I can possibly help it," she told him.

"But Philippa will return, and it is probably from those who people the court that we will choose Philippa's husband, Rosamund. It cannot hurt you to make friends," he explained patiently. His cousin had always preferred her own company and that of a few relations over strangers, but that needed to change.

"I suppose you mean to introduce me to some people," she grumbled at him.

Tom grinned at her. "My habits, dear girl, may not conform to most, but I assure you I know many people of the right sort. I am considered witty and amusing, you know," he said mischievously. "Now that you have concluded this business with both of our dear monarchs and you have been commanded to Windsor, it is time for you to meet others of your own kind, cousin. How do you expect to find the right husband for our Philippa if you do not mingle among the nobility?"

She laughed. "That is the difficulty, Tom. I think Philippa too young for a proposed marriage."

"Of course she is," he agreed. "But it will take us two or three years to find the right connections, and then another year for Philippa to decide which among her suitors will please her. These things must be done delicately and with finesse, my dear girl. One does not purchase a pig in a poke, Rosamund."

"You make it sound so calculated, Tom," she told him.

"It is," he agreed.

"But I want Philippa to fall in love and be in love forever," Rosamund said.

"If only life were that simple, my dear girl. With luck, she will indeed love the man she marries before they wed — if they have the time to know each other. But more than likely, that love will come afterwards. Your marriage to your cousin was arranged to keep Friarsgate in the family. Your marriage to Hugh Cabot was for the same reason. You were too young to know of love then, but when you were wed to Owein Meredith, you did not love him, did you?"

Rosamund shook her head.

"But you came to love him because he was a good man and he respected your position as the lady of Friarsgate. With careful planning, dear girl, we shall gain the same good fortune for Philippa. But unless we begin our search now, what chance have we? And do not, I pray you, bring up the love that you and Lord Leslie shared, cousin. It was unique and rare. Few in this world have such love."

"I know," she whispered to him, feeling the tears coming again.

"Dear cousin," Tom said, and he brushed the tears from her cheek, "be grateful that you knew such love, but also be sensible where your child is concerned."

Rosamund nodded. "I will meet these people you seek to introduce me to," she said with a small smile. "But can I meet them another day? I have had all I can bear today, cousin. I want to go home and sit out in your garden to watch the river."

"And think, mayhap, of your brazen

Scot?" he teased her.

"Aye," she said, surprising him.

"Take your own barge, dear girl. I will return later with Lucy and Philippa," he told her.

Rosamund leaned over and kissed her cousin on his smooth cheek. "What, dear Tom," she said, "should I ever do without you?"

"If the truth be known, dear girl," he responded, "I shudder to even contemplate it." And he grinned.

Rosamund arose. "Do not remain too late," she said. "It is Philippa's first day, and we will be leaving shortly for Windsor."

He nodded, then watched as she departed the Great Hall.

Rosamund's little vessel was brought to her, and after entering it, she sat down on the blue velvet bench and closed her eyes. "Take me home," she told her rowers.

The air was warm as they rowed, but some of the smells in the air were distinctly unpleasant as the barge moved along. Her servants rowed in midriver, as the tide was low now, and the mudflats along the bank were visible to the eye and discernible to the nose. Rosamund sighed to herself. The worst was certainly over now, she thought, and having thought it found herself longing for Friarsgate. But Tom was right. If she was to one day see her daughters matched with men of eminent families, she must socialize and make contacts now. A smile touched her lips as she considered that just a few short years back she had been considered a girl. Now she was a woman of twenty-five, widowed thrice and looking for husbands not for herself but for her three daughters. Yet the need for love had not deserted her. Surely not.

Rosamund knew she was lonely. But did she want to marry again? Did she want Logan Hepburn? It seemed she had been running away from him her whole life. Or he had been running after her. She hadn't, of course; nor had she even known of the Hepburn of Claven's Carn until . . . God's wounds! Was it that long ago that he had sat his horse atop a hill overlooking Friarsgate and told her he wanted her for his wife? Eleven years. Nay! It could not be eleven years ago! It had been just before she married Owein, and Philippa was now ten years of age. The realization dawned upon her. It was indeed eleven years ago that she had sparred indignantly with him and forbade him to come to her wedding. But he had, of course, with his brothers in tow. They had brought whiskey and salmon, and they had played their pipes for the bride and groom. Eleven years!

Yet she did not know him. Not really. She knew he was determined and that he was stubborn. She knew he had been willing to let his lands go to his brothers' sons rather than marry another. For her. For Rosamund Bolton. Never before had she considered Logan Hepburn in any other way but an annoyance. She had called him a crude borderer, a Scots scoundrel. And she had meant it.

She had dismissed his offer of marriage because rather than saying he loved her, he had talked about sons. When she had upbraided him for it, he had claimed that he had always loved her, that he had thought she knew it. But he had not said it, and until this moment she had not understood that a man who was willing to give up his birthright for a woman did indeed love her. I have been a fool, Rosamund thought silently.

But it still did not answer the question of whether she was willing to remarry. And all of her newfound knowledge would not answer that question. She needed to get to know this man she had been so busy scorning out of pride that she could not comprehend the depth of his devotion to her. He would be awaiting her return, she knew, and suddenly she was more anxious than ever to return home. But if he won her, would he be satisfied with his victory?

Or would that victory merely cause him to lose interest?

Rosamund felt her little vessel bump the stone quay of her cousin's house. She opened her eyes, blinking once or twice to clear her vision as the sunlight filled her sight. She took the servant's offered hand and stepped up from the craft, then hurried into the house. The summer gardens held no interest for her today. She needed to think. If she was going to allow Logan Hepburn into her life, they were going to have to get a few things straight before anything progressed beyond friendship. She remembered how kind he had been with her daughters and how they all liked him. Well, that was one point in his favor, she considered. But he was still a Scot. And there was certain to always be difficulties between England and Scotland. Yet would that matter in their tiny corner of the world? she wondered.

Lord Cambridge and Philippa arrived home as the long summer twilight was beginning to deepen into darkness. Rosamund's daughter could hardly stop talking of the sights she had seen and the people she had met.

"We are going to Windsor, mama, aren't we? Cecily will be at Windsor. Her family always goes on progress," Philippa said.

"And who is Cecily?" Rosamund inquired, smoothing her daughter's disheveled hair. "Is she someone Uncle Tom has introduced you to, my daughter?"

"She is Cecily FitzHugh, mama. Her father is the Earl of Renfrew. She has two brothers, Henry, who is the heir, and Giles, and two sisters, Mary and Susanna. They are younger than Cecily, who is the oldest girl. We have become best friends!"

"Gracious," Rosamund laughed. "All in a single afternoon, poppet?"

Philippa ignored her mother's teasing, saying, "It is her first time at court, too, mama. She has been left at home with her little sisters in the past. Her brother Henry is one of the king's gentlemen, and her other brother is a page. We both like to ride."

"Well," Rosamund said, "it would appear that you have had a fine day, Philippa, but it is your bedtime now. Run along with Lucy. I will come and kiss you good night."

Without protest, Philippa obeyed her mother.

"And what have you been doing alone and by yourself?" Lord Cambridge asked his cousin.

"I have been thinking of Logan Hepburn, Tom, and whether I do indeed want to remarry. And if so, whether it is he I want to wed," Rosamund said frankly.

"And what have you decided?" he asked.

"I do not know," she answered. "I need to really get to know him, Tom. I will not remarry simply for the sake of having a husband. Do you understand that?"

He nodded. "I do. Still, I think you wise to reconsider your former position on the matter, cousin."

"What you mean," she teased him, "is that you think I am becoming too long in the tooth for another husband. I am, after all, twenty-five now."

He laughed. "You will never be too old for another husband, Rosamund. You are too fair and too clever by far. Why, if I were a man to take a wife, I should seriously consider you above all women," he told her.

"Why, Tom, that is a lovely thing for you to say to me," she exclaimed.

"Alas, I am not a man for a wife," he told her with a smile.

"It would be so simple if you were," she considered.

"It most certainly would not, dear girl! Your laird once threatened to kill me if I admitted to being your lover," Lord Cambridge said with a shiver of remembrance. "He was very fierce, and I quite believed him."

Now it was Rosamund who laughed.

Then she said, "Tell me about the Fitz-Hugh family to whom you have introduced my daughter, Tom."

They sat companionably in the Great Hall of the house, ensconced in the window seats overlooking the river as they spoke.

"Edward FitzHugh is like your Owein, of Welsh descent. His holding is not large. It is in the marches between England and Wales. His wife, Anne, comes from a good family of English landed gentry in Hereford. Her dower was more than generous, for her family was delighted to have made a match with the son of an earl. Ned was the third son. He was never expected to inherit, but both of his brothers predeceased him. The eldest from plague one summer. The second son returning from Spain, where he had made a match. The ship upon which he traveled went down in the Bay of Biscay in a storm. The old earl died shortly thereafter, they say of a broken heart, and his third son inherited. Ned had been educated for a time with the king, for it was thought he might take holy orders one day. When he became the Earl of Renfrew, he used that ancient connection to bring his family to court. His lamented second brother had been betrothed to a distant cousin of Queen Katherine's. The family is also devout, so the queen favors them. It is said that little Cecily will eventually be offered a place in the queen's household as a maid of honor. She is too young now, of course, but if she and Philippa remain friends, your daughter might also serve as one of the queen's maids of honor one day."

"Thomas Bolton, you are amazing!" Rosamund said admiringly. "How on earth do you know all of this? I do believe you have surpassed yourself this time with your intimate knowledge of others."

"Nonsense, dear girl," he said, delighted with her words. "The Countess of Renfrew's father knew my grandfather in London eons ago. They had some dealings that turned out well for both of them, but especially for the countess' papa. The connection has been kept. I was even invited to the earl's wedding to his wife years ago, when he was simply a third son. I was generous in my gifts. After all, dear girl, one never knows."

"You are thinking of the second son for Philippa, aren't you?" Rosamund said.

Lord Cambridge nodded. "Giles Fitz-Hugh is fourteen now. He is still involved in his studies, and he is serving the queen. He will soon be too big for her household, Ned tells me, and will not return to court in the autumn. He will be sent to France and then to Italy to study. His brother is sixteen and has served the king since he was six. He will be married in August to a Welsh heiress. Giles, for all his half-noble bloodlines, has a bent towards business. Philippa will need a husband who understands such things."

"What if his brother dies?" Rosamund asked.

"Is that likely to happen again?" Tom said. "Besides, the heir's bride is already with child. Both fathers wanted it that way."

Rosamund was somewhat shocked. "I should certainly not allow my daughters —" she began, but he waved away her indignation.

"This was a unique case, dear girl. Ned wanted to be certain that his eldest son's heir followed them. The bride's father wanted the title for his daughter. Both the young people, healthy and lusty, were content to comply with their parental demands," he chuckled with a wink.

"It could be a girl," Rosamund said dryly.

"It could," Tom agreed cheerfully. "Both FitzHugh sons, however, are, praise God, healthy. The heir will continue to get children on his bride until there is a son or two, perhaps even three."

"What if Philippa and this boy do not get along?" Rosamund asked.

"They have not even met yet, dear girl. That will happen at Windsor. But our lass is only ten, and the boy is not ready, by any means, for a betrothal. This is merely a small fishing expedition at best. I know other families with eligible sons."

Rosamund nodded. "But after Windsor, I want to go home. I have some business of my own to take care of, Tom. And before we depart London we must meet with your goldsmiths and choose a factor for our little venture."

"Agreed!" he said. "Tomorrow, after we deposit Philippa with her new friend, we shall complete our own business, dear girl. And when I get home I must go to Leith to see how our ship is coming along. I should like to call this first vessel after you, cousin."

"I think I have a better name than mine, dearest Tom," she told him. "I think we should call our ship *Bold Venture*, for it is indeed a bold venture that you and I undertake."

He nodded. "Aye, I like it. *Bold Venture*. Aye!" he agreed.

The following morning they took Philippa to court, leaving her with Lucy to find Cecily FitzHugh. They then went on to Goldsmiths' Row, where the banking of the day was conducted. Lord Cambridge introduced his cousin to Master Jacobs, his goldsmith. Rosamund put her signature upon a piece of parchment several times so the goldsmith would have it to compare with any message purporting to come from her. Lord Cambridge had brought Master Jacobs a copy of his last will and testament for safekeeping and so that the goldsmith would know that Rosamund and her daughters were his heirs. He brought the agreement they had both signed for their enterprise, giving the goldsmith a copy of it, too.

"My cousin and I will both be depositing funds and withdrawing them, Master Jacobs," he told the goldsmith. "Lady Rosamund is a large landowner in Cumbria, where I now make my home."

"What will you use the ship for, my lord?" the goldsmith asked.

"We will export my cousin's woolen cloth to Europe. There is none finer, and the Friarsgate Blue will be the most sought after," Tom explained.

"What will your ship return with in exchange?" the goldsmith inquired.

"Tom!" Rosamund said. "We have not considered another kind of cargo. We cannot have our vessel returning with an empty hole. There is but half-profit in that."

"I have relations in both Holland and the Baltic, my lord, my lady. For a small percentage of your profits, they could fill your ship for its return journey," Master Jacobs said.

"It can be nothing that stinks," Rosamund said. "We would never get the smell out of the wood of the hole. The next shipment of cloth would pick up the aroma. No hides or cheeses. Wine. Wood. Pottery. Gold. But nothing that would leave a noxious fragrance. My captain will have such orders, Master Jacobs. He will take no cargo that smells."

"Of course, my lady. Now I comprehend your need for a new vessel. The fee I suggest is fifteen percent," he told her, smiling. "It is a modest fee."

Rosamund shook her head. "Nay," she said in a hard voice. "It is too much."

"Twelve," he countered, and seeing the look in her eye quickly said, "Ten is the lowest I can go, my lady." His mouth puckered nervously.

"Eight percent and not a penny more, Master Jacobs. I am being generous with you for the sake of your long-standing arrangement with my cousin. We have built the ship, grown the wool, and woven the cloth. The risk is all ours. Eight percent for bringing in return cargo is more than fair."

The goldsmith's pursed lips turned up into a smile. "Agreed, my lady!" he said. Then he turned to Lord Cambridge. "She both bargains and reasons well, old friend."

"Indeed she does," Tom said proudly.

"What are we to do about a factor?" Rosamund asked him when they were once more in their barge on the river.

"I think there is time for that," Lord Cambridge said thoughtfully. "Perhaps we need not find someone on this visit to London. My instincts tell me to wait."

"Your instincts have always proven reliable before," Rosamund said. "We will wait."

The following day the court decamped Westminster Palace and London for Windsor, where the king was looking forward to a summer of hunting in his green park. They rode with the royal progress, Lucy, Tom's man, and the cart with their belongings mixed in with the baggage train and their own men-at-arms. Philippa rode with her friend Cecily FitzHugh and Rosamund and Tom with the Earl and Countess of Renfrew.

The earl was a large man with gray eyes and sandy-colored hair. His wife was petite and dark-haired with fine blue eyes.

"I remember your late husband, Sir Owein," Ned told Rosamund as they traveled. "He was an honorable man and a devoted servant to the House of Tudor. I, too, have Welsh blood."

"Owein barely remembered the place of his birth, my lord. He went into service as Jasper Tudor's page when he was but six," Rosamund told her companion.

"My wife and I spend more time at court now than in the marches," the earl admitted. "Our son and his wife need to learn how to manage the family estates. It will be theirs one day. Tom tells me you have a large holding in the north."

"Friarsgate," Rosamund said. "My parents and brother perished when I was three. I became the heiress to Friarsgate. Philippa is my heiress. I have land, cattle, and many sheep, my lord. Now Tom and I have begun a new venture, exporting my fine woolen cloth. We are building our own ship, for the cloth must be transported carefully."

"And your daughter will inherit all of it one day," the earl said.

"Aye," Rosamund replied. "Her second sister, Banon, will inherit Otterly from Tom. As for my youngest daughter, Elizabeth, she will be given a very large dower portion. I seek a title for her."

The Earl of Renfrew nodded, understanding completely. Family connections were very important. "My second son, Giles —" he began.

Rosamund interrupted him. "Philippa is too young, my lord, for me even to consider it yet, but I thank you. When she is old enough, in another three years, perhaps your son will still be available, and we may speak."

"You are a good mother," the earl told Rosamund.

They reached Windsor, where Tom had provided them with an entire floor of a fashionable inn. He had even arranged housing for the men-at-arms, telling them if they wished to earn extra coin they might hire themselves out. They must, however, be prepared to depart Windsor in late July, when Rosamund wished to return home. They hardly saw Philippa, for she and her new friend were part of a group of young girls of good families following the progress. They rode to the hunt during the day and spent part of the evening dancing and playing games. Philippa had never known such a life existed, but she liked the court far better than her mother ever had and said so.

"It will be so dull to return to Friarsgate," she said one morning as she prepared to depart for the day's hunt.

"Nonetheless, it is where you belong for now, my daughter," Rosamund replied.

"Oh, mama! You treat me like a child, and I am no longer a child!" Philippa cried.

"You are ten years of age," Rosamund said stiffly, "and a long way from being grown, whatever you may believe."

Philippa rolled her eyes at her mother and emitted a deep sigh.

"We cannot go home too soon," she told Tom after she had repeated the conversation to him. "I see Philippa has a stubborn streak in her that must be controlled."

"I wonder where she has gotten that," he murmured, casting his eyes heavenwards.

"Tom! I always did my duty when I was her age," Rosamund protested.

"I cannot say, dear girl, for we were not acquainted then," he told her with a grin.

"Edmund will tell you it is so," Rosamund said heatedly.

"We are departing in another few days, cousin," he soothed. "Let her have her fun. Soon enough she will be back in the hall studying with her sisters and Father Mata."

"And the sooner, the better," Rosamund muttered. Philippa was suddenly making her feel very old.

Windsor Castle was a most impressive castle. It sat upon a hilltop overlooking green meadows and lush woodlands, the Thames River below it. The castle had been begun by the Normans in the year 1080. It was one in a nexus of nine castles being built to encircle and protect London.

In the beginning it was no more than a wooden keep used as a hunting lodge by its Norman kings. The first of the Plantagenet kings, Henry II, rebuilt the castle in stone. Runnymede Meadow, where King John had signed the Magna Carta, was nearby. In the year 1216 Windsor had withstood a great siege. Henry III, John's son, had the damage repaired and enlarged the royal apartments as well. A fire in 1296 destroyed much of Henry's rebuilding.

Edward III, born at Windsor, loved the castle and did much to add to its beauty and its use. Silver-gray stone from a nearby quarry at Bagshot was used in the new walls and buildings. Edward IV began building a magnificent chapel he dedicated to St. George, but it was not finished in his reign. His grandson, Henry VIII, was now in the process of completing the chapel. Henry Tudor loved Windsor for its great forest where he might hunt at his leisure all day.

While Rosamund found the castle an impressive edifice, she thought Greenwich fairer. Windsor had no gardens or walks to enjoy. Philippa didn't care. She was out a-horse with Cecily FitzHugh almost every day. And when the two girls were not hunting, they were with the queen, who might or might not be with child again. Katherine called Rosamund to her the day before the lady of Friarsgate planned to depart.

The queen did not ask, she simply said, "I will want Philippa sent to me when she turns twelve, Rosamund. I have decided to have her as one of my maids of honor. Young Cecily FitzHugh will also be one of my maids. You know I will keep your daughter safe and chaste while she is with me."

Rosamund was not pleased. Philippa had taken too easily to court life, and if she were ever to remain at court, what would to happen to Friarsgate? Still, one did not argue with a queen. She curtsied to Katherine and said, "This is a great honor, your highness, and I know that Philippa will be thrilled to have received it. Am I to tell her, or will you?"

"I have already spoken with her and with the Earl of Renfrew's daughter, as well," the queen replied.

Rosamund curtsied again. "With your highness' permission, I will withdraw now. We are departing in the morning for Friarsgate."

"You are eager." Katherine smiled. "You have always loved your home, Rosamund. Go, then, and travel safely with God. I will pray for you."

"And I will pray for your highness," Rosamund replied as she backed from the queen's presence.

When she told her cousin of the queen's words, Lord Cambridge was delighted. "The trip has been a great success, dear girl. You are back in favor, and Philippa is to be a maid of honor in two years' time. Wonderful!"

They were seated in the small private dining room of the inn, having their main meal of the day as they spoke.

"Philippa likes the court too well for my peace of mind," Rosamund said. "If she becomes involved in the life surrounding the king, she will neglect Friarsgate. I do not like it, but there is nothing I can do about it."

"It is but a phase she is going through," Tom said. "Philippa has extraordinary common sense and will not allow herself to be lured by the pleasures the court can offer her."

"I was not like that at her age," Rosamund said.

"Nay, you were a dutiful chatelaine with an ancient husband at ten," Tom reminded her. "The weight of Friarsgate was heavy on your shoulders, cousin, but Philippa is not you. It is a different time in which she lives. Besides, at court she is safer from Henry the younger."

"I wish we would go back to learn he has been hung," Rosamund said darkly. "I do not relish the next two years, if he survives.

Keeping Philippa from him will not be easy, Tom, but as God is my witness, I will do it!"

"I know you will, dear girl. Why, you frighten me half to death when you get that look in your eye," he teased her.

"Are the men-at-arms gathered together now?" she asked him.

"We will depart as early on the morrow as you can arise, cousin," he said.

"I am most eager to get back," Rosamund said.

"To Friarsgate or to your brazen Scot?" he asked, a single eyebrow cocked.

"To Friarsgate, of course!" she said immediately. "I do not know what is to happen with Logan Hepburn and myself. We shall see."

Tom did not pursue the subject further with Rosamund. He knew what was going to happen even if she didn't. She was going to marry the laird of Claven's Carn, and damned well about time, he thought. He didn't know how Logan would bring off this miracle, but it would happen. The Scotsman loved his cousin deeply, even if she was too stubborn to see it. They had both been through much in their lives, but now it was time for them. And Lord Cambridge intended to see it happen. He knew that Edmund and Maybel were in agreement with him on this. It was just a matter of making Rosamund see reason. It amazed him that his cousin, an intelligent and clever woman where Friarsgate was concerned, could be so foolish in the matter of her own emotions. He did not doubt for a moment that Patrick Leslie would always be in her heart, even if she spoke little of him anymore. But there had to be room in her heart for another love, as well. For the first time in a long while, Tom prayed.

A knock at the chamber's door opened to reveal the same page who had escorted Rosamund to the king at Westminster. The lad bowed smartly, saying as he did, "His majesty wishes to see the lady of Friarsgate before she departs. Please come with me."

"Where is the king?" Rosamund asked the boy.

"At the edge of the wood behind the inn, my lady," was the answer.

"Come, Tom. For my reputation's sake, I beg you to accompany me," Rosamund said.

He nodded, standing immediately, and together they followed the boy out the back door of the inn, through the kitchen courtyard, and across a small swath of meadow to the edge of the forest where the king stood half-hidden in the trees. The page and Lord Cambridge stopped, while Rosamund moved forward and curtsied to the king.

"You are determined to ruin my reputation with the queen, Hal," she greeted him.

He laughed. "And you, fair Rosamund, are determined to be what you were born to be." Reaching out, he took her small hand in his big one and kissed it. "I came only to tell you that you will always have my friendship, as you have Kate's. I wanted there to be no misunderstanding between us on that point."

"I am glad, then, that you called me to you," Rosamund told him. "It is a wise woman who keeps the friendship of both her king and her queen."

Again he laughed. "Direct and honest as you ever were, madame. I am sorry we may not take up where we left off. No one has ever spoken to me as you do, Rosamund."

"I am a countrywoman, my liege, and we do see things differently," she told him.

"Then this is *adieu*, fair Rosamund," he told her as he drew her into his arms and kissed her lips.

Now it was Rosamund who laughed as she drew away, shaking her finger at him. "You will always be the bad lad," she told him. Then she curtsied, saying as she did, "I am grateful for your friendship, Hal. My daughter Philippa will be coming to serve the queen as a maid of honor in two years' time. I hope you will grant her your friendship, as well. She is Owein's child, and the Merediths were ever loyal to the House of Tudor."

"I will watch over her as if she were my own child," he said. *If I had a child.* The unsaid words hung in the air between them.

"There will be a child, Hal. I will pray for it," Rosamund promised. Then, with another curtsy, she backed away, finally turning to rejoin her cousin, the page passing her as she went.

"He wanted to say good-bye," Tom said. "How charming. It is good to know that you still retain his favor."

"If I had remained, if we had taken up where we left off, he would have soon been bored. Hal has always sought the unattainable. It is the chase he enjoys far more than the possession," Rosamund noted.

"Then it would appear that our business here is done, cousin."

She nodded. "Aye, Tom, and I am indeed eager to get home to Friarsgate."

Chapter 18

"I wonder how long it will take the laird to know that you are home." Tom teased Rosamund as they rode down the road to Friarsgate.

"Did you not see the clansmen on the hilltop?" she asked him, laughing.

He grinned at her. "You can't blame the man for being eager. How long has he been waiting for you?"

"Tom, I have not said I would marry him. He has not even asked me," she protested.

"Do you doubt for a moment that isn't his intent, dear girl?" he replied.

"Perhaps I just want him for a lover," Rosamund answered him. "What is the purpose in my marrying again, Tom? I have three heiresses. He has an heir for Claven's Carn. I am English. He is Scots. I will not give up Friarsgate until I die. He will not give up Claven's Carn. We are, I am coming to realize, very much alike."

"Two like beings — a perfect partnership, dear girl!" Tom insisted.

"We shall see," Rosamund said again, as she had been saying all the way home.

Lord Cambridge clamped his lips together. If he heard her utter those three words again he was simply going to scream. Or shake her until she got some common sense. He would remain overnight, and then he had to get home to Otterly. This whole situation was beginning to wear on his nerves. He did not wish to be around while his cousin and Logan Hepburn sparred with each other. He did not envy the laird of Claven's Carn, and as much as Tom loved his cousin, she could sometimes be very difficult.

Reaching the house, Philippa was off her horse before her elders, throwing herself into Maybel's arms and chattering a mile a minute about all her adventures and her best friend, Cecily FitzHugh. Maybel hugged and kissed the girl, then set her aside firmly, looking to Rosamund. Rosamund dismounted and went wordlessly into Maybel's outstretched arms.

"God's blood, old woman, it is good to be home again!" she said, hugging Maybel. "Has all been well while I have been away? The sheep are looking fat enough."

"Edmund will tell you everything you need to know and some things that you don't, but I can't stop him," Maybel replied. "You look better than I have ever seen you returning from court, lass."

"That is because I stayed but a brief time, and having made my peace with the king and his queen, took little part in the activities of the court. I was able to eat and sleep enough, which my daughter was not, for she loves the court, I fear." She linked her arm with Maybel's, and the two women strolled into the house, seating themselves in the hall together on a settle by the fireplace. "Philippa's good manners, more your doing surely than mine, have won her the queen's favor. She is to return in two years to take her place among Kate's maids of honor," Rosamund told Maybel.

"What an honor!" Maybel said, but then she fretted, "She will yet be a child, Rosamund. How can we let her go?"

"There is no choice in the matter, Maybel. But I would trust my daughter with the queen, for her household is orderly and chaste. Her maids are the most virtuous girls in the kingdom, I am certain. And Philippa has made a good friend in Cecily FitzHugh, who will serve the queen with her. She is the daughter of the Earl of Renfrew. The younger of her two brothers may be a possible match for Philippa. He is fourteen, and having served in the queen's household is now being sent to France and Italy for more studious pursuits."

Maybel listened, nodding as Rosamund spoke. "Does Philippa know of this lad?" she finally asked. "What does she say?"

"I have not spoken to her about it, for it is too soon, but you can be certain that she knows. These little girls at court know more gossip than even the servants do," Rosamund laughed. "Besides, they may grow acquainted and decide they do not like each other. Nothing has been formally discussed or settled. There may be another boy better suited to Philippa. I have time, but Tom frets like an old lady."

"And with good cause, dear girl," he said, joining them. "She does not understand the necessity of looking about now and winnowing the possible from the impossible."

"That's all right, Tom," Maybel said calmly. "As long as our Rosamund has you to rely upon, she'll not go wrong. Of course, she may take another husband one day, and then your influence would certainly wane."

"His influence will never ebb with me, Maybel," Rosamund said. "And as for marriage, we shall see."

Lord Cambridge gritted his teeth so hard they hurt.

Edmund and Father Mata joined them at the high board late in the day as the meal was served.

"Has all been well, uncle, in my absence?" Rosamund asked him.

He nodded slowly. "But I have been grateful for the laird's clansmen, lass, for there have been strangers on the heights, of late, observing Friarsgate."

"Who are they?" she wanted to know. "I saw one as I rode in and assumed it was a Hepburn."

"I cannot be certain, for each time we have attempted to approach them, they run," he said. "I suspect they may be of your cousin's ilk."

"Damn him!" Rosamund swore softly. "He is after Philippa, the devil! I will catch him and hang him myself!"

Father Mata crossed himself at her words, saying, "Lady, there must be another way to solve this matter."

"Tell me, then, good priest," she answered him. "I have said plainly that my daughter will not marry Henry Bolton the younger. I have said it more than once. What else can I do if he will not listen?"

"Young Philippa must be guarded closely at all times," the priest agreed. "You must be frank with her and explain the dangers involved."

"It is time," Edmund agreed, and the others about the high board nodded.

"What must I be told?" Philippa asked them. She had been bored the entire ride home from Windsor. Her mother and her uncle had paid little attention to her.

"My cousin Henry wants to steal you away and force you to marriage so he may get his hands on Friarsgate, Philippa," Rosamund told the girl. "So you must be protected."

"But I am to marry Giles FitzHugh someday," Philippa said.

"That is not so!" her mother said quickly. "Who told you such a thing?"

"Cecily did. She said she overheard her father and mother discussing it when they did not realize she was nearby. Giles is very handsome, mama."

Rosamund shook her head wearily. "There has been no discussion between the Earl of Renfrew and me, Philippa. Giles FitzHugh might make you a good husband one day, or he might not. And there are other possibilities to consider before any decision regarding your future is decided."

"But I like Giles FitzHugh," Philippa said stubbornly. "He is so handsome."

"So you have said, Philippa," her mother remarked dryly, "but there are other requirements in a husband that are more important than just his features. And besides, you are much too young to be thinking of marriage. I will not even consider a match for you until you are fourteen."

"Oh, mama! You were wed three times by the time you were fourteen," Philippa countered.

"We are not discussing me, Philippa. We are speaking of your future," Rosamund said in a steely voice. "Now, if you have finished your meal, you may be excused."

Philippa slipped from her place, and as she did so, one of the laird's clansmen arose to follow her. Was this how it was going to be from now on? Rosamund wondered. She looked to the priest.

"Mata, send to the laird on the morrow," was all she said.

"Very good, my lady," the priest answered her, but they both knew he had already done so.

"Now," Rosamund said, turning back to her uncle, "other than strangers looking down on us, all was well?"

He nodded. "We're beginning the harvest now, niece. It will prove to be a good one, as the fields are lush with their crops. The orchards, too, will give us a bounty, but the fruits will be a bit smaller this year, for we have not had quite the rains we have in most summers. Still, the apples and pears will be the sweeter for it."

"The wool?" she asked him.

711

"Of excellent quality," he said. "The sheep are fat and content this year. The cloth woven will be the best we have had yet. We'll be ready for next year. We've withheld enough this year that the merchants in Carlisle are complaining already," he chuckled. "I've noised about what we intend to do, and they are not happy."

Lord Cambridge smiled and nodded. "Have you begun the dyeing yet?"

"We will once the harvest is in," Edmund replied. "The dyeing and the weaving make for good winter work for the Friarsgate folk, Tom. But by springtime, I promise you, we will fill your ship's hole with fine cargo."

"We shall be very rich by this time next year," Tom said with a grin. "The Friarsgate Blue cloth will bring us a premium, especially as we shall not offer much of it. You must hold back at least half of every year's stockpile in the warehouse, Edmund. We alone will regulate the sale of the Friarsgate Blue woolen cloth."

"Should we not be more generous the first year and then hold back later in order to drive up the price of the cloth?" Rosamund asked him.

"Nay," he said. "There may be among our mercers some more clever than others, who will hold back from their own meager supply in order to enrich themselves. We cannot take that chance, for that would then cut into our profits. Nor will we permit it," Tom said. "Any mercer who does not sell his entire supply will receive none the following year. We will know how much they sell by how much we sell them, and we will demand proof of the sale of their entire stock."

"I think," Rosamund told him, "I shall leave the stratagem to you, cousin. I shall simply watch over Friarsgate and all that entails."

Logan Hepburn came late the following day. Rosamund looked at him as a man for the first time in a long while. He was still handsome in his rough-hewn way. His eyes remained that blue-blue color that had once had the effect of making her weak in the knees when she looked into them. She wondered if they could do that again. But was there the faintest touch of silver at his temples amid the ebony of his thick hair? He slid easily from his mount, and coming to greet her, he smiled.

"Welcome home, lady," he said.

"You did not bring my daughters back?" she asked him.

"Nay. I think it best they remain hidden at Claven's Carn with me until we have solved the difficulty of your cousin," he told her.

"You know?" But she wasn't surprised. The priest was his kin and would have told him, of course.

He nodded. "His men have been watching Friarsgate, and we have watched them, though they know it not," Logan said with an engaging grin.

"I don't know what to do," Rosamund said honestly. "I cannot keep looking over my shoulder forever. And I cannot have Philippa frightened over this."

"Then we must find a way to defeat Henry Bolton the younger, for good and for all," the laird told her frankly.

"How?" Rosamund asked.

"Perhaps we may even use your Lord Dacre against him if we are clever. Henry is raiding on both sides of the border right now, lady. Lord Dacre is raiding on the Scots side, though he has been told to cease by his king. Still, Henry Tudor makes no effort to enforce his edict with Lord Dacre, which leads me to believe he raises havoc in the borders with private royal sanction though your king cries otherwise."

"What do you propose, then, my lord?" Rosamund asked him.

"Your cousin raids out of his lust for riches. He has no loyalties to anyone but himself, having never been taught otherwise. Lord Dacre raids not simply for what he may carry away, but out of a sense of loyalty to his king and to England. Lord Dacre hates the ancient enemy. He fights to the death. What if he believed that your cousin and his band of ruffians were renegade Scots? What if he and his men met up with your cousin and his men?" The laird of Claven's Carn smiled wolfishly.

"You hope that they will kill each other," Rosamund said, "thus relieving us both of an enemy. You do not do this just for me."

"I did not say I did," he replied. "We are far enough to the west in the borders to have been safe so far. But what if Lord Dacre comes to Claven's Carn unexpectedly? He will not ask if any of the inhabitants are English. He will simply slaughter everyone he can find, lady."

"Then bring my daughters home," she replied nervously.

"Dacre has not cast his eye in our direction. Your lasses are safer with me," he reassured her.

"This is how you would court me?" she demanded of him suddenly.

"I have not come to court you, Rosamund Bolton," he told her. "I have come to strategize with you to our mutual benefit. Perhaps one day, if I think you are ready, I will indeed come to court you. I am not of a mind to marry again quite yet." He smiled.

"Good!" she said. "Neither am I, Logan Hepburn." But she was thinking, He was a devil if she ever had met one. All that soft talk he had used before she had gone down to court, implying that he loved her yet and wanted her for his wife. He hadn't changed at all. It had been nothing more than a deception. He was probably revenging himself on her for refusing him once. Well, she didn't need him, but she did need his clansmen. "May I retain the use of your men?" she asked.

"Of course," he said, smiling again. The look of surprise on her face when he had said he hadn't come courting her had almost caused him to laugh aloud. The clansman who had ridden through the night to fetch him had brought a message from Tom Bolton. Rosamund's cousin had advised the laird of Claven's Carn to pretend he might not be as interested in remarrying as he had previously indicated. Rosamund far preferred a challenge and would respect him more if she believed she must work to regain his love. Follow your instincts with her, Lord Cambridge had advised the lord of Claven's Carn. And so he had. The results had been far better than he had hoped for.

Rosamund, he knew, had believed that she would control their courtship. She thought that he wanted her enough to dance to her tune. And he did. But he realized now that Tom knew exactly what he was saying when he suggested play difficult to obtain. It had been just the right thing to do. Now the next move in this game they were playing would be up to her. He wondered what she would do.

"You will remain the night," she said. It was not a question on her part.

"Nay," he said. "I think it better I return to Claven's Carn, lady. I must think on how we may bring your cousin and Lord Dacre into serious conflict with each other. I will return when I have the answer to my questions."

"Very well, my lord," Rosamund answered him. He was not staying. Why would he not remain? Could they not have spoken together and made a plan? "Perhaps if we dealt with the matter together, Logan Hepburn, the solution might come easier and sooner," she heard herself suggesting.

"Do you think so?" he said. She was asking him to stay.

Rosamund nodded. "Certainly Claven's Carn is well protected in your absence, as your son resides there," she reasoned. "And it would indeed be a quicker ride home for you in the daylight."

"You may be right," he said casually. "Very well, lady. I will stay."

"Come into the hall, then," she invited him, and turning, she led the way.

Logan winked at Lord Cambridge, and then he followed her.

"What was that all about, I should like to know," Maybel demanded. "What mischief are you up to, Tom Bolton?"

Tom grinned at the old woman. "I have simply advised him how to win her. He must pretend his interest in her is beginning to wane so it is Rosamund who will have to convince him that they should be man and wife," he told Maybel.

"Oh, traitor!" Maybel said, and then she laughed. "My child would not be happy if she realized how well you have come to know her, Tom Bolton. But you are right. If we are to see her married again, and happy at last, it must be her own wish, not ours."

"You'll not tell on me?" he said, his eyes dancing with their conspiracy.

"Nay, I'll not," Maybel promised. "You have been her guardian angel since the day in which you came into her life, Tom Bolton, and I thank the Blessed Mother for it."

"Thank you," he said softly. "But you well know we have been a blessing to each other, Maybel. Come along, now, and let us see what is transpiring in the hall. Are you not curious? I know that I am."

That evening, after the meal had been served, Rosamund, Logan, Father Mata, Maybel, Edmund, and Tom sat together in the hall plotting. Philippa had been sent to her bed, her windows barred, Lucy on the trundle by her bedside, and the Hepburn clansman on guard outside the girl's door.

"The bait must be something tempting to them both," Rosamund said.

"Then the trap must be baited twice," Logan told them. "Once for Henry the younger and once for Lord Dacre."

"If Dacre believes that Henry and his men are Scots," Rosamund considered, "that should be bait enough for him. But what will bring them together at the same time and in the same place?"

"There is a deserted abbey near Lochmaben," the priest said. "What if Lord Dacre learned that gold, previously hidden there, was to be transported from that abbey across Scotland to Edinburgh for the little king's use? He would want to take that gold. And what if Henry the younger learned about the same gold? The abbey is in a desolate area. Both men would consider it an easy haul. Lord Dacre would be warned of this band of renegade Scots in the neighborhood. Henry would not be warned of Lord Dacre. If they came upon each other, certainly a battle would ensue."

"I remember once," Edmund remarked, "my brother Richard saying you would go far in the church, Mata. Your talents are indeed wasted in this rural outback."

The young priest grinned.

"To get them to the same place at approximately the same time," Logan noted, "that is where our problem will lie."

"Not if Henry believes the shipment will be unguarded for only the first five miles of its trek. That it will meet up with the king's men where the abbey road and the Edinburgh road join. That means he must attack before the gold reaches it guardians. If he is clever, he will wait until the shipment is halfway between the junction of the two roads. We will make certain he does this and then we will make certain Lord Dacre knows it," Logan said. "Your cousin is basically a coward. He is not looking for a fight, but rather easy pickings."

"How do we do this?" Rosamund asked him.

"I will go to Lord Dacre," Tom said. "I am English, and he will believe me, particularly as I will bleat about this bandit who threatens my estates at Otterly and those of my cousin the lady of Friarsgate, who is the queen's dear friend, just back from court, you know, where her daughter was chosen to be a maid of honor in two years' time and may be matched with the Earl of

Renfrew's son. His lordship is a snob. He will listen carefully to what I have to say and think to gain greater favor with the king by stealing this gold for him and protecting the queen's friend in the bargain."

"And who will tell Henry the younger of the gold?" Rosamund asked.

"I will," Edmund spoke up.

"You, old man? Are you mad?" Maybel demanded. "Am I to be widowed in my old age, then? You will do no such thing, Edmund Bolton!"

They all laughed, but Edmund replied to his wife, "Nay, old woman. I will go to my nephew and tell him this tale of gold. I will say I heard it from our neighbor, the laird of Claven's Carn. That I have come to him in hopes that by telling him of this bounty that can be his, he will leave Friarsgate and Philippa Meredith in peace. That the gold he may steal will give him the opportunity to begin a new life somewhere else. I am his uncle, his blood kin. He knows how much I love Friarsgate and our family. He will believe me, for he could never conceive that I would be duplicitous with him where the safety of Friarsgate and its inhabitants are concerned."

"He is right," Tom said.

"Aye, and brave, too," the laird remarked. "You'll take an armed guard with you, Edmund, for without them your nephew might be tempted to do something foolish."

"And just where is this gold going to come from?" Maybel demanded. "And how will you gain the monks' cooperation in this charade?"

"Remember, the abbey is deserted, Maybel. But neither Lord Dacre nor Henry the younger will know that," the priest said. "Monks' robes are easily available, and some of the laird's men can don them to make it appear to anyone watching that the abbey is populated. Two monks will drive the cart up the abbey trail towards the road. At the first sign of trouble, the drivers will leap from the cart and flee into the woods. No one will chase after them, for it is the gold they want, not a pair of cowardly monks."

"You still have not said where the gold will come from," Maybel insisted.

"There is a supply of bricks stored away from when we made the new bake ovens," Edmund said. "They can be wrapped in cloth and tied with yarn. Piled in the cart, they will appear to be just what Lord Dacre and my nephew have been told. Gold."

"It must all be done with perfect precision if we are to succeed," the laird said. "Tomorrow we will set up the steps to follow."

"What will Lord Dacre think when he discovers the bricks?" Rosamund wondered.

"He will undoubtedly head for the abbey, and discovering it empty, realize he has been duped. I suspect he will believe there was indeed gold but that it was transported earlier in some secret manner to foil the English," Tom said. He stood up, stretching and yawning broadly. "Oh, I believe I am ready for my bed," he said. "All this plotting is absolutely exhausting, dear girl." He bent, and kissed Rosamund upon her forehead. "Good night, and sweet dreams, cousin. Logan. Maybel. Edmund." And then he was gone from the hall.

Edmund arose quickly, and taking his wife's hand, bid Rosamund and Logan good night as he hurried his wife from the hall. Maybel, who had opened her mouth to protest their swift departure, suddenly realized what her husband was all about, and her jaw snapped shut as their eyes met in understanding.

"Where am I to sleep, lady?" the laird asked his hostess.

Why was he in such a hurry? she wondered. Had he met another woman while she was down in England? "Bide with me a while, my lord," Rosamund said, and she arose to pour him a goblet of her best wine. After all these years of his alleged devotion, he was going to desert her for some other woman? Most certainly not until she decided if he was worth marrying! She swallowed her temper, and smiling, handed him the wine. "This is my favorite time of day, or rather, evening," she told him as she brought her own goblet back to her seat by the fire. "Everything is quiet, and there seems to be a peace on the land as at no other time." She sipped her wine.

He couldn't resist. He enjoyed it better when she fought him openly. "Are you attempting to ply me with good wine and then seduce me, madame?" He cocked a black eyebrow questioningly at her.

"Have you always had such a fine opinion of yourself, Logan?" she demanded with a show of her old spirit. The beast! Could he read her mind?

"Always, my darling," he told her with a brash grin. He saw her fingers tighten about the stem of her goblet. "You are contemplating hurling the contents of your vessel at me, aren't you?" he said.

"Yes," she admitted through clenched teeth. "Oh, yes!"

"I have a better idea, and it will save my doublet and not waste your good wine," he told her with a grin. Then, setting his own goblet aside, he stood up. "Get up, Rosamund, and I will help you calm your temper," Logan said. "But let us put your wine aside first," and he took the goblet from her hand and set it upon a table. He drew her to a standing position. "From now on," he said, "when you wish to do violence to me, you will instead kiss me."

"What?" Surely she had not heard him aright, but then he was folding her arms behind her as he pulled her into his arms. His head was descending to meet hers. His lips were pressing themselves to her lips. With the touch of his flesh on hers, Rosamund's knees gave way, but he was holding her so firmly that she did not fall. Her eyes had closed of their own volition, and her head began to spin.

Then he raised his mouth from hers and said, "Kissing is much nicer, Rosamund, than quarreling. Didn't anyone ever teach you that?"

"I have never quarreled with anyone the way I do with you," she said as her head cleared. "You are the most annoying man."

"You are no longer angry at me," he teased her.

"Nay," she said. "I do not think I am."

"You see?" he said as he released her from his embrace.

"Will I have to fight with you in order for you to kiss me?" Rosamund asked him provocatively.

"For now, aye," he told her. "You are not an easy woman, and I must bring you to reason if we are ever to marry, my darling."

"Bring me to reason?" Her outrage was more than evident. Her little balled fist hit him a blow on his arm. "Not an easy woman? Who the hell are you to criticize me, Logan Hepburn? Do you think you are some paragon of perfection? Even Jeannie, God assoil her sweet soul, knew better than that!"

He wanted to laugh, but he did not. Instead, he yanked her back into his arms and kissed her until she was breathless and half-swooning. "I will master you, you impossible wench, if I must spend the rest of my life doing it," he said to her. Then he kissed her again and again and again until she was whimpering with pleasure. Finally he set her back on her feet, holding her arm lightly as she swayed for a moment. "There," he said. "You should be calm again. Now, show me where I am to sleep this night, Rosamund Bolton."

She shook her head to clear it, saying nothing. He was irritating! He was impossible! He was overbearing! But God's wounds! His kisses were divine. She was surprised to discover that she could move her legs now, and so she led him upstairs to the guest chamber. Opening the door, she stepped back to allow him through. "Good night, my lord," she said softly.

More softly than she had intended, but at least she could speak, Rosamund thought.

He stepped past her, and then turning, said low, "Not tonight, Rosamund, but another night, we will share this bed together."

"I have not said I should marry you, Logan," she replied quickly.

"I have not said I should ask you, Rosamund," he told her. "I have simply said that one night soon we will share this bed, you and I. Good night, madame."

Astounded, she stepped away from the door as he reached to close it. Her heart was beating madly. She began to consider what it might be like in his arms, and then she thought of the last time she had lain in a man's arms. "Patrick," she whispered, but even as she said his name she knew that the Earl of Glenkirk would never deny her the happiness with another man that he could no longer give her. And with that thought came the realization that the premonition they had both experienced when they had first met had finally come to pass. She would never see Patrick Leslie again in this life. And with that knowledge Rosamund knew she was suddenly free to love once more. She would always love Patrick. She knew that. He would live hidden in that secret place in her heart known only to her. But her life had to go on, and she knew now that she could not live without love.

Logan stood, his back to the closed door, breathing slowly. Deeply. Her mouth had been far sweeter than he had remembered. The sensation of her full breasts against his chest had made his senses reel and his manhood ache with his need. The boldness of the words he had just spoken to her burned in his throat. Instinct had warned him it was too soon, but how he had wanted her in his bed this night. Tom's advice had been good, but he could not play this game with her forever. He had not the patience for it, he knew. He loved her too much. Logan wanted Rosamund as his wife. And his wife she was going to be sooner than later. He slept badly. As did Rosamund.

Her dreams were wild, jumbled impressions that left her tossing and restless and more awake than asleep. She awoke bleary-eyed and irritable, but she was ready to begin preparing the trap they had devised the previous evening to rid Friarsgate of her cousin Henry Bolton once and for all. For all of her life she had been troubled, first by her father's youngest brother and now by his son. Her uncle's bones rested in the family burial ground. But Rosamund knew she would not feel safe until her cousin lay beside his father.

To her surprise, she found Logan gone when she came down into the hall. He had, a servant informed her, departed at first light with just a few of his clansmen. Then her uncle Edmund entered the hall.

"You are awake at last, niece!" he said jovially. "Logan has left me instructions for our part in this charade. We must begin today, for the sooner this is over and done with, the better for Friarsgate. I do not relish a winter defending ourselves from not just four-legged wolves, but two-legged ones, as well."

"He might have said good-bye," Rosamund said, annoyed.

"I thought you might have said farewell to each other last night," Edmund murmured innocently.

She threw him an evil look. "I showed him to his chamber and went to my own," she said. "I assumed he would be here when I returned to the hall and would speak with me himself instead of giving instructions to you, uncle." She felt her anger beginning to rise, and then the oddest thing happened. She remembered her anger of the previous evening and how he had calmed her. She could almost feel his lips on hers now, and as she did, the anger began to drain away. "He was wise to leave early," she said suddenly, surprising Edmund. "We must be scrupulous in our execution of this plan, or we will fail miserably. What would the laird have us do, uncle?"

"We must prepare the false gold and transport it in secret to the abbey near Lochmaben. And we must do it without your cousin's men observing us. To that end, the laird's men are scouring the few caves in our hillsides where an intruder might secrete himself to spy on us. Others of the Hepburns are posted upon our heights. But we must work quickly, Rosamund, for we do not want to arouse Henry the younger's suspicions."

"Have the bricks brought into the house through the kitchen garden door," she said. "Not all at once, but a few at a time over the day. We cannot be certain we are not being watched, and I would not have anyone's curiosity aroused by a constant stream of men and women going in and out of the house. At twilight and in the darkness of the evening the rest of the bricks may be carried inside."

"Where do you want them?" he asked.

"In the hall," Rosamund said. "We will wrap them here."

The morning meal was brought and eaten. People came and went throughout the day while Rosamund, Philippa, Maybel, and several of the servingwomen carefully wrapped each brick in a natural-colored felt fabric and then tied the wrappings with wool twine so the contents remained well concealed. The pile of wrapped bricks never grew any larger, for as each brick was covered with felt and tied, it was removed from the hall. Finally all the bricks were wrapped and gone from the hall. They had been taken over the long day and early evening to a barn, where they were loaded in a covered wooden wagon that would be transported first over the border to Claven's Carn and from there to the deserted abbey where the wagon's cover would then be removed. A tarpaulin would replace it, being tied down for effect. But the transport would remain in Rosamund's barn until the laird returned and gave the word it was to be moved.

And he did return several days later. "Twenty of my men are now populating the abbey," he said. "We will transport our gold over the border tomorrow and from there to Lochmaben. When I return again we will be ready to inform Lord Dacre and Henry the younger of the gold they may steal." He laughed. "You have done your part well, Rosamund. The bricks make quite a convincing shipment of gold."

"Aye, we worked hard to be certain there is not the faintest sign of what is really between those wrappings," she told him.

"In two days Tom will seek out Lord Dacre, and Edmund, Henry the younger. I know where both are now located. Leaving at the same time, they should reach their quarry at approximately the same time. The trick will be to return to us at the same time with the news that they have both taken the bait."

Two days later Edmund, six men-at-arms with him, rode to where his nephew hid himself between his border forays. Henry the younger was surprised to see his uncle, but he greeted him cordially enough. Edmund did not dismount his horse.

"This is not a social call, nephew," he said bluntly.

Henry felt at somewhat of a disadvantage standing by his uncle's mount. "Get down, Edmund Bolton, so we may speak eye to eye," he said. "Come in and have some wine. I have an excellent keg I relieved a traveling merchant of recently." And he chuckled as if it were all a jest.

But Edmund remained atop his mount. "Nay. There is something I have come to say, Henry," he told his nephew. "I want you to cease harassing Friarsgate. I want you to put all thoughts of marrying Philippa Meredith from your head. A match is being arranged for her with the second son of an earl. It is what the family wants. However, in return for your cooperation, we are willing to direct you to a rather large cache of gold, yours for the taking, nephew. Easy pickings, unless, of course, you are afraid of a band of Scottish monks," he said scornfully. "You have no real love for Friarsgate. Would you not be content instead with gold?"

"Perhaps," Henry said softly. "Tell me more, uncle."

"Your word first that you will cease seeking to kidnap little Philippa. She is yet a child, Henry, and would be more troublesome than useful to you. And you could not keep her from her mother for long. Rosamund is a strong-willed woman, as your father learned."

"Rosamund should have been my wife," Henry the younger said. "It could be my son who inherited Friarsgate, and not another girl, uncle."

Edmund's laughter was brittle. "What are you now, nephew? Seventeen? Rosamund is twenty-five, and she would kill you before she would marry you. You do not want Friarsgate, lad. That was your father's dream, and where did it get him but a narrow plot in the family's burial ground? His lust for what was not his drove your mother away. It turned her from a vapid but decent girl into . . . well, lad, you know what Mavis became. And you? You are hunted and will be one day caught and hung." He paused for a long moment. "Unless you decide to change your fate, Henry. Give me your word that you will leave the Boltons of Friarsgate alone, and I will make you rich, so rich you may leave here and begin your life anew. You were not meant to be a bandit in the borders, nephew. Do you really want your mother to come upon you one day, hanging at the side of the road? Would you break her heart that way? With the gold I offer you, you can rescue her from her shame and let her live out her life peaceably."

For a brief moment Henry the younger's face softened. Then his eyes narrowed, and he said, "Tell me!"

"Your promise first," Edmund replied.

"You would accept my word?" Henry the younger sounded surprised, but he was also flattered. No one had ever agreed to accept his word before. "You have my hand on it, uncle. If you will tell me where this gold is, and if I can obtain it, I will leave Friarsgate and its inhabitants in peace. I will go south, as Thomas Bolton's antecedent did. Perhaps I will have the same good fortune as he did." That is not to say I will not return one day, Henry the younger thought silently. But Friarsgate was not for him, and he knew it. Besides, he hated the stink of sheep.

Edmund took his nephew's hand and shook it. "The gold is at an abbey in the borders near Lochmaben. I learned of its existence from a Hepburn clansman. The laird's cousin, the now-deceased Earl of Bothwell, had stored it there for King James before the war. Now it is needed to support the little king, and the queen regent has sent for it to be brought to Stirling. There is but one place where it may be safely taken, nephew. The vehicle bearing the gold will travel from the abbey down to the Edinburgh road. It is a distance of but a few miles. Midway between the abbey and that junction in the road is the ideal place to snatch it. The wagon will be driven by two monks. It is hoped such an equipage will not attract any attention," Edmund said.

"You have remarkably good information, uncle," Henry the younger said suspiciously.

"Of course I do," Edmund agreed. "We hired out Hepburn clansmen to watch over Friarsgate. We pay them, and house and feed them. We are borderers no matter which allegiance we espouse when our kings go to war, nephew. The Scots have become comfortable with us, and they talk a great deal, for they are lonely for their families. They are also proud of their family connections, and the Earl of Bothwell, Patrick Hepburn, was responsible for hiding this gold at Lochmaben. I am sure that if Lord Dacre learns of this transport of gold he will want it, too. But that is unlikely, nephew. So there it is for the taking, if you are not afraid."

"I am not afraid!" Henry the younger said quickly. "Do you know when this gold will be moved, uncle?"

"They say in three days' time, nephew, but if I were you, I should go to Lochmaben as soon as possible and wait in hiding so you do not miss its departure." Edmund turned his horse's head as he prepared to leave his nephew's encampment.

"Uncle," Henry the younger called after him.

Edmund twisted in his saddle. "Yes, nephew?" he asked.

"If you have lied to me, I will come back and kill you," Henry the younger said.

Edmund laughed harshly. "You are surely your father's son," he said, and then he rode off with his escort of clansmen to return to Friarsgate, where he found Tom just returned from his visit to Lord Dacre.

The two men entered the hall of the house, where Rosamund awaited them anxiously. "Well?" she said.

"Your cousin said as I was departing his camp that he would kill me if I lied to him," Edmund chuckled. "He has taken the bait, niece."

Rosamund turned to her cousin. "Tom?"

Lord Cambridge nodded. "At first Dacre was not certain that I knew what I was talking about. 'Dear boy,' I told him, 'I have not ridden across half of England for my own amusement. The information I have practically comes from the source.' Then I went on to tell him he had really been quite naughty continuing his raids in the borders. I happen to know, I said, for haven't I just returned from court, that the king has told you it must stop! You are endangering all of us who live here. My cousin, Lady Rosamund Bolton, Queen Katherine's dear, dear friend from their shared childhoods at court, has a large estate, Friarsgate, nearby. Then I lowered my voice and became quite chummy with Dacre. 'Her daughter has just been chosen to be a maid of honor in two years' time. If you do not stop, dear boy, you endanger Friarsgate, for the Scots will surely retaliate and come marauding. Now,' I continued, 'one of the men who guards Friarsgate has a sister married to a Scot over the border. And he has told her that a large shipment of gold that has been hidden at Lochmaben in an abbey is to be transported across the country to the queen regent for the support of her son, the little king. Now, if you seized that shipment of gold, our king would be very pleased. His sister, the Queen of Scotland, is being most difficult with him right now. If our dear King Henry had her gold, then she would have to be more amenable, wouldn't she? Of course, if you are fearful of that band of renegades that have been about of late, well, I might understand, dear boy, but would King Henry?' "

They laughed, and Rosamund said, "You really are quite wicked, Tom. He listened to you, then?"

"I told him exactly where and when, dear girl, and suggested he would not be amiss leaving sooner than later. Like Edmund, I left behind a man to observe, who will return to us when both of our unsuspecting victims reach Lochmaben, when the battle is over and done with. Lord Dacre and his men are really quite well armed."

"Henry the younger will fight harder," Edmund said.

"Perhaps, but he will be overcome," Tom told them.

"Then we have but to wait for news," Rosamund responded.

"Where is your brazen Scot, dear girl?" Tom asked her.

"He is not mine, Tom!" Rosamund exclaimed.

"Of course he is," Lord Cambridge replied with a grin. "Now, where is he?"

"He has gone to Lochmaben," Rosamund said. "I will not believe that Henry the younger is dead unless I see his body and bury it."

"God's wounds, dear girl!" Tom exclaimed. "I am quite relieved not to be your enemy."

"I do not do it out of vindictiveness, Tom, but I must be certain that Philippa is safe," Rosamund told him. "And he is my cousin. Our blood. He should be interred here. Like his father, it is all he will ever have of Friarsgate."

So they waited, and ten days later Logan came riding over the border and down the hill to Friarsgate with his men. Among their number was a riderless horse that carried a body. The body had already begun to stink, but in anticipation that he would not fail her, Rosamund had seen the grave already dug and the shroud ready. The body was put into its burial cloth. Rosamund looked upon Henry the younger's face. In death he was a pleasant-looking young man who did not seem in the least dangerous. She nodded silently, and then she sewed the top of the shroud closed herself before they buried her young cousin.

"It is over at last," she said as they all

sat together in the hall that evening. "For my whole life I have battled Henry the elder and Henry the younger. Thank God it is finished." She looked at the three men with her. "Thank you," she said simply.

"Was it as you planned it?" Maybel demanded, wanting to know all the details.

"Exactly," Logan said. "I have never in my life known any plan to be so flawless in its execution. Both parties of men arrived unknown to the other. They secreted themselves on opposite sides of the path. They were silent and determined. Your cousin struck first. At his attack the drivers leaped from the wagon and fled into the woods. And then Lord Dacre swooped down on Henry the younger and his men. He thought them Scots, and he was savage in battle. There were no survivors among your cousin's men.

"Dacre then undid the covering on the wagon and pulled forth one of the bricks. He felt its weight and grinned, delighted. He unwrapped the brick, and seeing what was inside, he swore an oath. Then he began, with all his men, unwrapping the bricks until there wasn't a one left. He spoke some of the most colorful language that I have ever heard," Logan said, smiling.

"What happened then?" Maybel asked, leaning forward in her chair.

"He and his men galloped down the path to the abbey. They found it deserted, of course. They came back up the path, and dismounting, examined the wagon most carefully. I was near enough to hear the English milord. He decided that the monks had run away to hide in the woods knowing the wagon was empty of gold, but that the gold must assuredly have been there at one time because of the renegades who attempted to steal it before he attempted to steal it. He came to the conclusion that somewhere between there and Stirling there was a wagonload of gold, and he would attempt to find it before it became too dangerous for him and his men. He had his men unhitch the horses and then rode off with his troop."

"So you lost two horses. I am sorry," Rosamund said. "I will replace them."

"There is no need," Logan said. "We stole them back that night."

They all laughed, and then the servants began bringing in the meal. It has been agreed that the laird would spend the night at Friarsgate.

"And you will return my daughters tomorrow?" Rosamund said.

"If you want Banon and Bessie back," he told her wickedly, "you must come to Claven's Carn and fetch them, Rosamund Bolton." The blue-blue eyes were dancing.

Rosamund felt her temper rising. But when she glared down the high board at him, he pursed his lips in a kiss to her. For a moment her head spun at the memory of the last time he had cooled her tantrum. She was, to her family's surprise, silent, and she could see he knew exactly what she was thinking and was restraining his laughter. I will not let him make me angry, she decided, and then she lifted her goblet to him in a taunting gesture and drank deeply. She heard his chuckle as she set the goblet back down on the high board.

Edmund and Tom played a game of chess before the fire afterwards. Maybel dozed, her feet turned towards the warmth of the hearth. Several dogs sprawled about them, and a single cat lay dozing in Philippa's lap.

"Am I really safe now, mama?" Philippa asked. "And Friarsgate, too?"

"We are all safe now, poppet," Rosamund told her daughter. "One day you will inherit Friarsgate, and your descendants after you. With me, the Boltons die. There will be none afterwards to harm you or yours." She put an arm about her child, and Philippa dropped her head for a moment upon her mother's shoulder as she had done when she was younger, seeking security and solace.

"I do not think I could ever be as brave

as you have been, mama," Philippa said.

"I wanted you and your sisters to have a happier time in your childhoods than I did," Rosamund told her daughter. "But you have had your share of sadness, too, my child. I know how hard it was for you to lose your father."

"But if you married again, mama, we could have another father," Philippa said.

"We will see," Rosamund murmured, not noticing her cousin Tom wince.

"When will my sisters come home, mama?" Philippa asked.

"Soon," Rosamund said. "Now find your bed, my daughter."

Curtsying to her elders, Philippa left the hall. And soon Maybel and Edmund were gone. And Tom, after pouring himself a goblet of wine, swiftly sought his own chamber.

Rosamund arose from her place on the settle where she had sat with Philippa. "Come, my lord. I am certain you remember the way, but I shall lead you." She glided from the hall, the laird of Claven's Carn's footsteps behind her. Reaching the guest chamber, she opened the door for him, gasping as he drew her inside and shut the door behind them firmly. "My lord!"

He stopped her mouth with a hard kiss. "Tonight, madame," he told her, "we will begin to get to know each other as we should have years ago but that you kept marrying other men. We are getting too old for these games, Rosamund, my darling." His arms tightened about her.

"I have not said I would marry you," she whispered breathlessly.

He took an index finger and ran it from the top of her head down her nose and over her lips and chin in a tender gesture. "I have not asked you to marry me, Rosamund," he told her softly. "I have just said it is past time we got to know each other, my darling."

"You want to make love to me," she answered him.

"Aye, I do," he told her.

"Logan . . . oh, Logan, I do not know if I can ever love you as you love me," Rosamund despaired.

"So you finally see that I love you," he replied. " 'Tis a start, my darling." He kissed her face gently, moving his lips from her forehead to her eyelids to her nose and finally to her sweet mouth. Then the blue-blue eyes met her amber ones. His big hand caressed her cheek. "You will never love me as you loved Patrick Leslie, Rosamund, but you will love me. I promise you."

Tears slipped down her face, and he kissed them away. Then, turning her about, he began to unlace the bodice of her plain brown velvet gown. His lips found the soft nape of her neck and pressed a kiss upon it. Rosamund sighed, wondering as she did why she had this sudden feeling of relief. He removed the bodice, laying it aside on a nearby chair. He undid the tapes of her skirts and lifted her from the puddle of material that slipped to the floor.

"You seem to be quite expert at this, Logan Hepburn," Rosamund told him, beginning to regain her equilibrium. She was facing him now, and her fingers were undoing his doublet unimpeded.

He smiled a slow smile down at her. "I am," he admitted modestly. Then he lifted her up and set her down upon the bed. Kneeling, he removed her slippers and stockings.

"I haven't finished undressing you," Rosamund said boldly.

"I can do it quicker," he told her. "And I think it necessary tonight, my darling." His hands undid his breeks. He removed his sherte and then sat to remove his shoes and his wool stockings from his big feet. He stood again, pulling his breeks off, then got into the bed with her. For modesty's sake, he had left her in her chemise, but he was as naked as God had made him.

"You are a very big man," she said, eyeing him.

"I am," he agreed, untying the ribbons that held her chemise closed. He drew back the folds of fabric and stared. "God's wounds, madame, you are incredibly beautiful," he said admiringly. He did not touch her.

"Would you like me to remove my chemise now?" she asked softly. He was such a handsome man with his blue-blue eyes and his unruly black hair. Unable to help herself, she reached up and ran her hand through that hair.

"Nay," he told her. "I want to absorb your beauty a little bit at a time, Rosamund. I am not a greedy man." The dark head bent, and he kissed a single nipple.

She shivered with the pleasure that small touch offered her. It had been almost two years since she had lain in a man's arms and received the homage of his love for her. "That was nice," she told him.

"Good," he said. "I want to know what pleases you, and then you shall learn what pleases me, Rosamund."

"What if we discover that we do not enjoy each other?" she asked him.

"Why, then we shall go our separate ways, madame," he replied blandly.

"What?" she cried. "You would seduce me and then desert me, you Scots scoundrel!" She pushed him away.

"Madame, 'twas you who introduced

doubt into our passion," he returned.

Rosamund sat up. What was she doing? She jumped from the bed, looking to gather up her other garments. "You shall not have me, you monster!"

"Oh, but I shall, my darling," he said, rising and following her, drawing her back into his arms, drawing the chemise off of her. Her breasts were crushed against his lightly furred chest. Her belly pressed against his.

"Dammit, Logan! Would you commit rape?" she demanded of him. God's blood! She had never felt so very naked before. She hammered against him with her fists. He enclosed her face between his big hands and kissed her, his mouth insistent, demanding, and moist against her lips, her face. He would not be denied, and the truth was, she realized, she didn't want to be denied, either. She needed him as much as he needed her.

"If you truly want to go," he said, suddenly releasing her, "then go, damn you! But if you remain, Rosamund, these fevered bodies of ours will shortly be one." The blue-blue eyes looked straight at her.

"I don't know," she whispered.

"Yes, you do!" he said fiercely.

"Do you *really* love me, Logan Hepburn?" she asked him.

"For as long as I can remember,

Rosamund Bolton. *Forever!* And I always will," he told her in a sure and quiet voice.

"Please God that I am not a fool," she said.

He smiled at her. "We will talk about that on the morrow, my darling," he told her, holding out his hand in silent invitation.

She took it, and he brought her back into the comfort of his embrace. Then they walked back to the bed. They lay together, slowly and tenderly exploring each other's bodies. He caressed her breasts. She pressed kisses on his flat belly. Their mouths met again and again as their limbs intertwined, rolling this way and then that. Finally she lay beneath him, and with the most infinite care, indeed as if she were a virgin, he entered her body, pushing his thick length slowly, slowly and filling her full with his long-pent-up desire for her. Moving with a leisurely rhythm until she was whimpering softly and her head began to thrash with her rising pleasure. And when their need for each other reached its peak, they rose together, their fingers intertwined, until with great joy they fell back together into the abyss of warm and soothing release, fulfilled.

And afterwards he told her that on the morrow she would return with him to Claven's Carn and they would be married.

"If, of course, my darling, that is your wish, too," he said smiling into her face, devouring her with his love until she could no longer bear it, for it was simply too sweet.

"I cannot live at Claven's Carn always," she said. "I am the lady of Friarsgate."

"I cannot live at Friarsgate always," he said. "I am the lord of Claven's Carn."

"Then we must be like the wealthy nobles who go back and forth between their homes and estates, Logan," she told him. "Sometimes we will live in your house, and sometimes we will live in mine."

"And if our countries continue to war?" he asked her.

"Then you must stay on your side of the border, and I will remain on mine," Rosamund teased him with a smile.

"Of course," he told her, "if we remain free of political entanglements and know nothing of the world outside of Friarsgate and Claven's Carn, we shall never be separated." Then he kissed the tip of her nose.

"What a clever man you are," Rosamund told him. "I think I will marry you after all, Logan Hepburn."

"And one day you will come to love me?" he said hopefully.

"I think some small part of me has always loved you, Logan," she admitted. "And I will be a good wife to you and a good stepmother to your son. I promise."

"And I will be a good father to your girls," he vowed. "I remember their father, and he was an honorable man. I can be no less to you, or to them."

"And if we should have bairns, Logan?" she asked.

"They will belong to Claven's Carn," he told her firmly.

She nodded. "Then it is settled, my lord. But if we are indeed to have bairns, you will have to pay more attention to me than you have been," she teased him.

He grinned down at her. "Madame, I have already put a bairn in your belly, but until he objects, Rosamund, you and I will enjoy our bed sport."

And Rosamund laughed aloud, her heart soaring with her happiness. Aye! She was indeed happy again, and she knew that with Logan Hepburn by her side she would be happy forever, no matter the world about them.

Epilogue

They were not married the next day, but rather a month later, on the eighteenth of October, St. Luke's Day. The ceremony took place not at Friarsgate or at Claven's Carn, but rather in the hills between both estates where the border between England and Scotland was acknowledged to be by both parties. The bride stood on the English side of that border. The bridegroom stood in Scotland. Both were smiling as they joined hands across that border. It was a perfect autumn day. The sky above was a clear, strong blue, and the bright sun was warm on their shoulders. The hills were dressed in russet and gold, and the air about them was soft, but there was no breeze.

The simple ceremony was performed by Prior Richard Bolton and Father Mata. The invited guests were few: Maybel, Edmund, Tom Bolton, Philippa, Banon, and Bessie Meredith, little John Hepburn. And when the formalities were over and done with, the laird of Claven's Carn took his bride up on his horse and invited them all back to his keep for the celebration. There in the hall, as the day waned, his clansmen and clanswomen raised toast after toast to the newly wed couple, the pipes wailed, and there was much dancing. John Hepburn spent most of that afternoon curled in his new stepmother's lap. Rosamund frequently caressed the little boy's dark hair, wondering if the child she now carried would be dark-haired, too.

And eight months later Rosamund discovered that he was, when Alexander Hepburn was born into the world to the delight of his three half-sisters and his half-brother. He was christened at Friarsgate Church by Father Mata, Edmund and Tom standing as his godfathers and Maybel as his godmother. And watching, Philippa Meredith could but consider if this was the last of her mother's children she would see born, for in ten more short months she was to go to court and join the queen's household. In ten months she would see her friend Cecily FitzHugh again. She would be twelve years old. Old enough to be considered a possible match for the right young man. She wondered if that young man would be Giles FitzHugh, or perhaps another, someone she had yet to meet. Someone she did not even know. Someone with whom she would fall madly in love. As her mother had with Patrick Leslie.

"I cannot wait!" Philippa said softly to herself. *"I cannot wait!"* And she smiled as she contemplated her life to come.

A Note from the Author

I hope you have enjoyed Book Two of *The Friarsgate Inheritance.* I will tell you that no one was more surprised than I was to have Patrick Leslie, the first Glenkirk earl, and the father of my very first heroine, Janet Leslie, a.k.a. Cyra Hafise (*The Kadin*), appear as the great love of Rosamund's life. I had always wondered what had happened to him.

In Book Three of this series I will have some other surprises for you. Look for it in October 2004. In the meantime I hope you will visit my Web site at www.BertriceSmall. com or you may write to me at P.O. Box 765, Southold, NY 11971-0765. God bless, and much good future reading from your most faithful author,

Bertrice Small

About the Author

Bertrice Small is a *New York Times* best-selling author and the recipient of numerous awards. In keeping with her profession, she lives in the oldest English-speaking town in the state of New York, founded in 1640, and works in a light-filled studio surrounded by the paintings of her favorite cover artist, Elaine Duillo. Because she believes in happy endings, Bertrice Small has been married to the same man, her hero, George, for forty years. They have a son, a daughter-in-law, and three adorable grandchildren. Longtime readers will be happy to know that Nicki the Cockatiel flourishes along with his fellow housemates: Pookie, the long-haired greige and white feline; Honeybun, the petite orange lady cat with the cream-colored paws, and Finnegan, the naughty black kitty.

CP
10/06

MG ✓
3/06

4/05

ML